JENSEN
A DARK COWBOY ROMANCE

RAYA MORRIS EDWARDS

Jensen

By Raya Morris Edwards

FIRST EDITION

Dev edits by Lexie at Morally Gray Author Services
Proof & copy edits by Alexa at The Fiction Fix

Cover by Maldo Designs
Cover photo: Michelle Lancaster @lanefotograf

Save a horse, ride a tatted cowboy's mustache?
If you smiled reading that, this book is for you.

AUTHOR'S NOTE

This book is set in rural Appalachia and contains dialect, sentence structure, and phrases which may be unfamiliar to you, however I assure you, they are intentional and correct.

This is a work of fiction. For the purposes of storyline and character development there are many instances of characters doing things that I recommend against in real life. That includes some of the spicy stuff. Yes, I'm talking about the Crisco too.

Please do not look to fiction for accurate kink and BDSM representation.

Additionally, this book is dark and contains sensitive topics that may be upsetting to some. I highly recommend that you check out the content warnings before reading if you have concerns.

Please go to rayamorrisedwards.com/jensen to read a full, detailed breakdown of the content in this book.

CHAPTER ONE

JENSEN

AGE SEVENTEEN

I meet Miss Holly the summer I turn seventeen.

I notice she's pretty, just a quick acknowledgement of that undeniable fact before moving along. Her son Kyle was my closest friend, that year and into the next. Even if I were a legal adult, she'd be off limits. That's code. I might not have money or anything else, but I've got morals and shit.

There's no avoiding her though. My grandma, Cherry, works at the beauty parlor in Byway, a little no-count town outside Lexington, Kentucky. Holly works with her, but they're not friends because Cherry doesn't have those.

Cherry is a mean lady on the surface, but she's alright underneath. She took me in when my mother passed. Maybe because she's got some heart in her, or maybe because the social worker said she had to, but that's the closest thing to love I know in my short life.

I'll take it, no complaints.

After growing up in the armpit of Harlan, her trailer in Byway is pure luxury. Between what she makes at the salon and her late man's social security, we have it pretty good. I have my own room instead of a couch off the living area, and Cherry is alright, even though she smokes like a chimney inside, secondhand smoke be damned.

By nine AM, she's up and sitting at the table, bright red cropped hair spiked, going through a pack of Camels like nobody's business. She was like that from my first moment in her house, the day the social worker dropped me off in her yard. Just sitting at the table, staring at me like she's trying to figure me out.

"What do I do here?" I ask.

She coughs through the thick smog. "What do you mean?"

"I mean, I just got here," I say. "What do I do tomorrow?"

She clears her throat, frowning. "You go to school," she says. "After school, haul your ass over to the beauty parlor, and you can hang out until I'm done with my shift."

"And then what?"

"Then we'll eat dinner, and I'll watch my soaps. You'll do your homework tomorrow night, after your first day of school."

We're at the ancient table in the kitchen. Our plastic plates are empty of the sandwiches and chips she put together after I admitted I hadn't eaten. It was just deli meat and Miracle Whip on white bread, but it was the first thing I've had today, so no complaints. I'm a teenage boy, a vacuous pit of hunger. Any food I get is a win in my book.

"So...I'm not super involved in school," I say.

She narrows her black lined eyes. "What grade are you in, Jen?"

I think about it. "Not sure."

"What the fuck was your mother doing with you?"

I don't answer. My mother was sick for the last four years. Nobody came to the house when I stopped going to school after a while. Hell, I'm not sure anybody noticed.

Cherry looks at me like this isn't partially her fault for throwing my pregnant, teenage mother out on her ass seventeen years ago. I shrug.

"I did one year of high school," I say.

Her jaw works. "Were you any good?" she asks.

"Maybe," I say. "They didn't flunk me."

She looks at me, laser beam eyes narrowed. She's been mean since I showed up a few hours prior, but after that conversation, she softens a bit. We go out on the porch, and she lights a cigarette. I sit on the porch step and watch the chain link fence shake in the wind.

"Reckon I should get that fixed," she croaks.

I get up and go over to it, checking it out. My mother used to tell me I could fix anything, which I relay to Cherry. Not a brag, just imparting some information. She gives me twenty bucks and sends me to the feed store in town to get materials. I have that fence looking pretty good by the end of the night. Cherry is impressed—I can tell by the begrudging grunt as she inspects it.

The next morning, when I get up to get ready for school, there's my lunch packed on the table.

That astounds me. I was always a hot lunch kid, arguing with the school over my unpaid bills. There was a lunch lady, Miss June, who gave me my meals even though I couldn't pay up. *Fuck that*, she'd say, even though she wasn't supposed to swear in front of us. *They'll just throw it out anyway.*

As a growing boy with a hole in his belly the size of the US of A, I was pretty grateful.

Now, here I am, with my grandmother packing my lunch. Unbelievable. I grab it and vow I'll pay Cherry back by keeping in line and trying to catch up on all the school I've missed.

Things go real smooth for the spring.

Then, it's summer vacation.

Enter Holly and Kyle. Like my mother, Miss Holly was a victim of a man who sowed his seed and took no responsibility for it beyond court-mandated checks. She never married, just supported herself and her son by doing hair out of her camper until she got a job working at Cherry's salon.

First, I meet Miss Holly. Or, I see her from across the room and think *hot damn*. She's gorgeous, red-brown hair stacked up on her head, makeup all done like Angelina Jolie or something. Then, the door behind me swings open, and in walks Kyle.

I want a friend so damn bad.

Kyle is a cool guy with a pickup truck and a sparse mustache. He's about two years older than me, but he was held back two grades, so he just wanders around high school, a whole ass adult among the kids, flunking all his classes. I'm sure Cherry cringed when Kyle and I became best friends right off the bat, but I was good for him. At least, that's what Miss Holly told me.

Kyle and I are inseparable. Being broke and fatherless bonds us immediately. Inspired by his elite truck ownership status, I swing my focus on the thing that becomes my obsession for the entire year: getting myself one too.

Nobody has money for a truck at our age. The economy is flatter than flat, with no prospects of relief. None of us kids have anything to do but loiter and steal magazines from the dollar shop. Jobs are a rare commodity. Apparently, Miss Holly scraped together the money to get Kyle his truck, which Cherry is not about to do.

So, I decide if no place will hire me, I'll make my own luck. I go into the salon after school one day and announce I can do handyman jobs. One of the ladies says she needs somebody to paint her deck.

"How much?" I ask.

"Fifty bucks, if you strip the paint too," she says.

Done.

I shake her hand and show up the next day. That night, I have fifty bucks in my pocket. Holding that money feels like winning the lottery.

After that, it takes off. Anytime I'm not at school, I'm doing odd jobs for the salon ladies, and it all adds up.

I store it in my pillowcase. Then, after thinking it over, I go down to the gas station by Cherry's house. The gas station is at the intersection where the trailer parks meet the edge of town. It's walkable to the salon if you cut through a few backyards. Kyle comes along so he can buy cigarettes. I get a bucket of Crisco for one dollar and fifty cents.

We walk home. Kyle sits on the back stoop and smokes a Camel while I clean all the Crisco out and put it in gallon bags, wash the tin clean, and secure the lid on firmly with a pound and a half of duct tape. Then, I cut a slit in the top, big enough so money can go in, but not come out. One by one, I slide all my bills inside. Four hundred and thirty-seven dollars. I need about three thousand, five hundred more to get a truck.

Kyle and I spend the rest of the day talking about how to get more money. He's thinking of moving to Lexington in a few years. I want a truck by eighteen.

We both have goals.

So, we start a handyman business. Cherry has a printer we can make cards on. Using her sewing scissors, I cut them all out, earning myself a smack across the back of head when she finds out. Then, we hit the streets and put them on every doorstep in Byway. We're flexible, and our prices are competitive. By the end of the week, we're booked solid.

Every penny I earn goes into the Crisco tub. Then, the hot water heater breaks in Cherry's house, and we have to take some out, setting me back several hundred dollars. I couldn't say no to Cherry. She took me in without question when my mother passed. She keeps food in my belly, clothes on my back, and makes sure I'm getting an education. That makes her the first person to do that, and I owe her on that account.

I'm down about it for a day or two, but I get a new Crisco container and take it in stride.

My eighteenth birthday draws near, a momentous occasion. I graduate with incredibly average grades. Kyle, nonplussed that I'm no longer at school with him, drops out. Miss Holly grinds her teeth at the salon for weeks over that one, but Kyle doesn't give a fuck.

Instead of moving to Lexington, he decides to give up and blow all his money on booze.

Our handyman business is lopsided after that. I'm from nothing, but I know now what it tastes like to have money, and I want that damn truck so I'm not walking all over town for work, especially now that Kyle isn't showing up consistently. It's tough dragging all those tools around by hand.

My birthday comes and goes. I'm still four hundred dollars behind. Deflated, I trudge over to Kyle's house to play video games. He's in the living room, feet propped up on the couch. I take my boots off in the pristine hallway, grab the second controller, and sink down on the other end.

"Hey," Kyle says, not looking up.

We spend so much time at each other's houses, we don't knock. Miss Holly's place is a lot nicer than Cherry's. It's a real house, the walls painted white with cream rugs on wood floors. There's a hard and fast rule of no shoes inside and no beer out of the kitchen. Everything always smells like fresh flowers from the garden out front.

"I think we should cram some last minute jobs," I say.

Kyle grunts.

There's a click-click on the floor. I glance up and look away real fast. Miss Holly walks in wearing a skintight dress and towering heels, fluffing her hair, putting in earrings. I've never asked Kyle how old his mom is, but I've heard Cherry say she's forty-four. I'm not sure if I'm into older women, but I'm into Kyle's mom—not that I would ever, ever act on it.

"What are you boys doing?" she says, smiling brightly.

"Talking about how to make more money," I say.

She grabs her purse from the table. "Why? Your grandma not doing well?"

I shake my head. "Cherry's fine. I just fell short on my goal of four grand."

Her brows lift ever so slightly. "Goodness, Jen, I didn't know you'd had a birthday. Well, happy birthday. How short are you?"

"He's about six-three," says Kyle, not looking over.

"Shut up, honey," says Miss Holly. "How much do you need to hit four grand?"

"About four hundred," I say.

"Well, I got that job out in the backyard on the shed if you want it," she says. "We had it put in for the gardening tools, but I'd like to renovate it, make it into a tiny house so we can rent it out."

"I can do that," I say, interested. "What's it pay?"

"Probably like a week of work," she says. "At a rush rate."

I calculate. That's almost a thousand dollars. Without thinking, I nod, turning to Kyle. "You want to do that with me and split it?"

Kyle jerks his head. "Sure, whatever."

Overjoyed, I tell Cherry that night that I'm hitting my goals, albeit a little late. We toast with a splash of whiskey in the bottom of our coffee mugs. Then, I go to bed dreaming about finally having the freedom of four wheels. When I get up, it's to a text from Kyle saying he isn't going to make it. He went up to Lexington last night and ended up taking on a construction job that pays double.

I'm pissed, but it's fine. I won't have to split with him that way.

I gather my shit and walk down the road to Holly's house. The door to the shed is open. I go in and start taking measurements. I hear the back door open in the distance. Looking out, I see her standing on the back porch in a white bathrobe.

"I didn't expect you so early," she says. "You want some breakfast?"

I've spent so much time at her house the last two years, but for some reason, it feels weird today.

"I'm good," I say. "I ate."

"How about some coffee?" She cocks her head.

"Okay, that's fine," I call. "Just leave it on the porch."

She gives me a strange look, brows furrowed. Then, she goes inside. For some reason, I feel guilty as I haul the table-saw out of the garage and get it set up. Maybe she was just being nice, like she usually is. After a while, I look on the back porch, and there's a cup of coffee waiting for me.

I feel pretty bad about it. I think about it that evening and decide I'll be nice tomorrow. But when tomorrow comes, she doesn't offer me breakfast or coffee. Her car is gone when I get there, so I just start working on my own.

I break when the sun hits the middle of the sky. I sit in the shed with my back to the wall and open my cooler. Inside is the same meal I've been eating for lunch every day since I moved into Cherry's trailer—bologna sandwich with Miracle Whip on white bread.

The floor creaks. I glance up and freeze. She's standing there, looking like a million bucks in a tight shirt, her breasts overflowing like a badly poured beer, and high waisted jeans with flared legs. She smells like artificial cleanliness, lotion, soap, perfume. It's nice, but as someone who sweats all day into the same dirty shirt, it's jarring.

"How's it going out here?" she asks.

I swallow my bite of sandwich. "Fine. Making good progress."

"You can eat inside where it's cool," she says, turning on her heel and disappearing.

I think it over and decide I probably should. When I step through the sliding back doors, she's standing by the stove. There's a pot of sweet tea already bubbling. I sink down in my usual place at the breakfast bar. It feels weird to not have Kyle sitting with us. His presence was akin to fungus on the side of a tree, inert, but it kept things from feeling awkward.

"How's the shed coming along?" she asks.

"Good. On schedule."

She crosses her arms. "I appreciate you being willing to do it without Kyle. I really think this new job could be a breakthrough for him. It's been rough, him not having a daddy to help him get situated in the world. Of course, I know you both got that problem."

I just nod. She comes closer and leans on the breakfast bar. My whole body prickles. I'm a late bloomer, more focused on getting myself a truck and a steady income than girls, but I know some stuff from talking to Kyle. I've got a pretty good idea she's putting off signals.

I'm just not sure I want to be on the receiving end of them.

My life is carefully balanced, and she feels like she could upset it. I can't piss off Cherry because she took me in. I can't fuck up my relationship with Kyle because he's my best friend.

"You got a girlfriend, Jen?" she asks.

I shake my head. "No, ma'am."

"Why not? You're pretty. Real handsome."

It takes me a second to find my words again. "Um...just don't have time. Work and all."

She purses her lips. Then, she comes around the breakfast bar, and she's right up on me, standing between my knees. Heat pours through my body. Things are happening whether I'm ready or not. She leans in, and I catch a flash of her big eyes and cherry coke-colored lipstick. Then, she's kissing me, her nails gripping the front of my sweaty shirt.

I didn't get up that morning with the intention of swiping my V-card, but I do anyway, on the floor of Miss Holly's kitchen, my back against the cupboards. She's naked, her clothes strewn around. She's gorgeous like a movie star. Her hair smells good, her skin is soft, and she doesn't mind that I'm not doing a very good job overall. She just laughs, brushing back my hair, and tells me it's fine. We can try again later.

I could say no, get up, and leave.

But I don't, and I don't know why.

We get our clothes on, and I can't make eye contact. Shamefaced, I put my tools away and tell her I have to be somewhere, but I can put some more hours in on the shed tomorrow.

The walk home doesn't feel nearly as good as the walk I took to get there.

That night, I lie on my back and fight with guilt until the sun comes up. Then, I grab my shit, walk down the road, and knock on the front door, ready to confront Holly. This can never happen again.

She opens the door with two cups of coffee in her hand and nothing on but a little white nightgown. At first, she tries to pretend this is normal. We stand in the kitchen, coffee in hand, trying to make small talk. Finally, she snaps, takes my hand, and pulls me upstairs to her room. I've never been up here. Miss Holly's house is weirdly nice for a woman with a part-time salon job. I always assumed she was getting big child support checks or something.

I don't have time to think about it, because she's stripping my clothes off, and we're in her bed. She pushes me to sit against the quilted white headboard and rides me hard.

I feel sort of...used, but not enough to stop.

She pays me what she owes me, even though the shed's not done. I break open the Crisco tin for the last time and count everything up. I did it. I've got enough. The next morning, I walk down to the used car lot and pick out a truck. It sucks that Kyle isn't here to see me paint the logo of our business on the door.

But he'll be back, I'm sure of it.

It's not until the third time I sleep with Miss Holly that I start feeling something that isn't a kick to the gut. She's lonely, and she loves to talk afterward. I listen because I'm pretty good at that.

It's kinda nice.

I'm too young to go out with her, can't get into bars or clubs, so we start spending a lot of time at her house now that Kyle is staying in Lexington. I never told Cherry he moved out so she's not suspicious. Cherry is a no-shit kind of grandmother. If she caught us, it would be over for me and Miss Holly.

The fall turns into winter. I work less, but it's alright because I know it picks up in the spring. It's a cold season in Kentucky, and I spend most of it between the sheets in Miss Holly's bedroom. She knows all kinds of stuff, and I'm a quick learner. Roleplay, bondage, a little pain with our pleasure.

I'm hooked on her, to the point I hope Kyle doesn't come back for a while.

She smokes. I start smoking too, just to taste the same thing she does.

Spring comes, and I'm back to working long days outside, but I try to see her a few times a week. We fuck and drink whiskey on the front porch when it gets warm enough to be naked outside. The shed around back is done, but she never rents it out.

She feeds me real food too, no slight to Cherry. Her endless supply of cheap, processed meat saved me. It was better than having to ball up Wonderbread, squish it down hard, and eat it that way to keep it in my stomach longer. Holly loves cooking, and she makes me full meals, hot, with vegetables.

There's a lot of reasons I don't break it off.

"You think you'll ever leave Byway?" she asks one night.

I shake my head. "I don't have anywhere else to be. Plus, I'm making fine money. I should be able to get a house in a few years."

Her eyes are hazy. "What happens then?"

I glance sideways. She's biting her lower lip. "I don't know," I say.

She laughs. "I guess that's your business."

"What's that mean?" I press.

She shrugs, turning dewy lashes up to look at me. "I mean, I don't expect you to stay with me, Jen. You're young."

That's the first time I think about the future. If I want Miss Holly long term, that'll be a whole world of trouble when it goes public. It'll implode my personal life. The salon will be in an uproar. Every church in Byway will be whispering about it. But I'm willing to give it a try.

"I ain't leaving," I say.

She gives me a sad smile and doesn't answer. This is one of those times when I wish I had a father. I need somebody to talk to about all this shit, somebody who can give it to me straight. But I don't even have a name—Childress is the surname from my maternal side. It's not like I could track my sperm donor down and say *hi, can we talk*? Whoever that man was, he shook me off his shoes like dust.

Up until now, I found ways to ignore that void, but the summer I fall in love with Miss Holly, I think about it a lot.

CHAPTER TWO

JENSEN

AGE NINETEEN

One morning in early July, I take my truck out to see Holly before work. It's scorching hot. The air conditioner in the truck is broken, but I'm putting off getting it replaced because I need to fix something else that's rattling. Might as well do it all in one go.

I pull up under the willow and get out, wiping the sweat off my face.

And I stop in my tracks.

There's a man standing on the porch. He's got one hand in his pocket, the other holding a cigarette. He's wearing Sunday kind of clothes, but not the flashy ones. Good and simple dress pants, a starched shirt, open a few buttons and rolled up to the forearms. His tie hangs loose around his neck.

A tingle runs through my body. He's giving off the strangest aura. If the sun could come out at the same time as a storm rolls through, it would feel just like him.

I walk up the path to the porch. As I get close, I can see he's no younger than thirty, with a lean, handsome face. Almost an Appalachian Gregory Peck. His hair is colorless brown above hooded eyes with drooping lids. His whole demeanor is lazy, like a dog in the sun. All except for that sharp stare that follows my every move.

"Nice truck," he says.

The door opens behind him. Were they...doing something inside? My stomach is twisted with jealousy, but I'm relieved to see Holly is fully dressed.

No, I'm being paranoid.

"Hey," she says nervously. "This is a friend. He's looking for someone to help him with some odd jobs."

My shoulders sink. Okay, maybe this is innocent. It's not unusual that Holly hooks me up with clients. I lean forward, offering my hand. The man's face breaks into a smile, sweet as honey, and shakes it.

"You've got a good strong grip. I like that," he drawls. "Now, what's going on with that truck? I hear something rattling on it."

"Not sure. Once I get a chance to take the whole thing apart, I'm sure I can figure it out."

The man flicks his cigarette into a potted plant and dusts his hands off. "Let me take a look at it real quick."

I glance at Holly, who gives me a small smile. She's acting real cagey, but I know she's probably nervous about our secret getting out.

"What's your name?" I ask.

"Brothers," he says.

"Say what?"

He walks past me, and I hurry after him. He's moving confidently as he pops the hood and braces it open. "It's Brothers Boyd," he says.

"Brothers is your first name?"

He nods. "Yeah, what's yours?"

"Jensen," I say, "Childress."

He dips his arm into the engine bay and starts digging around. "Mind if I call you Jen?"

I shake my head. He takes the toolkit from the bed and starts working on the truck like we're good friends. I go along with it, because people are friendly in these parts. Miss Holly brings up iced tea after a while. She doesn't talk much, but I'm too distracted by Brothers to care.

Hell, I thought Kyle was cool, but Brothers is a clear winner.

He's a charismatic revelation. He talks slow and easy, like nothing bothers him, and he asks me questions like he cares about the answer. It's not lost on me that this is the first man, including Kyle, to work on my truck with me. That feels good.

I ask him what kind of work he needs me for. He says mostly delivery, pretty easy.

"What's the pay like?" I ask.

"Around a thousand a week, with room to move up," he says. "And room and board, for those who need it."

It sounds way too good to be true. I keep my face impassive and say I'll think about it. We finish up the truck around noon. Brothers says he's got to go and hands me his business card. Then, he invites me to Lexington, up to the racetrack, to see some of his horses train. I agree because I've never been.

I go, and it's a whole new world. Brothers knows everybody at the track. He can walk into a room and remember the names of three dozen men, their wives, their children, their dogs too. He chats his way through the crowd, introducing me left and right, shaking hands like a politician.

That night, I go home to Cherry's trailer like usual. The second I step through the door, I know something's wrong. Her raspy voice booms over the house, cussing somebody out in the living room. I walk in, and she turns on me.

"You fucking serious, Jen?" she yells.

The phone sails over my head. I duck.

"Jesus, what's the matter with you?" I say.

"Holly? Really?" She pushes a chair out of the way, coming close enough that I start backing up. "You fucking that whore? I thought I raised you to be better than that."

"I'm not fucking her," I say automatically.

"Yes, you are, and you got sloppy with it," she barks. "I just got off the phone with her, and she folded so fucking fast. Really, Jen? You've been fucking her for a year?"

My mind goes back to how scared I was that day on Holly's kitchen floor, but I don't know how to explain to Cherry that this wasn't intentional. It was like slipping on ice and sliding all the way down to a place I can't climb out of.

"Get the fuck out of my house," Cherry says, voice dropping. "Or I'm going to go over there and kill that bitch."

My whole body freezes. There's a pile of things on the table that Cherry never cleans off. Magazines, keys, screws from me fixing stuff around the house. My eyes fall on it, and I realize underneath unopened bills sits my lunch box. The one Cherry packed for me every day my last year of school.

"Leave?" I whisper.

"You explain what the fuck you're doing with yourself, Jen, or you get out," she says, deadly quiet.

"I don't know," I manage.

That's the God honest truth. Looking back, I don't think I wanted to get into this mess in the first place, but now I'm neck deep and guilty as sin.

"You don't know?" she repeats.

I shake my head. There's a hollow in my chest.

"Alright," she says, standing aside. "Get your shit and go."

She means it. Numb, I go upstairs and gather my things. I don't have much, no leftover things from my childhood. When my mother passed, all my childhood toys were sent to the charity shop. I arrived on Cherry's doorstep with a backpack of clothes. I repack it, grab my cash, and walk downstairs. Cherry sits at the kitchen table, an entire glass of whiskey in her hand.

"You should be ashamed, Jen," she says.

"Cherry—"

"You're grown," she says. "Get out."

Silently, I go out onto the porch and take my flip phone out. Miss Holly doesn't answer, even when I call her three times in a row. I get in my truck and start driving, not sure what to do. I can park in a gas station and sleep there tonight. Then, I have enough money to get a tent and find a place they won't chase me off tomorrow.

My phone lights up. It's an unknown number, but I answer.

"Hey, Jen," a man drawls.

Brothers Boyd.

"Hey," I say. "Everything alright?"

He laughs, but I'm not sure why. "I just got the feeling you might need a helping hand."

I drive in the dark, state route flying by, dazed from just becoming homeless, and it seems like a miracle. Everything spills out, and it feels so damn good to have a listening ear. I tell him about Holly, about Cherry, about only having a backpack of shit in the passenger seat.

I'm taking a breath to start on Kyle and how much it fucking hurt when he just off and went to Lexington without saying goodbye when Brothers stops me.

"Come on over, Jen," he says. "I'll text you the address. I'm not letting anybody live on the street."

I'm unsure how I feel about it, but I agree. He sends the address, and I turn the truck around to the other side of Lexington. When I roll up, I have to give my name to get through the black metal gates. Then, all the way down the drive, I'm just staring with my jaw slack. I knew Brothers was well off on account of owning racehorses, but he's got a mansion.

The doors open. Brothers stands between them, a shadow in a golden glow. I park and get out.

"Come on in, Jen," he says. "You had dinner yet?"

I climb the stairs, backpack on my shoulder. "No, but I'm fine."

"Nonsense," Brothers says.

We're in a stately hallway leading to a spiral staircase. There are doors lining both sides looking into large, well furnished rooms, but it's not that I'm staring at. It's the woman standing at the bottom of the stairs in a short, silk dress that has me stunned.

I'm frozen.

"What's Miss Holly doing here?" I whisper.

Brothers waves a hand like he's shooing away a fly. "Oh, she works for me. How'd you think she could afford that house?"

Holly takes a step closer, like she's going to touch me. Brothers slides right in between us.

"You're dismissed," he says firmly, giving her a cold stare.

She goes, like a dog with its tail between its legs. Before I can react, Brothers has me pulled into one of the rooms to my right. It's a lounge with a big fireplace and leather chairs. He pours a bourbon and lights a cigarette, handing both to me.

"What's going on?" I say.

"Nothing," he says. "I run a delivery business. She's in logistics, makes sure I have the means to keep all the routes running."

"Is she your girlfriend?" I blurt out.

He leans back, laughing. "No, she's not mine. Not like that."

A man appears and sets a tray of food down. Brothers fills my glass again and starts talking, laying everything out. He owns a shipping and delivery business in addition to racing and gambling. They distribute liquor, weed, and other products he's careful not to name. It's a lot to manage, so he keeps the people who work most closely with him here on site. He'd like to try me out as a delivery driver. Room and board is free as long as I do a good job.

I agree, but deep down, I'm making plans to figure something else out.

He sends me upstairs to the nicest room I've ever slept in. Big four poster bed, my own bathroom. I'm almost asleep when I hear the door creak open. Bare feet pad on the floor. A little weight dips the bed. Then, familiar warmth crawls over my body. Holly kisses me, face wet with tears.

"I'm so sorry, Jen," she whimpers.

"It's not your fault Cherry found out," I whisper.

She doesn't answer but does yank the covers back. Her hand goes in my boxers, and she starts riding me, hand on my chest. She's crying at the same time. I keep going soft because I don't want to fuck her while she's sobbing. She digs her claws into my chest as I push myself up on the pillows.

Then, out of the blue, she slaps me across the face.

I reel back. I'm stunned and suddenly rock hard.

Something mean clicks into place in that dark room. We fuck, harder and dirtier than we've ever fucked. Then, she falls asleep in tears while I sit against the headboard with my face in my hands. It takes a while, but I must drift off, because I'm waking up to a bird singing outside my window and an empty bed.

There's a stack of clothes by the door. I shower and put them on, lacing up a new pair of leather boots.

The front hallway is empty. I walk down it, looking everything over.

"Jen."

Turning, I see him through the first door on the left. It's a dining room with a big oval table and windows looking out over the horse barns. Brothers sits at the head.

"Come and get something to eat," he says.

I sink down. Another nameless person appears, fills my plate, and melts away. The coffee is good, strong enough to wake me up. We start eating, and the silence is big and awkward. There's a steak on my plate next to the eggs. It's kind of freaking me out. I've never tasted steak before, unless I'm counting Salisbury.

Finally, Brothers clears his throat.

"So what did you want to be when you grew up?" he says.

Alive would be the correct answer. My mother wasn't the best at keeping food on the table, so every day was a race against the empty space inside, but I still have a faint memory of the luxury of wanting something more. It sounds pretty silly when I think about it now.

"A cowboy," I say. "But I was about five then."

Brothers laughs, but it's a nice one. "I like that, like it a lot."

Silence. I hope I'm not embarrassing myself.

"When should I start work, sir?" I say finally.

"I'll show you around this afternoon," he says. "This morning, we're going to church."

"Church?" I stare.

"It's Sunday." He says it like that's obvious. "Now, I don't mean to tell you what to do with Miss Holly, but I know she was in your room last night. Do what you will any other day, but there is no fornication or drinking on the Lord's day within these walls."

He says all this casually, his drawl easy.

"But...you drank last night," I say.

"That was yesterday."

"Okay," I say, deciding not to focus on figuring him out right now. "So you don't...you know on Sunday."

"Never," he says.

Curious, I push it a little further. "What if I did?"

He lifts two fingers and puts them to his temple, miming pulling a trigger.

"You'd shoot me?" I say, jaw dropping.

"No," he says. "Of course not."

"Okay," I say, relieved.

"I'll shoot her," he says.

"What?"

"Before Miss Holly, there was a woman very much like her. After Miss Holly, there will be another one. The same goes for you. Make yourself irreplaceable, Jen. Just don't drink or fuck on Sundays in my home."

He gets up, giving me a soft look. There's something about his face, the way he holds himself, that makes me want to trust him. It's weirdly paternalistic for his age.

"Stick with me, Jen, and I'll make sure you're always taken care of," he says. "Oh, and there's only one other thing. We don't abide Caudills, so don't consort with any of them."

I know who the Caudills are; they're one of the richest families in the state. They have businesses, but their real money is made at the track and on drug running through the eastern end of the state.

"Why?" I ask.

"Because we are compet-tit-tors." He breaks up the syllables in that word, for emphasis.

Before I can answer, he walks out. I cut the steak, put it in my mouth, and damn—I think he's got me.

That begins the most exciting year of my life. I do odd jobs, set up meetings, and don't ask questions. In return, I get paid a thousand dollars a week, I stay in the Boyd Mansion, and I still get to fuck Miss Holly whenever she decides to appear in my bed. Whether the last part is a good thing is up for debate. It's getting to be a more traumatic experience every time, but I can't seem to stop.

I have bigger things to think about now—a real future. Brothers takes a liking to me. I'm smart, despite not having a great education. When it comes to hands-on stuff, I learn quick. He likes that all he has to do is give me instructions once, and I can carry them out to the letter.

The only contention between us is that I like Brothers and Brothers likes me, but Brothers *does not* like Holly and pretends she doesn't exist when she talks in front of him. Me liking Holly feels like a vulnerable point in our growing relationship.

I ask him about it one day while we're duck hunting. He's tracking a bird, shotgun up, one eye shut.

"Money is money, Jen," he murmurs. "Business is business. Fucking is fucking."

I don't know exactly what that means, but it sounds like he's telling me who I fuck won't negatively affect my standing with him.

So, I don't break it off with Holly. By day, I'm Brothers Boyd's best worker and closest friend. By night, I'm Jen, the guy who can't make up his mind about what he wants.

Pretty soon, I become something of a right hand to Brothers, taking the place of his absent brother, Jem. He was supposed to help run the business, but he rarely shows up for work anymore, not unless he's forced. At first, I like Jem, and we work together a lot, but then he starts to feel a lot like Kyle, just checked out all the time.

But me, I show up in all ways. Brothers starts trusting me with the more delicate parts of his business, the parts that could get him in trouble if we mess up. In turn, I trust he knows what he's doing and follow his orders.

I like that trust. It makes me irreplaceable.

We're all over the town, in the speakeasies, the pubs, the racetrack, rubbing elbows with what Brothers refers to as the seersucker bourgeoisie. Not a day goes by where we rest—he's building an empire and he's building it fast. Brothers is always at Keeneland, shaking hands and leaving with his pockets heavier. I go from being a boy from Harlan County with nothing to sitting at the tables of Lexington's richest men.

Most importantly, for the first time in my life, I have something that feels like a real family. I never had a father or a brother, but Brothers Boyd comes so close. My life is good, beyond my wildest dreams.

Until it isn't, and everything crumbles in a single night. One mistake, and the whole thing is gone, leaving me standing in the rubble. I have nothing but my very first dream and my unbreakable will to live. On horseback, with only a revolver on my belt, I head west to cowboy country and never look back.

Fuck Holly.

Fuck Kentucky.

And most of all, fuck Brothers Boyd.

CHAPTER THREE

DELLA

FIVE YEARS AGO

AGE EIGHTEEN

It's spring, and I'm going to miss it this year.

I'm standing in the doorway of the only home I've ever had. Leland let me spend my last night here before the wedding. It was a long argument. *Why do you want to stay out there? I have a hotel booked for you.* But my husband-to-be doesn't understand. He doesn't want to understand me. He wants obedience.

A car is coming to get me soon. I have a few minutes to gather my overnight bag. Then, I have to walk down the dirty path to the gravel road, and I'll never live in this valley again.

My heart hurts. My eyes are dry from crying until past midnight.

Stepping outside, I shade my eyes even though the sun hasn't cut through the mountains yet. My little holler, deep in the mountains, always stays cool and shaded. The creek never dries up. I hear it bubbling at the bottom of the hill. If I walk all the way down the road, the mountains pull back, and everything is dusty and dry. But here, it's a little rainforest tucked away.

At the edge of the road, I close my eyes. The air is soft, warm, with a hint of coolness. I tilt my head and inhale—blossoms and greenery. Deep inside, I feel that flutter reminding me I'm not alone. My hand moves instinctively to my belly, where Leland's baby grows. A baby I never wanted, because now, I'm tied to him forever.

Leland Caudill is a criminal, a refined one who will never get caught because he's friends with the judges and police. But he and his family are the worst of the worst, loaded up with money from pills, rigged races, and other things he'll never speak out loud. I'm the unfortunate girl from Harlan County who got stuck waiting his table at the diner one day while he was passing through on a job from his father.

A tear escapes. I let it run.

I wasn't supposed to leave home. Hell, I'd have been happy living in the holler until they buried me in my family plot over the crest of the hill, but Leland is making me live in a house outside Lexington so he can turn me into something I'm not. I'll raise his son for him, be the perfect little mob wife. When it's my time, they'll put me in a big cemetery with no real family to keep me company.

Down the lane, a plume of dust rises. The shiny grate of an SUV appears.

My time is up.

Ducking inside, I gather my things and shove them into my bag. Then, I stand in the doorway as the car pulls up. I don't smile when the driver opens the door. Today, I'm grumpy and pregnant. My stomach is starting to show, at twenty-five weeks. He wanted to marry me before, but I took a lot of convincing. It wasn't until it sunk in that he was going to have me whether I liked it or not that I gave in.

No one says no to the Caudills.

I bite my cheek, lock the door, and climb into the SUV. The driver is a Caudill soldier, in a black suit and sunglasses. He gives me a curt nod as he pulls onto the road, ignoring my scowl. The backseat is shiny leather and smells like fresh paint. I sit in the middle awkwardly. There's no warmth here.

I stare out the window as the mountains fall away and the land grows flatter. Growing up, at our tiny high school, I was voted the funniest student. I might not have all the fancy education as Leland, but I can be quick. I've read every book I can get my hands on. I've devoured all the shows and movies. The principal even tried to get me to apply to college. I said no, knowing Mama would never be able to scrape together the money for a bus ticket, much less tuition.

Then, Leland came.

And I think my light might be dying.

I start peeling the skin back from my thumbnail at the thought of Leland. He says I need to stop using phrases he doesn't know. Why can't I put on a fucking pair of shoes once in a while? He says those things with a smile, like it's a joke, but it's not.

"You have a beautiful body, Della," he says sometimes. "I'll take you to buy better clothes for it."

I wear clothes from the salvage thrift shop. Big shirts with logos I don't recognize, basketball shorts, and slides from the dollar shop. We never had money. My mother worked the deli counter at the grocery store and had too much pride to accept charity. So, we made do.

Of course, the day I met Leland, I was wearing something different. That day, I put on a sundress on a whim. It was a tiny, cotton thing that always got me double the tips. He must have liked that, because he was knocking on my door days later.

I should have stuck to t-shirts and shorts. My mama likes to joke that dress broke the poverty cycle for future Cooleys. We were damned in her eyes. Then, in walked Leland, and now she's got a fancy house looking out over the river waiting for her after this wedding. That's the only good part. My mama worked hard after

Daddy died. Maybe this is a sacrifice I need to make to pay back my debt.

I'm a little sick by the time we pull up outside the Caudill Mansion. The Caudills are Catholics, but the Cooleys have always been Baptist, so we compromised on which church to get married in and decided to hold it at the enormous mansion where I'll live with Leland.

Red brick walls surround the yard. The house is modern, built about ten years ago. It sprawls out bigger than any house has the right to be. Big, white columns hold up the multiple porches. A silvery driveway winds over the hill, right to the front door. Everything is decorated in white roses wilting in the heat.

The driver pulls up and helps me out. Before I can get my bearings, a dozen women spill out the front door and pull me away to the back room behind the kitchen. There's a vanity set up. My dress hangs on the back of the door. A little plate of frosted strawberries and a bottle of sparkling water sit by the mirror. Hands push me to the bathroom and help me into the tub, not caring if I might want privacy.

Then, it's back to the vanity. I sit still while they do my makeup. These aren't my friends. They're all women hired by Leland.

I have no one coming today. My people aren't refined like his family and friends. Today, it's just me and Mama from my side.

And my baby. He's half Cooley.

Fists clenched, I sit perfectly still while they put me together. My dress is zipped up my back, and they rearrange the overlapping silk to cover my stomach like it's shameful. He doesn't want anyone to know he jumped the gun. Running drugs is fine in the Caudill family, but God forbid somebody gets pregnant out of wedlock.

The women dissipate when I'm done. I stand, my hips cracking. I've noticed they do that more now I'm pregnant. Things ache where they didn't before.

My lungs constrict. I need air.

Pushing open the door to the back porch, I step out and take a deep breath. The air is different here. Everything smells like the Magnolia grove to the left of the house. Carefully so I don't stain my dress, I sink down to sit on the concrete stoop. I'm not a smoker, but

I've stolen a few from the corner gas station before. And my daddy was a smoker, big time. I think it would get my head on straight if I could just hold a Camel and feel it burn between my fingers.

Deep inside, there's another flutter. A kick. I just started feeling those, almost like a hiccup suspended in the nothingness between my hips.

I lift my head and touch my stomach with my fingertips. A faint warmth stirs higher, in my heart area. I might not love Leland, but I think I could love his baby. Maybe he'll look like me, or my daddy—just so long as he doesn't look like a Caudill.

The door behind me swings open. I know without turning that it's my mother.

"Come on. We need to go," she begs.

I stare at my heels, pearl white. My perfect face is sealed under a mask of setting spray, my body carefully concealed in a tiered silk wedding gown to keep the little bump in my lower belly a secret.

Why it has to be a secret, I don't know. Everybody is going to know when I give birth months early.

I stand, brushing off the back of my gown. My mother is in blue silk, looking stunning. Ever since Leland put a ring on my finger, my mother has blossomed. Maybe that makes it all worth it. I don't know. I know for certain she's so much happier than she was trying to raise me alone.

I give her a weak smile. "Sorry, it's just hot in the back room."

"You need your makeup fixed?" Her brows crease.

I shake my head, moving past her into the house. It's so opulent, it makes my head spin. It towers over the river like Mount Olympus on a hill. When I stepped through the doors for the first time, it felt like somebody was squeezing my lungs. This will be my home. A hundred rooms. A hundred windows to look out and wonder if I'm a prisoner or a wife.

"My makeup is fine, Mama," I whisper. "Can you get my flowers from the cooler?"

"Sure. Why don't you meet me in the hall?" she says, gathering her skirt's train. "Don't go any further than the door, or Leland will see you."

I nod. She disappears through the side door. I know I have at least fifteen minutes because the cooler is in the basement. Carefully, I touch my hair to make sure it's perfect. Then, I step into the huge hallway to the living room.

They said Leland was doing right by me, marrying me after he knocked me up. I wish he'd be satisfied with being a deadbeat.

I never wanted to marry him, baby or not.

Sunlight falls through the paneled windows. Through them is the magnolia grove. They're young but already blooming. The wind picks up, blowing a few white petals into the sky, taking them away.

I could be like that. I could pick up my heavy skirts and run through the grove, over the hill, just keep going until I'm in a new place where nobody knows me. I close my eyes, leaning on the windowsill.

That sounds like heaven.

"Darling."

I turn to find my almost-husband standing just inside the door. He shuts it, coming close. I swallow the lump in my throat. Leland is handsome, like a movie star—big, broad, with a nice jawline, wavy dark hair, and blue eyes. He's got a white smile, a deep, rich voice, and everybody wants to be him or be with him.

Except me, the one person he's hellbent on getting.

He stops, hands in the pockets of his linen suit. This is his first look at me in my wedding gown. Warmth stirs, confusing me. Maybe I do love him. Maybe love just feels like anxiety and dread. I give him a brave smile, sweet, like the frosting on the wedding cake in the dining room next door.

He holds out his hands. I go to him, placing my palms in his. He leans down, kissing me discreetly so he doesn't mess up my makeup.

"My wife," he says. His eyes drop to the silk over my belly. "My son."

I just smile. I've always imagined my heart as a porcelain tea cup, easily breakable, and right now, there's a fine crack in it.

"You're beautiful," he says.

"Thank you," I whisper.

"We'll do the ceremony, then pictures in the Magnolia grove."

Turning my head, I look out at the rows of trees. Again, I see myself running through them. Leland touches my chin, turning me back to face him. He doesn't like when I give anyone or anything more attention than him. He's going to hate it when I have a newborn sucking up all my time and energy.

Through the door, I hear a cello playing, my mother's footfalls in the backroom. She comes through and starts scolding Leland for seeing me early. They laugh, joking with each other as she pushes him back into the living room.

I'm frozen to the ground, my flowers sticky in my hot fingers. If he hadn't gotten me pregnant, I really would disappear through the back door.

My gut is telling me Leland isn't safe, not after what he did.

So I don't run. Instead, I say my vows in the living room, surrounded by Caudills and their friends. Smile on my face, I dance with him for the first time. I cut the cake and let him feed me a forkful. Sugar melts on my tongue. His face is blurry like a bad dream. I endure all the comments made by his drunk friends as he carries me up the spiral staircase. And I let him fuck me, still in my wedding dress.

He sleeps. I lay on my side and cry without making a sound.

I barely know this man. We slept together for a few months, I wasn't even serious about him. Then *boom*—all my choices went right out the window. All it took was a misunderstanding and a little blue plus sign.

Now I'm his wife.

The next morning, he's gone at the crack of dawn. Slowly, I push myself up, knowing I have about a second. The sickness hits me, and I'm up, tearing across our enormous bedroom to the marble bathroom. I skid on my knees to the toilet and grip the edge.

Bile and water comes up. My vision wavers, heat and cold rolling over me. Then, it's over. That's the least I can say about this pregnancy. Once I throw up the minute my eyes open, the sickness is done.

Slowly, I push myself to my feet and turn on the shower. I smell like Leland, like his musky aftershave with notes of orange. It's no wonder, he was all over me last night. Stepping into the shower, I lean my head against the wall, and let the water wash him away.

Hunger comes with a new craving every morning. This time, it's for home. I want to be back in our trailer at the edge of the woods in the holler, the river glittering at the bottom of the hill. My heart is sick over never seeing those white-washed walls or curtains made from salvage shop sheets again. I'll never wake up to my open bedroom window, paint shards on the sill and wrens peeping in through the shades. I'll never walk into the kitchen and smell ham soup simmering on the stove.

My stomach clenches. A powerful craving for that soup, the texture of the beans, the saltiness of the ham, washes over me, all poured over sweet cracklin' bread.

God, I need some cracklin' bread right now. I could eat an entire pan of it.

I get out and dry off, putting on a plain white sundress. It's got thin straps that hang off my shoulders and a little flare at the hips. I wrap my hair into a bun at the nape of my neck. Then, I walk out into the enormous hallway.

I pad barefoot down the hall to the top of the spiral staircase. There's a maid wiping down the steps. I pause at the top awkwardly.

"Can I slip by you?" I ask.

She shoots to her feet, folding her hands. "Go right ahead, ma'am."

"Thank you," I say, offering her a smile. "What's your name?"

"Georgie, ma'am," she says, dipping her head. She's pretty, with wavy blonde hair and bright blue eyes. I wonder where she comes from, the way she speaks reminds me of myself.

"It's nice to meet you. I'm Della," I say. "Could you point me to the kitchen? I've never found it coming from upstairs."

Her brows knit. "Can I get you anything?"

"Just directions to the kitchen."

She's uncomfortable, but she points me down the hall. I go, in awe of the size of this great house. The ceilings are so high, they seem like a waste of space. The walls are off white, and Caudill portraits hang along the wall. Fresh flowers sit here and there, clean and curated, not like the wildflowers at home.

The kitchen is empty, but I can smell food. There's a linen apron over the chair. I grab it, wrapping the strings around my waist. Mouth watering, I start going through the freezer until I find what I'm looking for—a ham bone for broth. There's dried beans in the cupboard, along with cornbread mix and, shockingly, cracklings. I pick through the beans while the water boils, no time to soak them.

My mouth is watering. I need that fucking bread with soup, or I'm going to rip somebody's head off.

The side door bangs open. I glance up as a pretty woman with wavy brown hair and big eyes swishes inside. It's hard to tell, but we look about the same age. She's in a skintight mint dress and matching heels. Her eyes fall on me. She hesitates, then she smiles. I know her type—upper class Lexington, spray tanned, lots of makeup perfectly contouring her pretty face. I balk, feeling like I'm about to get judged for my appearance.

"Hey, Della," she says.

I hesitate.

"I'm Kayleigh," she says, sitting at the table. "Leland's cousin."

"Oh, I'm sorry," I manage. "I met so many people yesterday, I'm a bit turned around."

She gives me the most genuine smile I've seen in weeks. Before she can speak, I hear footsteps coming down the hall. I know who it is before I see my husband. Turning my back, I pour the beans in the water and reach for an onion. The door bursts open, and the footsteps stop short. I glance sideways for a second, and I swear, I see Kayleigh roll her eyes.

"Della."

I turn. Leland stands by the table in a dove gray suit. His eyes rake over me. For the first time since I got pregnant, I'm not hiding my growing stomach. He's looking at it, poking out under the apron, and he's proud of it, I can tell.

"What are you doing in the kitchen?" he asks.

I blink. "Making food. I have a craving."

He glances around the room. Kayleigh is eating cookies out of a tin, watching him like she just scraped him off her designer shoe.

"Have the maid cook for you or order something to the house," he says. "Why are you barefoot?"

I look down. Why do I need shoes? I'm not going anywhere. Kayleigh takes a bite of butter cookie and dusts off her fingers, mint nails flashing.

"How about you shut the fuck up, Leland?" she says. "Nobody asked your opinion, and they probably never will if they know what the fuck is good for them."

My jaw drops. Instantly, I change my opinion of Kayleigh. She's got some spice to her, and I like it.

"Why are you even here?" Leland snaps, going red.

"I was dropping some paperwork off," she says, jumping to her feet. "Paxton sent me. He's hungover from staying up all night after the reception."

"Well, show yourself out," he says.

She tosses her waves, sashaying to the door. Before she disappears, she flips Leland off behind his back and winks at me. I bite my lip so I don't giggle in front of him. That's all it takes for me to decide I like Kayleigh a lot.

The door shuts. He comes close, looking over my shoulder. "What are you making?"

I look up, giving him big, pleading eyes. They usually work. "Cracklin' bread with soup over it."

He stares down at the beans and bone simmering in the pot, and a crease appears on his forehead. "You're not supposed to cook. We have people for that. And I expect to see you dressed every morning."

"I'm dressed," I say.

"No, dressed up like Kayleigh," he insists. "I'll have your stylist come in this week and build you a wardrobe. You need to be pulled together. We have people coming in and out of the house for business most days. You are the matriarch of this family now."

I feel the emotion behind those words. It hurt him when his mother passed. I've got big shoes to fill. Quickly, I dip my head, and he takes my chin, lifting it back up.

"Understand, darling?" he asks.

I nod, sniffing. "Sorry. I'm not trying to embarrass you. I've been throwing up, and this is the only thing I wanted to eat."

He sighs. "Let me take you out instead."

Fuming, I snap off the stove and shove the half-cooked pans in the fridge. He doesn't understand. I don't just want the bread and soup. I want the particular way my family makes it, the memories that come along with it. But I just nod, blinking hard.

He takes me to an upscale restaurant in Lexington. I sit at his side while he talks to everybody who walks by. The Caudills are Kentucky's number one family, fast pushing out other competing empires. Leland can't go out in the city without having a bottle sent to his table. I don't eat much. The food is dull. There's no life cooked into it.

That night, after he's in bed, I go back downstairs and make the cracklin' bread and soup. It takes a long time, but it's worth it the minute I take the first bite.

I close my eyes, savoring that taste. Deep inside, my son kicks.

I smile. He likes it.

That becomes my routine for my pregnancy. In the morning, I wear what he wants and go out for breakfast in the city. People stare at my stomach and shake Leland's hand, like he did something extraordinary by knocking me up. Sometimes, we have dinner too, at places where nobody can ever get a reservation.

After Leland's in bed, I cook in peace down in the kitchen. My son is active during those times. I hum all the songs I know from memory to him. And he always kicks when I eat, especially the summer foods—spoonbread, salted tomato and corn, biscuits cooked in cast-iron with sausage gravy.

I leave a shopping list on the fridge. The next week, every item is in the cupboard. Georgie smiles at me, and I smile back at her. It's a small victory to have women in this house I can call allies.

I eat so damn much, but I burn it all off in my Leland-mandated maternity fitness classes the next day. He's very concerned that the baby comes out big and healthy. He even gets a doctor to give me a strict diet to follow.

That doesn't stop me. I'm starving every minute of the day, so I eat what I want at night. That includes making a mason jar of apple butter and eating the entire thing over pancakes and licking the jar clean. He doesn't understand how much work my body is putting in.

Or how homesick my heart is.

Kayleigh finds me late one night, and she joins in. I like her. She's different from me, but she's witty and kind. She doesn't give a shit what anybody in her family says. She does whatever she wants and spits fire if they criticize her for it. We bitch about Leland together. I cook her recipes from my family, and she eats them and asks for more. She teaches me how to be a Caudill woman, although I'm not brave like her.

Everything comes to a screeching halt when I go into labor. Traditionally, the Caudill women give birth at home with a doctor attending. I get my first wave of contractions around midnight, and fifteen hours later, I'm still writhing on the bed in agony, trying to push out Leland's eleven pound baby with no progress.

Kayleigh is there because I insisted. I don't want my mother around—she's not good under pressure. Kayleigh is white as a sheet, begging Leland to call an ambulance by hour ten. It's not until the doctor tells him there's a risk to the baby that he orders a helicopter to the backyard. I remember none of it, but they end up doing a c-section while I'm passed out.

My son is called Leland Landis Caudill, named for two of his paternal great grandfathers. I don't have a say because I'm unconscious. By the time I'm stitched back up and able to reach for my son, the ink is dried, and he'll never have my daddy's name. Kayleigh brings him to me, placing him in my arms, and I burst into tears at the first look.

He looks just like Leland.

I can't be calmed down. Kayleigh takes Landis, which is how he'll be known until he's grown, to the nursery. I sob, exhausted and scared. Every nerve in my body quivers. Leland asks me what's wrong. He's overjoyed. When I don't answer, he gets annoyed and orders me to stop. Finally, he leaves me to cry alone.

I can't do this.

I thought I could, but I can't.

This is over. I won't stay with Leland. There's something about laboring for fifteen hours with nothing but a Tylenol, only for him to name our son without asking my opinion, that wakes me the hell up. I won't raise another Caudill man to do this to some poor woman again. I'm done with being good and taking his dick and his fucking opinions without complaint.

I'm leaving him.

And I'll take my son with me.

CHAPTER FOUR

JENSEN

PRESENT DAY

The sky is overcast.

I stand on the crest of the hill. Today, I'm up at Ryder Ranch, working on cleanup after a fire on a neighboring farm. Deacon Ryder, the owner and namesake of the place, a close friend, always has endless jobs for my crew. This time, it's tearing down the scorched remains now that the warm weather is here and we can finally get equipment over the hill.

It took us about all week. Now, the last truck has hauled everything out. The ashes still need to be raked and taken away, but overall, we're done.

The wind picks up. It smells hot, like a storm.

I'm bored, and a little depressed. There are three months left until my fortieth birthday. The last few years, all my friends out in Montana have been settling down, coupling up and having kids. It's hard being the odd one out, but it's how I prefer it. There's always the possibility, even after nineteen years, that I might have to disappear in the dead of night.

I turn and walk down the hill to the ranch house. Deacon's woman, Freya, is on the porch, her dog panting at her side. My useless hound, Chicken, is passed out in the dirt on the walkway. He barely opens an eye as I ride up and dismount.

"You hungry?" Freya asks.

I shake my head.

"I've got to head out," I say. "But thanks."

The barn door slides back, and Deacon appears. He takes off his dusty hat and strides across the lawn, reaching into his pocket for the check. I take it, and click my fingers for Chicken, who doesn't even turn his head. Deacon sinks down on the steps and takes his handkerchief out to wipe his forehead.

"You staying for dinner?" he asks.

"He's got someplace to be," Freya says, sitting on the top step.

They're an odd couple. Deacon is about my age, roughed up from years of hard living. He's bullish and hardheaded, used to swaggering through life and getting what he wants. Freya is twenty-three, I think, and sweet with some fire to her. She comes from the mountains, same as me, but I don't talk about that with her—or anybody else. The last thing I want is to dig up the past. Deacon knows I don't like discussing it, so I doubt he's brought it up to her either.

"Where you off to?" Deacon asks.

I shrug. "Stockyards."

"Maybe you should consider going on a date or something," Freya drawls. "Like a real one."

Deacon laughs. "I don't think Jensen's the settling down type, sweetheart."

I shrug, slapping my thigh for Chicken. He stares vacantly before finally pulling himself upright, bones creaking, but that's as far as he gets.

"Oh, just leave him here," says Freya. "He's not hurting anything."

"Fine. I'll pick him up next time I drop by," I say, putting on my hat. Freya likes my dog, and that's alright by me. My dog probably likes Freya better than he likes me. "I'll see y'all around."

They sit on the porch and wave me off. Then, it's just me in the silent truck, eating up highway as I head towards South Platte. Just beyond lies West Lancaster, a little rougher of a place but with a better nightlife. Being out at Ryder Ranch, seeing Deacon so happy with Freya, has me feeling a bit hollow.

But there's a cure for that.

The stockyards are humming when I arrive. There was an auction just hours earlier, and the first people I run into are Westin and Sovereign, two friends who run one of the biggest ranches in the state. Westin is a tall, lankier fellow with a penchant for minding his business or getting into colossal trouble, depending on how he's feeling that night. Sovereign is a behemoth—not only in stature, but when it comes to the cattle business. We met a few years after I arrived in Montana and have been fast friends since.

Sovereign is counting bills, then pushing his wallet into his pocket. Westin leans on the makeshift bar, hat over his eyes.

"Y'all staying tonight?" I ask, pulling up beside them.

Sovereign glances up. "No can do. Got family stuff."

"Made out like bandits at the auction today, though," Westin says. "You're fighting again?"

I nod, leaning across the bar to tap the chalkboard so the bartender knows to add me to the list. He catches sight of me and nods.

"You should try actually dating instead of fighting," says Westin. "The end result might keep you a little warmer than winning a couple hundred bucks tonight."

I shake my head. "I can get laid if I want."

His forehead creases, and I know what he's thinking. Westin, Sovereign, and Deacon all settled down in the last few years. Now, they've got kids, and they come around the bars and stockyards less and less. That leaves me, the last person still knocking around my ranch alone. Unless, of course, I count—

"Jack Russell, goddamn it," murmurs Sovereign.

The uncomfortable fifth wheel of our group appears behind the bar.

"Did you miss me?" he says.

"No, I see you too much now," Sovereign says, taking his hat off the bar and fitting it on. "Come on, let's clear out."

He leaves, and Westin waves as he follows him, walking backwards until they're out of sight. Jack sighs, leaning his elbows on the counter. The only person who comes close to the mystique of Brothers Boyd is Jack Russell, cowboy assassin extraordinaire and professional manipulator. He was the first person I met in Montana, coming right up to me for my freshman fight in the stockyards.

He gave me a business card for his bar and told me if I ever needed help, to call him. It took me a while to figure it all out, but Jack Russell is what Brothers could have been if he wasn't the devil.

He's a talented killer for hire. Everyone knows when Jack Russell took some politician or businessman out, but nobody can prove it. The death is always so discreet, so clean, but so obvious that it was a paid hit.

Everyone knows, but they can't prove it.

He kills and collects, making him one of the richest, most influential men this side of the country. The other thing that helps with that is his face. We all make fun of him for it, and he doesn't mind because it's his greatest asset when it comes to getting himself laid. He's too damn pretty—dark hair, green eyes, a serpentine smile—but it gets him whatever he can't get with a bullet.

"I'm heartbroken," Jack murmurs.

"No, you're not," I say. "Pass me the tape under the bar."

Jack flips it over his back, catches it, and tosses it at me. The bartender appears, glancing sideways at him.

"What are you doing in my bar, Jack?" he rumbles.

"Can I bartend tonight?" he asks, flashing his Cheshire cat grin.

He shrugs. "Sure, why not?"

"Cool, thanks," Jack says, pleased. "I won't let you down, bud."

Jack Russell is loaded, beyond the rest of us. He doesn't need to own a bar or take on random bartending gigs. He's just chronically bored. I can relate to that. I own a construction company and a ranch, but I'm constantly plagued by the feeling of standing still.

"They're worried about you because you're single and sad," Jack says, watching me tape my hand.

"Thank you. I appreciate that," I say. "You are too."

"I'm single, not sad."

"I'm single by choice. You're single because you make people uncomfortable."

"Only because I'm gorgeous."

"I'm about to deck you in the face and fix that for you."

He laughs, taking a giant bucket of peanuts from under the bar, and starts cracking them. I think that's for the customers, but nobody here is about to tell him off.

"I'm not the one hiding from my problems with this macho shit," he drawls.

I give him a sharp look. Other than Deacon, Jack Russell is the only person in Montana who knows about my past. Despite his many flaws and the way he delights in annoying me, he's been there like a watchdog. He's got my back, checking to make sure no one from Kentucky tries to find me, keeping me hidden. Why? I don't know. Jack just decides he likes certain people and forces them to be his friend. I'm one of those people.

"Okay," Jack says, holding up a hand.

"What are you doing here tonight anyway?" I ask, pulling off my shirt and mopping my already sweaty face.

"Bored," he says, eyes sweeping the room. "No clients right now. If you're fighting, I might bet."

He leans forward to flick a peanut shell away. The silver dog necklace around his neck catches the light. To get ahead of the inevitable questions about his name, he branded himself and his businesses with a little silver terrier. His calling cards for clients are printed with a silver terrier, his bar is called The Brass Terrier, and he wears that damn necklace all the time. At this point, I wouldn't be surprised if he had a dog tattooed on his ass.

"Do you want to see a card trick?" he drawls.

"No," I say. "And no for next time you ask."

He rolls his eyes. "Alright, you better win, because I might put some real money down."

"I'll do what I do best."

The bartender appears again. "You want the first fight, Jensen?"

I shake out my arms. "Yeah, why not?"

Jack slides a shot over the bar, and I empty it, flipping it on the counter and leaving the bar. The crowd is thick, already gathered around the partitioned off area laid with plywood boards. There's a fighter warming up—my opponent, I presume. He's maybe a decade younger but about my weight class. Stepping over the tape, I glance him up and down as we shake hands. This shouldn't be too hard.

When I worked for Brothers, the rich fucks used to host illegal fighting rings in Red River Gorge. That's where I learned to fight for cash. Back then, I didn't need the pay out, but I did when I first got here, before I started construction. For the first five years, I lived off that money.

Now, it's just for fun.

To feel something.

The crowd is tensing up. The man who referees most nights climbs over the tape. My opponent is shaking his arms, pacing. He's got a smaller wingspan than I do, which can be bad or good, but I know how to play it to make it work in my favor. I circle, matching him, loosening my muscles up.

The crowd fades out. Excitement rises.

Finally, I feel something. It's a small challenge, but it's real, tangible. Despite all my years here, there's a big part of me that went numb after what happened in Kentucky. Now, there's always this strange feeling I'm watching someone else live their life, like I'm too self-aware, too careful. I can't live in the moment. It's like I'm a little action figure, moving myself around my life.

But being in the ring puts me firmly back into my own body.

The whistle goes off. Right away, my opponent swings, which I didn't expect. I duck, battering him back. He's got strength, coiled up in his shorter arms. But he doesn't have the reach to go on the defense the way I can, and he's tiring himself out fast.

This is my specialty—letting them wear themselves down. Then wham, bam, thank you ma'am, and they're down in a couple punches.

This guy is walking right into it. We spar back and forth across the ring. I'm enjoying myself, getting a little blood on my hands when he catches me below the eye and when I get him in the nose. It adds an edge to the energy in the room, and we're both here to put on a show.

I let it go on, watching him get more frustrated. My betting box has a lot of cash on it; I see it from the corner of my vision. It might be time to clean this up and move on—the next fight might be with someone who challenges me a little more.

He comes in swinging. I dip back and catch him with a right hook that sends him flat on his back. *Bam*—he hits the ground like a sack of bricks. He doesn't get up. He just lies there twitching. The referee squats, says something to him, then raises a hand. The fight is over.

I could go for another.

"We got the next round booked," the referee says as he walks past.

"I'll take the next open slot."

"That's fourth."

I shake his hand. "Good for me. Thanks."

Leaving the ring, I'm feeling good, loose, with just enough adrenaline to make me forget. At the bar, somebody hands me my shirt, and I pull it on. The bartender gives me a rag and a bottle of water. I have some, then dump the rest on my head and towel off. My drinks will be on the house tonight, so I order another shot of whiskey.

"Do you feel something yet?" Jack appears like a specter over my shoulder.

"Fuck off," I say.

His lids flicker, eyes focusing past me. "You're being watched."

There's something in his voice that has a chill going up my spine.

"What?"

He leans on the counter, jerking his head. I follow his gaze, and my eyes fall on a slender figure through the crowd. I open my mouth, then shut it. She's looking at me sideways through thick lashes. There's a little smile on her face, a come-on-over-here-and-find-out smile, one that tells me she knows how pretty she is, standing there surrounded by the chaos of the stockyards.

I can't move.

Hell, I can't speak.

Jack's saying something. I'm not fucking listening.

I've never seen eyes like those—big, deep brown, shaded by lashes heavy with glittering makeup. They're warm and a hundred miles deep. There's a little twinkle in them, like she can hold her own. I could trip and fall right in those eyes and be happy to drown.

Slowly, she lifts her hand, nails long and buffed beige, and blows a kiss, barely touching the tips of her fingers to her full mouth.

My jaw is slack. I clench it.

She shakes her hair out, a cascade of gold and brown falling down her back. I tear my eyes from her face and give her a glance over. Then, I go in again, because there's something here to appreciate.

Goddamn, she is pretty. She's all the things I shouldn't want but do anyway. Too young for me, several leagues ahead. Her body, beneath a tight, short, fringed dress that barely reaches the middle of her thigh, is lean with some curves. Enough ass to overflow my hand, enough tits to fill it.

But it isn't that that has me captivated. It's whatever is overflowing those eyes, that smile, like life is just spilling out of her, glittering, glowing, warm as the first day of spring.

She could stand in the middle of the universe, and it would revolve around her, drawn to the light.

The room is a dull roar in the background.

I have no idea where Jack went, but I swear I felt him slip something into my pocket. I don't care right now.

My boots start moving, and she's getting closer. The world is distant, and I'm looking directly into the sun.

CHAPTER FIVE

DELLA

PRESENT DAY

I get to the bar in West Lancaster, the Brass Terrier, just as they're closing. There's a blonde woman wiping down the counters when I walk through.

"Can I help you?" she asks.

"I'm looking for somebody," I say. "Jensen. He's working on a job for me."

She gives me a long look. Then, she shrugs, reaching over to turn off the neon sign. "He's at the stockyards. Fifty-five, South Ave."

"Oh," I say. "Can I walk there?"

"You can. Just cut through the backyards. It's at the bottom of the hill from the water tower."

It's a miracle I make it in the dark, but the tower is lit up with a spotlight. All I have to do is scramble through backyards and down alleyways until I get close. Underneath the tower sits two rows of metal roofing strung with lights. I can hear the crowd before I see it—or smell it. Everything smells like livestock out here.

It's so crowded and hectic, nobody bothers me when I slip under the caution tape around the pole barn supports. There's a counter on the far side selling drinks. Barrels are set up at all four corners, flames flickering from the round mouths. It's hotter than hell in here, the dust rising from the ground, choking me. Sweat etches down between my breasts, staining the front of my dress.

I have a picture of him, but it's from twenty years ago. I don't know what I'm looking for. Head down, I make it to the bar. The bartender gives me the up-down glance from above his handlebar mustache and leans in.

"You in the wrong place, sweetheart?" he asks.

"I'm looking for a man by the name of Jensen," I say.

He leans closer. "What now?"

"I'm looking for Jensen Childress," I shout.

He startles. "Jesus, you don't need to yell. He's in the ring."

I follow where he's pointing, to the partitioned section at the center. It's surrounded by people, shoving and shouting. My heart picks up. I might have grown up scrappy, but I'm out of my depth here. The tent is mostly men, some with women glued to their sides. Everything smells like beer and way too much testosterone for my taste. I just hope there's enough people around that nobody tries anything with me.

Slowly, I weave through moving bodies, closer and closer, until I'm standing on the other side of a circle of neon tape.

There are two men on the ground. Instead of dirt, there's a plywood board laid out for them to fight on. One of them, a man with a buzzcut, is falling hard. The other is swinging, knocking out the first man with a fist wrapped in what looks like medical tape. The referee hovers over them. The room is in an uproar, growing louder by the second.

The buzzcut man taps out. Right away, the other man helps him to his feet. They embrace, shake hands, and the referee helps Buzzcut out of the ring. The winner makes a slow circle, turning until I can get a good look at him.

Oh God.

Right away, I can tell this is an older version of the young man in the photo, and now that I'm seeing him in the flesh, I'm floored. He's fucking gorgeous. I came here with the intention of seducing him and cringing at the thought. I'd expected a gruff bounty hunter type, grizzled and far too old for me. Not my ideal man.

But Jensen is something different, something that feels a tiny bit like home, way out here in the wild. And he's so damn sexy, it's making me uncomfortable.

He's tall, over six feet, with a lean, well-muscled body that's flecked in sweat and dirt. His torso is bare, and on his chest, visible through the hair, is a tattoo of a half bullseye. There's more ink on his right arm, but it's faded, like the sun has baked it out.

My body feels like it's floating.

Why do I feel like I've met him somehow before? I know for certain I haven't. Maybe it's the pale blue eyes that sweep over the room beneath lowered brows. His face is angular, handsome in a rangy way I'm used to seeing back home. His curly brown hair has a colorless quality to it, and it's curled with sweat and flecked in grime.

He's not really handsome, but he is so deliciously sexy that he's gorgeous. He also looks...alone, like he's been on his own for a long time. Maybe it's the guarded way he accepts congratulations as he ducks below the tape. He's friendly, but he's keeping everybody at arm's length.

Another fight starts. I keep my eyes on Jensen as he works his way through the crowd and takes a towel, a shirt, and some water from the bartender. He empties the bottle over his head, rivulets streaming down the ridges of his stomach and over his lean shoulders. My body heats up.

If I have to seduce anyone, he's the ideal target.

He glances around the room. I swing my gaze back around, pretending I'm watching the fight. I know I look good, even after walking to get here. My dress fits me perfectly, cupping my curves. With the amount of hairspray and setting spray I used, I know every strand of hair and bit of makeup is still in place. Kayleigh taught me how to lock everything down.

I stare into the ring. Then, slowly, I glance to the side

He looks too, at the same moment.

The air in the room sizzles like sweat on hot pavement. He takes a step in my direction. My heart beats against my ribs. I like the way he walks. It's confident but careful. I can't figure out what to do with my hands, so I lift one and blow him a kiss. His jaw goes slack. His eyes glaze before he blinks and pulls himself together.

Then, he starts walking faster, until he's a few feet away. Our gazes lock. His thin mouth parts, showing a sliver of white teeth.

"Can I get you a drink?" he says.

His voice catches me off guard. It's low, with some husk to it, and there's still a clear Harlan County accent present. My body isn't warm—it's burning up all over.

"You were in the ring," I say. "Congratulations on the win."

He jerks his head, washed out eyes locking on the fighters inside. "Yeah, good night."

"Does fighting get you a lot of girls?" I say before I can bite my tongue.

He laughs. "No comment."

"You don't have to."

"I got one woman I'm concerned about right now," he says. "And I'd like to know what she's drinking tonight?"

He's got a strategy; eye-fucking me with that confident gaze. And it's working. Nodding, I follow him back to the bar on the other side of the room. He reaches for my hand, but I'm not ready for that. Instead, I lean my upper back against the counter, pretending I don't know how that's pushing my breasts out, making them spill over my neckline.

"I think I'll have a beer," I say.

"A classic," he says, leaning over to talk to the bartender. "Beer for the lady, on my tab. One for me too."

The bartender slides the beer across the counter. My stomach flutters, studying the muscled rise of his shoulders as he catches them, handing one to me. I take a sip. He cocks his head. I let the bottle sink down and flick my tongue across my lower lip. Eyes on my mouth, he moves close.

He smells like sweat, but in a nice, salty way that sets my blood thrumming.

"Are you looking for something?" he murmurs.

"Am I...what?" I whisper.

He leans in, face above mine. From this angle, I can see his eyes up close. There's no doubt he's from Harlan. There's only one place that produces eyes like that. Pale, almost shocked up close, like he saw something he'll never forget and it's burned into his brain.

"Are you looking for more than a drink tonight?" he asks.

"You're bold."

The corner of his mouth turns up. Lord, he's pretty, roughed up and still breathless from the ring.

"You don't like it?" he says.

"I am mortified, sir," I tease.

He can't stop smiling, and it's giving him a single dimple beneath his stubble. "I've got a feeling you can handle me," he says. "Might take both hands, but I believe in you."

I gasp, laughing out loud. "Well, look at you—"

"Go right ahead," he says, flicking something inside his mouth. "I like it."

His jaw ripples, and I see a flash of white. He's got gum between his back teeth. For some reason, I find that incredibly hot. Lord, he's reeling me in fast. I've never been flirted with before. Leland just pushed in like a bull in a china shop and tried to force our relationship. The feeling of being wanted by an attractive man feels like being drunk. It's shutting off the rational part of my brain.

"Let's see if you can earn it," I say.

"I'm a hard worker."

He shifts closer, his body inches from mine. He's leaning his elbow on the counter, beer in his other hand. His eyes drop to my cleavage rising above the tan fringe dress. I picked this dress because it's stunning on me, and I needed to look irresistible tonight. Clearly, it's working.

I glance down. There's a slight rise beneath his zipper.

"What's going on down there, cowboy?" I arch a brow.

He doesn't break eye contact. "Standing ovation for the prettiest girl in the room."

"Oh, well, in that case, let your flag fly." My face is on fire.

"I'll keep it at half-mast for now," he says. "Hoping for an opportunity to let it go full mast later."

"Lord," I whisper. "You are dirty."

He leans in, eyes filling my vision. "I'd be happy with a kiss and a phone number."

I smile, shaking my head. "I reward based on performance."

"I'm highly motivated."

"I can see that," I say, waving a hand at the crowd around the ring. "How long have you been fighting in the stockyards?"

He has a sip of beer. I see him up close, like a snapshot. His skin is tanned, like he works in the sun, and there are faint lines around his pale blue eyes that I find so sexy. Up close, his hair has a few grays at his temple, but he's fit, lean, and broad. It's hard to tell how old he is just by looks.

"About twenty years," he says.

"That's quite a while. Practice makes perfect, hmm?"

"In all areas."

"You have a filthy mind," I say.

He shifts to face the bar. Something warm and rough touches my bare thigh. Heart thumping, I glance down to see his hand, still wrapped from his fight, brush my skin.

Oh my God, I feel that between my legs.

Electricity, like a lightning storm in high summer.

I don't move. He slides his fingers against my inner thigh. God, he's so close, yet so far.

"You come on pretty strong, cowboy," I whisper.

He opens his mouth.

"Don't you dare," I warn.

He cocks his head, flashing the white of his teeth. "You know me already."

His middle finger has a callus on it. It's all I can feel, dragging up and down my inner thigh.

"What did you say your name was?" I ask.

He takes a drag on his beer. "Baby, you can call me anything you want tonight."

Thump. Thump. Thump.

My heart is trying to beat its way out of my ribs. Never in my life has a man made me feel this way.

"No, really," I press.

"Cowboy's just fine."

"How about Shotgun?" I say. "The way you're talking, I'm half expecting you to go off early."

He throws his head back, laughing. "Lucky for you, I've got a couple bullets in the chamber."

"Oh, really?"

"Yeah, want me to take you shooting?"

My brow arches. "If the shooting range is just your bedroom, and the gun is just your dick, I'm not so sure about that, sir."

His finger moves up, a fraction of an inch. There's a few inches of space left between my wet panties and his hand. If he makes contact, he's going to get the ego trip of his life. Without meaning to, I'm soaked. That's a shock— Leland never had the power to do that with his touch, much less a dimple and a few jokes.

We're in dangerous territory.

"So what do I need to do?" he murmurs.

I tilt my head back, letting my hair fall over my shoulders. "Isn't the fun of it figuring that out?"

He takes his hand from my inner thigh and starts playing with the strip of fringe crisscrossed over my waist. I sneak a peek down below. He's still flying that flag.

He wants me, a lot.

That makes me want him back, badly. Does he do this all the time? Maybe I don't really care tonight. The only sex I've had was with Leland, and I fucking hated it. Right now, my entire body feels like it's prickling with electricity. It's intoxicating, the way he's looking at me.

I came here to seduce him.

It's going to be easier than I thought. The only problem is...I think he might be seducing me right back.

"Is it warm in here?" I say lightly.

He's so close, his thigh is brushing my hip. "Scorching. The room's pretty warm too."

I laugh. "You always this quick?"

"Well, you did call me Shotgun."

"Click, click, and you're done, huh?"

He leans in. "Wouldn't you like to know?"

Actually, I would, but I'm having too much fun to cut this short.

"So if you won't tell me your name, how about where you're from?" I say.

His lids flicker. "You tell me where you're from."

"No names, no places it is." I tilt my head, giving him a sweet little smile. "You call me whatever you like, and I'll call you cowboy."

He taps the counter and catches the second beer the bartender slides across. His unoccupied hand goes from my fringe back to my inner thigh.

It singes like fire on my delicate skin.

"Can I get you another drink," he asks.

"I've got a half bottle," I say. "You've got that long to convince me to go to bed with you."

"Baby, you're already convinced."

I give him a look. "Oh, really?"

His throat bobs, pale eyes fixed behind me. His finger is moving in a little circle. "I think you might be dripping down your thigh."

My eyes widen, realizing his touch is wet. Mortification sweeps through me, but I keep my face perfectly still. Why should I be ashamed for wanting him? I'm single, and I can do what I want. I clear my throat. He glances at me, a glitter of triumph in his eyes.

"Who's going off early now?" he says.

"If you think that's going off, I'm about to be disappointed."

His throat bobs again. There's a red flush between his collarbones. When he leans in, his voice drops until it's just a rasp.

"Let me take you home," he says.

I keep my eyes over his shoulder. His hot breath on my ear is making this worse. His hand inches up.

"Don't you touch me with those dirty hands," I say.

"I won't," he says. "Just your panties."

My spine tingles. Heat flushes through my hips, centering where his finger just grazed the wet fabric. The room is full, everyone occupied at the ring. Nobody sees him put his hand up my skirt, and there's something thrilling about how boldly he does it out in the open.

His middle finger touches my clit through my panties. My thighs shiver, but I keep perfectly still.

"Think I found the trigger," he murmurs. "Safety on or off?"

"Off," I breathe.

He's touching me, back and forth, and my body is responding like it never has before. My breasts tingle, nipples hard. There's a raw ache inside me, and it makes me painfully aware of how much I want the emptiness between my thighs filled.

Up...down.

Oh God, I might come on his hand right here. That blows my mind, because I've never finished with anyone before. Tonight is full of surprises.

"You need to stop," I whisper.

His forehead creases. "Why would I do that?"

The crowd roars, and the third fight of the night is done. The bartender starts pulling winnings, and I know we're about to be swarmed. I don't watch these things often, but Leland used to host cage fights in Red River Gorge back home. He took me once, but I didn't have a taste for the gore and the heat. Watching Jensen fight, however...that's a different story.

The crowd descends, jostling us out of our trance.

"Fuck," Jensen swears, pulling his hand from between my legs.

"If you're going to ask me so nicely, I'll switch my no to a maybe," I say.

He doesn't reply. Instead, he takes the beer from my hand and sets it aside, weaving his fingers through mine and leading me from the swarming bodies.

My heart races. He pulls me outside, pushing me roughly against the side of the pole barn. His mouth is on the side of my neck. His hands are all over me, skimming over my waist, down my hips, caressing my bare thighs, callouses and dirty tape and rough palms.

Hands that feel nothing like Leland's did.

My toes curl in my boots and my head falls to the side. More, I need more. Desire feels less shaky and tender and more like a wild animal. Fuck, I need him inside me, on me. It doesn't make sense, but it doesn't have to.

My hands fall to his leather belt. I see a flash of his smile, white teeth, creases by his eyes. It's dark enough down there, I can't get the buckle undone. My fingers tug at it, but it's stuck. A frustrated whimper escapes my throat. He laughs softly, catching one of my wrists.

"I think that maybe might be a yes," he says.

I should push back, but I just nod, swallowing.

"Where's home for you, cowboy?" I ask.

He jerks his head to the north-west. "I live just between South Platte and Sovereign Mountain. It's night, the road's clear. I can make the drive quick."

Breathless, I nod. He reaches into his pocket and takes out a key fob. A truck a few feet away beeps. Extracting myself from him, I stumble, tripping on the grass. His arm shoots out and wraps around my waist.

I turn to the side. He's so close, our noses touch.

God, I want him to kiss me.

"What am I doing? You could be a serial killer," I whisper. "I don't even know what you do."

He laughs again. "I own a construction company."

"I'll bet you bury the bodies under all the concrete you pour."

He picks me up and dumps me into the truck. I shift across the leather seats, and he slides into the driver's side.

"The only burying I'm doing tonight is burying my dick in that pussy," he says, turning the key and slamming the door shut.

He glances over his shoulder as he backs up, spinning in a half circle and heading towards the road. I pull my seatbelt on, clicking it in. The sound feels...final.

I came here to do exactly this.

So why does it feel like I'm losing control?

He flips the cruise control on as he gets on the highway. Then, he braces his knees apart to lift his hips, adjusting his pants. There's still an alarmingly big rise beneath his zipper. I glance down, and he catches my stare.

"I'm tested, by the way," he says.

A wave of guilt comes over me, but the minute it comes, it's gone. I'm single. I can do whatever I want.

"I am too," I whisper.

That's true. Kayleigh brought me to the clinic so I could get tested. Even though I never caught him in the act, I know Leland wasn't faithful. There was no way, not with the men he ran with and the places they frequented. I considered myself lucky he was clearly wearing protection with them, because he never gave me anything. At least he afforded me that.

The memory of Kayleigh brings back the memory of Landis.

I wince, turning to the window. I'm not guilty over the thought of sleeping with Jensen. I'm guilty my body is enjoying it this much. This was supposed to be all part of the bigger plan. It wasn't supposed to light every nerve in my body on fire.

He reaches out and lays his hand on my bare thigh. Distracted, I stare down at it. He has a laborer's hands—rough, the tattoos on his right knuckles faded out by the sun. There are scars all over them. The longer I look at them, the more I believe he owns a construction company.

"What do you want?" His voice shatters the silence, low, raspy.

I glance at his profile. "What?"

"You want it rough? You like it sweet?" He turns off the highway, taking a state route. "What do you get off on?"

"I...don't know," I blurt out.

His brow creases. "You don't know what you like?"

Fuck, I shouldn't have said that. My brain goes into overdrive, trying to remember if there was anything Leland did that I enjoyed. My quick analysis comes up with nothing. I always felt completely disconnected from him when we slept together. He used my body, and I responded the way he wanted me to. A few times, early on, he tried to get me off, but it was a long, frustrating experience. After a while, he got tired of trying, and that was the end of my limited experience with pleasure.

"You've done this before, huh?" he says.

"Yeah, I just...haven't really...done a lot of that," I say lamely.

"A lot of what?"

My nail digs into my thumb, picking at the scarred skin. "I don't come from sex," I say finally.

"Well, you almost came on my hand. Is that what you need to get off?"

He's so casual about this conversation. Inside, I'm dying. Leland and I never talked about sex. It was just something we did. Jensen flexes his hand, digging his fingertips into my thigh. Pain shoots up my hip. Without thinking, I squirm because it feels good.

"I don't know," I push out.

"Just tell me if you get off on it rough or gentle," he says. "I'll take care of making you come."

Despite what happened at the bar, I have doubts that, as sexy as he is, he's going to actually get me to orgasm. Building me up is one thing, but getting me over the edge is another. But I may as well let him try. At the very least, it'll be exciting, and that's what I'm craving, from my tingling head to my feet—I want to be breathless, panting in bed when he's done, like I've seen in movies or read about in books.

"Rough," I blurt out.

His brows rise. "One rough fucking, coming right up."

"You're pretty sure of yourself," I say lightly.

"What can I say? I get results."

He's quick, and I'm not used to smart men. I study him again as he drives further and further out. I'm expecting it to take hours, but he's going very fast. It's only a few more minutes before he pumps the brakes and pulls off the road, following a driveway lined with floodlights. I can't see around us, but I can make out a big ranch house at the top of the hill. He pulls up outside and cuts the engine.

"You gonna take a shower?" I say, glancing him up and down.

"What? This is proof of my victory."

"You're on the hook for my UTI meds tomorrow if you don't wash your dick."

He takes the keys out and leans across the seat. I turn, thinking he's going to open my door, but he takes my face in his hand, fingers on one side, thumb on the other, and kisses my mouth.

My eyes flutter shut as my body goes up in flames. At first, all I can feel is my pulse and my brain humming. Then, I become aware of my own desire and how my body craves him. He kisses me, his mouth firm and exploratory. I part my lips for him, and his tongue grazes mine. Slow, thorough. Faintly minty tongue caressing mine.

He pulls back, less than an inch.

"You taste good," he breathes.

"So do you," I whisper.

He spits his gum into an empty water bottle in the console before pulling me in. Our mouths meet again. This time, I unfasten my seatbelt and ease in. His hand slides up my waist and cups my breast, rough thumb playing with my nipple through my thin bra. He's kissing me like he's starving. Everything is hot, tortuously slow, and it tastes like I might do something so filthy with him tonight, I won't be able to look myself in the eye tomorrow.

He breaks away from my mouth and bites the side of my neck. My toes curl in my boots. God, that's so good. Mindlessly, I shift closer and move my knee to slide onto his lap.

His body goes stiff. He pulls back a few inches and puts his hand on my knee, blocking me.

"Let's take this inside," he breathes.

"You don't like making out in your truck?"

"I prefer to be on top," he says. There's a hint of seriousness now. "That's about my only boundary."

I pull back, thrown off. He's half-shadowed by the porch light. "Okay, that's fine. I think I can suffer through being underneath you."

He smiles, and I tumble straight down into butterflies again. He's got such an attractive smile, with strong, nice teeth. I've never found men's teeth to be sexy, but Jensen's are. And I fucking loved when he bit me.

"I like being on top. I like being in charge," he says.

I nod. "I'm fine with that."

He kisses me briefly, cradling my chin between his finger and thumb. "Good girl. All you have to do tonight is come on my face and open your legs so I can come between them. Deal?"

Heat floods my neck. "Wouldn't I need to be on top to come on your face?"

"Facesitting is all good. It's just that other position...I'm not a fan of," he says, opening his door.

"Is that why you have that mustache?"

"Yeah, that's for precision parking."

He jumps out and circles the truck so he doesn't hear me giggling, which is good, because he doesn't need his ego inflated. I'm composed by the time he opens my door and lifts me out. I turn to take in the house, but before I can make a comment about it, he spanks me across the ass.

Gasping, I whirl. He smirks.

"Before we go in, show me that ring finger, baby," he says.

I lift my finger like I'm flipping him off. There's no dent on my hand where I used to wear my wedding bands. They were so expensive, most days, I didn't wear them, so they never left a permanent mark. He looks my fingers over and winks at me.

"All good," he says.

"I'm no cheater," I say, shaking back my hair.

"I don't know you." He slips a hand around my waist and ushers me up the steps to the front door.

"But you're fucking me," I whisper.

"I don't need to know you to make you come," he says, punching in the keycode.

"Tell that to my ex. He didn't know me or make me come."

He laughs, pushing in the door. "God, you got a quick little mouth on you."

He doesn't know the half of it. I step inside, and the lights come on automatically. He follows me into the pale wood hallway and closes the door, setting the alarm system behind us.

"Somebody did something bad to you, didn't they?" he says.

I turn. "Why would you say that?"

He finishes with the lock and pushes his truck keys in his pocket. We're standing so close, I can smell the sweat dried into his shirt. In the full light, I'm soaking him in like I'm dying of thirst and he's a tall drink of water.

"Because you're funny," he says. "And you're not scared of me."

"Maybe I'm just funny and brave," I shoot back.

He shakes his head. "No, you're a little fucked up."

He's right about some of it. I am fucked up, but that's not my fault. I don't think I'm very brave. It's just that for some reason, I'm not one bit afraid of Jensen Childress.

That doesn't mean he's not big, much taller than I am, and he feels a little dangerous. It just doesn't feel like he would hurt me.

He takes a step in. I take a step back.

"I was voted funniest in my class," I whisper, my back hitting the wood.

He braces a hand against the wall above my head and leans in close. "Now you're just bragging."

"It was a really small class."

His face creases into a smile as he kisses me, and I feel his teeth brush my lips. We kiss gently this time, exploring each other's mouths. His lean body sinks into mine. This time, I get to feel his erection harden against my stomach. It's a delicious lengthening that strokes my ego. He gives me some tongue, and I love it, even though I fucking hated it when Leland did that. With him, it felt aggressive and wet. With Jensen, it feels almost like slow sex with our mouths. I'm disappointed when he pulls back.

He lifts me in his arms and carries me into the kitchen at the end of the hall. It's clean but lived in. There's a clean dish and cup on the draining board. A calendar taped to the fridge with a bunch of appointments scrawled all over it. An old wedding invite beside it. On the counter sits an empty mug with a coffee ring in it.

He sets me down on the table and takes my boots off. Then, he lowers me until I'm on my back.

"I thought you wanted me to sit on your face," I say.

"I do." He leans over, hand planted on the table beside my head. "You said you wanted me to get cleaned up, so I'm going to eat your cunt first, then I'll shower and we can get to work. How's that sound?"

"Maybe I should shower first." I push myself up on my elbows.

"Nah, that's a waste of good pussy. Spread your legs, baby. I know you taste good."

"That's... You're nasty," I gasp.

He grips my thighs and pulls me in like I'm a whole meal. "Just wait."

I close my eyes, his kitchen fluttering out of sight. His hands graze my bare thighs. For the first time in my life, I feel the eroticism of wanting to be touched instead of dreading it. Guilt rises in my chest as his mouth traces my inner thigh. I was sent here to seduce him, but now that he has me, I don't want to hurt him. This isn't how I thought this would go.

He says something. I crack my eyes, and he's washing his hands at the sink.

Thoughtful.

Then, he's back between my thighs, touching my pussy, sending tingles and desperate pulses through my hips. The guilt lingers until he leans in and licks me, from pussy to clit.

After that, there's no room in my head for anything but him.

CHAPTER SIX

JENSEN

There've been times in my life when I was having fun but didn't realize it. That was disappointing, because I didn't get to savor it. Tonight, I am having the most fun I've had in years, but I know it. And that just makes it ten times better.

She is whatever is on the other side of my dream woman—gorgeous, funny, and unafraid to dish it back. There's something else, an aftertaste to her that's familiar, like somehow I've met her before, which is impossible. I've got a good memory. I would know this girl in a second if we'd slept together before. There would have been no way I'd let her walk away.

I bend in and kiss her inner thigh.

She's completely bare between her legs. There's no stubble, which makes me think she's had laser. The soft folds beneath her clit are soaked, and they glitter under the kitchen light. There's a freckle on the right side of her pussy. I have the sudden urge to kiss it and tell her it's pretty.

The whole thing is pretty. Just real fucking nice.

I lick my finger and touch the hood of her clit, drawing it back and spreading her open with my middle finger and thumb. It's smooth, flushed pink. My body reacts, groin tightening. I lean in, flicking my tongue over her pussy and coiling it up to her bare clit. Her head rolls to the side, eyes closed. Her breath hitches, a muscle in her thigh quivering.

She doesn't think I can get her there, I can tell.

In the interim between losing my v-card and tonight, I learned a thing or two, and I spent a good amount of time practicing it. Ten thousand hours makes an expert. Well, I wasn't keeping score, but I reckon I punched my card for those hours over the last nineteen years.

Her lack of confidence doesn't faze me. Tongue flat and gentle, I start real slow, warming her up until she's lifting her ass off the table and dripping into my mouth. That's when I know it's time to slip my fingers inside. She grips me, pumping around my knuckles. I find that spot just inside and stroke her until she reacts the way I want—eyes rolling back, lips parting, body shivering at every downstroke.

My fingers aren't fitting too well, so I switch to one. That works better. Then, I get to figuring out what she likes on her clit. That takes a little longer—she likes the left side best, at a pretty even pace. Once I get a rhythm, it doesn't take long for her to reach the point of no return.

I glance at the clock over the stove—fifteen minutes.

Her spine curves off the table. Her thighs clamp around my head. Pleasure rolls through her body and slips into spasms. She leaks out around my finger and stings my knuckles. Her hand flies down, digging into my hair. The pain of her nails sets me off, making my cock so hard, it hurts against my zipper.

Fuck, that is satisfying.

I readjust my fingers, going in for another, but she lifts her head weakly.

"Please," she breathes.

Resurfacing, I run a hand over the lower half of my face. "That alright for you, baby?"

She props herself up. "That was...yeah, that was amazing."

Keeping eye contact, I run my tongue from her pussy to her clit, cleaning her up. She shivers, watching closely.

"You don't want another?" I ask.

Her breasts heave under her little dress. "I want fucked," she blurts out.

That, I can do. Rising, I reach into my back pocket, where I usually carry a condom in my wallet. Instead, I find what Jack shoved in there earlier; a silver foil packet. I take it out and hold it up to the light. There's a tiny silver dog on it, because of course there is. I am going to kill that fucker when I get a chance.

"Let's go upstairs and get a condom," I say.

"That is a condom," she says. "What brand is that?"

"Not any brand I want to use." I toss it on the table and pick her up, wrapping her legs around my waist. She grips my shoulders, ducking her head as we ascend the staircase. In my bedroom, I hit the lamp and dump her onto the bed on her back.

She looks so pretty sprawled out, her thighs pressed together. That feeling of familiarity passes over me in a wave. God, I want to get lost in her, to fuck hard all night and try to feel it again and again. The thought of her leaving is a dark cloud. I think I'm going to pretend tonight will last forever.

She lifts her heels, bracing them on the edge of the bed.

"Fuck me," she whispers.

I reach into the bedside table. "You want me to shower up still?"

"No, just fuck me."

Her voice cracks. Arousal is a pounding drum in my groin. I pull my shirt off and unfasten my belt, unzipping my pants. Her eyes follow my every move as I rip the corner of the condom package and take it out, pushing down the front of my boxer-briefs. My dick is rock hard, and it slaps against my lower stomach.

"Oh my God."

I glance up, condom on my tip. "Huh?"

Her eyes are wide. Not breaking eye contact with my dick, she pushes herself to her knees and comes to the edge of the bed. I pull the condom back. She stares. I'm wondering if there's something wrong. But then, she leans in and wraps her soft hand around my length. The pressure almost makes my knees sway.

"Oh," she breathes.

"You like that?"

She glances up, tongue flicking out to wet her lower lip. "Yeah, a little bit."

A while ago, myself and a friend collectively lost a bet. He got his dick pierced, and I got a nineteen-forty-nine Ruger tattooed on the underside of mine. It's not a bad tattoo, though the application of it made me see God. It's held up despite frequent usage.

"You into tattoos?" I say.

Her brows crease. "The ink is nice, but the rest of it is more what I'm looking at."

"Thanks," I say. "How about you flip over, face down, ass up, and let me put it in your cunt?"

She hesitates, so I pick her up and do it for her. Her skirt hitches all the way up, exposing her perfect ass. It really is perfect, round with a hint of leanness and just enough jiggle to shake when I spank her.

She moans, and her toes curl. I spank her again, where her ass meets her thighs. Her cunt tightens, wetness dripping to her clit.

"You know it's huge, right?" she says.

I brace my knee on the bed, rolling the condom on. Of course, I've been told that in bed plenty of times, but that's standard dirty talk.

"You can take it, baby," I murmur, taking some lube from the bedside table and working it into her pussy. She whines, spine arching, pushing her ass up. She's so fucking pretty, I'm starting to feel warm in my chest when I look at her. That's not normal.

"Hurry," she breathes.

I position myself, the head of my cock pressed against her cunt. "How desperate are you?"

"Please," she pants. "I'm so fucking empty."

My brain hums, and I can't resist. My hips press forward and she stretches to take me. It's tight, maybe a little more than it should be. I stroke my hand from her shoulder to her hip, kneading the soft flesh, coaxing her to relax. She does, a little. I grip the back of her neck and push, but I can't get her to ease up enough.

She whimpers, turning wide eyes on me.

"It's not going in," she breathes.

I adjust, pressing her lower and draping my body over hers. "Arch your spine," I urge. "Try to relax your hips for me, baby."

She presses her cheek to the quilt. Gently, I push the head back inside her pussy, and she clamps down tight. Alright, this isn't going to work. I bend, kissing the back of her neck. She shivers, then she melts into the bed.

"Hey, baby, you sure you want this?" I ask gently.

"I do. I want it," she breathes. "You're just big, and I haven't had sex in a while."

I kiss her nape again. "You sure? You're tense."

She doesn't reply. I flip her onto her back so I can look at her face. There's a hint of vulnerability in her eyes. Bending, I kiss her mouth slowly, and my dick aches at how intimate it feels. When I pull back, she gives me a tiny smile.

"Maybe I'm a little nervous," she whispers. "The guy before you...he did a number on me."

"Would it help if you could watch?" I ask.

Her brows knit. "Watch?"

I extract myself from her and get up, going to the closet beside the bed. One of the advantages of being the owner of a construction crew is being able to build my house exactly the way I want. That includes rolling closet doors that flip to reveal two enormous mirrors. They reflect the room, the bed front and center.

She turns her head to the side. Her reflection gives me a shocked stare.

"What is that for?" she whispers.

I kneel on the bed, pulling her to lay with her head on the pillows. "Watching you take it from every angle."

She can't bite back her smile. I unzip her dress, tugging it over her head. Underneath, her breasts are cradled in a pale blue bra made of delicate lace. My cock is rock hard at my hip as I unfasten it and tug it free.

Fuck, her teardrop breasts are perfect. My head goes completely empty as I dip my head to capture her nipple in my mouth, soft, then slowly hard on my tongue. She moans, arching towards me. Distantly, I know she's watching me, but I'm too distracted with having the prettiest woman I've ever met in my mouth. I release her nipple and kiss down her stomach, stopping abruptly as I reach her navel.

She has a c-section scar between her hips.

Right away, I veer to the side. She's not the first woman I've fucked who had one, and I know some women don't want to answer questions about them. The last thing I want is to overstep her boundaries and bring up a topic that makes her uncomfortable.

I nip her hipbone. Her toes curl.

"You want my cock in you, baby?" I murmur, shifting up and sliding between her thighs.

"Yes," she breathes.

I ease her other leg up, cocking it. From this angle, her pussy is just visible in the mirror. It's breathtaking, soaked, a little swollen. I spit in my palm and wet her entrance, just for good measure. Then, I take hold of my cock by the base and guide the tip inside her. She gasps, eyes fixed between her thighs. I'm watching her reaction, arousal surging in my groin.

Her cunt stretches to take me, and this time, she doesn't tense up. Slowly, inch by inch, we watch together as I slide inside her pussy. Searing heat, all the way up. She's so fucking perfect, I have to take a beat. Her inner muscles grip me hard, pulsing. Her head falls back and to the side, watching where our bodies join.

I fit, but barely.

She's an indescribable feeling. Even with the condom, I'm right on the edge.

It's something else, something I can't quite put my finger on, like there was a part of me that was off-center, and now, it's back in place. But that makes no sense right now. So, I brace my knee and draw halfway out, easing back in with a slow stroke. Our eyes connect. She flutters her lashes, telling me she likes it.

"Watch," I order.

She rolls her head back over, eyes dreamy. Her hand rests on my side. I think she's feeling the roll of muscle as I thrust. Whatever it is, I like it.

"You feel good," she says.

I bend, kissing between her breasts. "You feel better."

Somehow, we're kissing again. I go from fucking gently to rutting my hips between her thighs, pumping into her so hard, she's dripping onto the sheets. Fuck not kissing my hookups—there's no way in hell I can stop myself. She tastes so good, and the pure energy that surges in me, through us both, when we kiss is enough to make me drunk.

I am. I'm drunk on this woman.

That's alright. We can sort through everything tomorrow. But for right now, I think I'm feeling chemistry for the first time, and it's like every cold nerve in my body is alight. A bonfire on a snowy mountain. A signal to the parts of me that never got a chance to light up before tonight.

I slide my hand between us and touch her clit in quick circles, building her with every thrust. She gasps as she comes, a hot breath against my mouth. The stutter of her hips when she orgasms, the sensation of her clamped down on me, is too much. I brace my forehead between her breasts and let my own pleasure roll in like a storm.

She shakes, bodies joined as deeply as they can be, until it's over. Slowly, I lift my head.

"You alright?" I breathe.

She nods, releasing a shaky laugh. "Yeah, that was...intense."

It goes from sweet and dirty to awkward. I pull from her and stand, trying to pretend it didn't get as intense as it did. "Let's shower. I want to go again."

Her eyes widen. "How many times are you wanting?"

I glance at the clock as I strip off the condom and tie it. "Until I'm shooting blanks."

"I don't think that's what that means."

"Let's just see how many rounds I have in the chamber," I say, lifting her up and turning towards the bathroom. I swat her across the ass, and she yelps.

"You're so fucking full of it," she says, but she's smiling.

I carry her into the bathroom, flicking on the low light. She sits on the sink like a good girl while I get the shower going. Then, she climbs in with me, arms wrapped around her body. I step underneath the spray, wiping my hair back and shaking my head.

"So what do I get?" I say.

"What?"

"You thought I couldn't make you come," I say. "What do I get for it?"

She lifts a brow. "You get the privilege of making me come again."

"I was hoping you'd say that."

We wash up quickly and make it out of the shower and into bed again. I'm back inside her the minute our bodies touch the sheets. I've worked a farm for a long time out west. I plow my own acres and plant my own seeds. Tonight feels like the first warm night after the frost is over, and I am on a mission to get all the plowing in I can before the sun comes up.

Now that she's relaxed and I can fit easily, she's meeting me where I'm at. The bed hits the wall. I'm sweating, and it's falling on her naked breasts. She has her sharp little nails in my back. Her hips are coming up in waves to meet my thrusts. My head is empty, and I like it that way.

If I let myself think, I'll have to acknowledge this might be the best sex I've ever had.

The deepest connection I've felt in decades.

I kiss her open lips. When I break away, she follows my mouth, so I let her have it. It's rare that I kiss during sex, but I can't help it. She moans as I pull her ankles over my shoulders, going as deep as I can, plowing my hips hard.

She takes it. Every time I turn the intensity up, she meets me there. It's way past midnight, but neither of us wants to stop. After her fourth orgasm, we break so she can have a glass of water. Then, she's on her belly, and my dick is so deep in her, I can feel the resistance of her cervix.

She whimpers that it hurts. I breathe out that I can stop, and she tells me *don't you fucking dare, cowboy*.

We're still going at it when I see a faint streak of color on the horizon. I have her on her knees, face pressed into the bed, hand braced on her spine. The realization that I fucked her through the night sends me over the edge one last time. I sink over her body, panting as I kiss her nape.

"We need to sleep," I say.

She whimpers. Gently, I pull my cock from her pussy and strip the condom off. There are six others in the trash by the bed. The room smells like good, honest sweat, latex, and cum. I push open the window, and when I get back to the bed, she's sound asleep. Her pretty face is relaxed. Her body is melted into the sheets.

I lay down and curl up behind her and pull her against my chest.

I think I might ask her to stay another night.

CHAPTER SEVEN

DELLA

My body hurts.

Slowly, I'm aware of a bright light. Peeling my eyelids open, gray mountains and hills fill my vision, especially a big one in the center. The sun sits above the horizon, shining directly into the window. My stomach is painfully empty. My head is full of static. There's a tender stinging down below.

With effort, I roll over to the other side. My eyes widen, and despite everything, I bolt upright.

He's asleep, on his back. The sheet is pulled up to the middle of his thigh, and his other knee is cocked. Everything is out in the open, before God and everybody. Everybody being me, in this case.

Guilty over staring, I wonder if I should pull the sheet up over his waist.

Except, I can't stop looking, and not just at his dick. He's pretty in such a rough way. Sexy, gorgeous, big and tall, with leanness that streamlines his muscles. The tattoos over his right forearm are blown out and faded, but I like it. I think I prefer that over crisp ink. Between his pectorals, over the half bullseye, is the perfect amount of hair.

I follow it with my gaze, down his stomach, back to the V above his groin. I don't know how he doesn't know he's big. I might have only been with Leland, but I'm not naive. Jensen is blessed in that department, and it's all out, laying soft against his thigh. The revolver tattooed up the underside is a nice touch to his rough charm.

I shift to sit on my heels and press my fingers between my thighs. It's sore, and it probably will be for a few days. It kind of feels like the day after I slept with Leland for the first time.

I think the fact Jensen made me come is more surprising than anything else.

After five years with Leland, I thought it was never going to happen. But then came Jensen, who just walked in and made it happen like it was no big deal.

Was it a matter of skill?

Or something else?

I sink back against the headboard and pull the sheet over my body. I can't deny there's something here, and that's devastating, because I came here to seduce him, to use him, not to be raised from the dead after Leland did his best to put my spirit six feet under.

No, I can't let this happen.

I'm here for one thing only.

He stirs, and I freeze. Then, to my horror, he goes hard, even though he's still out cold. Without thinking, I yank the blanket over his waist. He startles, sitting upright, reaching for the bedside table.

"Sorry," I gasp.

He stops, blinking. Then, he pulls his hand back and pushes himself upright. "What's going on?

I shake my head. "Nothing. I just woke up."

He's looking at me kind of funny for a half second. My nipples go hard under his stare. He leans in and takes me by the waist, flipping me onto my back. His warm body slides over mine. All my desire from last night comes flooding back as his mouth grazes my throat. My hands come up, and he gathers them, pinning them to the pillow above my head.

"Stay where you are," he says.

I keep perfectly still. He doesn't break eye contact as he kisses between my breasts, pausing to flick his tongue over my nipples, then down to my navel. His mouth skims over my scar. My breath catches as he kisses it, but he doesn't acknowledge it. He just watches my reaction. Then, he goes lower, and my toes curl at the warmth of his tongue.

Suddenly, it doesn't matter that I'm sore. I want him again.

"Goddamn," he murmurs, voice husky. "You taste like somebody was fucking you all night."

I touch his curly hair, smoothing it back. "Somebody was."

He lifts his mouth. "Was he any good?"

I consider giving him a snappy response, but seeing him between my thighs, looking up at me with those beautiful eyes, I can't.

"Yeah, he was really good," I whisper.

He goes back down, pulling the sheet over his head. It's sexy just watching him move beneath the fabric. I stretch my arms above my head, enjoying the slow rise of pleasure. This feels so luxurious, all I can do is gasp when I come and ride my pussy up against his mouth. He licks me clean and resurfaces, reaching for a condom on the nightstand.

He looks down at me, lids heavy, forearms flexing as he rolls the condom on. God, he is so effortlessly sexy. I really don't think he knows it either.

"You gonna be a good girl and take it?" he says.

I roll my eyes. He lifts my thigh and spanks my ass, flipping me onto my belly. Then, he's over me, hand beneath my hips as he lifts my body to work his cock inside. I'm so tender, I have to bite my lip. He sinks over me, letting me adjust.

"Fuck. Me," he murmurs, rolling his hips.

I glance over my shoulder, enjoying the way his muscles ripple when he thrusts. He's gentle this morning, like he's savoring every stroke. When he's done, he tells me to lie still while he gets a washcloth. Then, he wipes me down, rolling me on my back.

"You need to get to farm chores, cowboy?" I ask.

He shakes his head. "My horses and cattle have access to the outdoors, and they have water and hay. It's pretty self-sufficient up here because I only have a couple guys helping me out."

He gets up and throws out the condom, wiping himself off. I roll to my side to watch him pull on a pair of sweats. It's a nice view, seeing him in the early morning sun.

He's so backwoods pretty. Low slung pants give away a faint outline of his firearm underneath, all below a V that makes my mouth water. Shitty tattoos, a bruised thumbnail from smashing it in some scenario where he was probably shirtless and sweaty, tanned skin dotted with scars and hair.

I think I found out what my type is.

"You like coffee, baby?" he says.

I nod. He takes a pack of cigarettes from the bedside table and disappears downstairs. Maybe he means for me to stay in the bed, but I don't want to. I get up and open the dresser, taking out a white t-shirt. Then, I pad barefoot downstairs in it.

He's in the kitchen, opening cupboards, taking down a percolator. I creep into the kitchen, studying everything. The house has evidence of being lived in, but it's still sparse, like he's expecting to leave at any minute.

A muscle in his bicep flickers as he turns on the gas stove. It ticks, then ignites. I sink onto the wooden chair.

He turns, leaning on the counter. I get the sudden urge to ask him if he's like this with other women. Does he clean them up like a gentleman and make them coffee when he's done fucking them all night too?

Or could it be just me?

Instead, I say, "Want to show me around your ranch after coffee? You've got a nice place."

He shrugs. "Sure. After."

"After?"

He clears his throat. "Round two."

Heat creeps up my neck. "I think that would be round eight. You weren't lying when you said you had a couple rounds in you, Shotgun."

He smiles but doesn't answer. That gets me thinking about his age again. In the old photo I was given, he looked like an older teen. Fresh faced, boyish. There was a light in his eyes that isn't there anymore. Now, the peripheries of his eyes are subtly haunted.

"Why don't you like me being on top?" I blurt out, not meaning to.

That's been on my mind since he said it. Last night, he was careful to keep me underneath him. Maybe it's a fragile masculinity thing, like he feels he's somehow not in control if he's not physically on top. That doesn't seem right, but I don't know him well.

"I get claustrophobia," he says.

That makes sense, and it sounds like he believes it. The coffee is bubbling by his elbow. He flicks it off and takes down two beige cups and fills them. I rise and cross to him, accepting one.

"You got any milk?" I ask.

"Like cream?"

"No, whole milk only. No sweetener."

He opens the fridge, scanning it. "You're very specific."

"I know what I like."

He shuts the fridge. "Unfortunately not. I usually drink it bitter."

"That tracks," I say, taking my cup and sinking down at the table.

He walks past me and out into the hall. "Come on, let's sit on the porch."

That trips me up. Before Leland, I used to drink my coffee on the porch every morning when it was warm enough. It was my ritual. A little whole milk, my bare feet in the sun, watching the wrens squabble in the garden.

Then, I married Leland, and we had breakfast in the dining room with the shades still drawn.

He holds the door, and I step out, inhaling sharply. His house sits on a hill, surrounded by flat plains and distant mountains. One is much taller than the others, with a darker aura. The grass is already dry for the summer, and it moves in a dusty wave as the hot breeze hits it. Everything smells sweet, even the faint scent of cattle and horses coming from the stained wood barn maybe a quarter mile away.

This place is beautiful. It's different from home, but there's the same sense of peace here.

He sinks down on the bench, naked back to the wall. I stand at the edge of the steps, enjoying the sun's warmth.

"All this is yours?" I say. "You always lived out here?"

"All mine, but no, I haven't lived here all my life." He frowns slightly. "You ready to finally tell me where you're from?"

I hesitate, knowing I need to stick to the plan. It's hard, now that I'm here with him, feeling all the things he makes me feel. But I have to stay focused.

"Tennessee," I say.

"I thought you had a little accent," he says lightly.

"Some of my folks are from Kentucky, some from Ohio, West Virginia," I say. "I reckon I've got some accent from all over."

"It is a bit all over the place." His lids flicker, but his face stays neutral.

We decided saying a little bit of the truth but twisting it up was the best way to handle Jensen. He's smart, but easy to manipulate if you can get under his skin. That's what I was told. Now that I've met him, I believe that statement. Underneath all that cowboy roughness, I feel he's got a sensitive side. I hate that I'm taking advantage of it.

Am I really, though?

I study him. Whatever I'm feeling, it's not fake.

"So, you have farm hands out here helping you?" I say, trying to change the subject.

"Yeah, I got a couple who keep things running, but they'll be out in the fields by now," he says.

I have a sip of coffee, the bitterness spreading over my tongue. I was worried about what would happen when I finally got him alone. Would I feel safe? Or would I be wishing I had a pistol in my boot the way Leland had me feeling?

Instead, I feel the safest I've felt since my daddy was alive, sitting on his porch with this man I barely know. I swallow hard. It's not fair we had to meet under these circumstances.

"You got anybody else?" I ask.

He shakes his head. "I work a lot, stay pretty busy."

"No friends?"

He shrugs. "Yeah, I got some."

My coffee is about halfway done, and it's cooling off. I set it on the railing and close my eyes, turning my face up to the sun. My skin is hungry for touch, and my heart is starving. Snapping my eyes open, I climb down the steps, walk down the short path to the grass. It's soft near the house, just starting to brown.

He gets up and goes to the railing.

"You said nobody was around?" I say.

He nods, taking a pack of cigarettes out of his pocket. He lights one and inhales, holding it as he gazes at me. Slowly, I strip his shirt off my body, leaving me fully naked. His lips part, a little trail of smoke rising from them. I step backwards, letting the shirt drop to the ground for dramatic effect.

He lifts a hand and runs it through his hair. That's when I notice he's got a little cross tattoo on his ribs. Surely, he's not religious. That would be strange, considering what we did last night.

He reaches down to adjust the front of his pants. That's enough to distract me from the cross, my eyes moving to the outline of his hard cock hanging by his thigh. I let him look, hands tucked behind my back. But in my head, I'm trying to draw the lines between the bullseye on his chest, the cross on his side, and the Ruger on his dick. One plus one plus one equals...what?

Nobody told me what to expect when I met him. He's a mess of flavors I wasn't anticipating.

He clears his throat. "You trying to get me to make a mistake?"

"How is a little fun a mistake?" I tease.

He comes around the railing, standing halfway down the steps. "I don't have a condom, but that might not stop me."

My stomach flip flops, but not for the reason I thought it would. That shocks me from my head to my feet. Is it possible I could want him enough to sleep with him bare? After what Leland did? That has to be some kind of miracle.

"How about that parking spot you promised me?" I say.

He cocks his head. "Parking's free before noon."

"Oh, well, I'd better hurry up then."

He stabs out his cigarette and jerks his head. "Get inside, baby."

I could go...or I could make him work for it. I turn, shaking my hair back, and take a step. He gives me a behave-or-else look, but his eyes are glittering. This is something new and addicting. Leland never teased me, he never played with me. Everything was so damn serious all the time. Just real fucking grim.

I take another step.

He comes down the stairs. Then, he takes a quick step at me. I whirl and take off running, but he's faster than I anticipated. I get less than ten steps before his arm wraps around my waist. Cradling me, he drops us to the grass. Our eyes meet, and a thrill goes up my spine, then down again, centering right where I want his tongue.

I've never wanted anything the way I want him. It's pure, like a deep mountain spring bubbling up. All I want to do is roll around with him until we're both spent. Eat, drink, sleep it off, then do it all over again for days. Maybe weeks.

He kisses me, and he tastes like coffee, smells a tiny bit like tobacco. Maybe it's being naked out in the sun like this, but I swear, I feel everything more clearly than I've ever felt. The grass against my back and thighs. The warm weight of his body. The rough calluses of his hands on my wrists, the side of my face.

He pulls back. "You're a handful."

"I think your hands are big enough."

Instead of answering, he grips my waist and flips me as he rolls onto his back. I reel, but he keeps me steady, lifting me and setting me down, my knees on either side of his face. His eyes flash, pale blue. Then, he disappears between my thighs, and his tongue is hot on my clit. The muscles of my hips tighten, rising. My head falls back, only blue overhead.

His mustache rasps against my skin as he presses soft kisses to my pussy. His jaw is stubbled, prickly against my inner thighs.

"Relax, baby," he says, muffled.

I sway, unsure where to put my hands. One of them goes in his hair, but that doesn't seem right, so I brace it behind my back. Overhead, the pale sky is a clear arch. A breeze picks up, and it's sweet like hay. His tongue drags over my sex, dipping inside before moving to my clit. Then, he sucks it between his teeth and starts flicking it with his tongue.

"Oh, fuck!" My spine jerks back.

His fingers dig into my thighs, holding me still. He's stronger than I anticipated, even after last night. And he's merciless, keeping my clit barely balanced between his teeth and the suction of his mouth as he flicks it. There's pain, pleasure, and suffocating overstimulation, but he knows what he's doing, because I come out of nowhere, a wave of pleasure like falling into clear water.

My thighs give out, my weight sinking onto his face. He groans, slapping my ass as I come down. I'm shaking so hard, he notices and has mercy on me, lifting me onto his chest.

His eyes glitter. "What were you saying about me not being able to make you come yesterday?"

I'm too flushed to answer. It's not the pleasure that has me shaken. It's the crumbling of my own understanding of myself. I thought my body was just quiet, that I felt desire but didn't enjoy the acts it led to or the participation of another person.

I cried over my body refusing to respond to Leland and his lack of interest in doing anything to fix it. It turns out, none of that was my fault. I think I never felt safe enough to relax in his hands.

Jensen was supposed to be my savior.

But he might be my awakening too.

CHAPTER EIGHT

JENSEN

I think I'm falling in love.

The last nineteen years have been a tough existence. My little sparks of light came from fighting, working, and my handful of friends. But every night was the same thing: a dark ceiling and an empty room. On weekends, a body I didn't know and some liquor to get me through the night.

Then, I saw her in the stockyards.

Then, I touched her in my bed.

And it was like tasting a drug on the edges of my mouth for the first time. I keep pushing my face further in, trying to get more of it, trying to sink my teeth into whatever is so addicting about this woman.

It might be her body with her soft little curves, her lean legs that wrapped around my waist last night while I pounded into her pussy. It might be her startling eyes surrounded by thick lashes that remind me of something. Or the faint freckles I bit and licked on her tanned thighs, all the way to the naked pussy between her legs. She's so fucking good, all cinnamon and honey laced with something that's got a hell of a kick to it.

It might be the way she talks, all soft and drawling.

Or the way she has these quick, biting responses that keep me on my toes.

Whatever the fuck it is, I want to keep it.

I carry her back into the house and to the bedroom. Outside, I know I should check the animals, but I also know they're fine. So, maybe it won't hurt if I just take one day off. I don't have any jobs today with the crew. There's one this weekend I can't reschedule, so I think I'll soak her up before I have to go.

We fuck, the sheets and blankets on the floor. She comes again, gripping my dick so hard, it pushes me over the edge. Then, she lays against my side and traces her middle finger over the cross on my ribs.

It's a bizarre sensation, like when an old scar flares up out of nowhere. A little sore, but only when her nail scrapes it.

My dick is raw, but it still hardens halfway.

"What's your name?" she whispers.

That startles me. Did we never exchange names? I wrack my brain and realize that, while we exchanged sweat, spit, and other things last night, our names never came up. She wriggles up and lays her chin on my chest.

For a second, it's fine. Then, I'm on the kitchen floor, back to the cupboards, Holly in my lap.

My heart increases. Smoothly, I flip her onto her back, push her up on the pillows, and lay my cheek on her thigh. Her brows knit, but she doesn't say anything.

"What's your name?" I ask.

She smiles, just a little. "Guess."

I study her carefully. "You look like a Cassie or a Delilah. Something smooth, maybe ends on a vowel or something."

"It's Della," she sighs, sinking into the pillows.

"I had the right idea," I say, enjoying how warm her skin is under my cheek. "Mine's Jensen."

Her fingers slip into my hair. She has neatly kept oval nails, and they feel like heaven when they stroke through my hair. I think it's giving me an emotional boner, because I keep getting hard even though I'm not really aroused from it. She's just got magic in her touch.

"You look like a Jensen," she says.

I don't answer. My eyelids are getting heavy. She strokes my hair for a long time. The birds chatter outside. That sweet breeze is coming in through the window, and it feels good on our naked skin. Everything is gold, and I never want to move.

"Do you want me to go?" she whispers.

I open my eyes. She's leaning over me, soft hair falling around her face.

"No," I say.

She bites her lip, hiding a smile. "What are your big plans? Just lay around in this bed and fuck?"

"You got a better idea?" I ask.

She looks out the window, thinking. "Do they fight down at the stockyards every night?"

"No, twice a week. So yesterday and tonight."

"You want to go again?"

There's a hint of excitement in her face. Surprised, I push myself up on the pillows at her side. She gathers the sheets, pulling them over our waists. Her legs interlace with mine, and she slides her arms around my neck.

"Do you always fight when you go?" she asks.

I shrug. "Sometimes I do, sometimes not."

"Why don't you take me on a date?" she says, then freezes like she just did something wrong.

"To the stockyards?" I say. "I can take you somewhere nicer."

She shakes her head, hard. "No, I don't feel like going anywhere formal. I just want to be in a crowd so I don't have to think."

It's been a very long time since I went out on a date. My knee jerk reaction is to shy away—at least it was. But looking down at her, I don't think I want to fuck this up. No, I'd like to learn what it feels like to pursue her properly, not like my catastrophic or very short relationships of the past.

Now that I'm thinking about it, I'm not sure I've been on a real date ever.

"The fights usually start around seven," I say.

"Seven is fine," she sighs, sinking into my chest. "We should nap. We were up all night."

"I'm pretty tired," I admit.

We both slide beneath the sheets. Our mouths meet, and I'm lost, tripping, sliding all the way down to a place it took me ages to get out of. I think it's alright this time. There are no obvious red flags with her, the way there was back then. She's younger than me, clearly in her twenties at least. And odds are, she's not involved in organized crime. That last time was a fluke.

No, she's a perfect. Like somebody plucked my dream girl out of thin air and dropped her into my lap. No strings attached this time.

Our kisses slow until we're both too tired to keep going. Her eyes close, and I stare at the feathery lines against her cheek until I can't stay awake any longer.

My eyes close, but my brain doesn't rest. For the first time in nineteen years, I dream, and it takes me back to the worst day of my life—the one that makes no sense because I still can't remember how I got into that trailer.

BEFORE

The day after my twentieth birthday, I wake up in the aftermath of the end times.

Or at least, it looks like it.

I shake my head. There's a pounding between my eyes and a taste like engine oil in my mouth.

The room spins. A naked woman is laid out on the couch, a blanket over her lower half. One of Pat Pretty's guys is out cold on the floor, hands draped above his head. It takes me a moment before I remember who Pat Pretty is anyway—notorious drug dealer, the right arm of the Caudill family. Two more women in their underwear are curled in the armchair. Another Pat Pretty guy is slumped on the other couch.

I stand shakily, walking on the sides of my boots to the kitchen. My AK sits on the round kitchen table. I remember now—I put it there when I walked into the trailer around ten last night.

Shattered pieces of last night start to come together, Brothers' face swimming before my eyes as we talked. I think we argued. I drank or took something.

Then, my foot was on the gas, the road bouncing the truck hard as I sped over the gravel. The creek rushing to my left. The clouds rolling in, covering the stars as they came out. My boots crunching over rusted beer cans walking up to the door of Pat Pretty's trailer.

It was a job, a deal I'd been working on for a while. A momentary truce between Brothers and the Caudill family.

There was something I was supposed to collect—maybe money, maybe drugs. I remember the smell of body odor when I stepped into the singlewide. After living in luxury with Brothers, it was a shock.

Now, I'm wide awake in a nightmare, and I can't recall how I got here. My stomach churns, but I keep it together. Slowly, walking over broken bottles and clothes, I move through the kitchen.

The hallway opens, and there's a woman on the floor, naked. Silently, I roll her over with my boot, checking her for injury. She looks fine—at least she's breathing.

I keep going to the bedroom at the end. The door is ajar, and it smells inside, like...gutting an animal, raw as open muscle hanging in a butcher's shed. I shift the AK and bring my hand up over my nose, like that'll do anything.

Then, I kick open the door.

Jesus fucking Christ.

There's a body on the bed, cut in two. Not across the middle, but up and down, like the giant deli meat slicer of God took him out.

Fuck, I need to get out of here. I know Brothers and I are on the outs, but I'm not staying in this trailer with a body cut down the center, like he's about to be laid on ice behind glass. I need to get my ass back to the Boyd Mansion before this whole thing blows up in my face.

I stumble into the hall and step over the woman. She moans, rolling her head. I stop, turning as her eyes flutter open.

"Help," she whispers.

I need to go...but I can't leave her. She's pushing herself up on her elbows, terror in her eyes. I raise my finger to my lips, hunkering down to offer her my arm. She stands with my help, and I start hauling her down the hallway to the back door.

It's sickly warm out. I drag her onto the metal porch and shut the door quietly.

Then, we both hear it—footsteps.

Quick as a flash, I push her off the porch and jump down with her. It's only a few feet, but she falls into the tall grass and struggles like she can't get up. The door bursts open, insulation exploding from where it was kicked. Pat Pretty stands in the doorway, all six-seven of him, tatted up, bigger than a house. He has a Glock in one hand, trained on me.

"Don't you leave, Childress," he snarls. "We fucking talked about this."

Talked about what? I don't know, but fuck all this shit. Nothing is worth this. I'm barely twenty. I've got my whole life ahead of me, and now I'm sitting here, looking down the cold barrel of a pill pusher.

"Hey, I'm not here for nothing," I say evenly. "Just let us go."

He jerks his head at the woman in the grass. "That's one of Harlan's mules. You can't take her."

The woman rolls to her side, trying to get up. It's clear that even if she's physically unharmed, somebody drugged her the way they did to me. Even on her hands and knees, she can't keep from swaying. On cue, she starts vomiting, body recoiling like a cat trying to get up a hairball. There's a stirring from inside the trailer.

The living room window is yanked open.

A rifle pushes out.

I stare into the dark barrel and think back to the first time I pulled a trigger. I was a little kid, standing on the dirt road by my house. There was a snake coming at me—a copperhead—whipping hard back and forth. My mother stood a few yards off the porch, hands on her hips. I still remember her screaming at me but not daring to move in case it came at her instead.

"Put the damn gun back, baby."

Bam—I blew that motherfucker off the map. Then, I took the tail and nailed it to the porch as a sign to all the other snakes. *Pass over this house because there's a crazy six year old with a Smith and Wesson inside, and he sends snakes to meet Jesus.*

My mother beat my ass, which was her solution to everything. But she let that tail hang up there, because why the hell not? Maybe, deep down, she was a little proud.

I glance down at the vomiting girl, then back at Pat Pretty, then over at the rifle. Panic sets in. I'm getting out of this death house right fucking now. Tensing my body, I swing my AK up and pull the trigger, unloading the magazine like an amateur, but it works. Pat Pretty goes down, spilling out onto the porch, stuck in the metal bars. The rifle in the window disappears back into the trailer.

I can't run. They'll shoot me. So, I step over the woman and swing onto the porch, kicking the door open. There's another magazine on my belt. They didn't take that. I rip it out, pop it in the rifle, and stride into the kitchen.

All three men are up now, scrambling for their guns. I mow them down. One by one, quick and steady as that snake in the grass.

Parts of the couch flutter through the air. The woman on it is screaming, wide awake now. There's no threat to her. All the men are dead. Just to make sure, I walk through that house and kick open every door. Then, I go through the front, walking fast, to the gray Toyota parked at the end of the gravel drive.

Heart pounding, I hightail it down the gravel road. Maybe I should have gone back for the women, but there was nobody left to hurt them. They can run and have as fair a shot as me.

I don't know what happened to get me to this point, but I know I did something terrible. Pat Pretty is the man in charge of running all the Caudills' product. He's protected by all the power of their family. I don't think even Brothers Boyd can save my ass now.

This means war.

I don't stop. I get on I-75 and head towards the other side of Lexington without washing the blood off my hands. I don't take my iron grip off the wheel until I pull up in front of Brothers' mansion.

The gate pulls back as I hit the button. I drive up to the porch and get out, leaving the door hanging open. My body is stiff, and it's making me limp.

The security code doesn't work. I beat the front door with my fist. The cameras swivel and lock on me. The door swings open. It's Jem Boyd, who just got back from a trip overseas a month ago. He's wearing a tracksuit like he was about to go for a run. His brows rise, and he steps back, jerking his head, indicating I should go inside.

I spill into the foyer, just as Brothers appears at the top of the circular staircase. His brows rise, face a mask. I stand, gasping in the middle of the room. He descends and looks me over from head to foot.

"So you decided to come back," he drawls. "What the fuck happened?"

"Pat Pretty—he's dead," I burst out.

Jem freezes, and Brothers Boyd's face goes slack, all the lines easing out. His eyes round, then narrow. The curl of his palm tightens, knuckles going white.

His throat bobs. "You kill him?" he asks, voice flat.

I nod.

"You know he's protected by the Caudills?"

Everybody knows that. It's why nobody's ever touched that fucker. I nod, more scared than I've been in my entire life. The world's worst silence follows.

"Get inside, Jen," he says. "Don't leave my property."

But I do—I turn around and go home for the first time since Cherry kicked me out of her trailer. And the minute I walk through the front door where I spent the last few years of my teenagehood, I know why he told me not to run.

Sunlight filters through the broken kitchen window. Flies buzz over bloody linoleum. The microwave beeps, and I open it. There's a cold cup of coffee sitting inside that nobody will ever drink.

The Caudills were faster than a striking snake. They sank their teeth into my neck and injected their venom into everyone I ever loved.

NOW

My body startles so hard, I sit upright. Everything spins, and my skin is cold. For the last nineteen years, I haven't dreamed, at least not anything that wasn't a wet dream or the one where I get punched in the mouth in the ring and lose all my teeth.

Why can't I dream about that night I can't remember?

Maybe it would release me from my resentment if I could just remember what Brothers did to me, or said to me, that made me leave.

I run my hand over my face, dropping my head. Decades later, I'm still haunted by unanswered questions. I ran west. I became someone else with a whole new life.

I should be at peace.

But here I am, still dreaming of the horror that was home.

CHAPTER NINE

DELLA

BEFORE

I'm sitting at Leland's right, staring at the plate in front of me. There's a charger plate under it. I had no idea what that was until I married Leland. Now I spend all my time trying to figure things like this out. I'm getting good at it too, the way he wants me to be.

Leland is talking. The room is smoky, filled to the brim with men who do business with the Caudills, the boys in tweed from Lexington, the rich pieces of shit from out of state who come around only for the races. None of the men do his dirty work—this kind of dinner isn't for that. This is the room where deals get made.

I take a sip of wine and set it down. The man to my right, in a golf shirt that probably costs thousands, glances me over.

I'm perfect, a statue, a centerpiece for the new generation of Caudills. Skin tanned and lasered. Body lean from the mornings I get to escape to the gym and hide for a few hours. Flawless makeup. My body showcased in a rose gold dress that cups my breasts, cinches around my waist, and pools over my thighs to my ankles.

Elegant, beautiful, like the silver swans he has in the fountain out front.

Nobody would ever guess I grew up in a Harlan County trailer with sheets tacked over the windows.

Leland's palm touches my thigh. I flick my eyes over to my husband, but he's not looking at me. A conversation is happening, an important one, with a man from Chapel Hill. I paid attention enough up front to know his name is Richard St. Hilaire. His grandfather had money, and his father had even more. Richard has enough to buy my soul.

He owns horses. My husband knows how to get those horses to the finish line. They're a match made in heaven—or hell.

"She is," says Leland.

I flick my eyes between them. Are they talking about me? Richard St. Hilaire leans back in his seat, bourbon in one hand. He's looking at me, and I don't like it.

"Now I got somebody for you," Leland drawls.

"You're showing off, bringing your wife out looking like that," Richard says. "Letting us just look."

Leland must want this deal bad, because he leans forward, threading his fingers. Gold watches glint. The sun is setting, casting a deep yellow beam of sunlight across the table. It makes the red velvet curtains glitter.

"You can't fuck her, but if you put pen to paper, I'll let you watch," he says.

They both laugh.

The polite smile slides off my face. My mouth is dry, my cheeks on fire. Leland is possessive, but he likes me to be desired by other men too. It helps him with the business.

"Hell, show me where to sign," says the man to my right.

Everybody in earshot laughs, the sound shaking the table. I can't move. The laughter echoes as they banter back and forth. Apparently, that's funny, the thought of Leland letting them see me like that. This is a huge joke to all of them.

It's not a joke to me.

The laughter goes distant. I'm alone at the table, trying not to let my tears fall.

Crack.

My porcelain teacup heart breaks.

Hands steady, I take another sip of wine to bring me back. At this rate, I'm going to be one of those wealthy wives who stays just drunk enough to get through the day.

Leland's hand grips my thigh hard. The conversation shifts away from me to something else. I stay put until the dishes are cleared away and everybody gets up to go have drinks in the den.

I go last. Leland went first, but he comes back, cornering me in the hall.

"What's wrong with you?" he asks.

I shake my head. "Nothing. Just tired from the wine."

"You're a liar," he says. "You didn't like what I said."

I look away, then correct myself. He hates that. He tells me to look him in the eyes when we speak. He puts his hand on my waist, and my breath hitches.

"How do you think I pay for all this?" he says.

All this?

"What?" I whisper.

He runs his hand from my waist to my shoulder, unhooking the straps of my dress. The cowl neck falls, exposing the lace lining of my bra.

"You never look at price tags," he says, voice low. "You get to walk around with your head empty because of me. So you be a good girl and say yes sir when I tell you to behave."

I nod.

"Good girl," he says, cupping my breasts. He bends in and kisses me, and I feel something, a tiny spark in the darkness—not love, not lust, but hope that his feelings are enough to protect me from himself.

Leland loves me, I think. He just doesn't know how to love very well.

He pulls back. “You go upstairs to bed. I’ll be up later. Stay awake and don’t change, Del. You look too good in that dress not to fuck.”

I nod, because nothing he says surprises me anymore. His wife is a beautiful, fuckable doll to him. He brushes my lower lip with his thumb, and then he’s gone, striding down the dark hall. Pulling my dress back up, I circle the back way to the south staircase. Only once I’m in our room do I release the breath I’m holding and sink down at my vanity.

I want to rip everything off, but I can’t. Instead, I pull a mini bottle of vodka from the drawer and take a sip, telling myself it’s alright. That I’m not coping. That sip turns into the whole bottle, until I’m slumped in the chair with my head back, staring at the ceiling.

The worst part isn’t that he’s making me a drunk. It’s that by the time he comes upstairs to lay me down, I’ll be sober again.

NOW

I’m startled out of my sleep by Jensen shooting upright. He inhales, leaning forward and resting his elbows on his knees. His head dips, cross tattoo on his ribs exposed. My brain is fuzzy. It feels like Leland was there while I slept.

“Hey,” I whisper.

He glances over his shoulder. “What’s the clock say over there, baby?”

He’s so calm, despite having sweat dripping down his face. I glance at the digital clock on the bedside table.

“About six in the evening,” I say.

He gets up, wiping his hand over his face, using the sweat to hold his hair back. “You still want to go out to the stockyards?”

My forehead creases. “You feel good enough to go?”

He shrugs, reaching for the pants on the chair. “Yeah, why wouldn’t I?”

Maybe because he’s sweating bullets. I shrug. He goes into the bathroom and shuts the door. After a minute, he comes out, and he’s in his pants, boots, and a t-shirt that fits him very well. My dress and panties from the other night are in his hand. He tosses them onto the bed.

"I don't have anything else," he says.

"It's fine," I say, getting up.

My bra and boots sit on the corner chair. His eyes follow me as I pull them on and wriggle into the fringed dress. My purse hangs on the door. He must have gathered everything up at some point. I grab it, taking my emergency makeup out, and slip past him into the bathroom.

He leans in the door, still watching me.

"What?" I ask, bending in to apply my mascara.

His eyes narrow. Then, he shakes his head. "You're just real fucking pretty," he says. "And I think you know it."

He turns to go, but not before smacking me across the ass and grabbing the underside for a quick squeeze. His temporary bad mood is gone. I smile, and butterflies erupt in my stomach as he disappears downstairs.

My hand goes still, mascara hovering.

No, I can't actually fall for him.

And yet, I tripped on his big dick cowboy attitude and rolled all the way down the hill to a place I don't know how to climb out of. I'm not sure I want to get out.

Maybe this doesn't have to end the way I planned. Maybe he would help me, and there could be a future here when we're done. That thought has me smiling and blushing like a teenager as I apply my lip gloss.

I just need to figure out what he's thinking.

Then, maybe, I can tell him the truth.

He's waiting in the hall when I come downstairs. I go to him and turn my face up, even though it makes me nervous. I'm not used to interacting with men like I have free will. With Leland, I cowered and hoped to God he didn't notice me. Jensen smirks, putting a finger under my chin and bending down to kiss my mouth.

He's got something in his mouth. Dip? I wrinkle my nose. He flicks it with his tongue, and a hint of mint hits me.

"You didn't offer me any gum?" I tease.

He reaches behind himself to the brown cowboy hat on the coat rack. He takes it off in one hand, leaning over like he's going to kiss me. I part my lips, and he spits the gum into my mouth and puts the hat on my head.

"Let's hit the road, baby," he says.

Oh my God.

He takes my hand, leading me down the hall and out the front door. I stand while he locks it, trying to get control of myself. His hat smells like him, and the gum between my back teeth tastes like mint and Jensen.

Normally, a man spitting his gum into my mouth would make me gag, but I like him too damn much to care. I liked being underneath him in bed, his sweat dripping on my chest. I like the natural way he smells, the way he tastes, all the imperfections on his body.

He makes me want new things for myself.

We get into his truck. He lifts me in, making sure to give my ass another squeeze as I climb into my seat. I roll my eyes, but Lord, do I love it. He gets in, spinning the wheel to turn the truck around. Then, he rests his hand across my bare thighs as we head down the road. Everything is dusky golden. It's not dark yet, but it will be soon.

"So how much should I bet on you tonight?" I say.

"Bet everything you've got," he says.

"Oh, pretty confident you'll win?"

He squeezes my leg. Then, his fingers start circling where I have a freckle above my knee. Warmth blossoms. I watch his finger, distracted.

"You didn't think I could make you come," he says. "But look at you go."

I bite my lip and look away because I'm crushing on him so damn hard. I don't want him to see me smiling like that. He's already got an ego for days. He keeps stroking my thigh all the way into town. I try to pretend it's a casual gesture, but the longer he does it, the wetter my panties get. By the time he lifts me out of the truck at the stockyards, they're soaked and sticking to my pussy.

"All good?" he says.

I lean in, pulse pattering. "I don't know what you're doing, but it's working."

"How do you mean?"

Glancing at the packed building, I shift until his body buffers mine. Then, I lift the hem of my skirt in invitation. He slides his hand between my thighs, and his pupils dilate in the dim light.

"Fuck," he murmurs.

I lean in, his mouth grazing mine. "Win for me tonight, cowboy, and I'll let you fuck it."

He shakes his head once, the corner of his mouth turning up.

"I like thinking about you watching me with your pussy wet," he says. "Take your panties off and give them to me."

Obediently, I slip them off, and he holds out his palm. I never realized it before now, but he has a blurred letter tattooed on his thumb, right below the knuckle. Another piece of the puzzle that is Jensen Childress. I see it in a flash, then my crumpled panties cover it as he fists his hand. He pushes them into his back pocket.

"Little good luck token," he says.

He takes my hand and leads me down the hill to the barn. It's just as packed as the other night, maybe more so. In the middle, I can see there are a handful of men in the circle, just milling around, talking and taping their hands up.

"Let's get you a drink," he says, ushering me to the bar.

I find I like when he moves me around like this. It's not the same thing Leland did, but I don't know how it's different. Maybe because I always felt like I was being held hostage by Leland. But I want to be here with Jensen, so I bite down on his gum and follow.

He leans on the bar. Right away, like he erupted out of nowhere, a handsome man with jet black hair appears behind the bar. He swings his eyes on me and stares, lips parted. There's an animal-like quality to him, like he sees more than the average person. He also looks a little familiar; I think I saw him here yesterday night.

"Jesus Christ," says Jensen, startling.

"Almost," he says. He holds his hand out to me, and I shake it, confused. "Jack Russell."

"Like the dog?" I blurt out.

His jaw muscle flickers. Beside me, Jensen laughs, and Jack gives him a cool stare.

"How about you shut the fuck up, Childress," he drawls. "You all want anything to drink?"

I glance past him at the rows of bottles set up on the plywood board. The beer I had the other night was alright. I'm not a big beer drinker, but it also feels pretty silly to ask for wine at a stockyard fight. My eyes settle on a bottle of flavored rum.

"Can I have a shot of that?" I say, pointing.

Jack turns and fills a small glass instead of a shot and slides it over.

"Why are you bartending here again?" Jensen asks.

"Got bored and Lisbeth is on duty tonight," Jack says. He passes Jensen a beer, but he doesn't touch it. "You fighting?"

Jensen nods. "Thought I might."

"Go on then. They're taking names," Jack says.

"You hold my shit," Jensen says, taking a swig of beer before handing it back. He steps back and pulls his shirt off. There's a pleasant jerk in my lower belly, like I went over a bump in the road. He's so pretty, in a way Leland never could hold a candle to. Just raw and real.

My eyes trace the pattern of his tattoos again.

Ribcage cross.

Chest bullseye.

Ruger beneath his zipper.

Somewhere in that father-son-and-holy-ghost of ink lies the secret to Jensen Childress.

I can feel it even if it doesn't make sense right now. He passes his shirt over the counter. Jack hands him a couple strips of black cloth. My face is hot as I bolt the rum, trying to calm my fluttering heart.

God, he's got me tied up in knots.

Spellbound, I watch as he wraps his hands. Then, he leans in and gives me a kiss that pulls the breath from my lungs. I follow him as he moves through the crowd to the pit. Then, I stand with my jaw slack, watching closely as he talks with the referee. His name goes up in chalk. First fight of the night.

He looks at me through the crowd. Pale blue eyes washed out by firelight. Tanned skin glittering gold.

My heart won't stop trying to jump right out of my ribcage.

I want to fight for this chance. Some people get everything they want.

Why can't I?

CHAPTER TEN

JENSEN

I don't know if it's because she's watching me, standing there in that tight little fringe dress, but I clean house tonight.

The first guy taps out in ten minutes. The second takes a few longer, but he goes down and stays down. I bow out of the next fight because I'm getting tired. If I'm being honest, I'm worn out from staying up all night with Della. Even for me, six rounds, start to finish, is a lot.

I take her hand in my filthy one and lead her back to the table. Jack arches a brow as he tosses me a bottle of water.

"Peacocking pretty hard out there, bud," he says.

I flip him off. Della is already flushed, but she goes darker pink. I towel off and slide my arm around her waist, sinking down on a stool. She leans into me, but there's a faint tension in her body that wasn't there before.

"What did you say your name was?" Jack says, leaning on the counter.

"Della," she says, voice soft.

He doesn't speak, but I see his eyes narrow. It's bothering me that he's being such a buzzkill. For the first time in years, I'm on cloud nine. There's the most beautiful woman I've ever seen with my arm around her waist. Tonight, I'm going back home with her, riding the high of winning in the ring. Nothing can bring me down.

"You want to get out of here?" I say.

She nods. "Yeah, I'll go wherever you like."

Jack gives me a look, but I drop a twenty on the bar, take my winnings, and stand. He's not fucking this up for me. She puts her hand in mine, and I lead her back through the crowd. Jack's eyes follow us, like he's trying to figure something out. Then, he disappears as we leave the building.

"That was something else," she says.

I glance back at her, and my stomach jerks. She's so damn pretty, hair a glowing halo in the firelight. We get to the truck, and I can't stand it anymore. I pull her in and kiss her like I mean it, not like I'm just horny.

I want her again, slow and deep, until the sun rises.

She pulls back. "You alright there?"

"Yeah, you just look good," I say, opening the truck and lifting her in. "You want to get a drink with me before we go home?"

I get in the truck. I'm close enough now to see her blush.

"Yeah," she says, voice shaky. "I'd like that."

My heart is pounding all the way to the little honky-tonk place on Main Street. There's no way I'm showing up at Jack's bar tonight. I want privacy after his attitude. She looks up at the lights, and I swerve a bit off the road staring at her. She gasps, hand clamping on my forearm. I right the truck and pull into the city parking lot.

"Sorry," I say. "You just look so damn good."

She rolls her eyes. I take her by the back of the neck and kiss her again. My nerve endings tingle. There's a feeling of coming home with her that I haven't felt in a long time. Or maybe I've never felt it before tonight.

We break apart. Her eyes are huge.

"Let's go dancing, baby," I say.

She smiles, hesitantly. "You're gonna dance with me?"

I nod, pushing open the door. "I can dance alright."

"Alright," she says. "Let's get to it."

We walk across the street and enter the bar. It's pretty full, and there's a band playing in the corner. I check my phone. It's getting late. The music is slow and syrupy. The lights are low, and the space feels intimate. Keeping my arm around her waist, I guide her to the bar.

"What can I get you?" I ask, turning to her.

She studies the drinks, her nose wrinkling. "How about white wine?"

"So you're not a beer drinker?"

"It's alright, depends on the brand." She shrugs, smiling. "I was trying to fit in."

I laugh, leaning on the counter. "You don't seem like the type to care."

She leans in, sobering. We're so close, I can count the freckles on her skin. Her lashes are soft like a dark feather. When she smiles, she has laughter lines on one side, but not the other. There's a tiny overlap between her front teeth. The little details of her are what make her so familiar, I think, but I don't know why.

She lifts her fingers, touching the indent on my cheek. I have one dimple, and I see her looking at it when I smile.

She's noticing the little details too.

"You're so pretty," she says wistfully.

My brain goes in two directions at once. The first side makes me think of Miss Holly and her calling me pretty that day in her kitchen. How I felt kind of embarrassed, like I wanted to rub the back of my neck and look at the ground. The other side tells me it's alright when Della says it.

The room melts away. There's only her, looking at me with soft eyes.

She feels like grace, a break in the clouds.

Relief.

"Sorry, did I say that wrong?" she whispers.

"No," I say, leaning in. "You couldn't say anything wrong."

I'm tripping, falling, sliding all the way down to the bottom of a place I can't crawl out of. But this time, I don't want to get out. No,

I'm staying here all night, and in the morning, I'm asking her to stay with me for a while longer.

We don't know a lot about each other, but I have a feeling that will come.

Forgetting about the drinks, I slip my hand around her waist and steer her backwards to the dance floor. There are a few other couples, bodies close as they sway to the soft music. I want to be like them, normal and falling for somebody I could build a future with. I pull her near, and she goes, hesitant at first. Then, she melts and puts her head on my chest.

I feel it again.

Something new.

This time, when I think about the first time I fell for someone, it hurts less. With her body in my arms, perhaps I could move forward instead of just living in hiding. Maybe everything is alright. Maybe this is my break.

"You alright?" she whispers.

"I'm better than alright," I say.

We don't speak for a while. We just exist in a comfortable, golden haze.

CHAPTER ELEVEN

DELLA

He wasn't supposed to feel like being home, but here I am, in his arms, feeling like I'm back in my little holler and everything is right with the world. It's breaking my damn heart.

His hand slides down to the small of my back. Leland used to hold me there, controlling me when we'd leave the house.

It doesn't feel like that with Jensen. No, his hands feel like if I woke up from a bad dream, his touch might send me back to sleep, all firm, strong, and steady. I turn my head, the band blurry in my vision. His chin shifts, his mustache tickling my temple.

"You all good, baby?" he murmurs.

I swallow the lump in my throat. "Yeah, I'm just perfect."

He's breaking my already-cracked heart. If we dance any longer, I'm going to spill everything out here right now. Reluctantly, I pull back, and he releases me.

"I'm getting tired," I say.

"You were up all night." He takes my hand, pulling me against his side. "Let's get back, fuck a little, and get some sleep."

I nod, and the lump of guilt stays in my throat all the way back to the truck. The moon is out, reflecting off the mountain peaks in the distance. It blows my mind how vast Montana looks in comparison to the close set hills of Kentucky. At home, I'm used to being tucked away, but out here, I can see for miles when we get on the highway.

"You like living out west?" I ask.

He puts his hand on my thigh, shifting up my short skirt. His middle finger touches right below my panties, circling like he did that first night in the stockyards.

"Yeah, I do," he says. "It's different than what I knew, but I like it pretty good."

"Where you from? You've never told me."

He glances sideways at me. That's a look I'm getting used to, and it reminds me he's a fair bit older than I am. It's a stern little glance, like I'm stepping on his boundaries, and he doesn't appreciate it much.

"Here, there," he says.

"Everywhere?"

He squeezes my thigh. "Something like that."

We don't talk again until he pulls up outside his ranch house. I sit tight, knowing he's circling the truck. And he does, lifting me out and kissing me briefly as he sets me down. Everything tingles. Then, he takes his hat off and puts it on my head, spinning me around and slapping my ass.

"Get yourself inside," he says.

I flash him a smile, scrambling up the steps. He unlocks the door, and we're tumbling into the hallway. My body is ready, the guilt forgotten once again. He's got me pushed up against the wall in a second, hands all up and down my hips, shoving up my skirt, dropping to his knees.

He's still sweaty from his fight, but I don't say a thing about it.

"Ride my face, baby," he breathes.

Palms flat on the wall, I brace my knee on his shoulder and slide my pussy onto his face, right up to his mustache. His eyes flicker, lids drooping with arousal. My legs almost buckle as he starts licking my clit, moaning in his chest like I'm the best thing he's ever tasted.

My fingers curl in his hair. His eyes are still on me.

That's when I see something I've never seen in a man's eyes, but I don't think I've been treated well enough to know what to call that expression. It's one that better, more fortunate people get to see. I don't think Leland would have thought me deserving of it.

He was always quick to remind me what I am.

Never good enough. A charity case who should be grateful for the way he pulled me up.

Jensen breaks me out of my spiral by pushing his face in harder and shoving his tongue into my pussy. A little yelp breaks from my lips. My spine recoils. Fuck, I can feel him moving inside me, slow, deliberate thrusts.

"Oh God," I breathe.

He curls it, and I think he's hitting my g-spot, or he's very close. Shaking, I grind my clit down against his mustache, letting him tongue-fuck me while I'm at it. Maybe it's the combination. Maybe it's the way he rolls his eyes. But I come hard, a slight burning I'm not used to flowing through me. My body goes limp, and his hands come up to keep me from falling.

I shake, pleasure moving through my body in stronger waves than I felt last night. They wring me dry, leaving me weak.

He keeps going, tongue pulling from my pussy and heading back to my clit. My toes curl as he starts licking. This is too much. I'm going to crawl out of my skin from overstimulation.

"Jensen, please," I gasp.

He keeps going, pale eyes locked on mine. Desperate, I pull at his hair, and he moans before nipping my pussy gently.

"Please." I'm trying to wrestle his head up by his hair, fingernails in his jaw.

He lifts his mouth, my arousal dripping down his neck. "You looking to get put over my knee, baby?" he says.

Oh, well. Fuck me, I wasn't, but maybe I am now.

I shake my head, cowed and so turned on, my breasts ache in my bra.

He flicks my clit hard with his tongue. "Cause I don't mind making that happen."

My lips part, but no sound comes out. He stands, the front of his shirt absolutely doused. Did I do that? I don't have time to think about it, because he picks me up and carries me into the kitchen. The way he manhandles me is thrilling. It's so rough but still gentle, like he's fully aware of how much I can take.

He flips me onto my belly and lays me down, bent over the table.

My heart pounds. Oh God, he's going to do it. My fingers grip the edge in front of me, and my toes barely reach the floor.

"You want it to stop, you give me the red light," he says gruffly from up above.

"The red light?" I whisper.

"Just say red," he says. "That way, if you want to beg and struggle, you can, but you're still safe. You understand?"

It clicks into place what he's saying. He's giving me a safety lever to pull, but he's letting me have the fantasy of brute force. It's controlled violence.

No, that's not the right word.

Careful violence is a better way to describe it. Contained but still raw, visceral. My body responds to the idea so hard, it's embarrassing. There's something dripping down the inside of my right thigh.

I need this.

"I understand," I whisper, turning my head and laying my cheek down so I can see him.

The kitchen light is off, making him a shadow. My skirt has slipped down over my ass, but my thighs are out. Can he see they're wet?

Why do I want this?

It feels like I shouldn't, but there's this deep hole inside me that feels like it was scooped out with a serrated spoon. I've had it for the last five years. It's the inside voice that cried out for someone to do something when Leland appeared, the same one he starved out by stonewalling my every need.

I need. I need so badly, it hurts.

A firm hand, a gentle word. A guide through the things that terrify me. A lighthouse in the dark.

Clink.

He's unfastening his belt, stained with sweat and dust from the ring. It slides through rough fingers. Then—crack—he snaps it so loud, I jump, biting my lip to keep from gasping.

Between my legs is swollen, so sensitive, I can make out the rhythmic throb of desire where I'm soaked. His hand cups the back of my thighs. His inhale is so sweet, I have to close my eyes while he trails his fingertips through my arousal.

I had no idea it could be like this.

"You're a wet little bitch, aren't you?" he murmurs.

Heat floods through me, making my ears roar. His tone is soft, reverent, but his words are filthy. I don't know if I should be offended, or if I should grind back on his hand and come.

Before I can decide, he pulls back, almost flicking me as he does, bringing his palm down across my ass.

Pain ripples, followed by heat.

"Oh God," I whimper.

"I asked you a question, baby," he says, the hand holding the belt pressing on the middle of my back.

He slaps the back of my right thigh hard.

"Yes," I manage. "Anything you want."

He comes down on my other thigh. "Anything?"

I'm pretty sure he could ask me to sign my soul away, and I'd do it for him. Delirious, I nod. "Yes, just don't stop."

He shifts, crouching behind me. He pushes my skirt up over my ass and starts eating me from the back, licking me from clit to pussy in long, hungry strokes, sucking, biting. My nails scrape into his table. I hope he doesn't care that much about it.

"I think I can answer my own question," he murmurs, scraping his teeth against my inner thigh.

"What?" I whisper, floating.

"You are a wet little bitch," he says, slapping my ass again.

My pussy throbs. Never in my life did I think I'd get off on being called that word, but Lord, the way he says it, just all dirty and sweet, is too much. He bends in, flicking my clit, and I come again.

He's on his feet, and I hear the belt whistle. White heat bursts, followed by pain so intense, I cry out.

Everything is a mess of pleasure and agony. It's two flavors that shouldn't work together, but they do, like fireworks ripping through every inch of me. Shutting off my brain. Turning everything else on. Lighting me up.

I've never burned this bright.

The belt comes down across the backs of my thighs. Something wet drips on the floor between my feet. His hand slides beneath my throat, cupping the underbelly. His hands are so big and firm, holding my head steady, thumb on my jaw, pointer and middle beneath my opposite ear.

The belt whistles again. It cracks across my upper thighs.

I whimper, tears stinging my eyes. The belt comes down again, then one more time, on the same place, right where my ass meets my thighs. Then, it hits the floor. The dull thud of leather and clink of metal makes me open my eyes.

He's circling to my head, chest heaving, shirt stained with my arousal. The muscles in his forearms flex as he unzips his pants, unleashing his cock.

"You hit my side if you want out," he murmurs.

One handed, he flips me onto my back on the table. That's when I realize what he wants, and my stomach flutters. He's putting God knows how many inches in my mouth. My nerves hum—I think I can take this. I want to at least try. I've done this many times for Leland before, but this is the first time I've wanted it.

Wanted is a weak word.

Crave is better.

My lips part. He pulls me closer until my head hangs off the table.

"Open for me, baby," he rasps.

The table is the perfect height. My tongue flicks out, wetting my lips, although I don't know if that will do anything to help.

"I won't hurt you," he murmurs, cupping my right breast, teasing the nipple with his worn fingers. "Open your mouth and reach between your legs. Touch that pussy for me, baby."

I'm done, laid out and weak on his kitchen table. My fingers slide down my stomach to my clit, gathering my arousal, stroking myself the way he just did with his tongue. I close my eyes and part my lips, ready for him.

"Good girl," he praises.

The table creaks. I think he's bracing himself. Then, the big, hard head of his cock pushes past my lips. Maybe I'm imagining it, but I can feel the lines of the tattoo. I keep my throat slack, letting him feed the barrel of his Ruger into my mouth, pushing all the way to his groin.

My head spins.

I can't breathe. That's fine with me.

"Fuck," he breathes. "Look at you go."

He touches my throat like he's trying to feel himself through it. Then, he pulls back.

"Breathe," he orders.

Obediently, I inhale. He ruts his hips gently, filling me past the bend of my throat. Then, he pulls back until the head is on my tongue.

"Exhale for me."

I exhale.

"That's my girl," he says, voice hushed. "You keep touching that pretty, wet cunt."

Right now, I would do anything for him. He cradles my head, fucking my mouth with just enough force. The tension is perfect. The pleasure is buried somewhere beneath the pain, just enough so I'm dripping on the table as I stroke my clit.

"Fuck yourself, you pretty little bitch," he pants. "Put your fingers in your cunt and fuck them hard while you swallow my cum. I want to hear how wet you are for me."

Distantly, I feel myself obeying. My two fingers delve inside. It's loud, soaked, slipping down my ass.

"Fuck," he groans, shoving himself so deep, I can't breathe. His hips stutter, his finger and thumb pinching hard on my nipple. A final orgasm, like an afterthought, ripples through my hips as he comes. The taste of him, visceral as falling into saltwater, floods my senses.

I squirm. He pulls out and flips me onto my knees on the table, holding me steady. I'm shaking, swallowing the spit and cum pooled in my mouth. His thumb runs over my lips, wiping them clean, licking it off. He bends, eyes hovering over mine.

"Hey, baby," he says. "Look at me."

Dazed, I obey, tumbling into those beautiful mountain eyes that only come from one place on Earth.

"You're safe," he says. "And you were so fucking good for me."

My head spins, but slowly, I start feeling my limbs again. He bends in, his mustache tickling as he kisses my forehead. I melt, and he takes me in his arms, lifting me so I can wrap my legs around his waist. He holds me like he loves me, even though we barely know each other.

Now that I'm not high on him, reality comes back in full force.

The guilt is too much. I can't keep this secret any longer. I have to tell him the truth. Before I knew him, I thought it would be so easy to seduce him, con him into helping me. But now that he's holding me, close against his skin, there's no part of me that can hurt him.

It wasn't supposed to be this way.

But here I am, falling for him.

CHAPTER TWELVE

DELLA

Wrecked by guilt, I let him sink down to the floor with me. We curl up, backs against the cabinets, and he pours two shots of whiskey. He's still in his pants and boots, but he gave up his shirt for me. It smells like sweat, like the stockyards. That's alright. It's nothing I'm not used to already. And I love the way he smells.

Guilt is a heavy sin.

I take a sip from my glass. It's alright, not as good as what we've got back home, but it puts the fire back in my bones.

"I was thinking," he says.

"Yeah?"

He's staring straight ahead at his glass. "I was thinking I'd like to keep seeing you. How do you feel about that?"

The bottom drops out of my stomach.

"Jensen," I whisper.

He rolls his head to the side. "That's a yes or a no?"

"I've got to tell you something," I say, fragile, like the husk of my words are all that are left over.

My vision wavers. I have another sip, a bigger one this time. It's only making me drunker, and I need to keep my wits about me if he throws me out.

I blink hard.

"I need help," I whisper.

He sits upright, shifting to face me. "What kind of help?"

My lip trembles. "I got a baby, a little boy."

His eyes flick down. I know he saw the scar from my cesarean. He was just too polite to ask.

"He in trouble?" he asks, voice dropping.

Yes, he's in danger of growing up under the thumb of the man who destroyed my life. In danger of becoming a monster like Leland someday. And I'm in danger of looking in his eyes and not knowing him.

"His father took him from me, but he's not in danger," I push out. "I left him, and he took him from me. I can't see him unless I go back. He's a big, powerful person. I can't win in court against him."

The strangest expression crosses his face. As soon as it's there, it's gone.

"Who's his father?"

My tongue flicks out, tasting a bit of whiskey on my lip.

"Leland Caudill," I whisper.

He doesn't move, not an inch, but his pupils dilate like a bomb bursting. There's a silence. We're both tensed. Then, he reaches behind his back, and I surge forward, dropping my glass. It shatters as his hand snaps around my throat, shoving me back against the cabinets.

Click.

He's got his revolver pressed to my neck.

"Say that again," he breathes, inches from my face. "Louder."

The taste of his cum is still on my tongue. Now, it's edged with fear.

"Leland Caudill."

The words hang between us. The dark kitchen was cozy a moment ago. It feels so grim now, all shadows and the sober glitter of his eyes.

"How?" he spits softly.

"How?" I whisper.

"How'd he knock you up? One night stand?"

I shake my head, swallowing. It's hard past the cold barrel of the gun. "He married me."

"He *married* you?"

He stands, pacing the length of the kitchen, then turning. It's a relief to not be at gunpoint, but he's still standing over me, well over six feet of muscle and anger and betrayal.

"You know Leland?" I whisper.

That wasn't made clear to me prior to coming to Montana. All I was told was that Jensen had family problems with the Caudills, that he was uniquely situated to help me. Apparently, he's a talent when it comes to figuring tough situations out. The best of the best.

"I know the Caudills," he says flatly. "I don't know Leland well, but I'm pretty goddamn aware of who he is. I just didn't know he had a wife and a son."

Silence.

"And I didn't know I was fucking his wife, a Caudill woman," he spits.

"I'm not his wife," I interject.

He turns, gesturing with the gun. "Explain yourself then."

"Can I stand?"

"No. You keep your ass right where it is, thanks."

Cowed, I press my back hard to the cabinets. "I divorced Leland, but he won't let me have my boy. Nobody goes against the Caudills, so he got full custody, no questions."

My voice breaks. Inside my chest, it's like I'm peeling back the skin on a newly healed wound. Every time I think about it, I want to sob. Not cry, but curl up in a ball and just sob my insides out.

Landis is my baby.

He needs to be with me.

I bite the inside of my cheek. My thumbnail aches—I'm tearing the skin on it again. His eyes flick down, then up to my face again.

"And Leland Caudill just...let you walk out?" he says.

"I had help," I say.

He comes close, crouching to get eye level with me. "Who helped you?"

The only set of instructions I was given was to never answer that question. At least, not until I got him back to Kentucky. But that was before I fell right into his beautiful mountain eyes, his arms, and then his bed. Back when he was just a name and a face in a photograph.

"Tell me, Della," he says.

I swallow, trying to give him the pleading eyes that sometimes worked on Leland. But Jensen is ice cold.

I mumble, trying to get it out.

"Speak up," he snaps.

I tilt my chin up. "Brothers Boyd."

Nothing changes, but the entire room goes cold. He's looking at me like an animal, and I'm trying to figure out if he's going to eat me. But not in a nice way, not the way he looked at me in the bedroom. No, this is colder than the dead of winter. He could be a different man.

Abruptly, he pulls back. "Come here."

He takes me by the wrist and leads me out of the kitchen, up the stairs. Panicking, I start rethinking my choice to tell him. I should have stuck to the plan and told him in Kentucky, where Brothers could protect me. Now, I'm being pulled into his bedroom, and he's shutting the door.

"Clothes off," he says.

"What?" I whisper, backing up.

He uncocks the revolver. "Strip and get up on the bed. The faster you go, the easier this'll be."

The bottom falls out of my stomach. I'm usually pretty brave, but I don't like what he's saying.

"Please don't," I whisper, dipping my head to hide my tears. "I'll leave, tonight."

"No, you're not going anywhere."

The tears are coming so fast, I can't hide them. I sniff, wiping at my face. He mumbles something under his breath, pushing past me to the bedside table. The drawer opens, then shuts.

"Do you need me to count?" he says. "Get up on the bed. Now."

Miserably, I drag the shirt off. I'm so damn scared, I don't notice he's got something in his hand. Leland liked doing this kind of thing, pushing me to a place where I wondered if he was capable of being intimately violent. I look up at him, my lower lip trembling uncontrollably.

"I'm not going to hurt you, Della," he says quietly.

The bed dips as I crawl up it, sitting against the headboard. His mouth thins, jaw tight. Cold metal touches my wrist, and I whip my head around as he clips a pair of handcuffs around me and fastens them to the headboard.

He turns, taking up the gun, and circles to the end of the bed.

"Alright, baby," he says grimly. "You better have a real fucking good story to tell me, or we got problems."

I know we've got problems regardless of what I say, so I may as well unload the whole truth, start to finish.

"Brothers wanted me to bring you back to Kentucky," I say. "I think he wants you to work with him again. He knew I was trying to get away from Leland, and he's not friendly with the Caudills, so he offered to help. I'm sorry, but I'm so desperate, Jensen. I need help getting my boy back."

My voice breaks. He doesn't.

"What do you want me to do?" he asks.

"Brothers said you were one of the most talented men he'd ever worked with, that you had a reason to want to see the Caudills hurt, same as him," I say. "He said if you can't get Landis back, nobody can."

His jaw works.

"Brothers Boyd is the devil's assbackwards evil twin," he says finally. "You shouldn't be fucking around with him."

That makes me pause. His words are a little funny. Under other circumstances, I might have laughed if he weren't saying them so seriously. But there's real venom in his voice.

"What's he want from you?" Jensen asks.

I shake my head. "Just you."

He goes a little pale. "So you sold me out, huh?"

"I didn't know you," I shoot back.

"And knowing me changes this...how?"

"It changes everything."

The words burst out, echoing through the room. His eyes widen in a quick flare, pupils retracting. There's no way he's going to lie and tell me the last few days meant nothing. Because after meeting him and all the things his touch made me feel, I'm never going to be the same woman.

Neither of us speak.

"How'd you know where to find me?" he asks finally.

"There's a photograph in my purse," I whisper. "Brothers gave it to me, along with a list of places I should check."

He crosses the room, grabbing my purse and emptying it on the chair. The photograph falls out. He picks it up and goes completely still. His lips part as he stares at it, brow furrowed.

"Alright," he says. He puts the gun back in his holster and shoves the photo in my pocket. "I'm gonna go have a fucking cigarette,"

He walks out, leaving me chained to the headboard. Pain, the worst kind, settles in like a cold front. It aches from my head to my feet.

More than anything in this world, I want my son back in my arms.

But now, I also want Jensen.

I fell so hard and fast, I didn't realize I'm feeling things for him already, real, gut wrenching things that make me want to cry as he slams the front door.

I could have had this from the start. If Leland Caudill hadn't seen me walk up to his table in the diner and decided he just had to have me because of some two dollar, secondhand dress that made my tits look good. If he hadn't knocked me up and put a ring I never wanted on my finger, I'd have had the opportunity to meet a man like Jensen.

But no, Leland couldn't keep his hands to himself. For the sin of being desired, I was damned. And now, my heart is ripped in two—

one part back in Kentucky with my little boy, and one part sitting all torn up in my chest.

Bleeding out.

CHAPTER THIRTEEN

JENSEN

It feels like that one time I got kicked in the chest by a mule when I was in middle school. It wasn't even hard, but it was a mule, so of course, it knocked the bejesus out of me and sent me dry heaving over the edge of the fence.

Dazed, I step out onto the porch. The shadow of Sovereign Mountain hovers in the distance. Usually, it's a comforting behemoth. Tonight, it feels like the encapsulation of the threat breathing down my neck.

The wind hits the door and sends it slamming shut. I reach in my pocket and pull out the box of cigarettes, taking the last one out.

Brothers Boyd.

That's a name I'd hoped to never hear again in my life.

When I fled Kentucky, I took nothing but a horse and a revolver. I felt, at the very least, I deserved that much to take me onward. It was a silly dream, a child's dream, to be a cowboy. But when the sensible parts of the world fell apart, it was all I had left.

It worked. For nineteen years, I was left alone.

But not in peace. Every day, I look over my shoulder and wonder if the Caudills or Brothers will find me here. If I could do it over again, I'd have changed my name, but I didn't know enough then. I was a kid, and all I knew to do was run as far as I could until I found a place to hide.

Nineteen years is a lot of hiding.

My shoulders sag. I bring the cigarette up and inhale. The label taunts me, half crushed and flashing the emblem I used to look over and see on Holly's nightstand. Back then, I was too young to know better. Both Holly and Brothers got their pound of flesh before I came to my senses. I thought I'd gotten over that, but clearly, I haven't, because I couldn't let Della get on top of me like that.

I haven't let anyone, not since Holly.

Ghosts don't die, and mine are no exception.

BEFORE

Jensen - Age Twenty

I'm in my room, trying to get ready for church with Brothers. Holly stayed in my bed last night. There's a slight fear in my chest that he'll find out. But I'm more annoyed I don't have any clean shirts. That's my fault for shoving them on the floor instead of in the basket.

She's sitting up against my pillow in her red silk nightgown. Her eyes follow me as I sort through my dresser.

"You okay, Jen?" she asks.

I glance over my shoulder, guilty she's even in my bed on Sunday. Technically, we didn't do anything wrong. Everything was over before midnight.

She came in from doing whatever she does for Brothers early. Dinner was plated in the kitchen. She ate standing by the stove. I had a cup of coffee while I talked to her about my day.

She said that Kyle was back from Lexington and living with her now.

"Did you tell him?" I asked, stomach twisted with guilt.

She shook her head. "No, but he'd like to see you."

After everything that's happened, what I did with his mother, there's no way I can look Kyle in the eyes ever again. I might resent Holly for that, but I can't tell.

I don't know what I feel anymore when I'm with her.

She saw my face and said it was alright if I didn't want to see him. I went upstairs and left her to finish eating on her own. It's hard to believe Kyle was my family, and now that's been replaced. Now, it's Holly, Brothers, and me, the fucked up holy trinity of organized crime.

My eyes fall on a clean shirt, a pale blue button up. I pull it on and start fastening it.

"You're so handsome," Holly says wistfully.

I don't answer. I thought I loved Holly, but she's starting to grate on my nerves. Now that I work closely with Brothers, I see other couples and wonder why I can't have that normalcy. All Holly and I do is fuck in ways that kind of freak me out. I'm having trouble getting off from anything that isn't mutual pain.

"Thanks," I say finally.

She gets up, running her wine red nails down the front of my shirt.

"You want to do something later?" she asks.

I shake my head. "It's Sunday."

She pouts, frowning. "He won't know."

"He might." That's one thing Brothers Boyd is good at—knowing everything the minute it happens.

Her palm slides down, cupping me through my pants. "What about just a quickie, right now?"

I politely move my dick out of her hand under the guise of leaning over to grab my belt.

"I have church," I say.

She snaps out of seduction mode, crossing her arms. Now, she looks the way she did when she used to yell at me and Kyle for getting mud on the carpet. That bothers me. I finish fastening my belt and push my wallet into my pocket. The mirror says I look pretty good, clean-cut and up and coming.

"You spend a lot of time with Brothers," she says.

"Yeah, I work for him," I say.

"But church? You're not religious, Jen."

I turn, halfway out the door. "Can you stop calling me that? It's Jensen."

Her jaw drops, and right away, I feel terrible. Closing the door, I take her by the shoulders and kiss her forehead. She melts against my chest. I soothe her, rubbing between her shoulder blades.

"Sorry, I'm just stressed with work," I say. "But I do have to go. I'll see you at dinner, okay?"

She nods, giving me a weak smile as I leave the room. I'm not stressed about work—in fact, it's going incredibly well.

Everything is perfect, except for Holly.

I regret that day on the kitchen floor. At night, after we sleep together, I lie awake and turn the same question over in my head. Why? Why did I sleep with her in the first place? But I don't know the answer—I think I'm in too deep to figure it out.

Downstairs, I unplug from worrying about Holly. Brothers stands on the front porch in his best suit, waiting. I step out, and he puts a hand on my shoulder, looking me up and down.

"You look good, Jen," he says. "Ready to hit the road?"

I nod. "Let's go."

We do this every Sunday morning. Brothers is part of a Baptist church between Lexington and Byway, has been since he was a boy, according to him. We head down, attend the service, rub elbows with the people there. Then, we go out and have lunch with his business associates.

After that, if it's racing season, we drive all the way up to Keeneland and have dinner and do business. Brothers calls Sunday his networking day. He starts with God, then moves onto the seersucker bourgeoisie.

"God, then money," he always says. Then, he narrows his eyes, a sly smile on his face. "And by Monday, it's right back to bourbon and beautiful women."

Today is a perfect day. It's warm but not too hot. The sky is clear blue, and the bluegrass is waving in the breeze. We get to church with a few minutes to spare, and Brothers and I sit in his pew up front. The service starts, but for some reason, I can't stop thinking about my conversation with Holly this morning.

I don't think we're working out.

And that hurts.

I look up at the plain cross on the wall. I'm not religious or spiritual, but I envy the way Brothers' face transfigures when he walks into the building. I glance sideways. He's gazing at nothing, totally relaxed. At first, I thought it was a joke that he goes to church. He's an organized crime lord, essentially. But then, I realized there are no easy answers when it comes to Brothers Boyd.

My mind stays right with Holly. It keeps drifting to what we did last night. Then, I feel kind of guilty, because what if God is real, and here I am, thinking about bondage and sadism at eleven thirty on a Sunday morning? In His house too.

I give my head a shake.

"You good, Jen?" Brothers leans in.

I nod. "Yeah, all good."

I gather everything up and shove it down, hard. The service ends, and I float through, shaking hands with everybody I know. Then, I follow Brothers out to the cemetery around the side of the church. He's got two second cousins buried there, everyone else is in his family cemetery. We're both quiet as he walks beneath the willow tree, looking down at the headstones.

"You never told me where your mother is buried," he says.

"She was cremated," I say. "It was cheapest."

"Where did you spread her ashes?"

I shake my head. "I didn't. They're in Cherry's house."

"Oh, like a memorial urn?"

"No, she's in a Tupperware container in the crawl space."

He swings his gaze around. "Goddamn, Jen. Sometimes, you make me feel like my life was easy."

I shrug—what am I supposed to say to that? Now that Brothers has provided me safety, I've had a lot of time to pick apart my life.

I'm starting to realize I'm not a fortunate kid. I just never knew better than to be happy with the bare minimum.

"You know what? Let's go have lunch at the diner today," he says. "I'm tired of all this socializing."

He can tell I'm having an off day. Brothers is the first person to give a damn about what I feel. I'm grateful for that. He claps me on the shoulder, and I follow him to his fancy car parked around the side. We don't talk as his driver takes us through Lexington to a diner in the countryside to the west of the city. It's a quiet, hole in the wall place Brothers favors.

We go in through the side door. The inside always reminds me of my trailer growing up: wood-sticker walls, peeling linoleum floors. The difference is, the diner is spotlessly clean and smells like pancakes. We sink down in our usual booth, the second from the back, left row.

Our waitress, Ashleigh, appears. She likes Brothers, flirts with him every time, and he eats it up. Or maybe it's the other way around. She's about my age, curvy, with bombshell blonde hair and a sweet southern drawl.

"Hey, there," says Brothers.

"Y'all out causing trouble on a Sunday?" she says, setting our coffee down.

"You know it." He winks.

She rolls her eyes. "Alright, you want the usual."

I nod. "Yeah, but can I get bacon, no eggs today?"

"Coming right up, sweetheart," she says, scribbling on her pad. "And for you, Mr. Boyd?"

He leans in, dimple flashing. "Same as usual, ma'am."

She rolls her eyes again and leaves. Brothers flirts with everybody, drizzling honey all over every situation he walks into. But I've noticed he doesn't say sir or ma'am to his peers. It's only people who are less wealthy or powerful.

He's all yes, ma'am the minute he's at a diner or a strip club. Thank you, sir, but only to the person pumping his gas. I asked him about it once, and he gave me a thoughtful stare and said it costs nothing to be a gentleman, Jen, but it'll cost you everything to be a cunt.

"You doing alright, Jen?" he asks, having a sip of coffee.

I start to nod, then our eyes meet. His gaze is soft, real gentle.

I put my coffee down. "I've just been thinking."

"About what?"

It feels shitty to say it out loud, but I think I have to. It's eating me alive.

"I don't think Holly and I are working out," I say.

He flicks the inside of his cheek with his tongue. He does that a lot. Then, he sinks back, releasing a sigh.

"She doesn't seem like a good match for you," he says finally. "I hate to say it. I know she means something."

I don't answer. Brothers has been pretty clear about his feelings toward my relationship with Holly. He's just short of forbidding it, always telling me I need to find somebody my own age. Settle down. Maybe have some kids someday.

"I can't just let it go," I say finally.

He cocks his head. "Why's that?"

I shrug. "It's kind of personal stuff. Not Sunday conversation."

"You can talk about anything, Jen," he says, and he means it.

Something snaps inside, and it bleeds like it did the night Cherry threw me out.

"Okay," I say. "She's way too fucking much for me right now. I never wanted to fuck her in the first place. She was just all over me in her kitchen, and I didn't know how to say no. And then it just kept going and fucking going. And now, I can't even get off without some kind of weird shit."

He blinks, lips parting. "Jesus," he says.

"I think I have like a fetish or something, and I don't want it."

He shakes his head. "That's something different. You just need to pull back and recalibrate."

There's an awkward silence.

"Sorry, I gave you too much information," I say.

"No, you really can tell me anything," he says, voice gentle. "What do you mean by weird shit?"

I shrug, neck heating. "Hitting, biting. Saying all kinds of real mean shit. Choking her out. I don't know what the fuck I'm doing."

The lines on his face soften.

"That's alright," he says. "Lots of people like that. It's normal, you know, as long as you're both fine with it."

"That's the thing," I say earnestly. "I don't think I'm fine with it."

His brows rise. "She's forcing you?"

"No, no, everything we did, I could have stopped. I just didn't get what I was doing. I don't know... I think I need some time to have regular, boring sex with someone who isn't beating the shit out of me."

Ashleigh appears, a plate in each hand. Brothers and I stare at each other as she sets them down.

"Y'all need ketchup?" she asks.

"No, we're just fine as is," Brothers says, snapping into his usual charm. "Thanks so much."

She tops off our coffee and leaves. I poke at my charred bacon with my fork. Brothers lets out a long breath and leans on his elbows, rubbing his fingers together.

"I think you should break it off with Holly," he says.

"No shit," I mumble.

He gives me a paternal look. Sometimes, I forget he's only ten years my senior. There's an ageless quality to him that makes him feel like he's in his forties or fifties.

"I'm gonna tell you something I've been wanting to tell you for a while," he says. "But it's not good, and you might be angry with me. But I want you to know I never meant to hurt you. Alright?"

My stomach sinks. "Okay."

He clears his throat. His eyes shut for a second, then snap open.

"Miss Holly is a honeypot," he says.

"A what?"

"I have to be able to trust the people who work for me. It's sensitive materials we're distributing," he says, voice low. "Holly brings in the men for me, and I set them up and provide them work. She gets a cut per person she brings to me."

In the distance, I hear the slow whine of destruction.

We're both quiet.

"You had her seduce me?" I ask finally.

He shrugs. "I mean, I didn't know who you were until that day we worked on your truck. She called me, said she had somebody who was an excellent worker. I met you, and you were...really something, Jen. You've got grit, drive. You're like a cat, always landing on your feet."

Now I'm going over every second of the night Cherry threw me out. That low whine doesn't stop as the pieces fall into place.

"Holly told Cherry about us," I say.

He sighs.

"She didn't answer the phone on purpose," I whisper.

"I didn't plan that part," he says. "She just said I should call you."

I'm speechless, my gut twisted. Of course, I should have put all the pieces together, but some of it doesn't make sense.

"If you put her onto me, why try to get me to dump her?" I ask finally.

"I didn't put her onto you, I just said that," he says. "She picks the men and sends them on. I didn't expect her to find somebody who was just a kid. When I met you, that changed things."

"How? How did it change anything?"

He looks at me, and I wonder if this is the way my father might have looked at me if he were here right now.

That's when it hits me. This is what I was desperate for the entire year I was sleeping with Holly: a smarter, older man to listen and tell me what to do, one who cared about me.

"Because you were just a kid, Jen," he says quietly. His voice sounds the way it does when he's in church. "Miss Holly fell for somebody she wasn't supposed to. I've told her more than once to leave you alone, but I think she feels guilty about what she did."

My food is getting cold. I haven't had a bite yet.

"I think she loves me," I say finally.

"I think she does too. But I think she's angry about it," he says. "Guilt is a funny thing. It can make you pretty damn mean if you let it."

I can't figure out what to say. Once again, I'm in a mess, and I don't know how to get out. I set my fork down and cross my arms, staring out at the parking lot.

"Hey," says Brothers. "Can I say something?"

I glance over. "Sure."

"I'm real sorry," he says. "I really do mean that."

I feel the tug of sympathy, but I'm pretty cut up right now.

"Okay," I say.

"I want you to know I love you, Jen. You're family to me now."

Boom. There it is, the explosion at the end of the low whine. Those words hurt more than anything. More than Holly's betrayal and Brothers' hand in it. More than Cherry kicking me out. Because even though I'm hurting, I believe him. He does love me like his own blood.

We sit. He lets me have my silence.

Finally, I clear my throat. "Where's Ashleigh? I could use a warm up on my coffee."

He smiles. I'm choking, but I smile back.

"You can always talk to me, Jen," he says. "Anytime you're in trouble. I've got your back. Alright?"

"Alright," I repeat.

I forgive him. Because if I don't have Brothers, I have no one.

NOW

Hearing that name come from her lips broke the seal. Everything is coming back, and I can't keep it down. I'm sick, the way I was when he told me about Miss Holly.

I take the cigarette out of my mouth and lean over the railing, vomiting into the grass. As fast as the sickness came, it's gone.

I'm alright, I think.

Slowly, I sink down to sit on the steps. There's so much pain from that time in my life, and I can't figure out where it's coming from. Is the source Holly? Is it what Brothers did?

Or is it what the Caudills did in retaliation?

Because that was the worst thing of all. That was what made me steal my horse, Godspeed, out of Brothers' barn, ignore his warnings about staying under his protection, and run like an outlaw. That's what I've kept locked up deep inside, along with everything else.

That's what I can't forgive.

I run a hand over my face, wiping away the sweat. Brothers talked a lot about forgiveness. He said the Good Lord forgives every Sunday morning. So, I did the same. I forgave him. I trusted him.

I take the picture Della gave me out of my pocket.

My stomach turns over. There we are, looking young and brilliant. We're standing outside the diner, arms around each other's shoulders. Brothers is in a linen suit, holding his cowboy hat in his hand, big grin on his face. I'm in my Sunday shirt and pants, always creased because I stuffed them in the dresser instead of hanging them. My hair is wild and my smile is real.

God, I look like a baby.

The world is quiet. The mountains and fields are still. An ache worms its way through my heart.

Sometimes, I just wish it had all worked out. I want to know what happened the night I killed Pat Pretty, but it's all still a blur. Slowly, I flip it over, and my stomach drops.

There's a tiny scrawl, barely legible.

Come home, Jen.

This was written years ago. An intense anger floods my veins. Jesus Christ, this man cannot be content with ruining my life once. No, that's not enough for Brothers Boyd. He has to reach out through twenty years of estrangement and sink his claws back into me.

I'm not free.

I haven't ever been free. All this time, I've looked over my shoulder. I've slept with woman after woman, trying to fix what

Holly did. I've made friends, real friends, and yet, there's always this unanswered question hanging over me.

I am an unfinished story.

And I'm tired of it.

I don't want to run anymore. I'm done stepping on eggshells, hoping my past doesn't rear its head. I still can't let Della get on top of me without being right back there on the kitchen floor. It's ruining my hope for the future. I thought she was my dream girl, my chance to have a family like everyone else I know. Instead, I'm right back at the beginning.

I'm done. I won't do this anymore.

I'm going back home.

It's time to face him, to say the things I was too young to say back then, to face the Caudills and find out what happened the night I killed Pat Pretty.

I've lost sleep for years, wondering what I would do if I could go back and do it all over again. My chance is here to lay my demons to rest, maybe figure out some way to keep Della when it's all over. I don't know what I want with her, but I'm pretty sure I need to find out.

I'm back at the beginning. It's the same unholy trinity.

But the Holy Ghost is a different woman this time, and that makes all the difference.

CHAPTER FOURTEEN

DELLA

I don't cry.

I'm too devastated for tears.

The handcuffs cut into my wrist. An owl screeches over the fields. Jensen is still outside. I haven't heard the door slam or his boots on the floor again. The austere clock on the wall ticks the minutes away.

How long is he going to leave me here?

Rolling my head to the side, I watch clouds scud across the sky through the window. This house is beautiful, simple. It would be a good place to raise a family. Landis would love it out here, all the space to run. He's such an active little boy, always begging to go to the park or play ball in the yard.

My eyes sting.

Brothers said he and Jensen were on the outs. I just didn't expect such a visceral reaction. He recoiled like he'd put his hand in his pocket and pulled out a snake. Brothers Boyd is no saint, so whatever happened could range from drugs to murder to something worse. But he'd talked so highly of Jensen, I thought there had to be some positive emotion there.

Turns out, I was wrong.

The door slams. I push up, pulling the sheet over my breasts. He's coming quick, boots loud. The door swings open, and he's there in the flesh. Quite a bit of it, actually, given that he hasn't put his shirt back on yet. He shuts the door, takes the chair, and flips it backwards. Pale eyes on me, he sinks down and puts his gun in his belt at the small of his back.

We stare at each other.

He clears his throat.

"The kid...your kid," he says. He swallows like he's having trouble speaking. "What's he like?"

I stammer; that's a pivot.

"He's a really good kid, very sweet, very outgoing," I say.

He winces.

"He's kind, I tried to make sure he's always kind," I continue. "But I look at Leland, and I know what he's going to turn him into. But I'm...I won't let that happen. He won't be raised by Leland."

His jaw works. "Custody battles are ugly."

"This isn't a custody battle," I say firmly. "Either I die getting him back, or I get what I want. There's no afterwards that involves me leaving him with Leland."

Silence.

He leans back. "I could have used a mother with your backbone when I was his age," he says finally.

There's a flicker of vulnerability in his eyes.

"Your mother is still alive?" I ask.

He shakes his head. "Died when I was a teenager. Yours?"

That's a sore spot, but I can tell he's not in the mood to be lied to.

"We had a difference of opinion," I say. "I didn't want to marry Leland, and she wanted me to, real bad. She ended up remarrying one of Matthew Caudill's friends, and they moved to New York a few summers ago. I...I tried to get a hold of her when I left Leland, and she told me I was being stupid, giving up Caudill wealth."

"Money is the root of all evil, huh?"

"I think she was just desperate," I say. "But she did pick it over me and her grandson."

"Your father?"

"My daddy died when I was young. He's buried in my family cemetery, in a holler in Harlan."

His eyes flick up. "You say Harlan?"

I nod. "Why? What's it mean to you?"

He shrugs. "I'm from Harlan originally."

"Brothers say you were from Byway."

He lifts his head, and I should have guessed from those mountain eyes what county his people hailed from. They're pale as the lakes in spring, clear as the streams when the ice melts. He's got them in his veins, the hills I grew up with. That's why he feels like home, like life courses through his body.

Homesickness kicks the door down. I'm only twenty-three years old, but Lord, I'm so tired, I could lay down in the grave by my daddy and sleep. I'd rest, just watch the grass wave overhead, the trees flip their leaves, and the birds rustle at the edge of the clearing.

But I can't. I've still got so much living to do, even if it hurts. It's not my responsibility to bury this body—that's for Landis to do when the time is right.

"You miss it?" I ask.

He blinks, focusing on me. "What?"

"You miss the mountains?" I whisper. "The creeks, the hollers?"

His throat bobs. "Yeah, but I don't want to go back."

"I'd go in a second," I say. "I'd give it all up to just go home to my trailer in Harlan and raise Landis there. I'm fine with having nothing but my freedom."

The corner of his mouth turns up, and his eyes are so sad.

"Tell me about it," he says hoarsely.

Pushing myself up further, I let myself indulge in homesickness. "There was a long dirt road that turned into my drive. My trailer sat to the right, up on cinder blocks. It was old, but my mama kept it spotless. We cleaned every day at three, no exceptions. Up on the opposite side of the hill was a path that led to the clearing. Our family cemetery was on the left, and there was a grove of pawpaws that ran right up to it."

His lids flicker. "You eat them?"

"Grew up on them," I say, letting myself smile. "Pawpaw bread, pie, raw from the tree. I'd eat them until I was sick when they were in season."

He's quiet.

"What happened to your land?" he asks finally.

Anger seeps through the homesickness. "My mama let Leland sell it and give her the money. I think he didn't want there to be anything for me to go back to."

He's thinking. I see his eyes moving under lowered lids.

"You didn't want to marry him?" he says finally.

A wave of panic moves through me, and I breathe, letting it flow. The path that led me to being Leland's wife is confusing. There are parts of it I'm still trying to understand, but I know some of it for certain.

"He met me at a diner one day while he was passing through," I say, voice steady. "He came down the next day, just kept coming back. My mama wanted me to stay with him. She'd had a real hard time raising me alone, and I felt selfish not sacrificing."

His jaw works.

"Plus, he knocked me up," I say. "That sealed the deal."

"How'd he do it?" he says.

God, he's bold.

"With his dick. How do you think?" I snap. "After last night, surely, you don't need me explaining how babies get made."

His eyes narrow, studying me. He's sharp, and it's making me squirm. Finally, he stands and pushes the chair to the side. I cringe as he crosses the room and leans across the bed, reaching for the cuffs. They clink, then release. Frowning, I rub the red line on my wrist.

"That was overkill," I say.

"Get up," he says.

Shakily, I rise, wrapping my arms around my breasts. He jerks his head toward the door. "Put my shirt on and go downstairs and make me a cup of coffee. I got some phone calls to make."

“So…are you going to help me?” I whisper.

He checks his gun and puts it in the bedside table, locking it. When he turns, there’s a frown creasing his forehead.

“Against my better judgement, I am,” he says.

“Why?”

“That ain’t none of your fucking business, ma’am.” The whole Harlan accent comes out in that sentence. “You take what you get.”

He picks a linen button down off the dresser and tosses it at me. I catch it, stunned.

“But—”

“Della,” he says firmly, “make me a fucking cup of coffee.”

Cowed, I button on the shirt and go downstairs. He’s towering over me as we enter the kitchen, taking up so much space, my heart starts pounding. The chair is still pulled out from what we did earlier. I stare at it, heat bubbling on low in my stomach.

“Go on,” he says, sinking down in it.

Obediently, I take down the percolator and measure out the coffee. It takes a second for the gas stove to get it bubbling. Then, we wait in silence while it gurgles until the coffee is rich and dark. I take it off, fill his cup, and bring it to him.

Pale eyes on me, he has some.

“Good,” he says.

“What’s going on?” I ask.

“I’m trying to see if you can follow a basic order. Because if we’re doing this, you don’t get to question me. No back talk, no suggesting we do something else. You let me work and do this my way, or I send you back alone.”

I open my mouth, then shut it. “I can follow an order,” I bristle.

He tilts his head, studying me. “So far, the only orders you seem to be able to follow are the ones I give you when your legs are open.”

My brows shoot to my hairline. “How dare you?”

“Oh, I dare pretty often,” he says. “I mean this, Della. I got business with Brothers Boyd, and you don’t understand it. It means something that he sent you to bring me back. We’re going to

Kentucky so I can handle some shit. I'll get your kid from the Caudill house, and I get to put some bodies in the ground."

"Bodies?"

"It's a metaphor."

I study him, not so sure. Ever since I mentioned Brothers, a thick cloud sits over Jensen. The brightness of his eyes is cold like steel. His jaw is tight, grim. I have a feeling this version of him, the one I unwittingly resurrected, has a lot less to joke about than the version I spent the last few days with.

"My way or the highway," he says quietly.

Having to listen to a man again kills me, but there's only one way out of Montana and back to Kentucky. If I don't accept his help, it'll be just me against Leland, and I already know how that ends.

"Fine," I say.

He spits in his hand and holds it out. Our eyes lock. Unintimidated, I spit in my palm too, and we shake on it.

"It's a deal," I say.

"Good. Go to bed. I've some things to do before we leave in the morning."

CHAPTER FIFTEEN

JENSEN

I'm struggling to focus on putting a feasible plan into place. So, I leave her in the bed, not handcuffed this time, and go out onto the porch and call Jack Russell.

Not many people know how close I am with Jack. He doesn't like other people in his business, so he pretends he's everybody's enemy or casual acquaintance, depending on his mood, until proven otherwise. But Jack's one of my best friends in Montana. I've always been able to ask him for help.

He picks up, sounding a little groggy. "Hold on," he says.

I hear his footsteps. Then, a door shuts with a soft click.

"You got company?" I ask.

"Yeah," he sighs. "What's going on?"

I clear my throat. "She's from Harlan. Brothers Boyd sent her to bring me back."

"I thought something along those lines."

"You did?"

"She's got your same accent."

Frustrated, I run a hand over my face. "You could have told me."

"Suspecting is not the same as having proof. What do you need from me, Jensen?"

My mind turns, trying to come up with a plan. "I need two horses shipped to the Red River Gorge as fast as possible and a safe house waiting for us when we get there. We'll travel up through eastern Kentucky to avoid the cities and Caudill territory."

"And then?"

"Then, I'm getting her kid back," I say.

"She's got a kid?"

"She's Leland Caudill's ex-wife. He's Matthew Caudill's son, the guy who... You know what he did." My throat tightens, blocking the words. "She's trying to get her kid from him. I said I'd help."

He releases a sigh, that sounds a hint judgmental. "Why?"

I could lie, but Jack knows me too well.

"Because I think me and her...might have a shot," I admit.

"A shot? You're hauling your ass across the country and risking your life because you think there's a shot she might be the one?"

I look down at my boots, trying to sort through the emotions churning in my chest.

"You're lying," Jack says. "You're going back to face him."

"Two things can be true at once."

He's quiet for a while, and I know he's sitting at his desk, staring into space.

"Jack," I say.

"What?"

"Tell me the truth about something."

"When have I ever lied?"

I can think of a few dozen times, but not when it comes to serious things. No, on those, Jack is a straight shooter.

"I have to deal with my shit, don't I?"

He clears his throat.

"As a professional avoider of my own shit, yeah, you do," he says. "It might be time to stop looking over your shoulder. Time to stand and deliver."

I take the phone from my ear for a moment to myself. When I put it back up, I can hear he's still on the other end.

"I'm going back," I say. "I've decided."

"I'll send the horses and have the safehouse set up for you. I still have contacts in the area."

"What do you want for it?"

Jack Russell never makes a deal for free, not even for friends. As one of the best assassins in the country, he knows his worth, and he sticks to it.

"You're good," he yawns.

"What?"

"I said, you're good. It's nothing."

He hangs up, and I know he won't take another call tonight. Slowly, I pull my phone from my ear and stare down at it. Is it a bad sign Jack is doing me a favor for nothing? Is he expecting me to not come back?

Confused, I go back inside and climb the stairs to my bedroom. She's asleep, curled up in a ball under the covers. I sink down in the chair by the open window and have a Camel because, despite how many I've had in the interim, they still take me back.

They taste like home, the place that made me who I am.

It runs through my veins like blood. Deep down, there was always a part of me that knew I'd go back. The mountain of shit I left behind was too big to just walk away from. I don't think I've been at peace a day in my life, not until I saw her at the stockyards.

Maybe there's a chance Della Caudill, with all her baggage that turned out to be mine too, is a shot at fixing things.

I like her, a lot.

There's a future in my mind's eye where we have all the things normal couples do, the things my friends have now. God, they look so damn happy. In my mind's eye, I wake up, go out to take care of the ranch. She's in the kitchen when I get back, having her coffee. There's a faceless little boy sitting at the table.

My eyes snap open. Cold sweat trickles down my temple.

Is that what I want?

I don't have to answer that. From the very beginning, that was what I'd always wanted. The Crisco tin was never about money. The money was never about the truck. The truck was never about the business. It was all about making a home where somebody loved me and I got to love them back.

I'm sick of the barely-getting-by-kind of home. I need the real thing.

If I want a shot with Della, I have to help her. If I want a shot at ever finding peace, I have to help myself.

No more running. I hate to admit it, but Jack's right. From here on out, it's time to stand and deliver.

CHAPTER SIXTEEN

DELLA

He's quiet and distant the next day. I understand; I'm lucky he's even speaking to me after all the lying. But it still hurts that the romance between us had to be put on hold.

He doesn't touch me, not like he did before, when I go into the bathroom to get dressed. He just buttons his shirt, glancing at me in the mirror.

Then, he walks out.

I didn't expect instant forgiveness—we were lost in a honeymoon glow before, and now, there's a wound that will need a lot of fixing. The silver lining is, he appears to have a plan, and that gives me hope that if he does pull through, there could be a second chance.

It makes sense he's angry about being deceived. What doesn't make sense is his visceral reaction to Brothers Boyd.

Something big went down there. He told me he and Jensen used to work together, that he was the best of the best, the only man who could face down the Caudills. He also told me the Caudills did something terrible to Jensen a long time ago.

The enemy of your enemy is your friend, he'd said.

But he didn't tell me what *he* did to Jensen. I clearly only got the most convenient part of the story, and it all somehow ties into the empathy that Jensen appears to feel for my son's situation.

The thought of Landis has my eyes smarting. The last few days have been hell, trying not to think about him so I don't break down in front of Jensen.

Now, he's all I can think about.

I know he's safe with Kayleigh. And as terrible as Leland is, he loves his son. He wouldn't hurt him. But he would, and is, using him to crush my spirit beneath his heel. He knows I'll be back so long as he has Landis. It's the only fucking reason he signed the divorce papers.

I look at myself in the mirror and force a smile on my face.

Landis is safe. I will get him back.

Jensen calls from down below, saying we need to leave for the airport. I grab my purse, the only thing I took when I left, and go down to join him. Neither of us speak the entire ride there.

He lets me have the window seat. Then, he sits beside me and closes his eyes.

The last time I was on a plane, I was sick to my stomach from fear, not knowing what awaited me in Montana. This time, I'm just as sick, but it's not as bad because I'm not alone. I fidget, watching the patchwork quilt of the states roll along underneath. This is going to be a long plane ride. He shifts, stretching his legs out. There's not a lot of room for him.

I pick my thumbnail. He opens one eye.

"Maybe I should have sedated you for this," he says.

I give him a look. "I'm fine."

"You scared of heights?"

I shake my head. He opens both eyes and turns his head. "What?"

"I'm scared of Leland," I whisper.

A muscle in his jaw works. "I get that," he says finally.

The plane whirrs; the white noise is a little comforting.

"What do you miss from back home?" he says abruptly.

My brows knit. Is he trying to make conversation to calm me down? I glance to the side, studying his profile. The lean, hungry demeanor of him reminds me of home. The Appalachian Mountains are the only place that produces this particular brand of man—tough like nails, everything pushed down so hard, it'll never come up, eyes that lock the pain in until they're haunted.

I dig at my thumbnail again. "I miss being free. We might not have had much, but nobody fucking told me what to do when I lived in Harlan."

Silence. Then, he sighs.

"Yeah, I miss being free," he says.

I'm starting to like his voice, more than I should. It's deep, with a prevalent rasp that sounds like it's about to break. There's a Montana drawl mixed in, but I hear the Harlan County still. I roll my head to the side, watching him unabashedly, wondering what he was like as a young man.

"Can I ask you something?" I whisper.

"You can," he says, shutting his eyes. "Might not answer."

"Who is Brothers Boyd to you?"

"Hell on Earth," he says grimly.

"What does that mean?"

His brow creases. "Why don't you take a nap or something?"

"Okay," I say, making sure he hears the sass in that word.

We're both quiet until we alight the plane with his carry-on. I'm still in my tiny dress from the night we hooked up. Jensen picks up a rental truck, a big, white Dodge Ram, and we drive out of the Nashville airport, still not talking.

The air conditioner is on too high, and it's freezing my bare thighs. I turn it down and he gives me a sharp glance.

"It's hot," he says.

"Can we stop and get me some clothes?" I ask. "I'm about half naked in this dress."

He jerks his head in a yes. A few minutes down the road, he pulls off at a Walmart, hands me a wad of cash, and sits in the parking lot while I run in. I'm glad he stayed outside, because the last thing I need is him breathing down my neck while I try to buy myself a whole wardrobe in ten minutes.

I hurry through the store, and when I get back to the truck, he's staring into space. He never scrolls his phone. Maybe he's not much of a technology guy.

I knock on the door. He unlocks it, and I scramble in. The look he gives me is distant, and it's hard to believe this is the man who fucked me for two days straight. Now, the thought of him seeing me naked with that closed off stare makes me uncomfortable.

"Okay, you look away while I get dressed," I order.

His jaw flexes. "I have already seen every part of your body in detail. Just get dressed."

"Well, this is different."

"Let me just forget what your bare ass looks like real quick. That'll fix it."

"Oh my God, I can't believe I fucked you," I snap, crawling into the back seat and ripping my dress off.

He glances at me in the rearview mirror, eyes narrowed. I pull on my cotton panties and bra, work my t-shirt down over it, and wriggle into my jeans. They're bootcut, so they work with the shoes I already have. In ordinary clothes, I feel more like myself than I have in the last five years.

When I'm back in the front seat, he starts the engine.

"Alright, let's get going," he says.

"I'm hungry," I say.

"Jesus Christ." He pinches the bridge of his nose. "You need to use the bathroom too, huh?"

I think about it. "In a little while. Don't gripe about it. I can't just pull over on the side of the road and pee in the ditch like you can."

"I don't do that," he says.

"Every single man I've ever met pees on the side of the road," I say, tying up my hair in a ponytail. "Leland didn't, though, but he was all proper about everything."

"How many men have you known other than him?"

I shrug, turning to look out the window. It's incredibly annoying that he's demanding specific responses to a casual statement. That's typical man behavior.

When I glance back, the corner of his mouth is turned up. He doesn't speak again until I give him my order in the drive-thru window. Then, we're on the highway, heading east toward the border.

I tilt my body away, sinking into the seat. Hell is Real signs and adult superstores fly by for the next hour. I'm getting sleepy. After he left me in the bedroom last night, I tossed and turned until his alarm went off. Neither of us got much sleep.

Finally, he pulls over at a rest stop and lets me out. I'm surprised when he walks into the main area and waits outside the bathroom door, like he's guarding it. It puts a little smile on my face, but I don't let him see it. Then, we're back on the highway, and I'm feeling lighter. All it took was that little gesture from him to put me in a better mood.

I think he's hurt, but I don't think he hates me.

He lets the radio play, real low. My eyelids droop until I can't fight it anymore.

Then, he's shaking me awake. I blink, shooting upright.

"What's wrong?" I whisper, heart pounding. My nails are ripping into his forearm.

"Nothing. We're in West Virginia," he says, wincing. "Getting closer. Do you need food?"

I release him, trying to pull myself together. "No, I'll be okay."

"Last chance before we stop for the night."

"I'm fine."

My eyes burn. I rub them, blinking hard. We're driving in a remote area, but up on the hill, I can make out a handful of neon signs. They come into focus: curvy bodies, playing cards, lurid letters advertising gentlemen's clubs. We're definitely in West Virginia. Jensen clears his throat, glancing up at the biggest sign emblazoned with a barely clothed woman.

"I always know the second I cross the West Virginia border," he rasps. "Swear to God, you'd think the whole damn economy rides on a poker chip and a pair of tits."

"I only came here a few times," I say. "My mama would always tell me to shut my eyes when we drove past those signs."

Jensen's mouth thins.

"What? You think they should outlaw it?" I ask.

He shakes his head. "No, but gambling exploits people who don't have shit to begin with."

My brows rise. He's got a sense of justice. I didn't expect that.

"You've never gambled or went to a strip club?" I ask.

"You're a little too bold," he shoots back. "Do you go to strip clubs and casinos?"

"I'm not very experienced, about anything. You're the second man I've ever slept with," I admit before I can bite it back.

Tension hums, filling the truck cab. I didn't feel embarrassed about that before, but now, my face is warm. The silence drags for a good half mile.

"Is that true?" he asks.

"That you're the second man I've slept with?" I ask. "Yeah. Just you and Leland."

"Hmm."

I shift to face him, pulling the seat belt out to keep it from choking me. "What? I'm not a prude. I just didn't have an opportunity."

"How old are you?" he asks, a little forcefully.

"You're not supposed to ask a lady her age."

He hits the brakes, pulling to the side of the road. Pale eyes turn on me, and I'm caught in his headlights.

"How old are you?" he repeats.

Cowed, I shrink against the door.

"Twenty-three," I whisper.

His lips part. "But you have a son? How old is he?"

I wet my lips. "Landis is four."

He's calculating, brows lowered. Finally, he runs a hand over the lower half of his face, mustache and stubble rasping.

"What am I getting into here?" he asks. "Is Leland just your ex-husband, or is he a statutory rapist? Because I've got a quick and easy lead nose cure for the latter."

I shake my head, rattled. "No, I was eighteen when we met. I just got pregnant real fast. He married me before we had Landis."

His jaw works.

"How old are you?" I ask, desperate to get the spotlight off me.

"I'll be forty this summer. Old enough to be your father."

"Only if you got started real young."

"Only about as young as you did."

I gasp, and he leans back, popping his door open and stepping onto the curb. He reaches past me and takes a pistol and holster from the middle compartment. There's no response in me. I'm getting tired of going back and forth.

I watch as he stands at the edge of the road and fastens the holster around his upper thigh, buckling it to his belt. Then, he reaches out like he's going to slam the door.

"Where are you going?" I ask.

He looks at me, eyes blank in the overhead lights. "Gonna go urinate in the ditch," he says, and does slam the door.

My blood pressure is through the roof. I cross my arms over my chest and don't move a muscle while he's gone. My God, if he isn't the strongest concentrate of Appalachian male I've ever met.

I've never known a man from the mountains who didn't have sass coming out of his damn ears. Jensen has it in spades.

The door opens. He gets in, and starts up the engine. We're quiet as he rolls back on the highway. It's quiet—after our burst of conversation. We both have some thinking to do.

The road we're on cuts through the mountains. They get thicker and taller as we go. Then, I think from the flashes I can see in the headlights, the flora changes. It's more familiar, tangled vines coating the ditches.

My heart picks up. I stretch my neck, trying to see into the dark.

"Did we cross the border?" I whisper.

"Yeah." That single word is so tense.

I turn around, and his forearm is like iron, knuckles pale on the wheel.

"We're in Pike County?" I press.

He shakes his head. "Harlan."

Something settles over me that I can't name—a painful longing, a hollow in my heart. He's struggling with something too. I leave him be, keeping quiet until he pulls off on the side of the road.

We're outside a strip motel, a neon sign advertising hourly booking. He gets out, not bothering to hide the gun on his thigh. As we cross the parking lot, I see his eyes like searchlights, just roaming. I keep close.

There's a woman at the desk, young, with dyed black hair piled on her head, a tattoo of a butterfly on the side of her neck. She looks us over, chatting about the weather, and pops her gum. Jensen is tighter than a bow as he pays in cash and takes the key.

He leads the way to a room a few doors down. We go inside, and I turn on the single lamp by the bed. He locks the door. Everything feels different than I remember, like somebody went through my house while I was gone and rearranged everything. Or maybe, I just grew up.

I turn to face him. "You okay?" I whisper.

His tanned skin is dewy with sweat. I can make out the pulse between his collarbones where his shirt is soaked.

"I never wanted to come home again," he rasps.

There's no room now for the snappy replies we've been trading all day. He's shaken to his core, eyes haunted.

"I'm sorry," I whisper.

Tick. Tick. Tick.

The clock over the bed moves. There's a watercolor painting of Jesus on the face, looking down on us, one palm up, the kind that comes a dime a dozen at thrift shops. Jensen looks at the window, paisley curtains stiff with starch, and up at the clock, then back to me.

This feeling is something Leland would never understand, something he never wanted to understand. But Jensen understands.

He knows the Jesus clock isn't just a clock. It's the distant memory of being a kid in these hills. The getting by but barely. It's scraping together pennies to get an ice cream from the cooler in the dollar shop. It's my hair standing on end, wondering if I'm going to hell every Sunday morning. It's a hot gravel road leading to a two-bedroom at the end of it. It's becoming an adult and realizing everyone older was so broken, all the time, just barely holding it together. It's being on the other side of that and seeing it all with grown up eyes.

Somebody coughs outside, breaking the spell. He blinks, wiping his sweaty face with his palm.

"You take the bed," he says.

He's drawing a line in the sand. I understand, but it hurts. Numbly, I start pulling off my boots and jeans. The chair scrapes across the floor, then hits the door as he jams it below the knob. I slip out of my bra, leaving me in my shirt and panties. I've never been able to sleep in my clothes, otherwise I would. I crawl beneath the covers, not looking at him.

"Della," he says.

I lift my head. He's standing at the end of the bed.

"We'll get your kid back," he says.

I'm so close to tears. "Thank you," I whisper. "Please sleep with me."

He doesn't move.

"Sleep with you?" he says finally. "Or sleep with you?"

I start to speak, but he leans his knee on the bed. Cowed, I slide to my back. He moves his body over mine, and his mouth dips. Hot breath skims over my lips, but he doesn't kiss me.

"That clock on the wall," he says. "We had one like that when I was a kid."

We're not alone in the room anymore. Jensen's ghosts are standing all around us, watching how our mouths almost touch. I lay my palm on his chest. It's hot and damp.

"I feel something for you," I say. "Nothing changed for me."

He doesn't speak.

“Please sleep with me.” I push the sheet down and take his hand, pressing it to my chest.

He looks down at where his palm sits between my breasts. Then, he pulls back. “I’m not sleeping tonight,” he says. “You sleep. I’m going to sit in that chair and make sure no one comes through the door.”

He withdraws, tapping the lamp to turn it out. The chair creaks. My eyes adjust slowly as I sink into the musty sheets. He sits in profile—his head is leaned back, one knee cocked, one leg extended.

There’s a gun in his hand, rested on his thigh.

Tick. Tick. Tick.

The clock is the only sound in the room. I watch him until I can’t stay awake any longer, and he never moves from that chair.

CHAPTER SEVENTEEN

JENSEN

My heart thumps in tandem with the Jesus clock. The minute we stepped into this goddamn room, my eyes fell on it, and suddenly, I was eight years old again, trying to scrape a meal out of the food I could lift from the gas station down the street. My mother was always forgetting to buy food or spending the money on something else. Hunger makes an impression.

I tap the side of the pistol, staring at the opposite wall.

I never wanted to be here, ever again. The minute I see Brothers, I'm going to let him have it for dragging my ass back. That's going to be sooner than Della thinks because, while I was relieving myself in the ditch, I was also sending a text.

No hello, how've you been since you made me believe you could fill the empty place where I never had a father and then ruined my life? Just a place and a time tomorrow morning.

I'll drop Della at the location Jack secured for us and the horses.

Then, I'll give Brothers Boyd a piece of my fucking mind.

I close my eyes, leaning my head against the door. Without meaning to, I sleep soundly until the sun cracks through the godawful paisley curtains.

My neck cracks as I push myself upright. Della is still asleep, a little lump under the covers. I stand, shaking my leg to get the cramp from my foot. She stirs, sitting up, and my lower stomach jerks.

She's beautiful, hair messy around her face. It's easy to see why Leland wanted her despite her lowly beginnings. I know because I want her too, despite everything. I nudge the edge of the bed.

"Get up," I say. "We need to hit the road."

She grumbles, pushing off the sheets. She's in a t-shirt and panties, no bra. Her nipples are hard beneath her shirt. I look away, going to pull the chair from the door. By the time I'm done, she's got her clothes back on.

I leave the key on the pillow, and we get back into the rental truck. She's blinking in the harsh sun coming down the road, cutting between the mountains. It rained, and steam rises from the cement, the air thicker than cream.

"Let's get some food," I say. "Then, we'll get to the house Jack has for us."

"Where's that at?"

"Red River Gorge."

"Not too far, right?" she sighs.

"Not far. Better than being in that motel room with Clockface Jesus breathing down my neck," I murmur.

She laughs.

"What?" I say.

She shakes her head. "You're just...a mess of flavors I wasn't expecting."

"That a bad thing?"

There's a flash of the Della I met in Montana as she smiles, turning to look out the window. "No, I like it," she murmurs. "You're different. It's good."

I clear my throat. "I'm not angry with you," I say finally.

She doesn't turn to meet my eyes when I glance over, but I see her nose twitch as she sniffs. "I know," she says. "But if you were, I'd understand. You feel whatever you need to feel. I'm sorry for hurting you."

I'm lighter for hearing that, but I'm not evolved enough to do more than clear my throat and let the subject drop. Usually, I'm good at holding a grudge, but I can't be angry with her any longer.

She's not doing anything wrong. She's just trying to be a good mother, only twenty-three and already overburdened.

It's not fair—not for her, not for my mother, not for me, or for her boy.

I force my thoughts out of the past. Now that it's light, I'm soaking in the sight of the mountains, the green, brushy hills that boast foliage so thick, there are places where the sun never shines. We make good time on the state route, but we're choked up by all the little towns teetering over the roads. Most of them are empty, paint peeling on gas stations with flickering signs. Then, we're back in the open, and it's the most beautiful place in the world.

We stop and get breakfast to-go at a tiny diner on the side of the road. Everything is exactly how I left it. The mountains never change.

The house is thirty minutes through the winding roads of the Daniel Boone National Forest. I know these hills, but it's still a shock navigating the hairpin turns and places where the road is washed out. It's about noon when we finally pull off and travel a half mile up a gravel drive. At the end sits a small, whitewashed house with a porch off the front. There's a rusted out car covered in vines by the mailbox. I park next to it and cut the engine.

"This is it," I say.

She cranes her neck, soaking it all in. I can't tell for sure, but it looks like her lip trembles.

This is home to her, as it was to me.

I get out, grabbing our things, and step onto the porch. The wood groans beneath my boots. Jack said the door was unlocked. I test it, and it swings in, revealing a tiny lower level that looks almost like the trailer I grew up in.

My chest is tight. Della walks past me, looking around.

"This looks like the trailer I grew up in," she says.

I don't say anything. Up above us, there's a loft with a queen bed. I presume the door just off it is the bathroom. Downstairs has only a kitchen, a dining table coated in dust, and a couch beneath the loft.

"I might clean it up if we'll be here for a while?" she says.

"Indefinitely," I say.

My heart is beating sideways. There's something lodged in my throat that I just can't swallow. Silently, I set the bags on the table and cross the room, opening the breadbox. Inside is a pistol, a little terrier engraved into the handle.

"Thank God for Jack Russell," I murmur.

She watches as I take it out and set it on the table. "Who is he? You act like he's your guardian angel or something."

"More like the useful devil on my shoulder." I check the chamber, and it's loaded. "I'm leaving. You stay here until I get back and shoot anybody who walks up here who isn't me."

Her brows crease instantly. "What?"

"I have business," I say. "Keep the doors locked. I'm going to pull the truck into the barn with the horses."

"Horses?"

"Jack sent us two."

I leave, locking the door. She's confused, but I can't talk right now, or I might spill more than I should. My stomach is an uneasy void as I get in the truck. The entire plane ride, I wondered how I would feel coming back and seeing him again.

Now, I know—dread and anger.

I turn on the radio. Then, I turn it off. The hills fly by until they turn flat and become road signs along the fringes of the highway. Then, I'm through the outskirts of Lexington and on the west side. The closer I get, the whiter my knuckles go.

The parking lot lets up a puff of dust as I pull in. I cut the engine and sit in silence for a moment. I tongue the inside of my cheek, tasting a bite mark. I think I put it there in my sleep. The windows of the diner are tinted, and it looks like it got a new paint job. Other than that, everything is just the way I left it.

I get out and walk across the lot through the front door. Inside, the blast of air conditioning makes the sweat on my neck prickle. The interior got a makeover. Everything is clean, shiny linoleum and vintage metal seats.

The waitress behind the counter lifts her hand and calls out that I can sit anywhere. I nod, scanning the room.

My eyes fall on a sloping figure.

Now I feel something else, and it's fucking grim.

He's sitting on the left, second from the back row, in his Sunday clothes. No suit, more ruggedly casual than I remember him being. His face is lightly lined, his temples frosted. Age has been kind to him physically, but I see the years in the hooded eyes that turn on me.

I cross the room and sink down opposite him.

He takes the unlit cigarette from his mouth and sets it in his coffee saucer. I can smell him. He's wearing the same cologne or deodorant. We look at each other. I expected to feel like I'm nineteen again seeing him, but I don't.

Instead, I feel like I'm back from the wilderness, big enough to face him this time.

"Long time, no see," he drawls.

The waitress appears. I order a black coffee, same as him. Then, it's just us again.

I clear my throat.

"Where did you bury them?" I ask.

He clears his throat too. "How do you know I did?"

"Because I know you."

His lids flicker. "They're in my family plot."

"All three?"

He nods.

"How did you know where I was?" I say, keeping my voice low.

The waitress appears and sets my coffee down. They're still using the same mugs.

"It's still Folgers," he says.

"You heard my question," I say.

He sighs, leaning back in his seat. It's hard to believe he's real after years of him living only in my memory. But here he is, flesh and blood, with the same face, the same drowsy existence, like nothing phases him.

"You said you wanted to be a cowboy," he says. "I looked west. It wasn't hard to find you."

"Who told you?"

"You sleep with a lot of women, Jen. One of them was bound to talk."

"Jesus." I look out the window. "That's invasive."

He's quiet until I force my eyes back. His expression is soft.

"I still love you like my own blood," he says.

"I'm disappointed you didn't die," I say. "I'm sure you had ample opportunity."

His face splits into a lazy grin. "Still a funny guy, huh?"

My mind goes back to what I said to Della about her being funny because she's fucked up. That's another thing she and I have in common. I take the photograph out of my pocket and slap it down on the table.

"You dropped this," I say.

He picks it up. "Guess this doesn't mean anything to you?"

"No," I say. "And it was pretty low sending it with her."

"So you like her, though?"

"Don't talk to me about Della Caudill," I say.

His grin flashes again. "I thought you might."

I take a beat to calm down. "Actually, how about you talk about her? Why did you send her to me? You could have done this yourself."

He shakes his head. "The Caudills are more powerful now. Matthew Caudill is dead, his son, Leland, is encroaching on my territory. They're backing me into a corner, slowly."

I study him. Of course, an ulterior motive. "So you're gonna kneecap him by helping his wife take his son?"

"Yeah, something like that," he says. "I thought you might want to help, given what the Caudills did to you."

I narrow my eyes. "You can't manipulate me the way you used to."

"I never did—"

I lean in. "Yes, you did," I say. "We sat right here at this table, and you convinced me it somehow wasn't your fault that Holly did that shit to me. And I fucking believed you."

"Everything I said that day was the God honest truth," he says.

"Fuck yourself."

"No, thanks."

"I was a kid," I manage. "And you...you were old enough to know that."

He withdraws, leaning back. The unlit cigarette flicks against his thumb. It reminds me of the way Della picks at her nail until it bleeds. Controlled pain.

"I regret that," he says finally. "If I could go back and change things, I would do it in a heartbeat."

I can't speak. There's so much anger in me right now, I can't. There are no words to describe the nights I spent staring at the ceiling and wishing none of it had happened. I want to go back to before what Holly did changed me fundamentally. Now, I can't stop grieving over the man I could have been without her, without Brothers swooping in to pick over my bones when she was done.

"I could kill you," I say finally.

"I'd be honored."

Nothing is more frustrating than hating someone who won't fucking hate me back. Impassive, he flicks his lighter and inhales.

"God, you never stop, huh?" I run a hand over my face.

"Love is a terrible thing," he says. "I think mine is the worst of it. I've never loved anybody who wasn't worse off for it."

He must have changed, because he's right about that. Nobody's love was more destructive to me than his, except for Holly.

But understanding doesn't mean I owe him a damn thing. If we weren't in the middle of a diner with a few dozen people around, I'd hit him with a right hook and walk out with his blood on my knuckles—just because I can do that now, and he can't hurt me back.

None of them can.

I don't need anyone, so I don't owe anyone anything.

I push my cold coffee back and stand. "I'm gonna help Della. You stay out of my way."

He gives me a slow smile. "You haven't really changed, Jen."

"Goodbye." I tap two fingers down on the table, looking him in the eye. "And don't fucking call me Jen."

I turn to leave.

"You're gonna need my help getting Landis," he drawls. "Go check out that house and tell me if you think this is a one-man job."

"I'll be the judge of that," I say.

I walk out, knowing all my words went in one ear and right out the other. He's definitely going to contact me again. That's fine. Today was for me. I needed to get those words out.

All I can think about as I pull out of the lot and drive away is how Della feels like grace, like the first time I've been offered forgiveness instead of being asked for it. I wonder if I showed her all my scars, if I told her all the worst details of my past, she would still feel like that.

I have a notion she might.

Della is a sharp woman, but with me, I discovered softness I don't think she shows very often. I'm hurt that she was working with Brothers, but I hope she knows I really don't hate her for it. She's not a bad person. She's a victim. And yet, she let me walk out without insisting I hold her problems above my own.

She likes the bitterness in me. *You're a mess of flavors, Jensen.* She said it was a good thing we're two different people with iron wills, not caring that I'm damaged goods.

My very first relationship, the one with Holly, shaped the way I relate to sex, to love, so deeply. Since then, I've never been more to anyone than whatever the person I'm with needs me to be.

I learned to be charming, to be good in bed to earn that five star rating the next morning. But with Della, the minute the masks came off, I cared enough not to show her a false front. To her, I don't think I'm just a commodity, or she wouldn't have said those things in the car this morning.

The façade came tumbling down. We fought it out, but neither one of us walked away. And here I am, going back to her like we mean something.

My fingers tighten on the wheel.

Grace.

It hits harder than a right hook.

CHAPTER EIGHTEEN

DELLA

I pace the house, back and forth, while he's gone. There's no food, but I saw a gas station with an attached market on the way in. My stomach growls, and I know he'll be hungry when he gets back. So, I leave, even though I know Jensen told me not to. But it's a short walk, and I don't see anyone but the clerk.

There, I get some groceries. On the way back, I pass a farmstand and pick up some vegetables. They even have meat in a cooler in the back of their truck. I buy some cracklings and chicken, still half frozen, and lug it all back up the winding driveway.

The house is quiet as I unload my groceries and start cooking. It reminds me a lot of where I grew up. Simple, neat, with a pretty view out the window. The only unsettling thing is the pistol Jensen left by the stove.

Everything is so quiet. I turn on the radio and make cracklin' bread and chicken soup. It brings me right back to all those nights spent cooking in the kitchen while I was pregnant with Landis.

In retrospect, I'm not sure all that cooking was about anything more than trying to pull back a little bit of control. Tonight feels the way it did back then. I didn't realize how much I needed the comfort of familiar food.

The sun creeps towards the horizon, but he doesn't appear. Worried, I eat alone and set a plate in the microwave for him. He's still not back when it gets dark, so I go out and feed the horses in the barn and lock it up. Then, I climb the ladder to the loft and lay down, staring at the peaked ceiling.

Is he alright?

Surely, he didn't abandon me out here.

My stomach churns. Rolling onto my side, I close my eyes tight. It takes a while, but slowly, I slip away, only to be jerked awake a minute later by the front door opening.

Heart thumping, I listen. I'm attuned to the footsteps of men, and I know instantly it's Jensen.

Thank God.

I hear him move around downstairs. Then, his weight creaks the loft ladder. I see him in silhouette against the window as he unbuckles his belt. He looks so damn good, windswept and a little sweaty. The ache that only he ignites is back. He pulls his shirt up, revealing that trail of hair that goes down to his waistband.

Then, he comes to the edge of the bed.

"You awake?" His voice is a rasp.

I push myself up, shifting over. "Yeah. There's cornbread and soup in the microwave."

He leans over me, hand wrapping around my throat. For a split second, I think he's angry, and my heart speeds up. Then, his mouth meets mine, open and starving.

I inhale, tasting bourbon on his breath, but he's not drunk. I can tell by how deftly he picks me up and sinks against the headboard, upright.

I'm in his lap, thighs around his waist—the position he said made him claustrophobic. I'm so tensed up, I know he can feel it. He hits the bedside lamp, and it turns on, a pale yellow glow across the side of his face.

I freeze. His eyes are dark—so dark, they pull me into his undertow.

"Are you alright?" I whisper.

He shakes his head, hand slipping under my panties, grazing my pussy before tearing through the fabric. I gasp as he pulls my t-shirt up and tosses it behind us. His hands, rough in the way Leland's never were, cup my breasts.

His skin is hot to the touch, like he's been in the sun, and he smells of worn out deodorant and sweat. I didn't think that could smell good, but it must be all the pheromones mixed in, because it has me aching for him.

"Put me inside you," he says hoarsely.

I hesitate. He grips my hip, and I reach between us, taking the hard, heavy length of him and guiding it inside my body. He grimaces, muscle in his jaw twitching. I bite my lip, but a whimper works out. Our bodies ease together until we're joined.

I feel him, the blood pumping through him, deep inside.

Thump.

Thump.

Thump.

"Hit me," he breathes.

My jaw drops. "What?"

His unsettling eyes flash. "I said, fucking hit me, Della. Across the face. Backhand me."

My head is already shaking of its own accord. "No."

His hips start pumping, harsh and deep inside me. It hurts. He wants it to hurt. His hand wraps around my neck and squeezes, holding me still as he fucks up into me.

Every thrust is electric, tight, painful on purpose, forcing into me again and again, harder. Faster. I'm gripping his wrist, knowing in the back of my mind I can stop him if I want to, but I'm drowning with the desire to let him loose and see what he does.

He's as naked as he was in the motel room last night, and it scares me again.

"Hit me," he says through gritted teeth.

My jaw drops. His eyes flash like a thunderclap. We're fucking against the headboard, slamming it into the wall. I can't fight him. I don't want to fight him.

"Jensen"

"I said, fucking hit me, Della," he says from between his teeth.

"I don't understand," I wail.

He's fucking me so goddamn hard, vein standing out in his forehead. "Give me this."

His voice breaks at the same time I do, and I backhand him across the face. The slap is a gunshot through the night and a jolt of pain through my wrist. He grits his jaw, breathing out from between his teeth. A crimson stain appears on his tanned skin.

Our gazes lock.

"Harder," he demands.

Stunned, writhing on his cock as he slams it up into me, I obey, hitting him across the face a little harder. He takes a half second to recover, blinking, shaking his head like a dog. Then, his eyes lock back on mine, and he grips my hair, up by my scalp. Desire surges through me, pulling me down. I could have fucked a hundred men before I fucked him, but I know right now, nothing would compare to him.

He makes me feel everything after being dead inside for so long. He's a dangerous drug, and I'm tying up my arm, injecting him into the most delicate parts of me without knowing what he's made of.

"Hurt me," I gasp out.

I don't know where that came from. His pupils dilate, and he flips me onto my back, pressing me into the mattress. His hand encircles my throat, rough and broad.

I taste it—what he tasted, an edge that heightens everything.

"You hit my arm if you need it to stop," he breathes.

I flutter my lashes, nodding as best I can. His fingers burn the sides of my throat. My hips rise, begging for him. He braces his knee and thrusts into me, hard enough that I cry out at the shock of pain and ecstasy.

My God, he's big.

I need more of this, whatever it is. There's no judgement with him. So I look him in the eyes, his hand tight on my throat, and wrap my legs around his waist to pull him in.

"Fuck, you're a dirty whore," he grits out.

My brain buzzes.

I like the thought of being a whore if I can be his.

He ruts his hips into me, breaking me in a way Leland was never capable of. The bedframe begs for relief, screeching at its hinges. Pleasure hits me like a wall of bricks. He's not even touching my clit, it's just grinding against him every time he fucks in. But with him, that's enough. My hips lock and shake as I go over the edge.

Triumph ripples in his eyes. In one, smooth movement, he releases my throat and flips me so he's up against the headboard, and I'm in his lap, shaking on his cock.

"Good girl," he breathes.

The look on his face stops me short. It's like he's seeing me for the first time, really looking into my soul. But I'm a mess, and I can't appreciate it. My body convulses in his lap, wave after wave of pleasure rolling through. Slowly, lips parted and gaze locked on mine, he starts fucking up into my pussy.

"That's right," he murmurs. "You take it. Come all over my cock, baby.

I whimper incoherently. He digs his hand into my hair, fisting it. This is different from the connection we felt before. It's like the sharp edge of a knife. Dangerous, but God, so damn thrilling. Maybe because all our secrets are spilling out. We're not pretending to be perfect. He knows all the messy parts of my life, and I have a pretty good idea his are just as dark, if not worse than mine.

I love this.

I love the flip side of him.

I want it, so deep, it hurts. My hips pick up, riding him hard. We're going faster and faster, falling into a frenzy together.

"Put your nails in me," he pants. "Into my chest. Drag them down, baby, I want to see blood."

He tightens his grip in my hair. Pain shoots through my head and neck. Thoughtless with desire, I dig my nails into his pecs and rake them down, hard.

He groans, fucking haphazardly as the veins raise in his neck. I've never been the person who got to do things during sex. I was always on my back, legs open, trying to disassociate while things were done to me. Causing him pleasure, seeing his body respond to me, is a brand new feeling.

Bang.

Bang.

Bang.

The headboard hits the whitewashed walls. I'm grateful there's no Clockface Jesus over this bed, because I think this is some kind of sacrilege.

It's too much, too dark, too visceral.

He drags me close by the nape of my neck, our breath mingling. There's a dark trickle of blood and welt-like scratches on his tanned skin. It smells like metal and Jensen.

I touch the hair on his chest, between his pecs. Smearing the blood, I leave my fingerprints on his skin.

"Hit me again, baby," he breathes.

His hands grip my hips, his thrusts speed up. The sound of our bodies coming together fills the tiny house, wet and hungry. In the half second before the back of my hand meets his face again, I see something new in his eyes, all raw and painful, like somebody reached into his chest and skinned his heart.

I strike him hard, clenching my stinging hand. His cock jerks, and his eyelids flutter shut. A tremor runs through his body, and I feel him coming inside me, nothing between us. No condom this time.

But I'm not scared.

Our bodies sink, the position shifting my clit against his groin. Everything goes limp, and I sink into him. He cradles me against his chest. I bury my face in his neck, close enough to smell his blood, and I come hard, shaking on his cock, gripping him with crimson-stained fingernails.

I don't know if I take pleasure in his pain the way he does in mine, but when I give it to him, I encounter something real, a peeling back of shared wounds that have festered under bandages for too long.

This is the rough, raw underbelly of Jensen Childress.

And I need it.

The realization shatters what's left of me. I lie in his arms, on the verge of tears, panting.

He pulls me in, his lips pressing to the top of my head. I'm so damn worn out from that storm. We stay quiet until he stirs, taking my face in his hand to make me look up at him.

"You alright?" His voice is a rumble.

I nod. Am I?

"Good girl."

He gets up, depositing me on the bed, and goes to the tiny bathroom in the corner. My fists clench and unclench, sore and bloody. My fingernails feel tacky. He stands in the doorway in silhouette and runs a hand over his face. Then, he turns on the shower and disappears. I don't move, stunned.

"You coming in or not?" he calls.

His walls are up, good and hard, but he's still offering an olive branch. Like a cautious cat, I climb from the bed and creep to the shower.

He's a wavy, tan outline behind the fogged glass. I glance at the mirror. I'm a mess, faint crimson on my cheek where I laid my head against him. I wipe it back, desperate to get his blood off me.

"Get in here, Della," he says.

Head dipped, I obey. Our eyes meet, and I look away, turning my back to him. His energy is bothering me. It's...rude and pushy. I think I hear him laugh faintly, but before I can look, he's got his hands in my hair. I freeze as he starts washing it, working suds into my scalp, then down my neck, over my body. And finally, he washes the blood from my fingers.

I swallow. "Do you need me to clean you up?"

"I washed myself while you were deciding if you wanted to get in here or not," he says.

"I mean your scratches."

"No, I can walk that off."

I stare up at the yellowed wall, a fine crack where it meets the ceiling. "You in the habit of walking everything off?"

"Only way to go forward."

I let him rinse me clean. We stand there, naked in more ways than one. Finally, I offer him a tiny smile, even though I'm not feeling it.

"At least we did that here and not under the Clockface Jesus," I whisper.

His head drops back, and he laughs. My heart soars at the first sight of that dimple in a while. Up until now, I've found him sexy in a raw, offbeat way. But now, I see he's handsome, beneath all the wear and tear. He's blue-collar-backwoods-pretty. My type, it turns out.

"Clockface Jesus don't factor into this," he says.

There's a silence in which I try and fail to figure him out again. He shuts the water off, gets out, and hands me a towel. I watch him dry himself, shaking his hair like a dog. Then, he's gone back to the bedroom, and I hear him climb down the ladder.

When I step back out, he's in the kitchen in his boxer-briefs, leaning against the counter and eating his plate of food, scratched up chest and all.

I get back into bed.

I think he might be actually insane.

What does it say about me that I like that?

He eats. Then, he comes back and gets in bed. I'm getting whiplash trying to figure out what's going on between us, and some of that is my fault. But tonight, we're in a new place. He fucked me and ate my cornbread, and now we're going to sleep together like a real couple or something.

"Mind if I smoke?" he says finally.

"Open the window," I whisper.

He gets up, slides up the loft window, and takes a cigarette from his pants on the floor. Then, he puts the pants on, leaving the belt hanging. His lighter flicks. He inhales and holds.

"You going someplace?" I whisper.

"Might walk around a bit after this," he says. "See the horses before bed."

"You don't sleep much."

He shakes his head, releasing the smoke. "No."

I sit up, pulling the sheet over my chest. He watches me, lids low and one arm hanging out the window.

"If Clockface Jesus don't factor into this, then who does?" I ask.

His brows rise a minute amount.

"Let's start with Brothers Boyd," he says. "How did he factor into you, huh?"

"He didn't," I say.

He snorts, smoking rising from his lips. "I have been here and done this before, baby. And I did not, in fact, just fall off a motherfucking turnip truck. Brothers Boyd doesn't work for nothing."

I bite the corner of my mouth. "Can I tell you a secret?"

"My lips are sealed."

"You can't tell nobody. It's not safe."

"I swear." He lifts his palm.

"Kayleigh was sleeping with him. That's how we met," I whisper. "But you can't tell anybody, or she'd be in so much trouble. Leland might kill her."

His brows knot. "Who the fuck is Kayleigh?"

"Kayleigh Caudill, Leland's cousin."

There's a second when I know I've shocked him. His eyes widen as he takes a drag and sits on this information. Then, he shakes his head.

"Goddamn," he says.

"They met at his pub," I say. "Kayleigh's good people. She's the one keeping an eye on Landis for me. I need her on Leland's good side, or I have nobody in my corner."

"That's an explanation for how you met him, not why he chose to help you."

I lift my palms. "I don't know. But please, promise not to tell anyone about Kayleigh."

His lids flicker. “I won’t let your kid get hurt.”

His words are casual, but they hit me right in the heart. My throat has a lump. I clear it back. “Thank you.”

We’re both silent. He finishes his cigarette and latches the window. I slide onto my side, stacking my arms and resting my cheek on them. He’s sideways across my vision, fastening his belt.

Memory hazy, I recall how I saw him in Montana. The tattoos, the V of his lower stomach, the calluses on his palms. His big dick attitude about everything that doesn’t feel like ego because he’s so eager to please between the sheets.

“Where are you going?” I whisper.

“To walk,” he says. “See the stars.”

It’s been so long for him, I realize, since he’s been back home. His heart must ache for the hills and fields the way mine did all through my marriage. I pinch my eyes shut, listening as he goes downstairs. The door locks. His footsteps crunch on gravel.

Then, he’s gone.

CHAPTER NINETEEN

JENSEN

Two things wake me up around three in the morning. The first is my phone lighting up, a text from Brothers appearing on the screen. Right on cue, he's back, trying to pull me under again. Groaning internally, I roll over and lift it.

Meet me at my house, eleven in the morning. Bring Della. I just want to talk.

I ease myself up against the pillows and set the phone down. On my way back from the diner, I took some time to drive around Byway and the surrounding areas to get the lay of the land. I drove past the Caudill Mansion, and Brothers was right—getting a kid out of that place will be tough. That bothers me a lot, because I promised her I'd get Landis back, but now, I have concerns.

I stare into the dark.

Do I have it in me to cooperate with Brothers?

A little sniffle from her side of the bed breaks me from my thoughts. I turn, studying her inert form. Her core seizes, scrunching her limbs up into a fetal position. It's dim in the loft, but I can see she's still asleep. Her eyes are roaming beneath her lids.

She's dreaming.

I slide back down and roll to my side beside her. She shifts, like she feels the movement in her sleep. Her body goes rigid, and a whimper comes from between her teeth. Without thinking, I grip her elbow and give her a little shake.

Her lids fly open, and she rips her arm back, eyes dark. There's venom in them as she draws up against the pillows.

"Hey, Della," I say, keeping my voice low, staying back to give her space. "You alright, baby?"

She stares, brow scrunched. I don't move, waiting for her to come down from her nightmare. Finally, she gives her head a little shake.

"Sorry," she whispers.

She doesn't reach for me, and that breaks my heart, but she's not pulling back either. I get out of bed and turn on the lamp.

"You want something to drink?" I ask.

She nods. "We've got some chamomile."

I hold out my hand. "Come on, get out of bed. Shake it off and talk about it."

Her mouth cracks in a tiny smile, and she takes my hand, letting me help her down to the kitchen. It's raining. The droplets are loud on the tin roof, reverberating through the rocky ravine to the east. I take the kettle from beneath the sink, fill it up, and turn on the gas stove. She sits at the table, chewing the inside of her cheek.

I cross my arms, watching her. Finally, she looks up.

"Sorry to wake you," she says.

"What's going on?" I ask lightly.

Her throat bobs, and she digs at her thumbnail. "It's just hard being away from my son. I keep having dreams I'm holding him, and somebody snatches him right out of my arms."

She looks so lost, so small. I should feel pity, but instead, I'm angry. I've known men like Leland Caudill before, rich men with pockets that are never satisfied. They take until there's nothing left for the rest of us. Della is stuck under the thumb of one of the worst of them.

Her story is an old one, repeated again and again. And yet, she's fighting back.

“I’m getting your kid back for you, Della,” I say firmly.

She looks up, those eyes that glittered so bright in the stockyard, now dark.

“I want to believe that,” she whispers. “But I don’t understand why this really matters to you.”

My mind skims over the last twenty years out in Montana. It’s been a good time. Hell, maybe I wouldn’t trade it for a thing. But there’s this emptiness at the center of it. I didn’t have a name for it until I saw all my friends hitching up, having kids. Then, my house started feeling pretty big with only a single guy banging around in it.

She filled it up without trying, just walked in, and I was back in the cool valleys of my home, the parts of Kentucky I do miss.

I can’t stay here. My home isn’t my home anymore. But I could take this piece of it back with me in Della Caudill. I could make her my wife and get to feel golden sunshine every day until I die, but all those things...it’s too early to say them. So, I say something close to the truth.

“Nobody stepped in for me when I was a kid like him. I kinda feel like this is my chance to balance things out.”

She studies me. “You had a real tough time, huh?”

“The usual,” I say. “Nobody at home, better that way. My mom got knocked up with me when she was a teen, and my grandmother kicked her out. We lived in a rented trailer. She worked, but not enough to make ends meet. Then, she died when I hit about sixteen.”

Her lids lower. “And your father?”

“Pumped and dumped.” I flip the gas off and pour, steam rising. “Yours?”

“He mined coal until he busted out his back,” she says. “Then, he collected disability, and that was alright. But I think not being able to work just...really dragged him down.”

“How old were you?” I set the tea down.

“Seven when he finally went.” She touches the edge of the cup, skimming the tip of her finger in slow circles. “I don’t remember much.”

“Maybe that’s better.”

She gives me a weak smile. "Maybe it is."

We sit in silence, the weight of everything bearing down. Finally, she takes a sip and blows on the steam.

"It's good. Tastes like the fields," she says. "What's it like, being on the run?"

"I wasn't running."

"You were hiding like an outlaw."

She's smiling, and I can sense she's not wanting to talk about her past anymore.

"Well, I always wanted to be a cowboy," I say. "Got my wish. Did the whole ranch thing, worked with cattle on my friends' ranches. Worked the land."

She's watching me thoughtfully. "Think you found yourself out there?"

"I think it found me," I say, "right where I was at."

"But you weren't happy?"

"I was happy, just not completely."

She looks down. "I'd settle for almost happy."

"I think you can have the whole thing."

"I hope so." Her voice breaks.

Her shoulders slump. I'm not really a romantic guy, if I'm being honest. But she's changing me, deep in my bones. I go to her, holding out my hand.

Her eyes are questioning, but she puts one hand in mine and lets me lift her to her feet. A gasp escapes her when I pull her close, her breasts pressing into my sternum.

"What are you doing?" she says softly.

"I don't know," I whisper back.

There's music in the back of my brain. Clumsily, I start moving to it. Her lip trembles, then curves. She's steering me, subtly, and suddenly, we're dancing together, like we did back in Montana—turning, spinning, eating up the floor.

Outside, the rain beats a steady rhythm. Maybe that's what we're dancing to, the soft Kentucky rain. I can't tell if it's incredibly dark in the shadows of the room and beyond the windows, or if she's just burning as bright as the sun in my arms.

I'm worn out, embittered, but she makes me want to bring down my walls and be a better man. Maybe we stand a chance after all.

There's no end to the music, so we dance until she falters, letting her hands drop. The rain has stopped. Her tea sits cold on the table.

"We should get back to bed," she says.

I clear my throat. "Yeah. Brothers asked us to meet him in the morning."

The magic seeps out of the room. Reality is back, harsh and unwelcome.

"He did?" she asks.

"He just texted me. Eleven at his house tomorrow morning."

She glances at the clock. "Eleven this morning."

I brush her hair back, tilting her chin up. She's giving me big, wide eyes, the kind I don't know how to resist.

"You want us to go, don't you?" I say.

She nods, biting her lip. "I know you have history with him, but he's helped me."

This is my weakness. When she betrayed me, I had enough pain and anger to hold it back. But now that I've grappled with that and let it shift to the side, I find I can't resist the beautiful pleading face below mine. If a chain is as strong as its weakest link, I am a poor excuse for one, because I can't say no.

"You want to see if he's talked to Kayleigh," I say.

She nods. "I just...want to ask how my son is, to hear how Kayleigh is."

I clear my throat. "Alright. I'll take you."

Her hands slide up around my neck, her mouth finding mine. "Thank you," she murmurs against my lips.

"But you listen to me while we're there," I say. "And don't let your guard down."

She shifts back, but I keep her close against my chest. Brothers couldn't have picked a more effective weapon to use against me than this woman. At least, this time, I'm aware I'm being manipulated. I'm coming back to hell with eyes wide open.

"I'll do anything you want," she whispers.

I weave my fingers through hers, too numb for anything but the warmth of her body.

"I want one more dance," I say "Real slow. Then, we'll sleep."

CHAPTER TWENTY

DELLA

At ten, I climb down the ladder in my fringe dress. It's clean; I used the Maytag I found on the back porch to get our clothes washed up and hung them out on the line yesterday. He gives me a sharp glance as I step into my boots by the door. His mouth thins in silent judgement, and all the magic of last night dissipates in the wake of his general grumpiness.

"You don't like it," I say.

"I think half your ass is out," he says.

He's in a linen shirt, work pants, and his same old boots, like he doesn't give a fuck, which I've come to realize, he, in fact, does not.

"Aren't you lucky."

He puts a Camel in his lip. "Get outside and get in the truck, Della."

He's using his bossy voice again. Rolling my eyes, I turn to unlock the door, stepping out onto the porch. He grabs the dusty cowboy hat he set on the table the day we arrived and follows me, veering around to where he parked the truck. The engine revs, then the Dodge circles into view and stops.

He pushes open the door, holding out his hand. I climb in awkwardly, trying to keep my dress from riding up. Then, he does that sexy thing where he backs the truck up with one palm flat on the wheel. I look away, trying to get control of myself. I'm shameless. I can still feel what he did last night, wet between my thighs.

We pull out onto the road. His jaw is tight, his body tighter. I might struggle to read him sometimes, but not today. He's set up his walls good and hard, so I lean against the door, the way I used to do with Leland, and let my forehead press to the glass. Only, this time, Leland isn't there to tell me to sit up straight.

We leave the gorge, going out towards Byway. Then, we're back in rich folk country, surrounded by high, dark walls that protect millions in horseflesh. I see signs for the city, and they bring back memories I'd rather forget. Those roll by, and we're on the west side, out where the houses cost millions but somehow still less than the one I was kept prisoner in.

No amount of money can buy freedom.

I learned that, good and hard.

Something hurts. I glance down, noticing I'm picking back the cuticle of my thumbnail again. I used to push my hands under the dinner table and just tear at it while Leland talked to his guests. Something to focus on. Pain I could control.

"Stop that," he says softly.

I glance up, wordless.

"Don't hurt yourself," he says. "I won't let anything happen to you."

He's locked away still, but I know after last night, he's not angry with me anymore. I think his grumpiness this morning has more to do with where we're headed than me.

We pull off the road deep in the countryside. To the right, iron gates surround endless green hills and pear trees. Jensen leans out of the door and hits a button on the gatepost. There's a crackle, then: "Please state your name and purpose."

"Jensen Childress," he says.

He doesn't state his purpose.

The gates creak and slide apart, and he pulls through. I'm used to the grandeur of the Caudills, but the classic beauty of the Boyd estate as it rolls into view is something new. It looks recent, maybe built in the last twenty years. Everything is dark stone, big windows, perfectly kept gardens, a looped driveway of glittering white gravel. Jensen pulls the truck up to the door and cuts the engine.

"I maybe should have worn something dressier," I whisper.

He shakes his head, alighting the truck and circling to open my door. I start wriggling towards the edge, trying not to flash my panties. His hands encircle my waist, warm, strong. Heat travels out from his touch as he sets me down.

"Keep close to me," he murmurs.

"Brothers won't hurt me," I insist.

His jaw twitches. "You listen. That was the deal."

I nod. He guides me up the steps by the elbow. Before he can lift his hand to knock, the door swings open. There he is, in the flesh. Tall, lean, with a little lankiness, dripping charm so thick, I'm surprised he's not attracting flies like honey.

"Welcome back," he drawls.

He holds out his hand to Jensen, who shakes it, but in that grim way Leland used to with men he didn't like at the racetrack.

Then, he leans in and kisses just above my cheekbone. His hand grazes my waist, right where Jensen's sits. Jensen jerks back. Brothers pulls away with a televangelist smile.

"Y'all hungry? We've got lunch on the table," he says.

Jensen doesn't speak. His eyes are locked past Brothers, staring into the house like he's at the gates of hell.

"Yeah, that would be lovely," I say.

He ushers us into a vaulted front hall. "Excuse the mess," he says, waving at nothing. "We've been doing a little renovating."

We follow as he takes a sharp turn, and we're in a huge dining room. The table is set with three plates. Brothers sinks down on one side, pointing at the seats across from him. I'm glad he didn't take the head of the table. Leland always sat there. I hated it, the way he'd lord over everyone set me on edge.

Brothers gives me an easy, pleasant smile. My mind goes back to the day Kayleigh admitted she was sleeping with him. I was shocked, having never met him before. I just heard the stories swirling around the city. When she brought me to him so I could ask for help getting

Landis back, it all made sense. He's not my type, too refined, too horse money for me. But he's such an alluring personality, it's hard to resist him.

A man and a woman in black clothes appear and fill our plates without speaking. The doors swing shut behind them. Brothers shakes out his napkin, laying it over his thigh.

"I apologize for the lack of wine or beer," he says. "No liquor on the Lord's Day, but I'll get the cigarillos out with dessert."

"I'm good," says Jensen.

I just smile, and Brothers winks at me, like it's instinctive to him.

"Quit flirting with her," Jensen says.

Brothers raises his palms. "I wouldn't dream of it."

Boldly, I lean forward to pick up my silverware. "I don't think it's me he's flirting with," I quip.

There's a second of silence, then Brothers lets his head fall back as he laughs. To my shock, Jensen's jaw twitches, like deep down, he wants to smile. Innocently, I put a bite of brisket in my mouth. It's warm, tender, and a little spicy.

"Oh, I forgot how much I like you, Della," Brothers says. "You are a treat and a half."

"That why you helped her?" Jensen says.

Brothers' pleasant eyes narrow. "I helped her because my heartstrings were tugged by the plight of a mother and her child."

"God, that's such bullshit."

"Ease up, Jen. Nobody's out to get you," Brothers says, abruptly cold. That chills me to my boots. I've never seen him angry, and I have a feeling it's not something I ever want to witness firsthand.

"You were," Jensen says, not missing a beat.

Tension crackles. Jensen is chewing slightly. Then, he stops and smiles, but it's not a nice one. It's a watch-your-mouth-before-I-fuck-you-up kind of smile.

"You've got some bite to you now, Jen," Brothers says finally.

"Learned from the best."

"Could have done with some refinement."

"Sorry, my education got cut short by my entire family being gunned down by the Caudills," Jensen says. "Speaking of family, where's your brother?"

My jaw drops. Brothers' lids flicker as he waves a long-fingered hand.

"Oh, Jem? He got shot in the head."

The silence is startling. Brothers told me Jensen was no friend to the Caudills, but I didn't realize they'd killed his family. The admission about Jem Boyd isn't shocking, because we all saw it on the news when it happened, but Brothers' casual tone is disarming.

"Jem's dead?" Jensen says.

Brothers has a sip of his glass, like he's discussing the weather. "Yeah, Leland shot him behind a building at the racetrack about five years back. He was going for me, but I sent Jem to do my business for the day. Unfortunate."

I stare. There's usually a heartlessness around this type of man when they discuss death that I'm used to. Leland would put a bullet in someone and complain about the stain on the rug. But this is different. There's so much pain behind the forced lack of emotion in Brothers' face.

Jensen pushes out his chair. "I need the washroom."

He gets up and leaves, to my surprise. Brothers puts his hands together, releasing a sigh.

"Jem and Jensen weren't really friends, but they got along well," he says. "Worked together a lot at one point."

"I'm sorry about your brother," I whisper. "I never said that, but I should have."

He dips his head. "I appreciate that, Della."

I shift awkwardly and clear my throat. He lifts his eyes, and they're warm and friendly, sweet like honey.

"You can speak your mind," he says.

"Okay," I say. "Are you...you still seeing Kayleigh?"

His lids flicker and his throat bobs. "We do still...meet on occasion."

The memory of Kayleigh holding Landis is still painful, and it makes me bold.

"You mean you're still sleeping with her," I push.

He tongues the inside of his cheek. "On occasion."

"Can you give her a message from me?"

The door swings back open, and Jensen sinks down beside me. "Don't make deals with him, Della," he says. "You can't trust him to tell you the truth."

Brothers' sharp eyes dart between us. "And you trust Jensen to be truthful?"

I don't have an answer for that, because yes, I do, but I don't really know why I trust him more than any man I've met. Jensen zeroes in on Brothers, who offers him a paternal smile in return. Then, his focus shifts back to me.

"What would you like to tell Kayleigh?" he says, voice soft.

I open my mouth, but everything feels weak in comparison to how my heart is breaking. It's not enough to know she's protecting my son. I need to wrap him in my arms, press kisses to his round face. He is the biggest part of my heart, and it's torture being apart from him

My throat goes tight. A tear slips out, traveling to my chin.

"Shit," says Brothers, setting his napkin on the table.

"I'm fine," I gasp. "Just tell her I miss them both. And thank her for watching over him while I've been gone."

Beneath the table, a warm, strong hand slides over my bare thigh and holds it. I glance sideways, and Jensen flashes a look that warns me to be careful. I understand he wants me to keep Brothers at arm's length, but God, it's so hard when he's the only connection I have to my son.

"I will," says Brothers.

The dining room is so silent, I can hear a fly buzzing in the window.

"Would you like to see the colts?" Brothers says, standing abruptly. "I have them in the front barn, just a few yards from the back porch. They might lift your spirits."

I glance at Jensen, who doesn't move.

"Jen, we need to talk," Brothers says.

"Alright," Jensen says, rising. "But only if I can keep my eyes on Della."

Brothers dips his head, crossing the room on his long legs and pushing open the side door. Through it, I can make out a wraparound porch and black wood barn. In the pen off the side are two dark bay, wobbly-legged colts. I know they're trying to get rid of me so they can talk, but I don't care. Brothers was right; it might help me to step out for a second.

I get up, moving past Brothers and heading straight for the barn. The morning dew has dried off the bluegrass. It's starting to brown early this year from the heat, and it crunches under my boots as I lean on the fence, holding my hand out flat.

Behind me, Jensen and Brothers stand on the porch, watching me without speaking.

I feel like a bug under a microscope.

Jensen is still guarded, but he's different since Brothers mentioned Jem. The weight of their history sits over them like a cloud. I'm deeply entangled in this whole situation, but when it comes to the emotional side, it's clear to me I'm on the outside looking in.

There was a lot said at that lunch table between them without a word spoken. I'm third wheeling it hard out here.

One of the colts brushes its velvet nose on my palm. I keep them visible from the corner of my eye. Leland taught me to read men, to understand their body language to survive. I'm doing my best, but they are a couple of guarded motherfuckers.

Brothers takes out a pack of cigarettes. They both have one. The faint smokey scent reaches my nose. Now, they're talking, mirroring each other's movements. Usually, that's a negotiation tactic, but not with them. No, this feels more natural, like they're just...used to being around each other like that.

Jensen says something that makes Brothers frown slightly. He shakes his head, waving a hand as he replies. They both inhale.

Brothers is a repeat offender when it comes to nicotine—he inhales and really basks in it. Jensen breathes in, but only about half the time, telling me it's muscle memory, not an addiction.

Then, to my shock, they both laugh. Jensen sobers quickly, like he didn't mean to, but I saw that.

I turn back to the colt, trying to make sense of it all. Jensen speaks of Brothers like he's a striking snake. *Handle with extreme care.* But I never got that feeling from him. In fact, for someone who barely remembers their father, I felt strangely close to him in a way I'd only fantasized about.

I thought it was strange at the time. Brothers is maybe ten years older than Jensen at most. But there's just something about him that makes me think a paternal hug from him would fix the last fifteen years of my life. Maybe that's why Kayleigh started sleeping with him. She always had raging daddy issues.

The colt nibbles my fingers.

"God, we're all a mess," I whisper to it.

I sink against the railing, overwhelmed. A few minutes later, I hear their boots crunching across the dry grass. Jensen pauses a few steps behind, but Brothers leans on the fence beside me, long body draped casually.

"You like them?" he asks.

I nod, running my fingertips over the colt's star. "They're beautiful."

"We should wrap this up," says Jensen.

I push off the fence, following him back to the porch. We're at the door when Brothers clears his throat. We both turn.

"Can I talk to Della alone?" he says.

Jensen's eyes narrow, but I put my hand on his elbow. "Yeah, you can."

I know he's giving me those warning eyes, but I'm going to risk it and ignore him. Without looking back, I follow Brothers back into the dining room. Jensen leans just outside, one boot notched in the doorway to keep it open like he's my chaperone. Brothers strides to the far end of the room, by the doorway to the hall, and stops. I follow, a little nervous.

"What is it?" I ask.

He hesitates, jaw moving. He's got a habit of pushing his tongue into the inside of his cheek in a flicking motion.

"You have to go back in, Della," he says finally.

My mouth goes dry. "What?"

"You have to go back to Leland." He doesn't hesitate this time.

A cold wave of panic spreads down my spine. All at once, I'm back in my bedroom, listening to my husband's footfalls get closer until he's turning the doorknob. Then, it's just us, alone. He can do whatever he wants, and there's nothing I can do about it but be sweet in hopes of mercy.

"No," I whisper. "You can't ask me to do that."

"We need someone on the inside to get Landis out," he says. "Realistically, the only way you're pulling this off is if we get Leland away from the house for a night, and you take your boy and go."

I shake my head.

"Yes." He looks me in the eye. "You can. Jensen won't accept my help unless he's forced into it. The enemy of his enemy is his friend."

"Are you his friend?" I hiss back. "Or his enemy?"

He flicks the inside of his cheek. "Jensen and I have a complex relationship."

I bite my lip, hard.

"He has feelings for you," Brothers says.

"I don't know what he feels," I whisper. "Somebody, probably you, fucked him up so bad, he doesn't share anything."

Brothers is silent. I clear my throat, leaning in.

"You want to use me as bait," I accuse.

"No, I need someone on the inside to pull this off. You are Leland's only weakness."

I shake my head, feeling like I'm drowning. "I don't believe he wants me back that badly."

"You'd be wrong there," Brothers says. "He was so sure you'd come back, he let you divorce him on paper. He never meant to let you go. He didn't think you'd leave your son. It was a dark day here when you disappeared to Montana. I've never seen him like that. I pulled my soldiers back that night and stayed on the defensive."

I mouth soundlessly. Panic is a fist around my lungs.

"I can't beat Leland outright," Brothers says. "But with Jensen's help, with your help, you can get your boy back and I can...do something about what he did to Jem. Put the Caudills back in their fucking place."

"How sure are you of that?" I whisper, glancing at the shadow of Jensen through the door.

"I would bet my life on him," he says. "On it, I mean."

A heavy shudder moves through my chest. Overwhelmed, I cover my face, and that triggers my tears. In a second, I'm in his arms, and he's stroking my hair, shushing me in that comforting drawl.

"Hey now, it's alright," he murmurs. He smells good, like masculine cologne, notes of orange, cedar, vanilla. It's oddly familiar, and it makes my heart ache. My eyes shut, and I wish so hard everything would just...resolve itself. But it doesn't.

Brothers pulls back, hands on my shoulders.

"You know I'm telling the truth, Della," he says. "Jensen is going to figure out he needs me. When that happens and you see me next, you'll have an opportunity to do what needs to be done."

"What's in all this for you?" I sniffle.

"Unlimited power," he says. "There is not, in fact, enough room in this town for both Caudills and Boyds. It's time to collapse the Caudill empire, be done with this bullshit."

That, I believe to my core. Wiping my face, I pull back my shoulders.

"I don't think you and Jensen can reconcile," I say.

"Leave that to me."

I study his innocuous face and decide to ask the question I know he won't answer. "What did you do to him?" I whisper.

Flick—he hits the inside of his cheek with his tongue. His hands rest on his slender hips. "Something terrible and necessary," he says.

"But you can't tell me?"

“No, I cannot.”

The door creaks, and Jensen’s presence fills the doorway. “Time’s up,” he says.

Brothers concedes to him, staying in the entrance of the dining room as Jensen ushers me away. I go with him, letting him walk me around the house to the truck. Brothers only steps out when we’re heading down the drive. I see a flash of his tall body, hands still on his hips, watching us leave.

“What did he say to you?” Jensen says, voice low.

I shake my head. “Nothing important. What did he say to you?”

“Nothing important,” he answers.

We’re both quiet the rest of the way to the gorge.

CHAPTER TWENTY-ONE

JENSEN

We stop at the gas station on the way back. She stands by the meager options, staring at them and worrying her lip. There isn't much but dry goods. I wait around, then get a pack of gum and head out to fill up the gas tank.

Way back in the day, I dipped for about a year. To quit, I started putting a bit of mint gum in my back teeth just to feel something there. It helps me relax and fixate on something else.

I push the nozzle into the tank and snap it on. Using my tongue, I crush the gum and push it between my molars. It seeps down my throat, syrupy sweet and so minty it's cold.

A car speeds by, kicking up dust.

The nozzle clicks, signaling the tank is full. She's still inside when I go in to pay. It takes me a moment, but I find her by the freezer section. She's got a bag of rice, Crisco, and a jar of canned greens in her arms.

I stare at that Crisco, mint on my tongue.

"Can we stop at the farm stand down the road?" she asks brightly.

I blink, jerking myself out of my head. "That where you got the meat?"

She nods. "They had pork belly last time. How's that sound with the greens and rice?"

I jerk my head, taking the items from her arms and carrying them to the front desk. The clerk is zoned out at the register. I clear my throat, and he jumps, tapping at the keypad with one hand and reaching for a paper bag with the other.

"I got twenty-five bucks on the gas pump too," I say.

He nods, putting everything into the bag. The rice is the same brand Cherry used to buy, the same Holly kept in her kitchen. It's a white bag of the material chicken feed comes in, red lettering and a picture of a barn printed on it. Cherry kept a bag of it on the sink, in a gallon Ziplock to keep the weevils out. And the fucking Crisco—is there really no other cooking oil to buy in this town?

We leave the gas station, and I watch her ass sway across the parking lot to the truck.

What am I doing?

She hops into the truck, flashing her panties under that tiny skirt. Oh, yeah, that's why. Because Jensen Childress can't say no to beautiful women, especially not this one. I get in the driver's side, jaw tight, and we head down to the farm stand. There, I stand by her while she picks through the cooler, and I pay up after she finds some pork belly that satisfies her criteria.

We go home, and I take care of the horses while she cooks. When I get back in, she's about done making the pork, rice, and canned greens up.

She's subdued. Whatever Brothers said to her was upsetting, but she won't reveal a word of it. I know it had something to do with her son. I haven't been out to Brothers' house since the day I left. Seeing it again was surreal. I'm shaken too—by going back, by seeing the rice and Crisco tin.

She turns off the stove and removes the pots. I'm standing by the table, watching her. Her brows rise, asking me silently why I'm staring at her like this is our first time meeting. The house settles, creaking. I glance up, thinking I saw something that isn't there hanging on the wall, but no, just a knot in the wood.

"You loved what I did to you the other night," I say finally.

Her pupils spread. "I…I don't know."

"Don't lie to me, Della."

Her throat bobs, lips parting. "I liked it."

"How much?"

She shakes her head. "Enough to come from it."

I take a step closer. She lays down the rag slowly.

"I like your pain," I say. "But only if you like it too."

Her breasts heave. She's still in her tight little dress, the fabric clinging to her curves.

"Strip," I say quietly.

She obeys, eyes enormous. Her dress peels up and falls to the ground. Underneath, she's wearing the same bra from the night we met. Her panties are cotton edged with blue lace. They remind me of curtains, but I'm not sure from where. Maybe back home, a long time ago.

She unfastens the bra, dropping it. Her nipples harden as her breasts hang free, naked in the cheap glow from the ancient bulb in the ceiling.

"You know what word to say if it's too much," I say.

She nods.

"Out loud, Della."

"Yes, I do." She lifts her chin. "I'll say red if I want out."

"Good girl," I murmur. "Take your panties off and show me your cunt."

Her slender fingers dip beneath the fabric, loosening until it falls. She steps out of them. I soak her in. She's a wet dream, breathtaking in a raw, intimate way that makes me see red, knowing Leland had her too. Part of me wants to hear everything he ever did to her body. The other part knows it would only make this jealousy worse.

"Get down on your hands and knees," I order.

She bites her lip, hesitating. Then, she sinks down. Her spine elongates as she settles into position, tilting her head up to look at me. From my pocket, I take a knife. The half used bag of uncooked rice sits to my left. I pull it to the edge of the table and stab it, quick. Grains pour out, covering the aged floorboards.

She keeps still. I step back, boots crunching, until there are a few yards between us.

Then, I sink to a crouch.

"Crawl to me, you filthy little bitch," I say quietly.

Her lips part in shock.

"Focus, Della," I say, bringing her back with her name. "You know how to keep me from going too far. Say you understand."

"I understand," she whispers.

"Now, do it."

She starts crawling, her cheek twitching at the pain. I've done this before, with other women, but not here, back where I was pretending to be somebody I'm not.

She's wincing, but she moves until she's at my feet, gazing up at me, waiting.

"Sit back on your heels," I order.

She does, gasping at the pain. Her eyes are huge, her cheeks flushed. Without meeting her gaze, I circle the rice and step outside. She hung the washing on the line earlier. Some of it, worn out towels, are still there. I take one down, removing the two wooden clothespins that hold it up. When I return, she's sitting there like a good girl, not moving a muscle.

She loves this.

I crouch before her and brush back her hair. Bending, I kiss her forehead gently. She whimpers, breasts heaving. Then, I take her breast in my hand and pinch her nipple until it fully hardens. I clip the clothespin on it parallel to her body.

She inhales sharply. Her pupils blow.

"Good girl. Look at you," I murmur.

"It hurts," she gasps.

"Too much?"

She shakes her head, shifting her weight. "I'm...very wet."

I reach between her thighs and, fuck, she is soaked. It's halfway down her leg, so wet that when I press two fingers to her tight cunt, I slide inside with ease. Her body tremors. I stroke the swollen spot inside her pussy, torturing her before pulling free.

"Open your mouth," I say.

Her lips part, and the eroticism of her exposed tongue isn't lost on me. Waiting, receiving freely. I put my two fingers on it, pushing inside. Her eyes meet mine as she closes her lips, lapping up the underside and sucking her arousal from the tips.

My God, she's extraordinary.

I pull back, clipping the second pin on her other nipple. She gasps, palms on her thighs, head bowed. All the noise in my head is silent. I see her like a beam of sunlight in the darkness. My desire is a sadistic underbelly I once rejected. And yet, she lets me feel things I've pushed down for decades. This time, I don't want to reject myself.

I want to consume, just as I want to be consumed.

To give pain so as to take it.

She lifts her head, beautiful and ethereal. I take off my shirt, unfastening it one button at a time until I can pull it free. Then, I sink to a crouch and cup her chin. The tension is a hushed, shared breath between our mouths as I bend and kiss her. She tastes sweet—like Della, like home.

I press one palm to the ground, rice stinging my skin. Carefully, using my core to lower myself, I unfurl my body between the steeple of her thighs. Cradling her hips, I press her up until she's on her knees again. There's space for my head to rest between them. Pain sparks against my scalp, like fingernails down my back, as I sink against the rice covered floor.

I lean up, stroking my tongue over her cunt.

Sweet, soft. Euphoria.

"Does it hurt?" I murmur.

"Yes," she gasps.

I moan deep in my chest. Her hand skims against my pecs, barely reaching me. I work one hand free and gather her wrists, tucking them behind her back.

"Keep those there."

"Yes, sir."

My cock jerks hard in my pants, and I feel precum spill against my skin. Hot, uncontrolled. She wobbles as I lift my head and flick her clit. I push up on my elbows, rice digging into my forearms. Fuck, she's right—it hurts. The pain is pure mental clarity right to my brain, waking my every sense. Breathing hard, I press my face up into her cunt, burying everything in the sweet, wet softness.

She moans, then she whimpers.

I know it hurts to kneel on the rice, and I'll kiss every mark on her knees and shins when I'm done. But for now, I need her pleasure to flow like a river. My head is empty and crystal clear. There's nobody in this world but Della and me in this house that reminds me of home.

I lick her clit, lapping at it. Arousal runs down my chin, down my throat. She trembles, getting closer with each stroke. My tongue flicks again and again, pushing her, testing her limits.

She shakes, she's so close.

Her pleasure hits her, bending her back until I have to cup my hands around her thighs to keep her upright. Her pussy constricts over my lips, holds, then releases. Wetness fills my mouth, spattering my face like a dam bursting. Exhilarated, I pull my lips back and bite her on the hood of her clit.

She screams, but she doesn't try to get away.

And she doesn't safeword me.

I lose control, rolling from beneath her and pulling her down. We're on the floor together, and she's beneath me on her belly, panting. I dig the steel tip of my boot into the floor, bracing to keep her still. One hand digs into her hair, and I sink my teeth into the soft skin where her throat meets her shoulder.

She bucks, wailing.

That...that is adrenaline in my veins. I release her long enough to reach between us and free my cock. My belt clangs against the floor, my zipper hisses. I grip her hip, dragging her onto one knee. She's so wet, I slide up into her easily.

"No," she pants.

We pause, both breathing hard.

"You need to safeword me, baby?" I manage, mouth pressed to the nape of her neck.

"Not there." The words are barely audible.

Freezing, I glance down. She's as hungry as I am, but that catches me off guard and has me throbbing against the softness of her ass. I don't have any lube in the house, but there is that Crisco from the gas station. It's probably a bad idea, but I'm so fucking desperate, I'd use anything to get my dick inside her right now.

"You want that?" I murmur. "You want me to fuck your ass like that, baby?"

She whimpers, nodding hard. Pulling out, I lift up, getting to my feet. She lays where she is without moving, her cheek pressed into the rice and flaking boards. On the table sit the groceries. I push back one of the plastic bags and find the jar of Crisco inside, where she left it.

I peel off the top, and inside, one half is still crisp, untouched.

Untouched.

Something clicks in my brain, but I don't have the heart to follow that thought. Working quickly, I take what I need and kneel over her body, pushing the front of my pants down. Cupping my hand, I fist my cock, spreading it over my length.

"Hitch your knee up higher, baby," I murmur, leaning over her.

She obeys, biting her lip. I run my hand over her ass, leaving trails of oil on her skin. The low whine she lets out when I touch her asshole is euphoric. It brings me back over the edge, wiping my mind clean. My fingers slip inside, and I'm surprised at how relaxed she is—she wants this badly.

I want her like this too. Raw, surrounded by these things that made us.

My fingers pump, in and out, until I can't hold back anymore. She's loose, moaning with her ass pushed up as I pull my fingers out. Bracing my palm on the flaking floorboard, I guide myself into her. She tenses so hard, I can't get the head in.

"This your first time for this, baby?" I pant.

She shakes her head. "No, but it's been a while."

That makes me see red, but not at her—at the hands that touched her before mine. Rice digs into my slick palm. I brace my fingertips until my knuckles go white. My head dips, and I kiss the nape of her neck and bite down. Not as hard as last time, but enough to distract her for a second.

She relaxes. The head of my clock slips in. My vision flashes at how tight she grips me. Her spine arches, face to the side with her cheek digging into the rice, undulating her hips, begging for more.

My knee aches, torn open through my pants. She's a beam of light within long-empty walls, a cold war over, surrendered to these feelings that only she seems to understand and want as badly as I do.

"More, please," she begs.

I give her all of me, sliding in until she's warm against my groin. Then, we both break our last barrier, and everything is raw, animalistic sex. Fucking, moaning, fingernails raking into the floorboards. I can smell how turned on she is, on my face, on my hands. I can feel that I'm already leaking precum into her ass. I wonder if she feels it too.

"Please," she moans. "Please."

We're on a tightrope. I test her, and she tests me back. We fuck, her with her spine curved up, taking me. Me braced over her, panting hard as waves of heat and pleasure roll through. She's clamped down on me so hard, I don't know if I can finish like this. I've got Crisco down my inner thighs as I pump deep, rutting my hips against her naked ass.

"Jensen," she gasps.

I dip down, grazing her shoulder with my mouth. "Baby."

"Hard, slow," she begs.

Fuck.

I drag my hips back, pausing, and then slam into her ass. She arches, and I feel the pain shudder through her body. This time, it seems to soothe her, and she eases the stranglehold she has on my cock.

"You beautiful fucking bitch," I say. "God, you love taking me up your ass like a whore. Tell me."

She moans, barely audible. I take her chin, forcing her face to the side.

"Tell me," I order.

Her lashes flutter, eyes rolling back. I fuck slow and deep.

"I love it. I love taking you in my ass," she whispers.

I grind my hips, pressing her clit into the rice beneath her hips. She twists, writhing. Her lips part, and I push my fingers into her mouth.

"Suck them. Suck like you suck me off," I grit out.

She obeys, pulling them to the back of her throat. Then, she shudders, seizing, and she comes so hard, she's frozen. With the other hand, I rip the clothespins off her nipples, and she screams around my fingers. The Crisco is making a mess of the rice and peeled paint beneath our bodies. Through it runs her arousal, trickling over the floorboards.

White heat travels down my spine, and I let my forehead drop to the nape of her neck. My spine bows. My hips rut into her ass as I give her everything I've got. I've felt less beaten at the end of a losing fight.

And that's so fucking dangerous.

"Della," I whisper into her hair.

She moans, still quivering.

"Are you alright?" I press.

She takes a breath and lifts her head. I shift my thigh and pull my cock from her. There's pussy and Crisco and rice all over my pants, all down my thighs. Gently, I roll her onto her back and stretch out beside her. Her eyes are misty, blinking hard.

"Hey, come back to me," I tap her cheek.

Slowly, her breathing evens. I stroke her hair and hold her to my chest. When she's ready, I lift her to her feet. The sun cuts through in a beam, falling on her hair, making it translucent. I've never felt so naked with anyone before.

"We should wash up," she whispers.

I carry her upstairs and turn on the shower. She grabs the dish soap on the way up to get the slickness off our skin. Everything smells like cheap soap and sex as we wash it off. The drain clogs with bits of rice. I scrape them out, and she laughs, her shoulders finally sinking as the come-down hits her hard.

That's when I take her in my arms and kiss her like she means something. Slow, deep, exploring her mouth.

"Jensen," she says, pulling back.

I raise my brows.

She looks like she wants to say something, but then she shrugs. "I think it'll take both of us to clean up the kitchen."

I smile. "Yeah, think so."

We don't talk about what happened, not any more than we did the first time we mixed pain with our pleasure. I wash her, spreading her thighs to make sure I didn't hurt her ass or pussy. There are little marks on her delicate skin. I kiss them, remnants of blue dish soap bitter on my tongue. She washes me, and I let her, even though it feels vulnerable to be taken care of.

We get out, dress, and clean up the kitchen. It takes the rest of the afternoon, a few hours of not speaking.

Then, she reheats dinner while I feed the horses and lock up. I sit in my usual seat at the wobbly table. She sets down a plate of pork belly, refried in oil and served on a bed of rice and greens.

It's dark now, save for the single golden light bulb hanging by a string from the ceiling. She sinks down opposite me and hands me a fork.

I can't begin to guess what she's thinking.

We eat in silence until everything on our plates is consumed.

CHAPTER TWENTY-TWO

JENSEN

Neither of us talk about the Crisco again.

The next afternoon, I go into town to track the periphery of the Caudill estate and start to build a real plan. It's not the same one Matthew Caudill lived in when I was in Kentucky. It's bigger, more secure. Everything about the Caudills is more imposing than I anticipated.

That presents a problem.

I've done my fair share of breaking and entering, but this is different. The Caudill house is more of a compound. The fences are iron, and every corner is equipped with cameras. The only advantage I have on my side is that Leland Caudill won't recognize me, so there's a chance I can infiltrate. That would be the easiest thing—maneuver my way into his security team and slip Landis out. But that kind of plan will take time and money.

I have the latter, but on the former, we're running low.

The hills are on lockdown with Caudill soldiers. They're easy to spot. He employs them under the guise of a security company, so they all wear the uniforms. Brothers wasn't exaggerating when he said their family is growing more powerful. Around noon, I do a loop of the surrounding neighborhoods, and I see them, planted here and there. A car sits on the curb too long. An SUV repeats the same pattern twice. Men stand on the sidewalk with the faint outline of a bulletproof vest under their uniform shirts.

It's all there in plain sight.

But nobody looks. Nobody wants to see.

"Take me with you," Della begs as I'm strapping my gun to my thigh and fastening my shoulder holsters.

"No," I say.

She comes close, eyes big. "Please. I don't want to just sit in this house all the time."

"You wanted my help," I say gently. "Let me work."

This would be a lot easier if I had Jack, or maybe the boys from Sovereign Mountain. But I don't. I'm on my own.

This is my test, I think. Brothers, in all his biblical literacy, would call it my forty days in the desert. I call it figuring some shit out, but it's all the same thing in the end.

Either way, I'll have some sons of bitches in body bags, and she'll have her kid back.

And then, maybe, I get to keep her.

"Please, Jensen," she whispers, taking me by the front of my shirt just as I'm walking out the door to leave. "I can help. I lived there for five years."

I pause, looking at her face, knowing she's right. She's been less uppity with me since I fucked her on the kitchen floor. Not less sassy, though—I think that's there for good. But somewhere in the pain and Crisco, we established a new level of respect.

"Beg a little harder, baby, and I might come," I say.

"God, you're just the worst," she snaps.

My dick is hard, riding up on my zipper uncomfortably. I study her perfect face, the curve of her lower lip, down to her t-shirt, to her jeans. Her shirt shows a little bit of her belly, and between that and her waistband, sits a hint of pink lace. There's a subtle eroticism about her, even when she's not trying. It drives me fucking wild.

It's no wonder Leland did everything he could to get and keep her.

"I'm serious," I say.

Her brow arches.

"Go bend over the table," I say. "You want to go? Pay up for it."

"You're such an asshole," she breathes.

I lean in, taking the braid falling down her back and wrapping it once around my knuckles.

"You can always say no," I say, mouth almost on hers. "But you won't."

Her jaw works. Her arousal is subtle. It's in the deepening of her breath. The faint flush on her neck. The little rise of her nipples tightening beneath her shirt. Between her thighs, I know she's wet.

"Bend over the table and take your jeans down," I say quietly.

She goes, turning her back to me. My dick throbs as she undoes the front of her jeans. Her thumbs hook in the belt loops. I ache as she hesitates.

"Go on," I order.

She drags them down to the middle of her thighs, ass wriggling. She's wearing a pale pink thong riding up the curve of her hips. Slowly, she bends, spreading her ass as she lays her cheek against the table top.

I'm so desperate. I want to fuck, taste, hurt this woman to please her, make her come from all the dirty things I do to her perfect body.

I go to her and lean over her body, sliding my groin up against her ass. Fuck, that feels good. My head goes blank as I grind my zipper on her, running my left hand to the nape of her neck.

She wants it.

I lift her t-shirt up over her head and unfasten her bra, pushing them away. She whimpers as I trace down her spine, pushing back. There's a wet spot from her cunt on the front of my pants. I can smell it; sweet, laced with pheromones and Della. It's a scent that makes me want to do reckless things.

Like call her mine.

Or find Leland this afternoon, look him in the eyes, tell him I just fucked his wife in the ass, and then put a bullet in his head.

If only it were that simple.

When I wrap her braid around my knuckles again, she moans and arches her back. I peel her panties down. Her pussy is a little swollen, glistening with arousal. I run my thumb briefly over it—I don't want it to be too wet. Then, I spread her open and circle her asshole, where I fucked her last. She's beautiful there. Tight, responsive.

"You tell me to stop if you need to," I rasp.

She nods. Then, she gasps as I push my thumb into her, mostly dry. Her muscles tighten, fighting me, but I keep going until I'm inside.

"Fuck," she breathes, pupils wide.

One handed, I unzip my pants and free my cock. It's so hard, I don't have to guide it to her soaked entrance. But she's so fucking tight, I have to brace myself on my free hand and push to get inside. Her cunt is slippery, wrapping around my cock, pulling me deeper as I push myself up against her ass. The muscles around my thumb are so tight, it hurts.

Good. I like it when we hurt together.

"I want you to answer me when I speak, alright?" I breathe.

She nods, biting her lip. "Yes."

My hips pull back and surge. "Good fucking girl."

My thumb presses down, firmly and gently, until I feel it against my cock. She writhes, nails digging into the table, scratching into the peeling wood. My eyes fall above her head as I withdraw and thrust back inside. The knot of wood stares back at me.

This time, it doesn't feel dark.

No, I like this. I love the rawness of mutual pain. I like giving and taking.

I just needed to be given a choice.

And Della gave me that.

Here I am, in the place I never wanted to return to, and I think I'm healing. Or I'm so fucking close, I can taste it. She makes me the man I could have been. The man I want to be.

I close my eyes, sinking over her. I push my thumb in deeper, hearing her soft moan in response, and take her nice and slow. Feeling her from the inside with my cock and my touch. Reveling in how she takes it, how she eats my darkness and turns it into something beautiful.

My orgasm comes in a wave, and I empty myself into her bare.

She lets me. For a woman with her past, with a child from a man she hates, it feels like the greatest gift to take this risk together. I know she's on the shot, but she has to think about that tiny chance when I spill my cum inside her.

"Tell me how it feels," I murmur into the nape of her neck.

"How what feels?" she gasps.

Sliding my finger from her ass, I rut my hips, pushing it all deeper. "Having my cum inside you."

She bites her lip, suddenly shy.

"Tell me, baby," I urge.

"I don't know," she breathes out. "It feels so good."

She knows, but she's not ready to tell me, and that bothers me. Maybe it shouldn't. We don't know each other that well. That bothers me too. For what I feel when I look at her, we should have been married for fucking years.

That makes me a little angry.

I pull out and flip her on her back. Her breasts heave, nipples hard. I run my tongue down between her naked breasts to her soft, wet cunt. Sinking to my knees, I bury my face in it. I love everything about her body. I like that I can still taste her for hours afterwards, how I still smell her, or I think I do, the next day.

She arches, pushing her pussy up, riding it on my mustache. Goddamn, I'm rock hard again. Little whimpers spill from her lips. I eat her out like I have something to prove. A sick part of me gets intense satisfaction from the fact that I'm the first man to make her come.

She comes for me, dripping down my neck.

She never came for him.

I lift my head, long enough to slide my finger into her cunt. The muscles throb, pulling me deep. She's velvety hot, so fucking tight. I find her g-spot and stroke it, up and down. Then, I tap it lightly until she undulates her hips. They lift off the table. Then, they start to coil.

I lower my mouth to her clit and pull it between my teeth, keeping even pressure as I stroke it with my tongue.

She likes a little pain, like such a good girl.

My cum drips out of her, around my fingers. She's writhing, trembling. Then, she comes, and wetness releases over my hand, hitting me in the face, the chin.

Take me down, is the only thought in my head. *Take me down to the river between your legs and wash away all the shit I can't carry anymore.*

But I can't say any of that out loud.

So, I keep steady and let her writhe and grind on my face until she's done. Her body goes limp slowly, then all at once. Dazed, I slip my fingers from her and lick her clean, flicking her clit to make her wince. Then, I get up, tuck myself into my pants, and fasten my belt.

"Fine," I say. "You can come."

We fix our clothes, and I lock up the house. Then, I put her in the truck like she's mine or something. There's a warning in the back of my head about taking her from the gorge, but I understand why she wants to. That's her choice, she's a big girl and she knows the risks.

I just don't like it.

The thought that something could happen to her under my watch makes my pulse go hard.

We enter the neighborhood in the periphery of the Caudill estate. Everything seems normal. It's being patrolled, but their security is subtle today. All I see is the flash of a black SUV turning a corner and heading towards the front gate. Della sees it too, and a ripple of tension goes through her body.

I turn the truck, making a wide circle to get to the west side of the fence. There's an exit there for shipping and delivery. It's the biggest weakness in this fortress.

"Do you know the schedule for when shit gets delivered here?" I ask.

"What kind of shit?"

"Anything."

She leans forward, scanning the pointed tips of the fence. "All I paid attention to was food. That came every Saturday morning from a place in Lexington around nine."

"What's the company?"

She bites her lip, watching as the gate comes into view. "Maybella Catering, I think."

"Okay, that's a possible way in," I say.

The hair on the back of my neck prickles. Pumping the brakes, I flick my gaze between the mirrors. Beside me, she's staring up at the house in the distance with wide eyes. Her son is inside. I know her heart must be breaking that she can't just walk in.

I check the rearview mirror. A flash of silver comes around the corner, and I let up on the brakes, rolling down the street to the stop sign just beyond the gate.

A silver SUV cruises past the gate. Hand steady, I take a right turn. I can't tell what these motherfuckers are doing, but it kind of seems like they're following us. It's hard to tell.

"Where are we going?" she asks.

I check the rearview mirror. "Might have company."

She whips around to look out the back. "The SUV?"

I nod, taking a left turn into an alley and coming out on the connecting road to the state route. It leads over the river, down through some swamplands and back out towards Byway. There's nothing out here, no reason for anybody to be on my ass.

"They turned too," she whispers.

I should have left her home. Keeping my voice steady, I increase pressure on the gas until we're moving at almost seventy. This is a little out of my wheelhouse. I'm used to working outside the law in a wild, wild west kind of way, on horseback, revolver in hand. But a car chase? That's new for me.

"Turn around, baby," I say. "Keep your head up on that headrest."

She obeys, throat bobbing. "Are we okay?" she whispers.

"Yeah, we're fine," I say. "Just sit tight, keep your seatbelt on. Okay?"

She nods, breathing hard. "Okay."

"Good girl," I say without meaning to.

One hand on the wheel, I reach beneath the seat and take my semi-automatic pistol out. She glances down at it and bites her lip, but she doesn't speak.

We're driving over the narrow bridge, the river laid out on either side. The cliff faces to the left and right are brown and dry from the summer heat. It's making the trees sparse, not ideal coverage. Up ahead, there's a curve, where I'll have to make a choice where we're going.

What's the best place to fight back?

Or can I get away if we have enough road?

At the last second, I make the executive decision and whip the car to the left, heading into the swampland. The tires wail, and I grab her shoulder a second too late. Della flops to the side, throwing her arm up to keep from hitting the door. I have my foot on the floor, squealing the tires. We burst forward, engine screaming in protest. The trees thin, and there's nothing around us but pale water and rushes.

Behind us, the SUV turns.

And goes faster.

Fuck.

"Jensen," she whispers. "Are you sure this is alright?"

We both know it isn't.

"We're fine," I say evenly. "I'm handling it. Just put your head down if you hear bullets."

"Jensen—"

"Della, you hear me?"

"Alright, I do."

She sinks back, hands shaking. I glance over my shoulder, forcing myself to stop being terrified something will happen to her and start coming up with a plan. I don't think I can outrun these motherfuckers. But if I can get to higher ground, I can stop and pick them off before they reach us.

One thing I know for certain: I'm a pretty fucking good shot. Brothers Boyd made sure of that.

CHAPTER TWENTY-THREE

DELLA

I was brave when it came to standing up to Leland, but right now, I'm so damn scared. I'm not good at staying calm when there's immediate danger. Jensen doesn't seem to be bothered at all. His body is taut, foot on the gas, hand on the wheel. Pale blue eyes make their rounds from each mirror to the windshield every few seconds.

There's a gun strapped to his thigh and one in his hand.

I hope that's enough.

The truck is going so fast, the engine is whining, but Jensen doesn't let up. We're in the lowlands, by the bridge outside Lexington. This is a strip of no-man's-land. I hope he knows what he's doing, because the further out we go, the lower the chances we have of getting help drop.

I open my mouth, needing assurance. Then, I shut it. I trusted Jensen, went all the way to Montana to beg for his help.

"Are you sure he can help me?" I asked Brothers months ago.

"Jensen is a cat," Brothers said. "He always lands on his motherfucking feet."

Abruptly, Jensen veers the car to the right. My teeth rattle as we blaze over rough gravel and into sparse woods. The SUV barrels past, hits the brakes, and spins once. My heart pumps in my throat. Not missing a beat, Jensen spins the truck with one hand and takes a left, heading up the hill.

"Della," he says.

I glance sideways, still glued to the headrest. "What?" I gasp out.

"I need you to do exactly what I tell you, no hesitation," he says, jaw tight. "You understand?"

"What are you—"

"I said, do you understand me?"

My fists ball. "Yes, I do. I will."

We're traveling up a road so narrow, it barely fits the truck. There's a suggestion of gravel beneath us but not much else, and Jensen is going almost eighty miles an hour. Until he's not. He slams his foot on the brake, arm shooting out to catch me as I lurch forward.

"Get out and ball yourself up behind the tire," he says, ripping the gun from his shoulder holster and holding it out. "Do not use this unless I'm dead."

I see him like a snapshot, bathed in sweat but not afraid.

That's when something clicks into place that makes him so much less of a mystery. Jensen doesn't fear death, not at all. I think there's a tiny part of him that sees it, like the low whine of an incoming explosion, and knows he can't sidestep.

The haunted expression in his ice blue eyes isn't fear for himself. It's for all the people he expects to lose along the way.

Right now, it's for me.

"Yes," I whisper.

We have half a second, and I take it, spending it the only way I want to: by kissing his mouth, so quickly, he can't react. I want him to be the last thing I taste if we don't make it out.

His arm shoots out, hand wrapping around my neck as I pull away. He kisses me back so hard, our teeth clash. Then, he's reaching past me to shove my door open.

"Get down, baby," he says. "Stay down."

I drop, wrapping my arms around my knees. He tumbles out of the passenger door and eases to the left, positioning himself behind the back tire. From here, he scans the swampland below. There's a faint tearing sound from the SUV tires, getting close. All my senses burn with adrenaline. My head spins, and I have to force myself to breathe.

"Fuck," he murmurs.

I glance to the side. He's shoving the pistol in his holster and reaching into the bed of the truck. Faster than I can follow, he's pulling an AK from the truck bed and clicking a magazine into it. I think I'm losing my mind, because he's never looked sexier than he does right now: bathed in sweat, shirt plastered to his chest, wet hair curling. AK locked into place and eye on the sight.

His focus is intense, the barrel of the rifle moving slightly.

"Fuck," he murmurs again.

Something crawls over my foot. It's a furry caterpillar, the kind we had all over the holler back in Harlan.

Bang.

My entire body lurches.

"Eat lead, motherfucker," he says, like he doesn't even realize he's speaking.

My nails cut into my palms.

Bang.

Bang.

Bang.

Brakes screech down below. There's a colossal crash and a hissing noise like pressurized steam. Jensen lowers the sight and turns to the side, spitting the gum out of his mouth. He pulls back, lifting the hem of his shirt to wipe the sweat off his face.

"We need to go down and get the bodies out of the truck," he rasps. "Kill any survivors. You'll stay in the truck."

He puts the AK into the back seat and holds his hand out to me. I take it, letting him pull me to my feet. I'm speechless. So this is why Brothers said Jensen was his most valuable asset back in the day. He does not give a fuck about killing people. There was no hesitation there, not a second of it.

"Della, get in the truck," he says.

I can't move. Everything is unsteady. He doesn't shame me. No, he just lifts me up and puts me in the passenger seat. My fingers knot together. He settles himself into the driver's side, clicks the truck in reverse. His eyes flash as he pushes one arm behind my head, the other controlling the wheel with his palm flat, and hits the gas.

My stomach wavers.

The tires scream and gravel sprays, but he doesn't flinch. The muscles in his forearm ripple as he maneuvers the wheel, fingers flexing as it spins. He makes a hairpin turn backwards at fifty miles an hour, then he hits the brakes. I glance to the side. The silver SUV is crushed up against a tree, the entire front pulverized. Inside, a man slumps against the steering wheel, arm hanging out the shattered window.

Without speaking, Jensen takes his pistol and shoots. The body on the wheel flops from impact, falling to the side. The second bullet goes into the second limp body, making it jerk. They're both very dead.

"Jesus," I gasp.

"Not taking any chances," he says, pushing open the door. "Don't fucking move, Della."

There's no world in which I'm going to disobey this side of Jensen. I sit perfectly still, my hand wrapped around the extra pistol. He wrenches open the door and hauls the driver out by his jacket. Ignoring the seeping blood, he picks him up in a fireman's lift and tosses him into the bed of the truck. The other body is smaller but harder for him to dislodge. I want to get out and help, even though I'm trying not to gag, but he told me to stay put.

I close my eyes. The sick thud of the second body makes the truck bounce as it hits the bed.

Then, I feel his weight in the driver's seat. I open my eyes. He's putting the truck in gear, and we're heading backwards down the mountain.

Lord, I'm going to be sick.

My nails cut into my palms. We make it to the bottom of the hill, where the gravel road meets the state route. Instead of going back the way we came, he turns right and heads out into the swamp.

"Are you dumping the bodies?" I whisper.

"Yeah," he says, reaching into the dash. He's feeling for something.

"What do you need?"

"I'd like a cigarette," he says, voice hoarse. He's got blood on his fingers, and it's sticky on the gear shift.

I dig into the glovebox and find a pack of Camels. My hands are shaking, but I manage to light one for him. He takes it, leaving the paper bloody as he puts it in his lip. Warmth I've been too scared to feel until now floods through my body, pounding between my thighs.

Am I aroused by his violence?

If I am, what does that make me?

He stops in the middle of the swamp, miles out, and I sit in the truck and stare straight ahead. There's a distant splash. Then another. He stands by the door for a moment, finishing another cigarette. Then, he takes off his shirt and goes down to the water to wet it. Heart in my mouth, I watch as he washes the blood from his arms.

He gets back in.

"Thank you," I whisper. "For saving me."

He's shirtless, his tattooed arm resting on the wheel. I'm turning into some kind of feral cat seeing him like this, or maybe I just have an arousal response to fear, but out of nowhere, I'm crawling across the seat to him.

"Della," he says, turning.

My fingers dig into his buckle, pulling his belt free. It's thick leather, worn down. There's the faint outline of a pattern burnt into it, bumpy under my fingers. It's his initials, I think. God, I wish he'd wrap this fucking belt around my neck so hard, it would leave his mark on me the next day.

He doesn't push me away. Instead, his rough hand comes down on the nape of my neck.

I yank down his zipper, and there he is, all big and thick, lengthening as I shove his boxer briefs aside. Head empty, I wrap my fist around the Ruger and push him into my mouth all the way to the handle.

"Fucking hell," he breathes, legs flexing, pushing his cock further into my mouth.

He smells like blood, like sweat, but under it all, he smells like Jensen. He's all man, rough in a way Leland could never dream of being. The hand that cradles my head is firm, steady. His fingers weave in my hair and fist. He doesn't force my head down the way Leland used to, but I'm surprised to find I like the thought of Jensen doing that.

I curl my tongue, stroking him. Up, down. Licking the sensitive underside.

"Good girl," he grits out.

I don't need his assurances. I need the flip side. Hands tangled in his pants, I lift my head to meet his eyes.

"Call me a bitch," I beg.

He leans in, mouth grazing mine. "You want me to make you feel small, baby?"

"Yes." I'm practically panting.

Leland made me feel so small, but not the way Jensen can. With my ex-husband, I was nothing but a body to use, a story told over and over again. A man who gets what he wants and the body he gets off in when the day is done. But when Jensen turns his pale eyes on me, I feel like I'm in the sun.

Beautiful, degraded, free to be depraved.

He takes me by the hair and shoves my face back into his lap. My lips part, and I take the Ruger all the way to the back of my throat.

"You hit my thigh if you need out. Understand?"

I nod, choking around the head of his cock.

"Then suck, you dirty bitch," he breathes.

My pussy throbs, the seam of my jeans pushing against my aching clit. There's a darkness in me, and I think Leland put it there. It's a hungry, raw pit that knows what it's like to die of slow decay and fights back hard.

On my tongue, I taste the salt spilling from his body.

He's so alive.

The taste of his cock in my mouth is the underbelly of him. Rough, sexual, violent, but never to me. It's a force of life, flowing from him to the deadness in my veins.

I push deeper, feeling the head press against the back of my throat. But I don't gag, because I've done this before, many times. It's a small victory I learned how to deepthroat because Leland made me, but Jensen is the first man to let me enjoy it. Leland is a jealous man, and if he knew what I was doing right now, he'd be beyond furious.

A chill goes down my spine. Jensen takes me by the hair and pumps my mouth up and down his length. My breath cuts off. I swim in darkness before it floods back.

"Fucking whore," he breathes.

I moan around his cock, licking the underside with my tongue. This is my fuck-you to the man who destroyed me. He took my innocence. He made my womanhood come all at once until I no longer recognized myself. I didn't understand life before it had me by the throat and all my choices had been made for me.

I was a child, I think, when Leland came.

But with Jensen, I am a woman of my own making.

BEFORE

My mother leaves before the sun is up. She says she needs groceries, but I know why she's going. Last night, Leland asked to stay. She said he could if he slept on the couch. He promised to, but after she was in bed, my door opened.

He's a shadow. My window is open and the room is airy and pleasant. I wonder if he notices that, or if he only knows my room is so much less than what he's used to.

"Della," he breathes, weight sinking the bed.

"You're not supposed to be in here," I whisper.

He pulls the covers up over us. Hot breath touches my neck. My spine prickles—is this what arousal feels like? Kisses follow it up my throat. He pulls my nightgown down and exposes my breasts.

Mama said that's a sin, but does it count if the lights are off?

I don't have time to figure it out, because he reaches between us, and his zipper hisses. Then, there's a spark of pain, a second where I gasp out loud. Then, his body rocks, and all I can think about is how strange the concept of sex is when I really turn it over in my head.

He leaves very early. I'm stiff the next morning when I go out into the living room, expecting Mama to start yelling at me, but she's gone. There's a note on the table saying she's getting groceries.

Cold all over, I go back into the bedroom. My quilt is pushed back, and my sheet has a pale crimson stain. I sit down and touch it. The fabric is stiff. I lean over and look in the laundry basket I use for a trash can. At the bottom of the bag sits a condom, tied in the middle.

I'm angry, but I don't know why.

Head down, I tie up the bag and haul it to the trash outside. Then, I strip the fitted sheet off the bed, ball it up under my arm, and start walking down the road. It's hot and I'm on bare feet, still wearing my nightgown. My legs itch with sweat. The gravel digs into me with every step.

But nothing is stronger than my anger.

Slap, slap, slap.

My feet eat up the distance to the end of the road. Beyond that lies a fence, a flat pasture, and a river. Up on the other side is a tiny church. They don't mind when the local kids swim in the river, so they leave the gate open. I slip through and take off running across the field.

How dare he touch me?

I skid to a halt at the edge of the river. It's higher than it usually is in summer. Moving carefully, I step into the lazy water and wade out until it reaches the middle of my thighs. Stomach turning, I drop the sheet in and watch it soak through. A lump rises in my throat.

I scrub the stain out in the river until it dissipates in the cold, clear water.

I could have said no.

And yet, he should have known better.

Teeth gritted, I wring out the sheet and carry it all the way back to the trailer. Mama is in the kitchen, unpacking some grocery bags from the gas station. She glances at the wet sheet and goes pink, but she won't say anything about it. She never talks about anything indecent.

"Did Leland leave?" she asks, voice cheery.

"Yeah, and he can't come back," I say.

She goes still, hand in the bag. "He's a Caudill."

"So what?"

"I don't think people say no to the Caudills," she whispers.

My stomach sinks as I realize she's scared. Regret seeps in. Leland is wealthy, but more than that, he's got the power to destroy us both. That means he also has the power to make us.

"Della," she says gently. "I loved your father, but if I'd had the choice, I'd have picked a man with the means to support you."

My stomach is an ice cold knot.

"A man like Leland can protect you, provide for you," she says. "Money will keep you safer than love. I won't always be here, sweetheart."

I want to crumple, to beg her for a choice. I know a man with money can keep me safe, but what keeps me safe from the man with money? Instead, I lift my chin, remembering how much she's sacrificed to put food on our table, how hard it's been for her since my father died.

"I understand," I manage.

"Good," she says, a forced smile on her face. "Leland said last night he wanted to come for dinner this evening. Let's get some bread going so we can have it fresh."

She cooks one of my favorite meals, and Leland comes all the way from Lexington again to eat with us. He's an enormous presence in our tiny home. I sit beside him, his hand on my thigh, and wonder why he picked me. There are a thousand other women he could have gone after. He could have found one who wanted him back.

My mother excuses herself after the dishes are done.

"I'm really tired. I need to turn in early," she says, bustling down the hall. Her bedroom is on one side of the trailer. Mine is on the other.

Leland lets me sit and watch TV with him for a while. Then, his hand finds its way up my skirt.

"Not here," I say, staring ahead.

"Fine. Let's go to the bedroom," he says.

We go, and he shuts the door. This time, he doesn't lie with me. Instead, he sits on the edge of my twin bed and says he wants me to do something for him. I'm sheltered due to how rural our home is, but I'm not ignorant. It's obvious what he wants. I wet my lips and get on my knees beside my bed, like I'm about to start praying or something.

"I don't know how," I whisper.

He shows me, and it's not as bad as I thought. My head is empty, my mouth is full. Yet, he's the one eating from me, sinking his teeth into me before I was ready to be bitten. He keeps coming back, night after night, until I'm pregnant. And I wish he'd just given me a few years before making me his woman.

NOW

I feel the sweet pleasure of Jensen Childress. It fills my mouth and spills over my tongue, soapy, salty, and intoxicating. Recklessly, I push my face into his lap, taking him as deep as I can, letting him pump his cum down my throat.

He releases my hair and strokes down my back, gripping my thigh. The muscles of his thighs relax. His fingers cradle my chin, lifting my face.

"Show me." His pale eyes are wide, blown out.

My lips part, my tongue pushing out. His eyes drop, looking at his cum. Neither of us move until it inches to the tip of my tongue and drips. Then, his other hand opens, catching it. The fingers on my chin guide my head down. I know what he wants, and I want it too. It's not degrading. With him, it's so gentle.

I lick it from his palm.

"Swallow for me, baby," he breathes.

I do, because with him, I'm hungry. And this is what I want.

CHAPTER TWENTY-FOUR

JENSEN

My nerves buzz all the way home. Surprisingly, it's not from shooting two of the Caudills' men. No, that felt good, like revenge. It's from the way she looked at me when she lifted her head, eyes burning, face flushed, breasts heaving. Della is a wild thing, on the cusp of self-discovery. I'm not sorry to be the man she's discovering herself with.

We go back to the house. I glance over my shoulder the entire time, but nobody else follows us.

"Do you want help with the...blood?" she asks, climbing out of the truck.

I shake my head. "No. Go inside."

She obeys, leaving me parked under the tree. Flies buzz over the bloody truck bed. I make a slow circle to double-check there isn't a hose before I go to the barn, searching until I find two water tankards.

My horse, Godspeed, loiters in the barn. I take him out of his stall, tie the tankards together, and sling them over his back. We head down the hill to the creek. In the shadow of the pawpaws, I fill them up and secure them to his back so they don't slide off on the way up.

When I get back, she's out of her dirty clothes and in that blue sundress. It's tight, clinging to her body, and she wears it without a bra, pink nipples just visible. Her eyes narrow as she watches me haul the water into the truck bed and wash it out.

"You hungry?" she says finally.

"Yeah," I say, not turning as I hang the empty tankards back over Godspeed.

"Alright," she says. "I'll start dinner when you get back."

I turn to go, but she lets out a low whistle. My dick twitches, thinking about getting her into bed later. For right now, I drop Godspeed's reins and come to the edge of the porch. She gives me a playful smile. I reach out, pushing my hand under her skirt to grip her thigh, and pull her to the edge.

"Give me a kiss, baby," I say.

She leans in and kisses me, even though I'm still bloody and coated in dried sweat. If that didn't stop her sucking my dick earlier, it won't stop her giving me a kiss. I slide my hand up, touching just below her naked pussy.

I'm gonna miss her the minute she's out of sight.

Her eyes follow me as I take Godspeed back down the ravine to get more water. I'm filling the jug when I see a flicker in the mud. Crawfish, lots of them. Della would like that. Working quickly, I scoop them up one by one and take my handkerchief out, making a bundle to tuck under Godspeed's makeshift harness. Then, we head back up the hill.

She's sitting on the steps, bare feet in the sun.

"What's that?" she asks when I hold the handkerchief out.

"Crawfish," I say. "You can make them up for dinner so we have some meat. Think we're all out of pork belly."

She lifts it. "This is a lot. Thank you."

I open my mouth to thank her too, but then I shut it. How can I articulate what I feel when she makes a meal for us? The last time a woman cared enough to make me food was when Holly was feeding me in exchange for my body and time.

"Thanks," I push out.

She smiles, scrambling to her feet and going inside. I finish scrubbing out the truck and put Godspeed back in the pasture. Then, I go inside and wash the blood away in the shower. She comes to take my dirty clothes and disappears again.

When I return to the kitchen, she's at the stove. Everything smells good, like the spices used in jambalaya. Without speaking, she hands me a bowl. It's crawfish over rice and chopped greens. Spicy, warm, filling. I take a bite and swallow with difficulty past the lump in my throat.

She leans on the sink, eating from her own bowl.

"Can I ask you something?" she says.

I jerk my head.

"What Brothers said about your family...that's true?"

"Yeah," I say. "It's true."

"That must have hurt when you found out I was Leland's wife."

"You ain't his fucking wife," I correct. "But yeah."

She watches me scrape the bowl and refills it without me asking. I swear, it fixes me every time she hands me a bowl of food. It makes all the meals Holly cooked, before she destroyed me, hurt less in my memory.

"What happened?"

"My grandmother, Cherry, was at her trailer," I say flatly. "I guess Kyle must have not been too far, because he was there too—"

"Kyle?"

"My best friend. I fucked up a job for Brothers because I was on something, maybe drunk. I don't remember. But I was upset, and I shouldn't have been working that night. I shot one of the Caudills' best dealers. They killed Cherry and Kyle in retaliation."

Her lips part.

"I'm so sorry."

I shrug, scraping the bowl. "It happened a long time ago."

"Sometimes, I forget you're so much older than I am. Everything is...fresh for me."

"I don't forget."

A crease appears between her brows. It's true. Ever since she told me she was only twenty-three, I've been handling her with a little more care. She's got a lot more life experience than the average woman her age, but that's not a good thing. It didn't make a difference for me when I got involved with Holly.

I set the bowl down. She picks it up.

"You still hungry?" she asks.

Hesitating, I consider it. There's something about being home that makes me want to eat. I was always hungry until I moved in with Brothers. Truthfully, I don't know how I grew properly with how little food I ate as a kid. Everything after that was transactional. I was fed so long as I was useful to whoever was paying the bills.

Della...she just feeds me, and it has me starving.

Her food tastes like life. It's warm, spicy, and it sticks to my ribs.

"There's plenty," she says, taking the bowl.

I don't stop her as she fills it for a third time. This time, we sit at the table opposite each other. She's still working on her first bowl. I try to slow myself to match her pace.

"Clockface Jesus," she says.

I glance up. "What?"

"That knot on the wall," she says, pointing with her fork. "It looks like Clockface Jesus."

I pause, leaning back. "You go to church growing up?"

She shrugs. "Yeah, everybody did."

"What church?"

"Baptist," she says. "Leland's family is Catholic. It was more of a scandal in the holler that I got pregnant by a Catholic than by a crime lord."

I laugh, and she smiles. "Funny how that is. And we all end up in the same place in the end," I say.

"Where's that?"

"On a cooling board."

She sighs like she's thinking about it. "You're pessimistic. You don't think there's anything after?"

Into my head comes all the times I sat in church beside Brothers Boyd and wished I felt the way he did. That was one of the fundamental differences between us. He had hope, whereas I had no concept of something beyond.

I look at her, Della Caudill.

Maybe it's foolish, but I see something to hope for now. Up ahead, like a light at the end of a dark tunnel.

Her lips part, tongue darting out to wet them.

"You really don't think there's anything?" she asks.

"Honestly?"

She nods.

"I think if there is hell, it's the here and now."

The house goes silent. She sniffs, staring into my bowl.

"You really think it's all bad?" she says finally. "I'm not religious, but there's got to be something good somewhere, don't you think?"

I remember the night I saw her for the first time in the stockyard. How she blinded me, made me hopeful. That felt like heaven to me, but I can't say that aloud.

"I don't," I say, my voice so low, it cracks.

"Well, I think there are good parts in life," she whispers.

"Your kid. That's a good part, I guess."

Her mouth twitches into a smile, a little bittersweet. "Yeah, he is."

"We're animals, Della," I say. "People aren't good. We're conscious, evil animals. We're not above anything. We're below it—hell, animals wouldn't do the shit we do to each other. That's the only thing that makes any sense to me, after the things I've seen."

Her eyes are huge. I wish I hadn't said all that aloud.

She deserves to have hope.

"You're really hurt," she says finally, voice soft.

"It was a long time ago, Della."

"Jensen."

"I did some bad shit. I was the one who hurt people," I say. "Brothers might seem harmless, but he's just like any other crime lord. Some of the things we did changed my fucking brain."

Her throat bobs.

"Brothers said something to me once. He said, 'guilt is a funny thing. It'll make you mean if you let it', and I never forgot that. He was right."

A tear slips down her face.

"Jensen," she whispers. "You don't deserve the things that happened to you."

"Who deserved them then?" The words come out before I can bite them back. "My grandmother? My best friend? That's who took the bullet."

She wipes her cheek and takes a shaky breath.

"I wish Leland thought like you," she says. "He just hurts people and never stops to think about what he's doing."

"Maybe being self-aware is the only difference between him and I."

She balks at that, shaking her head. "No, you're nothing like him."

I'm not sure if I believe that. She gets up, pushing my bowl aside and sitting on the edge of the table. Her hand touches my face. Soft, gentle. She strokes down my temple, along my jaw. Her thumb traces over my mouth.

"You should get some sleep," she says. "You're tired."

I am tired.

We go up to the loft. It's hot, the air thick with humidity. We both strip, and I sink to my back on the bed. She stands in nothing but the soft darkness of her hair. I don't move. She leans in, touching the cross on my side. My lids flicker, and my body reacts.

Slowly, giving me the chance to say no, she straddles my body. My brain stays quiet. My body doesn't revolt; it wants this. I want this, want her.

"Ride me," I breathe.

She grips me in her hand, guiding me between her thighs. Her head falls back, exposing her throat, as she sinks down. We both gasp. There's nothing in the world but this tiny loft and our bodies, naked from desire and summer heat. I can't keep from touching her. She moans, hips working, when I put my hand on her stomach, grazing her scar, then up, to lay on her heart.

She rises, falling, lost in her pleasure, and all I can think about is who we could have been if we'd just been given the one thing denied us both—a choice.

CHAPTER TWENTY-FIVE

DELLA

I can't sleep after our conversation at the table. My heart is tender, thinking about Jensen, about Landis. Every day I can't hold him, breathe in the baby shampoo scent of his fine hair, is pure torture.

He's my baby. I need him within arm's reach.

And yet, if I let myself think about it, I'll break into a million pieces.

I'm getting damn good at not thinking.

The moon is so full, it's as bright as early morning. Jensen lays on his back, sheet pulled to his waist. I toss and turn beside him and think a lot about what comes next. There's a pull in me that tells me to trust him. But the other part, the rational side of my brain, doesn't trust men, not after my experience with Leland. Then, there's a third voice that tells me I don't have a choice. Brothers got me this far. Now, it's time for me to let Jensen take over.

I've gotten further with them than on my own.

He's breathing evenly, deeply. I glance at him. His hand rests on his stomach, perfectly still.

I ease to my right side, laying my arm beneath my head. "Jensen."

"Hmm?"

The sound is a low hum in the dark. I love his voice, all the husk to it. That deep, brittle rasp always sends a tingle down my spine.

"Who was the woman?" I whisper.

Silence.

"What do you mean?" he says finally.

I reach over and trace the cross tattooed on his ribs. He doesn't move, but down beneath the sheet, there's a twitch, then a slow lengthening.

Jensen is an enigma, a dark underbelly, a mind so quick that it keeps up with mine. But he's also slow decay, like a body left in a field. Yet, I see that he's fighting with everything he's got, trying to bring himself back to life. In that way, we're one and the same.

"Who did this to you?" I whisper.

"Nothing was done to me," he says.

I lift my head. He doesn't move, so I sit upright and slide my naked body over his, straddling him. He's hard beneath me, separated by a sheet so thin, I feel the hotness of his arousal through it.

"You are a liar, Jensen Childress," I say.

"So are you," he says.

That's not true, but it pokes a hole in my accusation right away. I bend over him, brushing his mouth with mine. He tastes like a man, all flesh and blood and strength that scares me if I think about it too hard.

And yet, it's my weakness, my downfall.

"Tell me," I breathe. "What was her name?"

"Holly," he says quietly.

"Who was she?"

He clears his throat, a hand on my waist. I straighten, his body smooth between my thighs.

"She was Kyle's mom," he says. "I was eighteen, she was about forty-five. We had a relationship that lasted a few years."

My stomach sinks.

"What did she do?" I whisper.

He releases a short sigh. "She was part of Brothers Boyd's drug operation, a honeypot for drawing men in, getting them in so deep, they couldn't get out. She pulled me in, and I had nowhere to go. So, I stayed, and then Brothers swooped in."

My chest aches for him. "What happened to her?"

"The Caudills killed her when they killed my grandmother and Kyle."

"I'm so sorry,"

He lifts his hand, flipping it. "I was so brainwashed, I had her initial tattooed on my thumb. Took most of that shit off with a power sander."

"What the fuck?" I whisper.

He shakes his head. "It doesn't matter. It was almost twenty years ago."

It does matter, and we both know it, or he wouldn't have reacted like that when I told him Brothers sent me to find him. I touch his chest, right where there's a smattering of hair between his pectorals. It rises, then falls slowly, but below his skin, I know he's hurting. It's so strange that our deepest wounds are rarely visible.

"Does it matter?" he says finally.

I wet my dry lips. "If it matters to you, then yes."

"It did," he says. "But I think about it less now."

It sounds like there was more to that sentence. I wait, but he doesn't speak.

"Why?"

His palm slides up my bare thigh. "You're a talker," he says.

A snarky remark comes up my throat, but I swallow it back. Truthfully, I'm not all that much of a talker. I was quiet for the entire four years I was married to Leland. It wasn't until I laid eyes on Jensen in the ring that I felt like I had something to say. Maybe because there was finally someone who wanted to listen. Now, I can't fucking shut up.

"It's my turn," he says.

"For what?" I frown.

"Asking you to be honest."

"There's really nothing you don't know already," I say, shrugging. "Leland is an asshole."

His touch is gentle, patient, like he's trying to soothe the truth out of me.

"If that were the case, baby, you'd have told me already," he says.

My throat tightens. There's a raw ache where my heart sits. He lifts me off his lap and sets me against the pillows. Then, he disappears down the ladder. His footsteps sound on the lower floor for a moment before he reappears with a bottle of bourbon in his hand.

"Here," he says, handing it over.

"Trying to get me drunk?" I ask, brow arching.

He shakes his head. "Let's play a game."

"A game?" I whisper, wrapping my fingers around the cold glass.

"Every time you want to lie, take a drink," he says. "The more you drink, the more the truth's gonna come out. Either way, we're both fucked, baby."

I stare down at the open bottle. The top must be downstairs on the counter. I can smell the faint scent of alcohol.

"The cross tattoo," I say. "What is it?"

"Goddamn," he says, and he takes the bourbon and drinks from it. "What did Leland do to you?"

I take the bourbon back and have some, shivering as it burns down to my stomach.

"What did Brothers do to you?" I ask.

"I don't know," he says. "It was something to do with a job he sent me on. I remember before and the morning after, but not what he said to me that night."

"Were you drunk?"

He nods, a quick jerk of his head. "I think so. Now, why did you really marry Leland?"

I meet his pale eyes in the dark. He doesn't back down.

"He got me pregnant," I whisper. "I was scared. He told me I couldn't do it without him. My baby is a Caudill, so he wasn't willing to just walk away."

A muscle flickers in his jaw. "How did you get pregnant?"

I shrug, unconsciously sliding into my default defense mechanism. "Sex. You know, how it usually goes. We've talked about this."

"Della," he says, voice low.

I take a drink, even though it's not my turn. "What?"

"Tell me the truth." His head is cocked, pale eyes boring into me.

I sniff, trying to ignore the lump in my throat. "It was a stupid mistake," I say, waving a hand. "We'd been sleeping together for a few months, he'd always used protection. That night, I thought he was wearing a condom, but he wasn't, and he thought I thought that was fine. We got our wires crossed, and I ended up pregnant."

I wipe my cheek, quickly so he doesn't see.

"Della," he says again.

I look up. His face is raw, just all naked in the darkness.

"If you could swing at him right now, would you?" he says.

My mind goes back to that night, just weeks after Leland and I met. The confusion, the sinking sensation in my stomach like I was being pulled into an undertow. The tingling shock that kept me from speaking the racing thoughts in my head. The denial, the grief, the slow erosion of anger I never allowed myself to feel.

And yet, with Jensen, right here, I think I can.

"Yes," I whisper. "Would you?"

His lids flicker. "I don't know," he says. "But what happened to me is different."

I shift closer until I'm in his lap. He takes the bourbon and has a drink. His arm slides around my waist, pulling me close. Our breath mingles, sharp with liquor.

"Let me hit him for you," he breathes.

I hear it in the distance.

A shattering.

The ending of one part of my life and the beginning of another.

I fall in love with him, all at once. My arms slide around his neck and our mouths meet. Hunger courses through my veins, drowning out all the pain. Distantly, I hear him set the bottle aside. Then, he's lifting me to the pillow and laying me down. Eagerly, I spread my thighs, and he puts his body down between them.

I shouldn't love him.

We barely know each other.

And yet, I have never known anyone as visceral and beautiful as Jensen Childress. He's complicated, damaged, and so damn stubborn. But from the moment I laid eyes on him, I've become more myself than I've ever been. I don't have to try to speak my mind. It just tumbles out. I never think about making myself different for him. We just fit together, like two broken pieces of one whole.

But more than that, he's offering me a choice, something Leland never gave me.

Revenge.

Or walking away.

I pull back, his taste on my lips. "I just want Landis," I whisper. "Then, I never want to see Leland again."

He doesn't speak. I run my hand over his warm, bare chest. His body feels so good, strong and firm. The corner of his mouth turns up, and he bends down to kiss me briefly.

"What was that for?" I whisper.

"You're a good woman, Della," he says. "You've got a quick tongue but a good heart. Better than he ever deserved."

His compliment makes my cheeks heat. "You seem to like my tongue fine when it's in your mouth," I say.

He kisses me again. God, he makes my toes curl. He pulls back. I lay my hands on his warm sides and run them over his skin. One hand skims the raised cross. I trace it softly with my middle finger. Slowly, his cock hardens against my lower belly. His eyelids flicker, like it's pleasurable and a little painful all at once.

"Jensen," I whisper. "Tell me."

"It's like a gang tattoo," he says roughly. "I had to get it when I joined Brothers' operation."

I touch the vertical line. "Does he have one?"

"Yes," he says, voice grim. "We all did."

"A cross is a little...hypocritical. It doesn't make sense, the way he is with church," I breathe. "Brothers says one thing, but he does another."

He shifts off me, sliding to his back. I roll onto my side, still resting my fingers on the cross. He doesn't seem to mind.

"Brothers is all fucked up," he says finally. "He's from one of those real fundamentalist sects, snake handlers. He lied, told me he was Baptist for a while. He's not religious, not the way you're thinking."

"Then why?" I whisper.

"I think he acts out his past," he says. "Maybe he hopes he can rewrite over what's already been written."

"But he doesn't actually believe all the things he talks about," I muse.

"Brothers Boyd is a deeply fucked up person," he says flatly. "Maybe I'm the same."

"How do you mean?"

He shifts, then he sits up and reaches for the bottle, but he doesn't drink.

"The pain, the rough shit, that's what she did to me," he says. "It was consensual, at least insofar as it could be. But it really messed with my head."

My heart hurts so badly, I can't move. Deep inside, I sense a part of him that speaks to the denial in me. Neither of us want to be victims. And yet, here we are, all wrapped up in our pain, naked in the sheets together with nothing but a shared bottle to dull the memories.

"You don't have to do it," I say.

He lifts his head, face sober. "I want to do it. I like hurting you when you enjoy it. And I like it when you hurt me."

I push the sheets from my thighs and spread them. He sets aside the bottle and lays back down between them. Our lips brush, breath melding.

"Then hurt me," I whisper. "All you want."

"Why?" He reaches one hand between our bodies. The head of his cock slides into me, stretching me, filling me with familiar heat.

"Because," I breathe. "It makes me feel like a woman."

He understands a lot, but not those words. I don't expect him to, but that's alright. He doesn't know he's letting me rewrite the past every time he gives me a choice. He's allowing me to open myself up in my own time, on my own terms, with a man that I'll never have to wash away in the river.

His stomach ripples as he thrusts, grinding hard enough in me that pain throbs deep inside.

"A woman," he repeats, barely audible. "Or my woman?"

My nails pierce his upper spine. "Your woman."

CHAPTER TWENTY-SIX

JENSEN

We fuck again, like we're trying to put a bandage over our wounds. She's hungry to have pain with her pleasure, so I take the clothespins from downstairs and pull her into my lap, back against the headboard. Her brow furrows in concentration, watching me twist her nipples and pinch them into place. If we get out of this, I'll get her real nipple clamps, but for now, these have the desired effect.

Her eyes meet mine, big, vulnerable. I spit in my hand, wetting her bare pussy, and guide myself inside.

She gasps, lids flickering. "You feel good," she whispers.

My cock slides in deeper, and there are no words for what it's like being this deeply connected.

This is coming home to somewhere brand new.

In the half darkness, I fuck her, and she rides me with her hand braced on my chest. Her nipples pink and tortured. Pussy so wet, I can hear it as she takes me. I don't feel anything but arousal, what I should feel during sex.

She comes, and I come right after, filling her up and laying her down. I know she's on the shot, but I like the thought of my cum inside her all night.

"You like that position," she murmurs.

I keep my eyes on the peeling paint overhead. "With you, I do."

She shifts, snuggling deeper into the pillow. "Were you really claustrophobic?"

"No," I say. "That's how she used to fuck me."

"Holly?" Her whisper is weak, sleepy.

I don't answer. I don't need to. She understands. The soft tip of her finger touches the tattoo on my ribs. A flash of pain ripples through my memory. It's a brand, underneath the ink. I watched grown men cry when the iron touched their skin, but I was so used to pain for pleasure at that point, I just got hard.

All my cum is inside her already, but I still feel the pressure of arousal beneath the quilt.

Goddamn it.

"I'm sorry, Jensen," she murmurs, barely conscious. "I'm sorry."

Her breathing deepens. I'm grateful she went right to sleep. The last thing I want is sympathy for her over something that happened twenty years ago. I've always hated when people say sorry for the past. It's awkward, and I'm usually pretty over it at that point.

Something is different tonight.

I think coming back here and facing down my past is changing me, giving me back my control. Back then, I got hurt before I realized what was happening. Now, I have my guard up. I'm used to defending myself.

Rolling my head to the side, I study the curve of her body.

I'm also defending her. Out in the swamp, I was on high alert flooded with adrenaline at the thought she might get hurt. Up until that point, I'd wondered how Della was with Leland. She talks about him like he's Satan himself, but she's so plucky with me. Now I know she gets scared, and that makes me pretty fucking angry at the man who hurt her.

I close my eyes.

I thought we could get out of this state without spilling blood. Now, I'm not sure I want to.

Sleep comes quickly, and it feels like just a moment before my eyes snap open. It's still dark, and Della is laying against my body, burning up at about a hundred degrees. Gently, I untangle her limbs and push myself up against the headboard. The clock says it's five in the morning, still dark. Residual rain drips from the trees to the roof.

The hair on the back of my neck stands up.

There's something outside.

Moving gently, I get up, covering her, and take my pistol from the bedside table. The extra magazine goes into the pocket of my sweatpants. Stepping on the sides of my feet, I cross the loft and lift the curtain an inch.

A flashlight sweeps over the woods.

What the fuck?

Did Brothers send someone after us? That doesn't make any sense when he can call my phone if he wants to talk nonsense in my ear again. Narrowing my eyes, I squint into the darkness, waiting.

An engine revs on the other side of the clearing behind the barn.

Alright, time to go. I don't want anyone setting foot in the house with Della inside. Moving quietly and swiftly, I get dressed, grab my boots, and climb down the ladder. I left my canvas bag sitting on the kitchen counter. Inside is my AK, my revolver, and two bags of ammo. I rummage through it until I find a suppressor and screw it onto the pistol in my hand.

I put on my boots and turn out the light over the stove. Softly, I unlatch the door and crack it, listening. There's a truck idling on the road to the left side of the yard. Men are moving around the backside of the barn. I can hear them talking in low tones.

These have to be Caudill soldiers. They must have found the wreck and tracked the truck into the gorge. That's the only thing that makes sense.

Brothers wasn't fucking around when he said the state was crawling with these motherfuckers. It's no wonder he's trying to get rid of them. The way they clocked us immediately and ran us down in the swamp is concerning.

Them finding us here is even more concerning.

I move out, keeping to the front wall as I move to the side. My senses are wide awake, the way they were in the swamp. There are four men at the barn. I can hear the slight changes in their voices. That puts me between them and their getaway vehicle, unless they have another car hidden somewhere. But I can take them before they get that far.

Gun at the ready, I creep around the west side of the house. To my right, I see their shadows in the pale light of the barn. Yeah, there's four of them motherfuckers, all in familiar security uniforms.

They're talking, real low. I wait until they turn their back to the house to make the quick dash to the front side of the barn. Back against the wall, I listen. They're talking, but it's so quiet, it takes me a few minutes of listening to realize I was right.

They're looking for us.

I know it's a rental, but I'm ripping the license plate off that truck in the morning.

The truck hums from the road. The men are still conversing, not moving off. I start edging back until I can slip through the side opening and into the dark barn. The horses are outside, sleeping. That's a relief, because Godspeed would be throwing his head, begging for food the second he laid eyes on me.

Their backs are to me. I could take them out with my pistol, but if there are others in that truck, it'll blow my cover, leaving Della exposed.

I push my gun into the front of my pants, beneath my belt. Moving silently, I leave the shadow of the barn.

"Hey," I grunt.

They turn, and my instincts kick in. The way they always have. The way Brothers trained them. I close my hands on the nearest man, ripping him back into me, and take his head between my hands. There's a moment when I see horror on the three men's faces. Then, I jerk my arms, snapping his neck, and his body falls like a wet rag at my feet.

They raise their guns, but they have the disadvantage of being barely a foot from me. I grab the barrel of the closest AK, jerk the owner forward, and slam my forehead into his nose.

Crunch.

He goes down, and I swing the gun around, whipping the man next to him across the face. The final man has the advantage. He stumbles back as I reach for his gun, pulling it from his body. Then, he spins and takes off running across the yard.

Livid, I take off, overtaking him by the tree just off the porch. He goes down, kicking hard. We both tousle, rolling and grunting until he manages to wriggle out from under me. It's dark as fuck under the tree, and I can't see well enough to know what I'm trying to hit.

He starts running at the house this time, taking a pistol from his belt.

Nope, that's not going to work for me.

Fear is a strong drug, and the second I think of her face to face with that pistol, I'm up and after him. He stumbles on the side steps. I swing and hit his elbow, sending it flying. My fist closes on the front of his shirt. I yank him up, using my head as a battering ram to slam his nose.

Blood pours over us both.

He's sputtering, begging.

Fist tearing into his shirt, I haul him up to shoulder level and slam his head into the porch railing. It's the kind of crunch I never get used to, no matter how many times I hear it. Just nasty and grisly. I'm impressed by how well the ancient railing holds up. It must be reinforced by metal.

His head is less lucky. It smashes in at the temple, blood and something thicker seeping out.

I haul him back and slam him into it again for good measure, mostly because I'm pissed. The white railing is deep red in the moonlight. His body slumps, tumbling past me to the dirt. An engine revs in the road at the same moment as a light goes on in the house.

No, no, stay inside, Della.

Heart pounding, I crash in through the front door. She's standing by the stove in her nightgown. Her face goes white, and she backs up as I burst in, soaked in blood. Swiftly, I move past her, taking up the AK from the counter.

"Caudill soldiers," I say, keeping my voice even. She's already scared enough. "You take that revolver and go up into the loft. Do not come down until I say."

Her lips tremble.

"Della, get your ass up into the loft," I order.

She nods, scrabbling in the bag, trying to get a hold on the revolver. I pause in the doorway.

"Della."

She turns, revolver at her side, fists clenched, shoulders back.

"Good girl, you got this, sweetheart," I say, giving her a wink like we're not about to get gunned down if I don't move my ass in the next second.

The truck revs, spinning around and barreling across the yard, heading for the house. There's no time. I step out onto the porch, brace the AK, and start unloading.

The truck veers, then straightens.

It speeds up.

God-fucking-damnit. I keep my finger on the trigger, not flinching as the truck heads towards the porch where I stand. Then, abruptly, it veers to the side, exposing the tinted windows. I can't get a clear shot at the driver now.

The moonlight glints on the sunroof. My mind works quickly as I glance around, trying to figure out a weakness.

I need a headshot.

There's maybe thirty seconds before the truck flies past the porch. I sling the AK back, jump on the railing, and pull myself up onto the roof. The AK jerks back, catching me on the cheek. Wetness trickles down my neck, but the pain only heightens my senses as I scramble to my feet on the shingles.

Moving fast, I run sideways along the edge of the porch. The truck narrowly misses the tree, eating up the space between it and the porch steps.

The window of time is so narrow. There's no room for error.

One.

Two.

Three.

Holding the AK out of the way, I jump. For a second, I think I misjudged, and I'm about to slam into the hood and vaporize into hamburger meat.

But no, the truck soars underneath me, and I hit the bed hard, bruising my knee as I roll onto my side. The adrenaline keeps back the pain.

The driver hits the brakes, and the truck spins out.

I'm on my feet, surfing across the bed of the truck, scrambling up until I'm upright with two feet braced on the rack on the roof, looking down into the cab. They don't see me at first, and that gives me the time I need to spin the AK back and rip the pistol from my belt.

The driver goes out, brain spattering across the windshield. The passenger raises his gun, but I pull the trigger faster than he can react. The entire truck lurches and starts rolling down the hill, fast.

I drop the pistol and take the butt of the AK, smashing out the sunroof and splintering the glass around the edges. The truck is picking up speed, rattling hard. I drop into the cab and yank the driver's body to the side, reaching down and slamming the emergency brake with the heel of my hand. It slows down enough that I have time to shove my AK down on the brake, bringing the truck to an abrupt halt.

Silence falls.

I'm breathing hard as I push the truck into park and peel myself upright. There's blood everywhere, and most of it isn't mine.

My body tingles as I slide from the truck and circle back. The clearing is silent. I run a hand over my face.

I need to do a perimeter check, but I'm pretty sure that's it.

"Oh my God."

I lift my head, and she's standing on the front walkway. Clearly, she's got a problem following instructions.

"I told you to get in the fucking loft, woman," I say.

"After that shit, I need you to fucking get inside me," she shoots back.

She turns around and goes inside, slamming the door. My legs take me to the front door before I know what's happening. The perimeter check needs to happen, but the way her ass sashayed up those porch steps has all the blood going from my big head to the other one.

I step inside, slamming into her on the other side.

Her eyes glitter. "You gonna fuck me, cowboy?"

I drop the AK back against the wall and pick her up, bloody hands on her naked skin. Our bodies fall against the wall between the door and the sink. My mouth is on her neck, my hand between us yanking my belt open. Her nails rake through my bloody hair, digging in so hard, it hurts.

"You turned on by blood?" I pant.

"I'm turned on by watching you fuck people up," she moans.

Bracing my boot, I shove the front of my pants down and thrust into her wet pussy. She cries out, head falling back.

"You're in luck. I've got a list of people to fuck up," I grit out.

She moans, hair falling around her face as I start fucking, bouncing her on my cock. The sex is hard, fast. The stove rattles wildly. I pound her into the wall, and she falls apart with her eyes rolling back. There's a freeness to her that isn't there when we have regular sex. She's dripping down her thighs.

I slam in, pinning her to grind into her clit. Her lips tremble. Her nails dig in. She comes so hard, I hear the splatter on my boot.

Part of me was afraid Della couldn't match my desires.

God, was I wrong about that.

She moans as I hammer so hard, I know it hurts. The wet sound echoes through the house. We're past the point of pretending we're rational people. Our eyes lock, and then hers roll back as I shove my cock so far inside her that her legs spasm, and come.

The clarity of my pleasure is mind blowing. My hips rut mindlessly. Sweat drips into my mouth, dragging blood with it. Her perfect skin is stained with crimson and the deep flush of pleasure. That perfect moment when we're both coming, bodies locked, seems to go on forever. I soak in every second of it, my forehead pressed to hers.

"Lord," she whispers, taking a shaky breath.

I kiss the side of her neck, leaving a bloody print. "You stay in the house. I'm going out to clean up the bodies."

She nods, wiping the sweat off her face. I grab the AK and shove my dick back in my pants, fastening my belt as I step on the porch. As I'm striding across the yard to the bodies before the barn, I take my phone out and dial Brothers Boyd.

He picks up on the first ring.

"Early bird, huh, Jen?" he drawls.

"Shut up," I say. "I just got attacked by Caudill soldiers. We need to talk."

Silence. I know he wants to say I told you so, but he also knows I might lose my shit if he does. He clears his throat.

"I'll be at the Bonnefield Tavern outside Byway tonight," he says. "Come by, and bring your girl."

The phone cuts off. I shove it back in my pocket. The Bonnefield is a historic hotel and tavern at the edge of town. It's where Brothers Boyd goes when he needs to do seedy business. If I recall, it's also where he hosts parties when the races start.

He was right. I can't do this without him.

And that's a bitter pill to swallow.

CHAPTER TWENTY-SEVEN

DELLA

The next day, he's up and gone before I can peel open my eyes. Everything hurts, especially on the inside. After I make breakfast and leave it on the table, I pull back the shower curtain and fill up the clawfoot bathtub with hot water. I swear, my eyes roll back in my head as I sink to my chin.

Right away, I start spiraling.

Back in the Caudill house, I spent a lot of time in the evening disassociating in the bath. It was where Leland left me alone. In the evening, I could have a long soak and postpone going to bed with him as long as possible.

"You take so fucking long at night," he'd snap.

"Don't you want me nice for you?" I'd ask sweetly.

"You take ages putting our son to bed too. Come here."

My eyes snap open. Right on the heels of the memory of his hands on me comes the pain of missing my son. The only consolation I have is that I know Kayleigh will put him to bed every night the way he likes: a story by the hearth in the nursery, a kiss on the head, and a song. Kayleigh's people are from the mountains, so she knows all the songs I tried so hard to pass on to him.

The door slams downstairs. I wipe my eyes. There's no point in misery, not when I have a bullet like Jensen Childress in my gun. If anyone can get my son back, he can. After last night, I see what Brothers was saying about Jensen being a cat. Watching him jump into a moving truck and shoot two men through the sunroof, I get it now.

He is a tough motherfucker.

Boots sound on the ladder. Jensen comes around the corner, taking off his cowboy hat and hanging it behind the door. His eyes linger on my body, brows rising.

He whistles, low. "Goddamn."

A flush creeps up my neck. "Hush," I whisper back.

He leans down, takes me by the chin, and kisses my mouth. The way his mustache tickles has my toes curling.

"We're going to Bonnefield Tavern," he says, pulling his shirt off and turning the sink on.

I sit up. "That's Brothers' territory."

"Brothers is the reason we're going," he says, splashing down his torso and toweling off. He takes his last clean white t-shirt from the pile of laundry I did the other day and pulls it on. "We're going to need his help."

I don't speak. I don't have any right to, not after dragging him all the way here. This is one of those times when silence is best.

"You're going to behave yourself this time," he says.

My feathers ruffle. "I was coming to help," I say.

He stops in the doorway. "I was a professional criminal, Della. I know how to kill people."

His footsteps die out, and I hear him pull a chair out at the kitchen table. Frowning, I sink into the water until it reaches my chin. The Bonnefield Tavern is where Brothers runs his bookkeeping business. It's between Lexington and Byway, the place to be during racing season. I've been there once with Kayleigh to see a band and place bets on the derby, earning myself a scolding from Leland. After that, Kayleigh had to go alone. That's how she met Brothers.

One thing's for certain: there won't be a Caudill in sight that deep into Brothers' territory.

Jensen spends most of the day outside. In the late afternoon, I walk the yard, coming upon a mound of fresh earth. Down below, I know are the men he killed. I stare at it for a long time. Hoofbeats pull my attention. He comes around the side of the barn on Godspeed, hat on his head. I watch him for a while, enjoying the view.

It feels so right, being in this house with him.

Like the home I've always wanted.

At first, I thought I didn't want marriage and children. I used to dream of running back to the holler and living alone, in peace. But now that I've met Jensen Childress, I realize I do want those things, but they better be on my own damn terms.

I just wanted the freedom of choosing my own way. I deserved to pick the man I wanted to be the father of my baby, the man I go to bed with every night, a man I love, one who loves me back.

I deserve a man who fights for me instead of fighting against me.

He disappears into the barn. I shake the thoughts from my head and go inside to get ready for tonight. Jensen comes in after a while. I get into my sundress, tying the ruched bodice tight, and put my boots on.

Then, I reconsider and retie the bodice to sit a little lower. I've got a nice body, and I like when Jensen looks at it.

My fingers falter.

I hated it when Leland looked at me; it made my skin crawl. It's so strange, rediscovering all these things with Jensen now.

I wait for him on the porch because I like watching the lightning bugs rise in the silence of the gorge. The truck looks different, and the license plate is gone. I think Jensen might have put some kind of tint on the side windows.

"You ready, baby?" He appears behind me, locking up.

He gives me an up-down glance that makes my stomach flutter as he follows me down the steps. His arm snakes around my waist, holding me back for a second.

"You behave yourself tonight," he says. "I mean that."

I nod reluctantly. "I know we're here to do business, and I trust you to do it."

He pulls back, spanking my ass, and opens the truck. "Good girl. Get in."

I'm so flustered, it doesn't occur to me until we're on the road that maybe Kayleigh will be there tonight. That thought keeps me going through the winding roads out to the horse farms on the north side. When we park on the street, a valet appears out of nowhere and takes the keys. He seems to know exactly who Jensen is. We're expected.

The tavern is a two story white building with green shutters. The front porch wraps around three sides, and the front door is open, light spilling out into the night. Music sounds faintly from inside. Through the wavy, mini pane windows, I can see there's already a crowd inside.

"You stay with me," Jensen says.

"Yes, sir," I say.

"Save the sass for when I can work it out of you." He puts his hand on the small of my back, guiding me up the steps and inside.

A wall of sound hits me, making me wince. A bluegrass band plays fiddle in the corner, a woman with a guitar singing into the microphone. Against the rich, red wooden walls are rows of bourbon, bottles glittering under the chandelier.

To the left are the betting stations, open for business. On the opposite wall, over the entrance to the upstairs hotel area, is an enormous TV showing the pre-race. And standing behind the counter, bartending, is Brothers Boyd. It's a stab of disappointment that Kayleigh isn't with him. I blink quickly, sniffing. It was a longshot, now that I think about it. I doubt she goes out in public with him at all.

He sees us and stops, lifting his hands.

"Hey, hey," he drawls. "Come here, Della. You're a sight for sore eyes."

I let him take my hands over the counter and kiss the back of my knuckles. Jensen leans on the bar, giving him a warning look.

"Flirt with her, and I'll shoot you in the dick," he says.

Brothers winks at me, turning to get down two glasses. "Nobody's trying to take your girl. Have a bourbon, Jen. It'll help your panties work that knot out."

"Christ," Jensen murmurs, but he takes the glass.

I sip mine to taste then shoot the rest. "It's good."

"Only the best," says Brothers. "Go on, put some bets down. It's on me if you lose."

Something I learned about Brothers is that he works hard, but Lord, does he play harder. Tonight, he's clearly in a great mood. His bar is crowded, I know he's put thousands down on a fast horse, and he's got Jensen right where he wants him.

I lean across the counter, bourbon already hitting my brain—I'm starting to feel pretty damn good.

"Can I bartend?" I beg.

He laughs. "God, I love you, Della. Come on, jump over the bar."

Jensen reaches for me, but I sidestep. "Let me back there. I'll be out of the way, and I can keep the drinks going so you all can talk."

He glances over the room then jerks his head. I might not be as deadly as Jensen, but I am the woman who convinced Brothers to help me in the first place. This isn't my first rodeo in getting what I want.

Brothers holds out his hands. I pull myself up, letting him lift me by the waist over the counter and set me down.

"You know how to do this?" he asks.

"You know I do," I say.

Truthfully, I've never done it to this level, but I served drinks by night when the diner became a bar for local events. Before Leland ruined everything. I think I can figure it out, at least for tonight.

"Alright, let's get a couple of Angel's Envy, neat," he says. "Jen, come here."

Right then, someone whistles, sharp and loud. The band goes silent. Brothers leans over and hits a button, the TV turning all the way up. There's something about the races that always gets my blood flowing. I go to the far end so I can see over everyone's heads.

The gates clang.

The entire bar inhales. I glance sideways at Jensen, but he's glued to the screen.

"Come on, come on," Brothers murmurs.

The horses go around once. The tension grows. Everyone moves closer, like it'll make their horse go faster. There are murmurs of *fuck yeah* and *come on, come on*. The energy shifts, rising as the horse in the middle breaks out into a clear lead. Brothers leans in, knuckles white on the bar.

"That's my horse," he murmurs.

"You own it?" Jensen asks.

"Yeah. Cost me a heavy stud fee to get that filly," he says.

"She's a good looking horse."

"Thanks. She's from Chariot Racer."

"Fuck, that's a stud fee. Better hope she takes it."

My brows are up by my hairline. They're talking, like it's all water under the bridge tonight. It's making Jensen's anger towards Brothers make a lot more sense. There was a strong bond there, once upon a time.

It must have been one hell of a falling out.

"Alright there, sweetheart," Brothers says as his filly picks up speed. His arms are crossed over his chest, body tensed.

The entire room starts clamoring, beating on the table with rising aggression. The filly blazes through the finish line, and the room roars, a huge wave, deafening me.

Brothers slaps the counter. "And that's how it's done, motherfuckers."

Everyone loses their heads, beating on the bar, moving in a surge to the betting stations. Brothers turns around and grabs the bourbon bottle, pouring Jensen and I another glass.

"Alright, let's talk," he says, putting a hand on Jensen's shoulder.

"Yeah, let's get to getting," Jensen says.

Well, his mood is improving. I wonder if this was all part of Brothers' plan; get him loosened up with something they bond over, then slide right in through the open door. Frowning, I watch them retreat to the end of the bar and start talking quietly.

One of Brothers' men leans on the counter. I glance up, screwing the cap off the whiskey. He's a burly man with bright blue eyes and a full, dark beard. I think he took over as Brothers' right hand after Jem died, if I recall.

"What can I do you for, Angus?" I ask.

"Good to see you, Miss Della," he says. "You bartending tonight?"

I glance back at Brothers and Jensen. "The boys are talking, so I've got to do all the work."

He laughs. "Get me a beer, your choice."

Reaching in the cooler, I take out a Guiness and pop it, handing it over. He has a swig then leans in.

"You know, it was a bit rough when you up and run off," he says.

"How's that?" My forehead creases.

His eyes dart to his boss, like he's breaking the rules. "Brothers is being pushed pretty hard by the Caudills. They've taken a good bit of territory. If Jensen doesn't help Brothers, well, it won't be pretty for anybody involved."

The hair on my neck rises. "Is it really...that bad?"

The bluegrass band starts up again, the fiddle going hard and fast. Everyone is drunk enough, they're dancing, shaking the floors and rattling the windows. I lean in, but that interim seems to make Angus rethink his words.

"Don't worry about it, miss," he shouts. "Shouldn't have said anything."

He pushes off the bar to leave. I glance back at Brothers, and for the first time, I think I see a little humanity. This isn't all about getting his claws back into Jensen the way he seems to think. It's more a matter of survival, a last ditch effort to bring in the best team to take the Caudills out.

A shiver runs down my spine.

I need to get my son and go. My home isn't safe anymore. It feels like the city is on the cusp of decimation.

Brothers and Jensen split about ten minutes later, and Jensen walks around to disappear into the back room. Brothers hoists himself up on the counter, sliding over and landing on his feet. He puts his hand on the small of my back.

"You give any thought to going back to Leland?" he says.

I freeze, looking ahead. "Is that still what you want?"

"Yes. Go back to Leland like I said, and I will draw him out of the house and provide you a safe route out with your son. But you have to be in the house, ready to go when I say. Understood?"

I stammer, wordless.

"Jensen knows he can't do this on his own," Brothers drawls. "We do this my way, or you lose everything."

The fiddle pauses. Everyone draws a breath. Then, they clap, and the floor shakes as they shout and the music starts up with a vengeance again. It's so fucking loud. Brothers' touch disappears. I turn, but he's already leaning over the counter, shaking hands and accepting congratulations on his win. The music hurts my head. There are too many people in this room.

My brain is going to explode. I put my fingers to my temples and shut my eyes.

"Come on," Brothers say, appearing at my elbow again.

Lord, how did he get back so fast? I open my eyes, a glass of bourbon hovering in my vision.

"Drink," he says. "Tonight is about yesterday. Tomorrow is all about tomorrow."

I reach for the glass, then hesitate. I'm at a crossroads, being offered a choice. A deal with the devil and a drink to seal it. I turn my head, and he's so close, I can feel his hot breath on my shoulder. He smells familiar, almost like my father's aftershave does in my memory.

"What's your real name?" I breathe. "I know your mother didn't name you Brothers fucking Boyd."

"The only reason anybody needs my name is for bedroom purposes," he says. "You don't have a use for that, Della."

My heart thumps in my mouth. My mind races through everything that's happened since we got back. The swamp, the attack in the gorge, what he's whispering in my ear right now. It's all falling into place, his design like dominos tumbling under the great and powerful hand of Brothers Boyd.

Flick, and they all fall, making a path right to my little boy.

"Jensen won't let me go back to Leland," I say, watching the back hallway.

"What Jensen doesn't know won't hurt him," he says, stepping back. "Come with me tonight. I'll take you back to Leland."

The high of bourbon and horse racing is gone. My breath comes short and fast. The music keeps getting faster, thumping with my heart.

I want to go, now.

Whirling, I push through the dutch doors and run across the floor, bumping directly into a broad figure. It's Jensen, steadying me, looking concerned. When did he come out of the back? And why does he have a bundle of AKs hanging over his shoulder?

"I'm leaving," I gasp, darting around him.

He steps back, eyes roaming over me, a crease between his brows. Behind him, I can make out the shape of Brothers leaning on the bar, head cocked, watching us with the smallest smile, like a cat playing with its prey.

My stomach churns.

He knows. He knows I have no choice.

"I'm a little drunker than I thought," I stammer.

"That's fine. I've got what I came for," Jensen says. "We can go now."

Just as the words leave his mouth, a folding chair flies out of nowhere and smacks him across the head. Dark blood blossoms on his temple. My jaw drops. He doesn't move except to reel back. The entire bar goes dead silent. Brothers is glancing around like he's trying to figure out who's responsible.

Click. Someone's whiskey tips over. It splashes, then drips.

"Who threw that?" Jensen says, still not turning.

A very drunk man lifts his hand. "Sorry... Accident," he slurs.

Apparently, that's not an excuse, because Jensen drops the AKs, kicking them back against the counter with the heel of his boot. He picks up the chair and slings it like a professional pitcher across the room, throwing the man off the table with a shattering crash. My hand claps over my mouth. The man flies back into the betting station. The rolling cover splinters. Brothers yells something, but nobody hears him, because suddenly, everyone has a fight to pick with the closest person.

All hell breaks loose. Brothers skids over the counter, snatching me around the waist and hauling me to safety behind the bar.

"Do something," I gasp.

He ducks through the swinging doors, grabs the nearest man, and punches him in the face.

"I meant stop fighting," I yell, "not fight more."

The man turns around and hits Brothers right back. Jensen appears, springing up like a jack-in-the-box, and takes out the man with a right hook.

"Thanks," says Brothers, face lit up like it's Christmas morning.

Somehow, it's Jensen and Brothers against the entire bar, beating the shit out of everyone who gets close enough like a well-oiled machine. Heart pounding, I reach under the counter and feel around. There's no way Brothers doesn't have a gun in here. My fingers touch cold metal, and I pull out a vintage Ruger.

It's the same kind tattooed on Jensen's dick.

That's...odd.

A shoe flies over my head and smacks the back wall, taking out a bottle of tequila. I'm backing away into the furthest point from the fight, gun in my lap in case someone tries something with me. I don't think I have to worry. They're all too occupied fighting the two man powerhouse that is Jensen Childress and Brothers Boyd.

I see it again, blurring over the chaos around me—a glimpse of the past. An explanation as to why it hurt Jensen so badly when

Brothers betrayed him. For all his faults, Brothers Boyd is the man who made Jensen, for good and for ill. It's clear, watching them fight together, that they were the dream team once upon a time. I just know they ran this city into the ground every damn weekend. Nineteen years and a lot of hurt later, they're still going strong.

I swallow, the metal of the gun digging into my palm.

Jensen will never let me go back to Leland. He's too protective. I saw the way he beat that man's head, stared through the kitchen window as he did it. While I'm not sure what to call what he feels, he definitely has very strong feelings toward me. Whether it's honor or something else, he's not letting me walk back into hell.

Which means Brothers is right.

And I have to help him betray Jensen one more time.

CHAPTER TWENTY-EIGHT

JENSEN

"I can't believe you two."

I glance up to where Della's sitting in the window, coffee in her hand. Not a single hair is out of place, despite the chaos of the evening. The bar is empty, and we're in the back room. Brothers went to lock up after taking Della's gun and threatening to shoot everyone if they didn't clear out.

I cock my head.

"You weren't a little turned on?" I ask.

She purses her lips. The swinging door to my left creaks, and Brothers appears with another cup of coffee. He hands it over. I ease back against the wall, stretching my legs out. Everything hurts, from tonight and the two days before. My body doesn't have quite the get up and go it used to.

Or maybe I'm just running it a little too hard.

"Well, I'll be closed tomorrow," he says. "But it's nothing we can't fix up."

"Where are my guns?" I say, rolling my head to look at him.

"In the front."

"What are the guns for?" Della interjects.

"Keeping us safe in the gorge until we're ready to move in," I say.

Brothers looks at Della, and she looks away fast. Brothers opens a cabinet beside the bookcase and pulls out a roll of bandages, some tape, and alcohol wipes. He tosses it all onto the chair beside me.

"Gonna wash up in the bathroom," he says. "Y'all stay right where you are."

He leaves, door swinging. Della sets her coffee aside and crosses to me. She's in the prettiest sundress that hugs her body, letting her breasts hang naturally. It drives me crazy, seeing them shift when she moves, but it's not half as bad as seeing her ass sway in the soft fabric.

I grip her thighs, pulling her in.

"Fuck, you look good," I say.

She gives me the littlest eye roll, turning to pick up the alcohol wipes. "I think you're just horny from the adrenaline."

I think she might be right, but it's hard to tell. I'm always horny when she's around. She rips open the pack and shakes out a wipe. I keep quiet because I like just looking at her, feeling her warmth between my knees and under my palms. She grips my jaw, turning it to the side. The wipe stings the gash left by the flying chair that started it all.

"You and Brothers are really a match made in hell," she murmurs.

"You can say that again."

"We need him, don't we?" Her voice softens.

I work my jaw, more against the pain than anything. For some reason, I can fight a room of people after being decked in the head by a chair, but the minute she's patching me up, everything hurts a hell of a lot more. Funny how a little of her sympathy makes me so damn soft.

"Yeah, reckon so," I say grimly.

She daps my temple, lips thin. Then, she tears off some tape and starts folding the bandage.

"So you're going to work with him?" she asks.

After the swamp and last night in the gorge, I don't have a choice, not when it comes to keeping her safe. They can't see her, or Leland will know for certain she's back. From what Brothers said, Leland wouldn't stop until he rooted her out and dragged her back. Apparently, he thought she was bluffing with the divorce papers, and it was a bloodbath when she actually left.

My grip tightens. She winces.

"Sorry," I murmur.

She tapes the bandage on and sets her hands on either side of my face, turning it up.

"I don't think you or Brothers know how to keep out of trouble," she says.

"I'm not like him," I say reflexively.

She purses her lips but doesn't speak.

"Della!" Brothers calls. "Where's that Angel's Envy?"

"It's under the bar," she yells back.

"Come here for a second. I don't see it."

She sighs, disengaging from me. I swipe at her, trying to smack the soft curve of her ass, but she darts out of the way. The look she gives me is a warning. I sink back against the wall as she disappears into the front. Their voices rise and fall. Then, she appears with a glass of bourbon in her hand, a sober expression on her face.

"Let me bandage up your knuckles," she says, holding out the glass.

I take it. She kneels between my knees, which isn't doing me any favors with how badly I want her right now. Brothers walks in and sinks against the window, knees braced and foot on the nearby chair. He takes a sip from the bottle of Angel's Envy.

"Hate me any less, Jen?" he drawls.

"The verdict is out on that one."

"Has been for a while, huh?"

I jerk my head, downing the bourbon and setting the glass aside. It's a little bitter tonight. Della takes my hand and turns it over, studying the scabs from the other night. Fighting in the bar broke them open. Rivulets of dried blood streak my forearm.

She sighs. "You're tore up, Jensen."

"I'll be alright."

She cleans me up so carefully, I'm transfixed watching her, forgetting Brothers is even there. I'm thinking about tonight, wondering when I went from the strait-laced kid who just wanted a truck to the man who tore up the town with Brothers Boyd. It was probably a little bit after that day in the diner, when he had me thinking he wasn't the one who fucked me up.

That was the day I officially broke it off with Holly. Of course, we fucked a few more times when I was feeling weak, but I told her to her face that I wanted out, that I resented what she'd done.

She cried and said she loved me.

But I never said it back.

My throat is tight. The room is a little hotter than before, and my head feels light, like I'm rising into the air. Down below, Della wraps my knuckles in crisp white. It looks like she's a million miles away. Maybe I hit my head harder than I thought.

"You alright there?" Brothers drawls.

I look up and fall forward like a rock. She darts to her feet, arms out, but it's Brothers who catches me.

"Easy there," he says, laying me back in the chair.

I'm slipping into darkness. The hit must have been a hell of a lot worse, because I'm crumpling. My mouth won't move. I'm trying to tell them I think I need a hospital, but they're just watching me. Della has her hand over her mouth, tears streaming.

"I'm sorry," she whispers.

No, this doesn't make sense, but it doesn't matter, because my eyes are rolling back. I'm sinking into darkness as warm and soft as a summer's day back home.

CHAPTER TWENTY-NINE

DELLA

Brothers calls Angus to carry Jensen out in a fireman's lift to his SUV parked on the curb. Guilt is a sharp knife in my ribs. I can't stop crying. Brothers offers me a tissue, which I take, but I shoot daggers at him when he touches my arm.

"You're so fucking evil," I snap, wiping my nose.

"You are the umpteenth woman to tell me that," he says, pointing to the door. I go, stepping onto the porch. He locks up and starts striding across the street.

"I'm riding with Jensen in the SUV," I say.

He stops in the middle of the road. It seems like he wants to argue, but then he shakes his head, walking back over. I scramble down the curb as he pulls open the side door. Jensen is draped in the back seat, face slack. I slide into the opposite bench, and Brothers gets in beside me. The ceiling is short, and he's a little hunched.

He taps the roof. The engine purrs, and we're heading up the road.

"I don't want to leave him until I have to," I whisper.

He stretches his legs out, releasing a sigh.

"You know, when I met you, I knew you two would hit it off," he says. "I just didn't realize how hard you'd fall."

I glare. "Don't try to take credit for this."

He shrugs. "You wouldn't have met him otherwise."

Silence while I wipe my nose with the damp, crumpled tissue. "Why did you think that?" I whisper.

"You're two sides of the same coin," he says. "Never met two people more alike."

"Maybe that's a bad thing."

"I don't believe in the notion of opposites attracting."

"What about you and Kayleigh?" I point out. "You're nothing like her. Honestly, I have no idea why she's going out with you in the first place. What do you even talk about?"

He clears his throat. "We're not going out."

"You break up?"

"No," he says firmly. "We don't talk about anything because we're just fucking. It's not serious. Don't need to have anything in common."

"How old are you?" I glare sideways. "Aren't you, like, fifty?"

"You're full of invasive questions tonight."

I sniff, getting some satisfaction out of making him uncomfortable after everything he put me through. "Well, Kayleigh's too young for you."

He turns his eyes to the window, street lamps flickering in them.

"You hurt, Della," he says softly. "I'm sorry about that."

Neither of us speak. He's right—I hurt, and I'm lashing out because he's right there to take it. I don't know how to respond. My words are all worn out tonight. Everything aches, but my heart most of all. Sliding back against the seat, I close my eyes and count the twists and turns until he shakes my elbow.

"We're home," he says.

I peel open my lids. The Boyd mansion is a blur in my tired eyes.

"How much time do I have to get ready?" I whisper.

"Not much."

He gets out of the car and goes straight like an arrow to the porch. His driver gets out to unbuckle Jensen. I tear my eyes away from his slack face, riddled with guilt. I can't help but notice this is the most relaxed I've seen him since Montana.

"Della," Brothers calls.

I touch Jensen's limp hand on the way out and hurry to where Brothers stands on the porch. There's something bothering him, that's obvious. Maybe he feels guilty too, but I keep my mouth shut as he leads the way inside.

"Go upstairs, three doors on the right," he says. "When you're done, come down. I'm going to get Jensen into bed to sleep off the drugs."

He doesn't wait for a response. I stare after him as he disappears back outside. Then, I'm alone, heart pounding. It reminds me of the first night Kayleigh brought me to see him. That was in a hotel, at the bar in the private lounge. I'd felt so guilty, so evil, meeting with a man to discuss my husband's downfall. I'd have felt better about it if we were having an affair.

My feet ache as I climb the stairs. The third bedroom on the right is open. I slip inside and stop short.

There's a dress laid over the bed, along with an open case of jewelry. I move close, my heart pumping faster than a moment ago. It's starting to really sink in that I have to see Leland tonight. I'll sit down opposite the man who did that to me, who robbed me of my future, who fucked me up so badly, I can't think of the word for what he did that night. I can't crack, or I don't get to see my son again.

It's so unfair.

Yet, it is.

But I am strong enough to carry this.

Blinking back tears, I shut the door and go to the adjoining bathroom to shower. There's makeup, soap, and perfume on the sink. He must have let his staff know I was coming tonight, because everything I need is laid out, waiting for me, like they're preparing to sacrifice me on the Caudills' altar.

Ignoring the shiver running down my spine, I try not to think about that as I clean up. The dress is sparkling beige, so tight, I have to wriggle to get into it, with matching shoes. Everything was selected with Leland's eye in mind, from the cloth that clings to my curves to the diamonds that match my former engagement ring.

Nothing gets by Brothers Boyd.

I clip downstairs in my towering heels. After being on the road, in Montana, and in the gorge, it's surreal being dressed up. It's like none of it happened, like Jensen and his backwoods pretty face was nothing but wishful thinking.

Brothers is standing in the hall, on his phone. His eyes glint as he hears my step, and his face softens the closer I get.

"Is this alright?" I ask stiffly.

He puts his hands on my shoulders as that achingly familiar paternal expression crosses his face.

"You're a brave woman, Della," he says quietly.

My throat tightens. I clear it. "I want my son back."

"You might have to fight very hard."

I lift my chin.

"I know," I say. "And I will."

He puts me in a car waiting in the driveway. The driver is to take me into the city, to the speakeasy where Leland always goes for business on Friday nights. We pull out onto the road and head into the city in the dark.

There's a partition between me and the driver, so I'm all alone with my thoughts. They get away from me, going to the one thing I've never let them entertain. What happens if I get everything I want? Could I really get Landis and Jensen? Could we be the family I'm too scared to even dream of?

I close my eyes, jostling with every turn.

He's guarded, a little bitter, but beneath his rough exterior, he's got so much heart. I think I'd be proud if Landis grew up to be like Jensen. Of course, I'm getting ahead of myself. We've never even spoken of what our lives would look like after all this is done.

But I still close my eyes and dream of it all the way there.

CHAPTER THIRTY

JENSEN

We're sparring in the back yard. It's a hot day, and all the work is done until we run a shipment this evening. Brothers is in his casual clothes, fists up, wavering before my vision. I've been working for him for only two weeks, but in that time, a lot has changed. He's taken over, doing all the things nobody ever did for me. Today, we got into a discussion about who would win if we fought. I admitted I'd never fought outside the schoolyard. He says he's going to teach me how to stand, how to hold my fists.

We're sparring under the oak tree behind the house. He says I'm way better than he expected. That feels good to hear, but it doesn't stop him from flipping me onto my back, all the air from my lungs leaving me as I hit the cracked dirt.

He's crouching, asking me if I'm okay. He says, sorry, should have gone a little easier on you there, Jen.

I say, no, let's go again.

"Jen."

My eyes snap open. Overhead is a sickeningly familiar ceiling. I've laid in this bed and looked up at it a hundred times before. My body seizes, and I bolt upright, scrambling back against the headboard.

My things are piled beside the bed. My belt, my gun. Otherwise, I'm still dressed.

"You're alright."

My eyes focus, sticky. He's standing in the window, in his pants and undershirt, suspenders hanging loose. It must be early for him not to be properly dressed yet.

"Della," I whisper. "Where is she?"

He turns, mouth thin. "She went to Leland."

The bottom falls from my stomach. "No, no. When did she go?"

"As soon as you were out."

I push back the covers, swaying. "You drugged me."

"*We* drugged you."

"Why?" My chest hurts so fucking bad.

He gives me a soft stare. "Because she wants her son back. The only way I can do that is to put her on the inside. Then, we draw Leland out and give her a chance to steal him away."

"She's not safe," I breathe.

"He won't hurt her."

"How do you know that?" My voice rises.

"Because he loves her," Brothers says, voice going hard, the way it does when he's tired of explaining himself.

"That won't protect her," I snap back.

The air crackles. I'm so angry at him, I don't trust myself not to put a bullet in his head. He's gone and done it again—playing with my life to suit himself.

"Della's a big girl," he says. "She knows what she's doing. You need to respect that."

"Della is a fucking victim."

I'm on my feet, steady, circling the bed. He takes a step closer, and everything snaps. Maybe it's the memory of him teaching me to fight, or the fact that last night, it almost felt like old times again. But God, I am so sick of him.

Quick as a flash, I reach over the bed and grab my gun, training it on him.

"Jen—"

"No, you shut your fucking mouth," I whisper.

His palms go up. Sweat etches down the side of his lean face. I'm so tempted to pull the trigger, my hand is shaking. But I can't, not while Della is behind enemy lines. That doesn't stop me from playing with the idea, fantasizing about what it would feel like to erase him from my life.

"Jen—"

"No," I spit. "You don't get to talk right now. You listen."

He nods, swallowing.

"You might not have meant to, but you ruined my life," I say. "You fucked me up, fucked me over. And now you dragged me back here, and for what? For *what*?"

He flicks the inside of his cheek. "I wanted a chance."

"For what?"

His shoulders heave, sinking. The room is unbearably hot. We're both sweating hard.

"It was supposed to be us, Jen," he says finally. "You're my blood."

My jaw grits so hard it hurts.

"You are not my father," I say. "Not my brother. Not my friend. You brought me back here to use me to take out your enemies. I am a useful idiot to you."

His eyes glitter. "I didn't bring you home to use you," he says. "I want you back, Jen. Come home, take this city with me."

There's a clock ticking somewhere. The sound drags me back, to my mother's trailer, to the motel in Harlan. It's making it hard to think.

"You were meant for this," he says.

I wasn't, though. It was the path I was spit out onto, a boy with nothing but the need to fill his stomach, to feel love. That path led me west. It made me into a calloused man, and that man doesn't have it in him to forgive anymore.

In my head, we're standing in the summer heat, beneath the oak tree. I toss the gun back onto the bed. He takes a step closer. I surge, and this time, when I swing my fists, I'm better than him.

He takes it, head whipping to the side. Blood spreads over his cheekbone. Then, instinct kicks in, and he's hitting back. My lower spine collides with the edge of the bed. My already-bruised body sears. I vault to my feet just as he comes at me, catching me in the chest. Fuck, he's still strong.

I turn on him, vision red.

His hands rise in surrender, palms out.

"Stop, Jen. Stop it." He clears his throat, jaw twitching as blood leaks from it. "She went of her own accord. I just facilitated it."

"Of course, she went," I breathe. "He's got her son."

"What was your plan? Tell me how you were going to get her son back from Leland. Because you can admit it—you have no cards."

"I was going to go in there and take the kid," I say. "And run."

It sounds pretty stupid now that I'm saying it out loud, but I've done this kind of thing out west before, and it worked. But that was with the Sovereign Mountain boys, with Deacon Ryder, sometimes Jack Russell. Here, I'm at a disadvantage. But I can shoot a quarter in the dark, and I can fight like hell in the pit. I could have done it. It just would have taken some figuring out.

The anger drains out of me. Being fucked over by him is a broken record at this point. That's all he's ever done.

"Look at me," he says.

I drag my eyes up. He's shining with sweat, scuffed up.

"You killed Pat Pretty," he says. "Not me. I didn't drive you west. I would have kept you safe."

"I would never have been in that trailer if it weren't for you."

"And you'd never have been here if it weren't for a couple thousand other things," he drawls. "Time to face up, Jen. You can't keep blaming me for what happened to Cherry."

My chest is tight and cold. "So who's fault is it?" I whisper.

"Matthew and Leland Caudill. They killed your family. They killed my brother."

"So, what? So I help you take them out, you get all the Lexington territory unopposed," I snap, taking a step closer. "You get everything you wanted, and I just have to help you, or I lose Della?"

His eyes glint. "Not everything I wanted."

The air is heavy with the last twenty years of my life. I'm hollow, like the empty place left by the man who fathered me and scarred by the man who stepped into that space but failed to fill it.

"What do you want from me?" I manage.

He lifts his hand. "Just for you to know...I never meant to hurt you. Everything I told you in the diner was the truth."

My eyes sting. Maybe it's sweat getting in my eyes.

"So you want me back because Jem's gone?" I spit. "Swap out one warm body for another, huh?"

His face stays the same, but his tongue flicks the inside of his cheek. The light goes out in his eyes, and he's behind walls again. Finally, he clears his throat.

"I promised Della I'd get her son back," he says. "I will, with or without your help."

"You know I'll help you," I spit before I can bite it back. "I don't have a choice, not when it comes..."

I falter. He doesn't have to ask what the next words were—we both know. I have no choice when it comes to Della. For the second time, he made me fall for a woman without my consent. It was so easy this time, sweet and natural. He must have known the moment he laid eyes on her what she would do to me. Nobody knows my weaknesses better than the man who was supposed to heal me and hurt me instead.

He's always known me better than I know myself.

"I want a promise," I say.

He jerks his head.

"I help you take down the Caudills, get Della back," I say, "and you never speak to me again. I never want to see your face after this is done. I'm not your victim...and I'm not your fucking son."

CHAPTER THIRTY-ONE

DELLA

The back of the chair digs into my spine. The lights of the speakeasy blur. I'm not crying, but my eyes hurt. If I wasn't all done up, I'd rub them, but I can't. I have to look the way he always wanted me to—like a doll without a voice.

I check the clock over the bar. Brothers said Leland would be here by eleven, which means I have ten minutes.

My heart beats so hard. I'm sick to my stomach. The room spins and wavers.

He never hit me. He never had to. I understand exactly what he's capable of. He laces it through his words, through his touch, through the unused condom in the back of my mind.

I'm going to have to put on the performance of my life.

The waiter appears. I order a martini, because he liked ordering those for me even though I've never loved them. The door opens. Two women and a man walk through and sit at the bar. They're beautiful, dressed in elegant club clothes. The women sit with their backs curved, shoulders back, legs crossed over the other so their feet can be seen in glittering heels. I correct my posture, trying to look more like them. They have confidence. I have none when it comes to facing Leland.

I take a sip of my martini, hand shaking.

The door opens again. My heart stops, vodka still on my tongue. The salty taste of olive trickles down my throat. Leland walks in, dressed in his good pants and a quarter zip. He's exactly how I left him, down to the bored stare and cut jawline. I saw that face up close so many times, right before shutting my eyes to block him out.

He is so handsome, so charming.

And yet, there's nothing emanating from him.

After letting Jensen touch me, fill me with his warmth, I understand why Leland is so unnerving. He's got no energy, no mind of his own. Nothing but a set of rules. An expensive suit. A moral code that never made any sense to me. A last name he carries around like it's pure gold. The paintings of his ancestors on the wall of his mansion mean more to him than anything.

He is a vacuum, a black hole at the center of my life, sucking me in, draining the warmth from me.

I dig at my thumbnail. He glances over, looks away, then reels back to stare as he realizes who I am. His lips part, eyes widening. I'm beautiful, Brothers made sure of that, but more specifically, I am beautiful in the way Leland likes.

Neither of us move.

I have to pull it together. I will not let my son be raised as a Caudill. Taking an even breath, I give him a soft look across the table, across the room. He walks over like he's in a dream and sinks down opposite me. I dip my head like I'm ashamed.

"Della," he says.

I look up, and there it is—a glimmer of triumph. My stomach roils, but I push it back.

"Leland," I whisper.

"What are you doing here?" His voice is stiff.

I look up, and I don't have to try to make tears fall. "I'm so sorry," I manage. "You were right. I didn't want to leave. I don't know why I did in the first place."

He's staring, his guard up. "Is this you trying to come back?"

God, I want to vomit at the smugness. He's trying to conceal it, but I know him well enough to read it behind his mask. I sniff, taking the napkin and dabbing my face before nodding.

"Yes," I say.

There's a long silence.

"How can I ever trust you?" he says finally.

In a burst of courage, I hold my hand out for him to take, palm up. He looks down at it, at my long nails done the way he likes.

"I'll do whatever it takes," I say.

He doesn't speak. The clock over the bar keeps etching on. Finally, he clears his throat and spreads his knees, leaning back.

"You embarrassed me, Della," he says in that refined Southern drawl. "Everyone knows my wife left me and our son."

Rage bubbles. I never left my son. No, he was taken from me, a bartering chip in the fallout of our marriage. Taking a beat, I force myself to stay tearfully penitent.

"I know," I whisper. "And I'm so sorry. I'll make up for it."

He clears his throat and lifts a hand to the bartender. I sit in silence, hands folded, while he gets a drink. It's the same old, a whiskey from the top shelf, neat. When we're alone again, he drags his empty stare back to me. This time, he lets himself look me over.

"It's my Achilles Heel that you have a body like that," he says. "It always has been."

I can't help but think about how Jensen wants my body as well, but never makes me feel used the way those words do. We fell into bed together the night we met. And yet, I never felt surface-deep. How does he do that?

I don't answer Leland. He doesn't want one.

The clock ticks. A few more customers come in and sit at the bar. Leland releases a breath.

"We have a lot to talk about," he says finally.

That's when I know I'm in. He's folding faster than he did the first day we met at the diner, when his eyes followed every step I took. He's the man who ruined my life, but I still feel a twinge of guilt.

Deep down, I think...I hate to admit it, but I think Leland might love me.

His version of love is brittle, self-centered, but it exists.

"Please take me home," I whisper.

He stands abruptly, holding out his hand. I drain my glass, swallowing the last of my pride with it, and let him guide me around the table. He doesn't try to kiss me. I didn't think he would, not with the way we left things, but it's still an enormous relief. He pays the bill with his hand on my waist. It's possessive but so cold. I might know his weakness, but I'll have to move carefully to gain a fraction of his trust back.

We step out onto the street together. His car loiters at the curb. His driver appears, and I see the shock on his face for a second before it's gone. He keeps a professional mask as Leland guides me into the back seat, settling in beside me and tapping the roof.

We drive but don't speak.

I'm aware he's there. How could I forget? But nothing is stronger than the realization he's taking me back to the Caudill Mansion. Back to my son, the only person I've fully loved before Jensen. It hasn't been that long, by calendar days, but every one of those days has felt like an eternity.

I bite the inside of my mouth and count the seconds. We're turning onto the long driveway to the mansion when Leland clears his throat.

"There are conditions to this," he says finally.

"I understand," I whisper.

"I can't trust you," he says. "I have to be able to trust people on the inside. So, you'll have to be monitored. No phone, no internet access, and you may not leave the house without me."

Stomach aching, I nod.

We pull up outside the door. It's like walking to the gates of hell but knowing the person I love the most is on the other side—confusing, terrifying, heartbreaking. The driver gets out, and there's a second when we're totally alone. Leland shifts, taking me by the jaw to turn my face up. In the half shadow, he sends a chill down my spine.

"You will do as you're told, or you'll never see Landis again," he says.

Anger floods my veins, reaching my eyes. I hate how he sees our son as his, not ours. I gave up my future, carried Landis in my body for nine months, almost died giving birth to him, and yet, he's just a Caudill to Leland.

"I'd better not see that look again," Leland says.

"What look?" I whisper, blinking.

He releases my face as the door opens and he gets out. My heels are so high, I can't scramble out on my own. He has to take me by the waist and lift me to my feet. We're close, body heat tingling.

"Defiance," he says quietly.

I shake my head.

He frowns. "You answer when you're spoken to."

My pride bubbles up, and I swallow it down. "No, sir."

He's looking at me with intensity. I'm eighteen years old, standing in my kitchen, where he tells me I don't have a choice about marrying him. I caved, I crumbled in his hands, but not this time.

"I won't make trouble," I say.

His mouth thins. "This is going to be a long conversation," he says. "For tonight, go see Landis."

Up until now, I kept telling myself I wouldn't see Landis until tomorrow, so I didn't lose control. But the minute he says that, tears start streaming. I'm through the front door, heels clacking on the staircase and down the hall. Landis' room is three doors down from the room I used to share with Leland. There's a strip of blue glowing beneath the door from his nightlight.

I turn the knob. Inside, everything is the same. A dinosaur print bed set Kayleigh gave him for Christmas. A matching lamp I bought him for his birthday. A little mound under the covers.

My body is floating, free falling. Somehow, I'm across the room, sinking onto the bed. I peel back the covers, and he stirs, eyelids flickering.

"Mommy?"

My heart breaks into a thousand pieces. He's confused. Then, he focuses on me and his face changes to shock. My arms are out. He's falling into them, and I push my face into his dark hair, inhaling. My pulse races almost as fast as the tears falling from my chin.

He's here. I can feel his chubby arms wrapped around my neck. He smells like toddler shampoo and Landis, the best smell in the entire world.

"Mommy, where did you go?" he asks, struggling to pull back.

I release him, brushing his hair from his eyes. "I just had to take a trip, but I'm back. I won't leave again. I promise, I won't."

He frowns. "Daddy said you went home."

"It's hard to explain," I manage. "But I'm home. Tomorrow, I'll spend the whole day with you. I won't leave you again, I promise."

The door creaks. I glance over and see the outline of Leland in the doorway. He's got his hands in his pockets, leaning on the wall.

"You say goodnight to your mother," he says. "We'll eat breakfast together in the morning."

"But I want Mommy to sleep with me," says Landis.

Leland shakes his head. "No, not tonight."

My heart hurts so badly, I'll be up all night cleaning the porcelain teacup shards of it and piecing them together. Landis stares at his father, and a strong crease appears between his brows. I'm taken aback. That face...that's my daddy's bullish expression, the one he wore every day until he died. Maybe there's more Cooley in my baby than I realized.

"Say goodnight," says Leland.

There's the old Leland, brisk, authoritative, and used to being obeyed. I take Landis' face in my hands to kiss his forehead, again and again. His arms wrap around my neck, and I bury my face in his hair. He feels like pure sunshine, like a morning in the house I grew up in. When he pulls back, I kiss him again, laying him back and tucking him in.

"I'll be here the minute you open your eyes," I say. "I promise."

His eyes are heavy. A little smile touches his lips.

"Goodnight, Mommy," he whispers.

The door creaks. I press one last kiss to his forehead, even though I know I could never hug and kiss him enough times to make up for everything. Then, I go out into the hall and let Leland shut the door. He's dead silent, watching me from the corner of his eye. This is the part I'm scared of, when we figure out what happens between us at night.

"Leland," I say, "I—"

"I think it's better if you sleep in the guest room," he says stiffly.

Relief washes over me, and I dip my head. "That's fine."

There's a step below us, and I look over the railing to see Georgie. She comes upstairs with a stack of sheets in her arms. Our eyes meet. She dips her head and skirts around us, going to the guest room down the hall. I'm going to talk to her the second I can get away from Leland. I have a feeling that's going to take longer than I imagined.

He stands in the doorway as Georgie gets me settled in. She leaves, hands folded over her stomach. Then, it's just him and me. He clears his throat, hand on the doorknob.

"Was there anyone else?" he says finally.

"What?"

His eyes flash. "Did you fuck anyone after you left?"

A dozen images tumble through my head, but the one my brain settles on is the first night Jensen fucked me in the loft. Frantic hands, hips rising and falling, blood on my fingers, pain stinging up my arm. The heat—Lord, he's pure hellfire, burning me up for the sin of wanting him so bad.

I shake my head. Leland's shoulders sink.

"No," I whisper. "There's only been you."

CHAPTER THIRTY-TWO

JENSEN

Brothers leaves after dinner, taking two of his men. They're lean, versatile types, like me. He's got a particular kind of man he recruits to his team, the kind that fights hard and works well without rules. I have nothing to do but go to bed, so I return to my old room upstairs. This is what I imagine coming home as an adult to feel like. Everything is the same, even the sheets on the four poster bed.

I pour a bourbon and sink against the headboard.

I'm wishing I was back in Montana, where my past was locked behind bulletproof glass. But more than that, I wish Della was here, safe in my arms.

The moon is a pale sliver over the magnolia trees outside. It's getting late. I empty my glass and set it aside, sliding to my back, but I can't sleep. There are too many memories in this house. I toss and turn until almost three in the morning. People come and go, then things settle to silence.

I get up, pulling on a pair of sweats. Brothers had a maid leave me some clothes. Of course, they all fit perfectly. Then, I leave the room and wander like a ghost down the empty hallway. Downstairs, the kitchen is shut down. The dining room feels like a graveyard, chairs like markers in a row.

I lean my temple against the doorway.

I lost my innocence in this house at the hands of people older and more capable. Maybe that's why it's important to me that Della gets her boy back. I've never seen him, I might never put eyes on him, but he reminds me of myself.

I push off the doorway and circle around to the back staircase. There's a faint sound from the door on the opposite side. It's dark down there, but it leads up and around to the second floor. Curious, I move silently down past the open door. There's a faint glow coming from inside. Tucked away in the shadows, I pause and look through the gap.

It's Brothers' office, I knew that. Half the desk is visible. Brothers sits on the edge, disheveled. The whole front of his Sunday shirt hangs open. He's talking quietly, a glass in his fingers. There's a disturbance, like someone getting up from a couch, and then the sound of heels on the floor. A woman in lingerie walks into view and goes to stand between his knees.

She says something, touching his jaw. He smiles and puts his hand on her waist, absently playing with her garter belt.

I'm taken aback by the way he's gazing up at her. Is Brothers Boyd...human? There's a softness to his face that only deepens when she leans in and kisses him, blocking my view with her dark curtain of hair.

That's...Kayleigh Caudill.

If I bet on what kind of woman would have Brothers Boyd wrapped around her little finger, this one wouldn't even make the list.

She's everything I thought he resented. Lexington bourgeoisie—young, spray tanned, luxurious brown hair falling to the middle of her back, neon pink nails holding a crystal glass. Her lean body is curvy with a little waist, highlighted in full lingerie the same shade as her nails. I think I can see the Victoria's Secret emblem in rhinestones right above her ass.

I shouldn't be here, and yet, I can't move.

My brain kicks into overdrive. Brothers said he wanted to topple the Caudill empire and take their territory a long time ago, but is it possible there's something personal in this for him as well? I know he'd never admit to having feelings, but I'm not sure he has to say it out loud.

I'm looking at it.

She pulls back, and he's gazing up at her like she hung the damn moon and stars. He says something, and she laughs, hair rippling. They both set their glasses aside. Then, she sinks to her knees between his boots. Her neon nails dig into the clasp of his leather belt.

That's my cue to get the fuck out. I've already been scarred by Brothers enough. I don't need to see him get blown.

Soundlessly, I go back upstairs and lie down. I'm pretending I can't sleep because everything I just saw puts Brothers in a new light, a more human one. But, deep down, I'm staring up at the ceiling and wishing Della was back in my bed where she belongs.

My eyes burn when I peel myself out of bed around six. The spacious bathroom got an update. Everything is sleek gray, and it takes me several minutes of cursing to get the shower on. The dresser is stocked with clothes, the kind I've always worn. I pull on a clean t-shirt, work pants, and boots. He even bought my favorite brand with the thick soles, good for Montana winters.

I go downstairs. The house is empty, save for the dining room. There's a security guard on the porch. Brothers sits at the head of the table, the Lexington Herald in his hand. He's got the same breakfast he's always eaten laid out—three strips of steak and a peeled orange.

I sink down. He looks up, offering a mild smile.

"How'd you sleep, Jen?"

"I didn't." I take a plate from the stack and fill it. A woman in a kitchen uniform appears and silently pours my coffee cup. "You probably didn't get much rest either."

His brow draws together. "How's that?"

"I came down to the kitchen and walked past your office on the way back up," I say, not giving a shit if I offend him anymore. "How's it feel, inviting a Caudill into your home?"

His eyes narrow, and he leans back. "You already knew about Kayleigh."

"You're a sick fuck," I say quietly.

"Oh?"

"You know what Leland will do to her if he finds out."

"She knows the risks." He flicks his cheek with his tongue.

"Same way I did?" I say. "Same way Holly did?"

An image of Holly on my grandmother's kitchen floor pierces my mind. Dead eyes open, blood matting the hair she used to brush out in the mirror before wrapping it carefully in curlers. It felt like blasphemy to see all her beautiful hair ruined. I hope the funeral home fixed it for her before they put her in the dirt.

He sighs, steepling his fingers. "You have to put the bitter pill of what I did to you between your teeth and swallow it," he says finally.

He's right. There's no working together if I can't handle my resentment.

"I want to talk to Kayleigh," I say. "She's my only link to Della."

I half expect him to say no, but he nods. "Fine. I'm seeing her for lunch today. You can come."

"Alright," I say. "Where are we going?"

"Down to the lake country," he says. "Kayleigh's particular. She likes this little place down there. Serves the wine she's partial to."

"She says jump and you say how high?"

He shakes his head, a flicker of exasperation in his eyes. "If I'm being honest, she's got me by the balls."

"Good," I say. "I hope it hurts."

He sighs, getting up. "I've got business. We leave at eleven."

I watch him go, gazing out the window at the green fields outside. It's a nice day, the sky bright blue and the bluegrass swaying. After everything, I need a second to breathe, outside of this house. I fetch my cigarettes from upstairs and leave through the side door, down the winding path beside the barn. The horses are out, glimmering chestnut in the sun. I lean on the fence, watching them absently.

I miss her. She's been gone a day, and I miss her so much, it hurts.

We travel almost two hours from the city for lunch. Brothers is quiet most of the way. I'm glad for it. After yesterday and the things I said, I know he's sore and pretending he's not. When we pull up and the windows roll down, I can see we're in a small town with shops lining the main street. Brothers gets out, buttoning his jacket. He's in a gray suit. I'm in a button down and good pants.

He leads the way through the door of a restaurant with darkened windows. Inside, everything is sleek black and gold, more opulent than I'd expected. A woman in a well cut suit appears out of nowhere, smiling like she knows Brothers.

"Right this way, Mr. Boyd," she says.

Brothers starts asking her about her family as we move through the tables. We dip through a velvet curtain. The back room is sleek wood with high top bourbon barrel tables. In the corner on a bench seat in a booth sits the same woman from his office the other night—Kayleigh. She's dolled up in a tight rhinestone dress with a scooped neck that shows everything, hugging her body all the way to the ground.

Brothers crosses the room, leaning in to kiss her cheek. She gives him a smile that says she knows who she's got wrapped around her little finger. Up close, she's younger than I expected, maybe a few years older than Della.

"This Jensen?" she says, leaning forward.

I shake her hand. When I do, her gold rings and long pink nails dig into my fingers, then release. Brothers sinks down beside her, leaning back and crossing one knee over the other. His hand rests on her thigh.

I sit opposite. "Nice to meet you," I say. "Have you talked to Della?"

She purses her lips. "Leland's being a cunt. I asked if I could see her the night she came back and he said no."

Her accent is thicker than I expected. She draws out the word—*cuuuunt*—letting me know there's no love lost between them. Before

I can respond, the woman in the suit appears again to take our drink orders. Brothers and I get a bourbon, and Kayleigh gets something tall and gold with edible flowers overflowing down the side.

"Is there a way you can get to her?" Brothers asks.

She sighs. "I'm working on getting Leland to let me take her to the salon to get her hair did. He likes her to be all done up."

"Which salon?" I ask.

She has a sip of her drink. "No, I'm not having you show up. Leland will lose his shit if he thinks she's not serious about going back to him."

"Kayleigh's right," Brothers says.

"Thanks, baby," she says, nestling under his arm. "Give me a cigarette."

He takes one from his breast pocket and holds the lighter for her. She inhales, leaving a crescent pink moon on the white paper.

"If we're getting her out with Landis, it's got to be real subtle," she says.

I study her carefully, trying to figure her out. "Where are your people from?"

Her brows lift. "I'm a Caudill."

"No, you're something else too," I say.

"My mama's from Pike County. She married Matthew's little brother," she says, a flicker of something unreadable passing over her face. "She wasn't too different from Della. I got cousins with silver spoons in their mouths and cousins mining coal."

Everything makes a little more sense with that information. Still, my guard is up. She is a Caudill, after all.

"How long have you and Brothers been dating?" I ask.

She laughs, slapping his thigh. "Oh please, I'm not dating him," she drawls.

Brothers sighs. "She's my mistress."

"Shut up. More like you're my boy toy." She elbows him in the side, and he gives her a look that lets me know they're about to butt heads later. I wonder what that looks like, probably plates and insults flying a mile a minute.

"I'd like to draw Leland out," says Brothers.

"How's that?" I say.

She leans over and taps her cigarette out in his drink. His mouth thins, and he moves his arm from around her shoulders.

"Jesus, you quit acting up," he says.

She rolls her eyes subtly, but I can tell she loves egging him on. "Anyway, Brothers is going to see if they can meet in the gorge on Monday. Can't do Sunday like I wanted."

"Why?" I ask, realizing the answer as I do.

"Brothers doesn't do cage fighting on Sundays," she says. "That's the Lord's Day."

"Oh, obviously," I say. "How could I forget?"

"Still got a little sass to you," Brothers drawls.

"Hush and go get yourself a new drink, honey," she says. "This is my plan. You're just here to look pretty."

His arm moves, and she jumps like he pinched her under the table. I look between them, people as different as night and day, and hope I threw my lot in with the right ones.

"Why in the gorge?" I ask.

Brothers sighs, tongue flicking the inside of his cheek. "Because the Caudills still run the pit fights in the gorge. That's the only place to get him face to face and make sure he's staying put."

"Then I'm gonna go in and grab Della and Landis," Kayleigh says.

"Is it...that simple?" I press.

Brothers shrugs. "Yes and no. The gorge is the place where he's least protected because it's remote, so he brings all his men. That leaves the house relatively unguarded. At least, the most unguarded it'll ever be."

I think it over. "Alright. So how are we getting him there?"

"I propose a cage fight," says Brothers. "One of my men, one of his."

"Have you done that before?"

"Sometimes."

They're both sitting there, looking like this is a foolproof plan. "So...what do you do? Send him a text?" I ask.

"No," Brothers says. "I'll send him an email."

Kayleigh giggles. "Isn't he funny?"

I release a slow sigh. There's something in my face that sobers them both. Brothers leans forward, pushing his ruined drink aside. "We send a paper invitation for the fight," he says. "It's all sport, but serious. If he accepts, he'll send back the name of his fighter. I accept. We go about it like gentlemen."

I'm quiet.

"What do you say?" Kayleigh asks.

I turn my eyes on her. "Can you get Della out?"

She takes a second to answer. "I'll have to iron out the details, but I'm confident I can get her as far as Byway. After that, you have to be there to pick her and Landis up."

"I will be," I say firmly.

Her face softens. "I always hoped she'd end up with someone like you."

"We're not really together, not yet."

"Oh, but you love her. I can tell."

I'm silent. Brothers watches me, face unreadable. I finish the last bit of bourbon and push my glass aside.

"I don't know her well enough to discuss that with others," I say.

"Oh, sure you do," she says, ignoring my discomfort. "You'd make a fine daddy for Landis. He needs a better example than Leland. Don't you think, honey?"

She turns to Brothers, who gives a minute nod. That's enough for her to smile and pat his thigh. "Brothers would make a good—"

Brothers' arm shoots around her head, and he clamps his hand over her mouth. "That's enough. We need to move on."

He releases her, and she gasps, jumping up. "Now I have to fix my lipstick. Fuck you," she spits.

He lets out a sigh from deep within. She grabs her purse and exits the room, disappearing through the curtain. He picks up his napkin and wipes the makeup off his hand.

"You've got your hands full," I say.

"Well, I don't like being bored," he says. "And I never am. Now, let's figure this shit out, huh, Jen?"

"Fine," I say. "Who's your fighter?"

CHAPTER THIRTY-THREE

DELLA

The morning after is the most awkward of my life. Leland must have sent for some clothes during the night, because there's a row of shopping bags outside my door. I pick through them until I find a simple blush dress that hits my knees with some matching heels. After my shower, I curl my hair the way Kayleigh does. Then, I push my shoulders back and practice a sweet little smile in the mirror.

I think I feel a brand new crack in my heart.

I go downstairs. In the huge dining room, Leland sits at the head of the table. Landis is in his booster seat. When he sees me, he bounces up, but Leland clears his throat in warning. The disappointment on Landis' little face as he sits back down breaks my heart, but Leland is staring at me with ice cold eyes. Head lowered, I sink into the chair at his side.

Kayleigh walks in, her brother, Paxton, at her side. I've got no use for Paxton. He's not any different than Leland, but the sight of Kayleigh lifts my spirits. I offer her a small smile. She checks if Leland's looking before winking at me as she sits down by Landis. He pats her arm absently, like he's used to reaching for her, and looks up at me.

I give him a little smile. He smiles back, but I can tell he's confused.

"It's good to have Della back," says Kayleigh.

Leland sinks back but doesn't answer as Georgie appears to fill our plates. Everyone is quiet, fake-pleasant expressions in place until she's gone.

"It is," says Leland after the door shuts.

Paxton has some coffee, turning narrowed eyes on me. "Any idea where you went off to, Della?"

I shrug. "I just went home," I say, voice rasping.

"To Harlan?" Paxton drawls. A smug smirk appears. "Funny. We checked out your trailer, and there wasn't anyone there."

Kayleigh rolls her eyes. "God, Paxton, you just get off on the sound of your own voice, don't you?"

"That's more than you get off," he snaps. "Haven't seen you go out for four damn years."

"So what?" She flips her voluminous ponytail. "At least I'm not a cheater like you two."

Leland's eyes snap up, flicking between his cousins, and my stomach sinks. I know he wasn't faithful to me during our marriage. It hurt me then, a lot, but I feel like it shouldn't hurt as much anymore. I do a quick check-in on how I'm feeling. It's not pain this time around, just dull disappointment.

"That's enough," Leland snaps.

I clear my throat. "I don't know if we should talk like that in front of Landis," I say softly.

Everyone goes quiet, turning to Landis. He's swinging his legs, eyes glued on me. I smile again, and he smiles back, but it's shy.

Kayleigh breaks the silence, reaching for the juice pitcher. "Here, honey. Let me get you something to drink," she says, filling his little cup. "I was thinking I'd go to the botanical gardens. You want to come, Della? We could take Landis."

"I told you, I don't want Della leaving the property," Leland says. "You may take Landis if you'd like."

Kayleigh gives him a cold stare while he's turned away. I shake my head ever so slightly, and she sinks back against the chair, like it's killing her to bite her tongue.

"That's fine," I say quickly, blinking back tears. "You both go without me."

"Daddy." Landis' voice cuts through the noise.

Leland turns to his son. "What?"

"I want Mommy to go," he says, scowling.

"She can't. She has to stay home," Leland says.

"What if you sent a couple of your guys along?" Kayleigh pushes.

"It might be good if you took him, Kayleigh. I think Leland and I could use the opportunity to talk," I say.

She shrugs. "Alright, that's fine."

She goes back to eating, unbothered. Kayleigh missed out on a career as an actress. When she was helping me get through my divorce, there was absolutely no indication she knew anything. I know she put on the performance of her life when I disappeared.

Paxton grunts and changes the subject. We eat while the men talk, droning on in the background. Then, I help Kayleigh get Landis ready to leave, and I'm allowed to stand in the doorway to wave them off. Paxton and Leland go into the study for a while. I sit in the living room, trying not to feel the empty space where Jensen sits in my mind.

I woke up last night and reached for him. I've never reached for a man at night before. I used to move away from Leland so he couldn't touch me.

The study door slams open. Paxton walks through the living room, towards the side door.

"Leland wants you," he says.

He gives me a disgusted look, lip curling, and goes outside. Heart thumping, I get up and walk out into the hall. Through the open door, I can see Leland at his desk. He glances up and beckons me with two fingers. My stomach is a cold lump. I hate that we're alone, nobody but Georgie in the house. She's as powerless against Leland as I am.

I slip inside.

"Shut the door," he says.

I obey. He leans back and releases a sigh of exaggerated patience. He's in a tan linen suit, his hair slicked back neatly. Leland has gotten more handsome with age. He also looks more and more like his late father every year. Someday, the same things will happen to Landis.

"What am I going to do with you?" he says finally.

Tucking my hands behind my back, I keep silent. He's not looking for an answer. He sighs again and points at the chair opposite his desk. I sit down, back straight, heels tucked. He opens a drawer and takes out a folder, tossing it down.

"My lawyer is reviewing the conditions of you returning," he says, like he's doing a real estate deal. "Obviously, if you want to stay, you will comply."

I nod. "Okay. May I ask what they are?"

"You will behave yourself, as befits your place in my family," he says. "You'll attend events, dinners, and so on, as I choose. At home, you'll run the household. Anyone you speak with, anything you consume, will be run by me first."

I stare. "Consume?"

He gives me a hard stare back. "Media. Somehow, you got it in your head to leave. It came from someone, something."

It takes everything I have to keep my face passive. He thinks I don't know about divorce on my own, that I got the idea to leave him from somebody else. Or, apparently, a book I wasn't supposed to be reading.

"You'll marry me with a prenuptial agreement that specifies all of this," he says. "And outlines next steps for our family."

The silence is deafening.

"Next steps?" I whisper.

He nods. "Landis is four. If we want more children, the time is coming up. I don't want them too far apart in age."

I'm too horrified to hide it. "I thought you were angry with me. Now you want me to get pregnant again?"

He stands, turning to the window. It's on the same side of the house that looks out over the magnolia grove. "I always knew you'd come back. Yes, I was angry, but I don't hate you."

That makes one of us. I hate him with everything I've got.

"I feel like we should maybe...do some marriage counseling first," I say.

"We can do that," he says. "But you will go right back to being my wife before anything else. Georgie is moving your things from the guest room into our suite. I expect things to return to the way they were with minimal interruption."

The memory of Jensen's arms around me in that little bed in the loft is so strong. The thought of letting Leland touch my body again makes me sick. I'm quiet for so long, Leland turns around. His brows knit, eyes staring at where I'm tearing the skin back from my nail. I drop my eyes to the floor.

"What?" he says.

"Um...there was something...something that really bothered me about when we got together," I whisper.

"You can look at me when we're talking."

I obey, remembering the night I got pregnant, how I laid there for a moment and waited for him to get up to throw the condom out. But he didn't, so I turned on the lamp. That's when I realized what he'd done.

I squeeze my eyes shut for a brief second. "I wish we'd done it right and waited."

"Waited?"

"Until we were married," I say, voice hoarse. "Mama raised me to wait until I was married. Our wedding night was nice, but I regret not waiting."

He's clearly caught off guard. "It's a bit late for that."

I give him my biggest, most innocent eyes. "Maybe we could wait this time around. Get married at the courthouse and have a proper wedding night. It would...make me feel better."

His jaw flickers, tightening.

"We could go on a real honeymoon this time," I say, offering him the sweet smile that usually pacifies him.

He's just looking at me. I go silent, unsure what he's thinking.

"Your shot still up to date?" he asks finally.

I nod. "I'm still good for about a month."

"Good. I want it in the contract you cannot get it again without my permission."

My stomach roils, but I can't show it. Instead, I tilt my chin and nod. "Just give me this one thing, and you can have everything else."

He thinks hard for a minute, then jerks his head in a sharp nod.

"Fine," he says.

"Thank you."

Carefully, I get to my feet, clearly indicating I'm looking to leave, but he doesn't dismiss me. Finally, I clear my throat.

"May I go?"

"Yes," he says. "You're not permitted to leave the house today. When Kayleigh returns, you'll take Landis to the nursery and watch him for the rest of the day. Both of you will meet me in the dining room for dinner."

I nod, turning to leave. I get as far as the door, my hand on the knob, when he taps the desk. Heart thumping, I glance over my shoulder.

"The least you could do is thank me for taking you back," he says coolly.

My mind goes blank with rage. All at once, I'm not in his office. I'm back in Montana, up in Jensen's bedroom. He's on me, inside me, the way he was that first night. He's loving me with his hands, his body, his words, and I'm realizing my body was never broken. All I needed was Jensen to make it come alive, to make me want more for myself.

When I was younger, I thought Leland robbed me of my home. But after meeting Jensen, I realize it's more complicated. He robbed me of a future that will never happen now.

I could have met Jensen back then, loved him of my own free will. I could have willingly had his baby and watched him become a father to my son. I could have been happy, innocent, untouched by fear. The ghost that haunts me is a single question: who could I have been if not for Leland?

Instead, Leland wrote my story, and it can never be unwritten. I have to live with that, every day, every night.

But he won't write the next chapter for me or my son.

That belongs to me.

I lift my chin and give him a passive smile, like I have nothing in my head.

"Thank you," I say.

CHAPTER THIRTY-FOUR

JENSEN

The day before we're supposed to meet in the gorge, I get up early and leave the mansion. It's so hot and dry, I'm surprised the Earth doesn't crack down the middle. The sky is clear, and it'll stay clear for a while, maybe through the month. Now is the dry season in Kentucky, when it's dangerous to flick a cigarette in the woods. I take the water bottle in the dash and split it open with a knife to tap mine out in.

The road to Byway isn't long, but I feel like years are adding on, not falling off, as I return to my stomping grounds. Everything is different now. Investors, real estate moguls, and anybody looking to snap up cheap land moved in since I left. Now, it feels like a suburb of the city.

That sits like a rock in my chest. I don't think a no-count boy like me could have made it in Byway nowadays. The price tags alone would have eaten me up.

I pull off the highway and drive through town to the neighborhood behind the salon. That's gone. I go by it slowly. The building is a chain donut store now. I turn and go out further, to where the land is flat and deep enough for willows to grow.

The house creeps up on me. I swing off the road and cut the engine.

There it is. Miss Holly's house. It's in good condition, paint fresh and lawn mown. Somebody lives here now. I get out of the truck, and the humidity hits me like a brick wall, soaking my t-shirt. It smells the same out here, a bit like the creek that runs through the neighborhood, like mulch and wet moss.

I stand by the truck, frozen in time.

Fuck. I didn't realize it would hurt this bad.

The front door opens, and a man of around forty in a baseball cap steps out. He lifts his hand, coming down the steps. I start up the walkway, but I can't get any further than halfway.

"You from the gas company?" he calls.

I shake my head. "I knew somebody who used to live in your house. Thought I'd stop by and see it."

He puts his hands on his hips. "Oh yeah? We bought it about eight years ago, so whoever they were, they must have up and left."

I shake my head. "She died."

His brows shoot up. "Oh. Not in this house?"

"No, not here," I say. "Is there still a trailer down the road, under the big willow tree?"

He's a bit shaken up, but he nods. "Yeah, it's condemned. Nobody's hauled it off the property, though. The willow tree got hit in a lightning storm about three years ago, but half of it's still there. How long has it been since you left?"

I sweep my gaze over the shutters, remembering when they were baby blue. The window to the right of the porch was Miss Holly's room, where we spent hours together that year.

"Nineteen years," I say. "My best friend lived here growing up. His mother was the one who passed."

That sounds a little more normal. The man's shoulders ease.

"Lot's changed," he says.

"Yeah, you could say that again," I say. "Listen, thanks, I appreciate it. I'll get moving now."

He nods, lifting a hand as I walk back to the truck. I'm not feeling anything at all as I get back on the road and drive the few blocks to the corner. The willow comes into view, and that man was right. It's split right down the middle. I pull off and get out, walking down the slope. Beyond the remaining half of the tree sits what's left of a trailer. There's a single piece of tape across the front door, rippling in the breeze.

My chest seizes, and I'm right back where I never wanted to be.

BEFORE

I'm so scared, I keep choking on my dry tongue. It's twelve-ten by the clock on my dash. I'm in my clothes from last night, flecked with blood. Brothers' voice, ordering me not to leave the mansion, is still ringing in my ears. But I went anyway. I burst through the gates and drove straight to Byway without slowing down for a minute.

My heart is pounding so hard, I might throw up.

I screech off the road and hit the brakes, leaving my door hanging open as I run across the yard. The front door is wide open. It's always a bad sign when a front door is hanging open like that. I catch a flash of the knob, splintered, as I surge through.

The hallway is empty. I reel, turning the corner into the kitchen, and stop short.

God, no.

My entire body feels like nothing, just the faint tingling sense of doom, like the whine of a bomb dropping.

Cherry sits in her chair, the landline belly up on the table. Her ash tray is cold. There's a cigarette beside it. It's the brand she used to smoke, Camels—the same as Holly smoked. Her head is back, hanging loosely. She's got a bullet hole in her temple, right by her dyed red hair.

I take a step, and my foot hits something.

No. No. No.

It's Kyle, on his belly. I drop down and push him on his side, but his blue eyes have departed. This is my first time seeing him since he went to Lexington. I never visited him after moving in with Brothers, the guilt too much. He grew a beard. It's not a great one, but it qualifies as the real thing. I'm staring into his eyes when I realize who comes next.

She's halfway in the hall, halfway in the kitchen, on her back, still in her white nightgown.

All her beautiful hair is matted in blood.

My stomach heaves as I rise, turning in circles, trying to soak in all the death around me. The air is thick, smelling like the inside of Pat Pretty's trailer, like fatal wounds. I stumble through the kitchen, up the hall, and burst out onto the porch. The yard is empty, but I see tire marks. Somebody left in a hurry.

Crossing it, I fall against the chicken wire fence and empty my stomach.

I did this.

I got involved in things I didn't understand, and now, everyone I ever loved has paid the price for it. The most obvious thing to do is run back to Brothers Boyd and let him do as he promised—protect me from the Caudills. The problem is...I can't remember, but I have this sick feeling Brothers has blood on his hands as well.

There's a vague memory of something happening, more like a feeling, of an argument. Then, something so horrifying, I've blocked it out.

I sink into the front seat of my truck. There's nobody here for me but the man who made me a criminal. Now, I never thought I would be the damn president, but I did think I'd at least have a nice little handyman business, a wife, some kids. I worked hard, and I had a fighting chance. But Brothers stepped in and took that.

He did that.

That sinks in for the first time.

And with it, comes a hell of a rage.

NOW

I blink, Cherry's trailer swimming into focus. After we fought and she threw me out, we didn't speak again. The next time I saw her was dead at her kitchen table. It's a small consolation she doesn't have to feel what I feel when I think about the past.

She was rough, a little mean, but she meant something to me. Cherry was my only blood left, a good woman.

I know now she was trying to protect me. She just did a shit job at it.

Kinda reminds me of somebody else.

My mind goes back to that day in the diner, when Brothers told me what Miss Holly was to him, that he didn't know anything about me when he took me on. For the first time, I see the entire situation in perspective. It's painful to admit it, but Brothers was more right than he was wrong.

He didn't do this to me. He was just there for the aftermath. Holly saw me, her son's best friend, a vulnerable kid on the cusp of adulthood. There were some weeks when I practically lived at her house, playing video games and loitering on the porch with Kyle. She knew her house was a haven, a place where I could get a meal and some stability.

And she still chose me.

She could have walked away, never told Brothers about me, never fucked me on that kitchen floor.

But she didn't.

All these years, I hated Brothers so badly, I wanted to hit him. Now, standing outside the remains of Cherry's trailer, I'm starting to realize Brothers Boyd was a convenient stand-in for my rage. Holly was a woman, and I was never going to show her my anger.

But Brothers, he can take that punch.

He has taken that punch.

I close my eyes, lifting my face up to the sky. All the times Brothers made a snarky remark about Holly being in my room filter through my mind. He was constantly telling me to break it off with her, even going so far as threatening to fire her once if I didn't.

My chest hurts.

In his own clumsy way, he was trying to protect me.

Brothers is guilty of getting me involved in the seedy underbelly of the city and what that did to Cherry and Kyle, but he never groomed me. I think, looking back, that it killed him to see he'd accidentally had a hand in what Holly did. Sometimes, I forget Brothers was pretty young too. All of fifteen years younger than Holly...and yet, he understood the situation better than I ever did.

My fist tightens on the truck keys.

Hindsight is twenty-twenty. I wish a lot of things had gone down differently. I wish I'd begged Cherry not to kick me out. I wish I'd told her everything the day Holly fucked me in the kitchen, and let her protect me.

But my head was so messed up, I couldn't see anything clearly.

That's what Holly did to me.

I can't go back and change what happened, but I can do something right here and now, for Della and her boy.

I leave the yard without going into the trailer. In the truck, I'm the emptiest inside I've been in a long time. I'm turning over the last nineteen years and how I've tried to fill it with everything to fix what happened. Sex, fighting, booze—the macho shit, as Jack would say. Then, Della walked in. She touched a nerve so deep, it gave me the courage to come back home and face my past.

It's going to give me the courage to save her. I'll make the Caudills pay for what they did to Cherry and Kyle and Della. I'll set myself free and end this cold war. When it's all done, I'll take her and Landis back to Montana, and I'll never look back.

If I want this woman, I have to fight our demons and win. Absently, I crack my knuckles.

Fighting.

That's something I can do.

CHAPTER THIRTY-FIVE

DELLA

Leland is busy all day Sunday and into Monday afternoon. I spend most of it in the house with Landis. I've never felt a mix of dread and relief like this before. Every few seconds, I hug Landis just to feel his little arms around me and remember he's there. Then, I remember I'm back in this house, and Leland's foreboding steps could appear at any minute.

It's torture.

I lay on the couch in the nursery and listen while Landis chatters. It hurts my heart how much he looks like his father, but it helps that he doesn't act anything like him. I think he's getting Kayleigh's personality. That puts a smile on my face.

I feed Landis in the nursery. Then, while Georgie is putting him to bed, I steal down to the kitchen to find some wine to help my nerves. There are a couple bottles leftover from dinner the night before. I pop a cork at the same moment as the back door clicks.

I whirl, heartbeat rising. "Oh God. It's just you," I breathe.

Kayleigh stands with her back against the door. She's in a matching dress and heels, minty fresh against her smooth, tanned skin. Her hair is loose, extensions cascading down her back.

Sometimes, I wish I could be as put together as Kayleigh, but we're just two different types.

"Get me a glass," she says, voice hushed. "And be quiet. Leland can't know we're talking alone."

I pour her one, and she sinks down at the table. I sit next to her.

"You alright?" I whisper.

She leans in. "Listen, we're getting you outta here tonight. With Landis."

A tingle of hope appears.

"What?"

She pops her gum. "Leland and the boys are all going out for a fight in the gorge tonight. I've got a driver we can trust to take us to Byway. Then, I'm sending you on to a safe place to meet with Jensen."

My heart leaps. This is the distraction, the way Brothers plans to roll the dice and give me a chance to get Landis out. "Really?" I whisper.

"Yeah, keep up," she says, having a sip of wine. "Yuck, this is awful. Anyway, all you need to do is be at the door, and I'll get you out."

I take a beat.

"I don't like you getting involved with this," I say finally.

Her face softens as she taps her nails on the table, thinking. Finally, she crosses her arms and lets out a little huff. "If I could make a break for it, I would. I'd like you and Landis to get out."

She doesn't need to explain why she can't leave. Kayleigh was born and bred into this life. She has no way to make it on her own. Eventually, if she doesn't make a change that could cost her her life, she'll be married off to some rich man who gambles at the same tables as Leland. She's wealthy, but she's not free.

"Are you sure?" I whisper.

She nods. "I've never been more sure."

Neither of us talk for a while. I wish I could have a glass of wine, but I'm worried about it making me sleepy. I need my wits tonight. Finally, Kayleigh pushes back the chair and stands.

"Be at the back door, off the kitchen, at eleven," she says, voice low. "Brothers has the driver waiting on the other side of the fence. We just have to cross the yard and get into the SUV before the security notices."

"And if they notice?"

"We'll be in the car and on the road before they can alert Leland," she says. "He'll be over an hour away, by the highway, into the gorge. Security can't get there faster than that."

"There's no signal," I say, remembering the time I joined Leland for the fight.

"Nope," she says.

Hope rises in my chest. "This could actually work."

She shakes back her hair. "Well, it was my idea, so yeah, it's a pretty good one."

We both laugh. Then, impulsively, I hug her hard. She melts into me, holding me close. Kayleigh always smells good, like sweet perfume, and she leaves traces of glitter from her body spray wherever she goes. I love it, it's like her signature. When she pulls back, her eyes are wet, makeup a little melted.

"Kayleigh," I whisper. "What happens to you if you get caught?"

"I won't," she says.

"Why don't you leave?" I burst out. "Go to Brothers after we're gone, get your happily ever after."

She sniffs, wiping her face. "It's not that simple."

"But why?"

"Because I'll just be trading one crime lord for another," she says. "Brothers is a good man, but he's a terrible person. What am I supposed to do with him if I got him? I'm twenty-five, he's...like fifty. Plus, if he lost the territory war, that would be it for me. I don't think Leland would let me live."

Everything she's saying makes sense, but the part of me that healed when I met Jensen wants to believe they could make it.

"I'm pretty well trapped," she whispers. "Unless I grow wings and fly away, this is my life."

There's a step in the front hallway. She coils back, listening. The footsteps come closer. She backs up to the side exit and pulls the door open.

"Eleven, right here," she says.

Then, she's gone. I grab her wine glass and put it in the dishwasher just as Leland strides in, still wearing his suit from his day at work. It takes everything not to recoil at his presence. It's dead air, a slippery slope down to hell. His eyes narrow as they settle on me, and a chill goes down my spine. Why does he look like he's plotting something?

"Hi," I whisper.

"By now, it's around town that you're home," he says, sitting on the edge of the table.

I just nod, unsure how to respond.

"I'd like you to eat with me, upstairs in our room," he says. "Dinner is at six. I have an engagement afterwards."

"Oh, I...um...that's fine," I stammer out.

He's got his hands folded, working his wedding band. He never took it off when I divorced him.

"I laid out a dress on the bed," he says. "Wear it."

Before I can respond, he gets up and walks out. I catch the faint sound of his phone ringing, and then the door to his office slams. My hands tingle, and I look down, realizing I'm clenching them so hard, they're red.

Steeling myself, I leave the kitchen and march straight upstairs. I've endured hundreds of terrible dinners with Leland. Tonight is no different. I just need to get through it and get him out the door.

Then, I never have to see him again.

Our old bedroom is open. I slip in and flick my eyes over the room. Everything is exactly the same, except my side table is empty. There's even that ugly family heirloom Leland valued so much hanging over the bed—a gold knife with the Caudill crest on the handle. I used to look up at that while he was fucking me from behind, hoping it would fall and skewer him. Then, I'd feel guilty for having thoughts that dark.

There's a blood red dress, short and tight, on the edge of the bed. My stomach sinks. That's not my color. I look terrible in red.

God, that makes me so angry, I could crack a tooth from how hard I'm gritting my jaw. I've told him that so many times. Red washes me out, I'd say. He'd narrow his eyes and let me know I should wear what he liked best.

Wrathfully, I tear off my clothes and pull on the little red dress, adjusting my breasts so they're spilling out over the top. There's gold jewelry on the bench at the end of the bed. I slip it on and go to the closet to find a pair of shoes. My things are still here, lined up in rows. I grab the closest pair of brown leather cowboy boots and step into them.

The door opens, then shuts. I back out of the closet to find someone came in and pulled the two person dining table out, setting it up before the fireplace before leaving. There are two silver covered dishes waiting. A bottle of wine. Two glasses.

I stare.

Now would have been the perfect opportunity to poison Leland, just slip it in his drink. Nobody would even have to show up for the fight tonight. I could grab Landis and run. But even after everything he's done, I know I don't have the heart to murder him.

No, I just want him gone. He can live out his miserable life knowing I took everything.

The door creaks open again. My pulse picks up like a racehorse in the final lap, and I sink down at the table without turning. The chair is hauntingly familiar; we used to eat in the bedroom a lot, back when Landis was little and still nursing and we didn't have guests.

He sinks down, filling my vision. I blink, eyes blurry.

"I thought you might like to join me tonight," he says.

He pours the wine, handing me a glass. I bring it to my lips but don't drink.

"Thank you," I say finally.

"I meant for my engagement later on," he says, lifting the covers off our food. "There's a fight in the gorge tonight. I want you to come, as my wife. Wear that dress."

No, that's not right—I have to stay here tonight.

Wordless, I shake my head. He pauses, leaning his elbows on the table to look at me head on.

"Are you saying no?" he asks softly.

I wet my lips. "I just... You know I didn't really like it last time."

He puts a slice of chicken in his mouth, chews, swallows, then pauses. "You know, I actually don't give a fuck if you like it or not. You came back, and we agreed you would be a good wife. That includes attending any and all events I need you to."

"I'm just so tired—" I burst out.

He slices through the chicken on his plate. "Della, you will go with me tonight."

"Leland—"

He sets his utensils down. "This is not a fucking democracy."

His harsh voice cuts through the room, letting me know this conversation is over. I look down at my food, white sauce pooled over chicken and steamed asparagus. It's good, but it's not the kind of food I crave. I close my eyes, willing the tears not to fall.

Behind my eyelids, I see Jensen standing on the porch with a handkerchief full of crawfish. We stood at the sink, eating it and the gas station rice out of chipped bowls. It was the best food I'd ever had.

A tear escapes.

It isn't about the food. It never was. It was about all the life cooked into it, about having a man like Jensen who loves me, who makes every minute of my life feel like it's worth more than gold.

"Stop crying," he says.

Hastily, I wipe the tear away and nod. He goes back to eating, not caring that I'm silent. He's used to it. Jensen would have noticed, because all I did was talk his ear off.

We finish our food in silence. I sit miserably at the table while he gets ready. Then, I let him push me numbly out into the hall. My heart is so sore. Not just from this, but from the last few months. Instinctively, my body pivots to the nursery, hoping for a glimpse of

Landis asleep before I go, but Leland turns me around and points me down the stairs.

We're in the front doorway when I look back and see Kayleigh, her shocked face peering out of the hall.

"I'm sorry," I try to say with my eyes.

She shakes her head, giving me a watery smile.

"I've got this," she silently mouths. "I'll do it."

My heart is pounding in my throat, but I nod, trying to smile back. Leland pushes me through the door. He holds the door to the SUV open, though not on account of being a gentleman. I think he's always a little afraid I'll reach back into that Harlan scrappiness and make a break for it.

If I didn't have Landis to think about, I just might.

CHAPTER THIRTY-SIX

JENSEN

It's Monday night.

I take Godspeed from his stall and start brushing him down a little before dinner. My nerves are steel, the way they always are before a fight. That will hit me a few minutes before they lock me in the pit, but I need that. The only fights I've lost are the ones where I wasn't nervous beforehand.

Godspeed raises his head, turning to the doorway. I lift mine to look. Under the entrance floodlight stands Brothers, a lone shadow. He doesn't move. I take a step out and wait, but he just runs a hand over his face.

"Hey," I say.

He comes closer, putting his hand on Godspeed's nose. "I was pissed when you took this one. I could see even when he was young that he was going to be quicker than hell."

"He's fast," I say simply.

"He's about ready to be retired," he says.

"I plan on it."

He looks up, face half shadowed. "One last ride, huh?"

I nod. "He'll get us where we're going. I trust him."

Brothers smiles, but there's something about him that unsettles me tonight. His shoulders sit lower, like he's resigned. Considering we're about to walk into a fight, I don't like the aura of defeat around him. Thinking hard, I saddle up Godspeed and put him in the pen in the corner to wait. When I return, Brothers sits on a bench, smoking, his legs stretched out.

He's sober. No jokes or digs tonight.

"Hey, you good?" I say.

He's distant. "Kayleigh's doing it for Della, not for me. She traded her cousin in return for Della and Landis going free, but she didn't barter anybody else's life."

"So...what does that mean?" I ask.

He finally looks up. "It means, when I kill every person in her family I can get my hands on, we're going to have a long, hard road to forgiveness."

Dead silence. I clear my throat, still not following.

"Are you planning to do that tonight?" I ask.

He shakes his head, inhaling smoke deep. "We'll see."

"You can talk straight to me," I say.

He leans against the wall, releasing a sigh. There's a wet patch on his Sunday shirt.

"You know why they called me Brothers Boyd?" he says.

I shake my head. "Never thought you'd answer if I asked."

"Jem commissioned the sign over the door of our first bookie business. It was supposed to say *The* Brothers Boyd, but they didn't seal the paint correctly," he drawls, eyes disconnected. "After a while, through time, the first word wore out, leaving it just Brothers Boyd. Jem was a slower moving kind of guy. He liked an easy life. See, back in the church, I was the eldest son. I had all the responsibility. The yoke, as it were, was thrust on my shoulders. But Jem...he just kinda ran to keep up, you know? I was moving, shaking, and Jem was fading out because he couldn't keep up. Eventually, I become both halves of The Brothers Boyd."

I study him. It's hard to think of Brothers as anything but an adult man.

"Is that why you wanted to bring me on to replace Jem?" I ask.

"Yeah, Jem fell behind." He points at me with the cigarette. "But Jensen Childress, he didn't just catch up. He flew like a fucking arrow."

I grunt, uncomfortable.

"It wasn't hard work," I say.

"It was. You were just good at it," he says. "People called me Brothers for a good while. Then, I was at the races one day. You weren't there, but you were working for me at the time, and one of the owners of the Derby winner that year saw me from across the room. He said Good God, it's Boyd, and it came out so loud, the whole room laughed. He was a big guy, Scotch-Irish, booming voice. Now, down at the racetrack, they call me The Good God Boyd."

I'm quiet. I'm not sure he wants me to answer. He's just talking. I think people don't listen to him talk very often, at least, not like this. He rolls his cigarette between his finger and thumb, brow creased.

"Kayleigh... When I met her, she thought that was so damn funny," he drawls. "So I stopped minding it so much."

He falls quiet, smoking, thinking. Finally, he clears his throat.

"I've been called near everything but my own name," he says. "I like that just fine, but I like it better when Kayleigh says my name, my real one."

I don't ask him what that is—he won't tell me anyway.

"I am a round peg in a square hole, Jen," he says finally. "Been weird, little off-beat, my whole life. Don't think I had a chance after the way I was raised, but she makes me feel...like that's alright."

My head goes back to Della, to how accepting she'd been of my past and how it shaped me. Brothers drops his head, stabbing out his cigarette on his boot. We sit for a while.

"Grace," I say.

"What's that?"

"She's giving you a little fucking grace," I say. "Feels pretty good, doesn't it?"

He stares, then he smiles. Sweat etches down his forehead, and he wipes his face with his palm.

"Yeah," he says finally. "I don't actually know what the point of all that was. It just came out."

"I heard what you were saying."

"Maybe you can enlighten me on what that is."

"You have a good thing going on," I say. "At the crossroads, if I were you, I'd pick that woman over taking down the Caudills and getting the city back. Power don't love you back."

"No, but it keeps you safe," he says.

"I'm fighting tonight like we planned," I say. "Then, I'm getting my girl and her kid, and we're going west. I don't need revenge for what happened to me."

"So what was the point of returning? I know it wasn't just for the kid."

"You asked me once what I wanted to be when I grew up," I say. "Ask me again. I'm grown."

He's got the saddest smile. "What do you want to be when you grow up, Jen?"

"I'm a cowboy," I say. "And I reckon there's a woman in the Caudill mansion right now who wouldn't mind settling down with a cowboy like me. So, I'm gonna get in there tonight, win this fight, and get my girl. You fuck your life up if you want and fumble Kayleigh because you can't give up your hold on this city. I won't."

He drops his head, laughing. "You are a firecracker."

"I know what I want," I say. "And tonight, I'm getting it, come hell or high fucking water. I couldn't care less what you do. I'll be on that plane to Montana you promised me by morning."

He stands, releasing a heavy sigh. "I respect that."

"Alright," I say. "Let's get moving."

We don't speak again until we're both in the rented truck. I drive, and Brothers sits on the passenger side, the headlights reflecting in his unreadable eyes. Following behind us is a cargo truck of his men with weaponry. I've been here and done this with Brothers before. We both know the pit will be the most heavily guarded place tonight, from both sides.

The further we go into the woods, the darker it gets. Then, after we've been in the forest for almost an hour, I catch a glimpse of firelight. The trees grow sparse. Trucks and ATVs appear, parked in the dusty ditches along the edge of the road. Men mill around, some of them with women. I see the glint of their eyes as we drive past.

It feels different this time. Even in the past, when I fought for sport, I was always the underdog.

Not this time.

We pull up outside the pit. Surrounding it runs a fence made up of spiked stakes that run to my shoulder. On the other side, by the trees, sit a handful of tents. Some of the men who fight often, usually for money, stay here through the summers. They're a rough bunch. I've spent a few nights out here myself.

I swing out of the truck. Brothers does the same, circling to me. He's dressed down tonight, work boots and pants and a gray t-shirt. It makes him look a lot younger. Or maybe that's the shadows, the flickering light, but he looks the way I remember him back then.

"You ready for this?" he says.

I jerk my head.

"Knock 'em dead, son," he says, taking his AK out of the truck bed and slinging it over his shoulder.

I don't tell him not to call me son. A dozen pairs of eyes follow us as we climb up the short bank and go through the opening in the fence. Inside, it's packed, absolutely jam packed beyond anything I've ever seen. Caudill soldiers are gathered in groups, I can tell because their guns are branded with Leland's crest. They glance up as Brothers and I walk up the pathway to the pit. There's a strong sense of unrest.

My body is eating the anticipation up and turning it into pure adrenaline.

I'm hungry to fight again.

I pause at the edge of the pit. It's a hard-packed basin with a dusty floor, deep enough that the wooden walls can't be climbed. Over top stretches a thick wire cage. There's one way in, a set of stairs built into the dirt. On both sides above the pit are two platforms for the fighters to prep and recuperate.

On the platform to my left loiters a group of Leland's soldiers. The one to my right is empty. Brothers and I move there, his men trailing behind. We step up under the overhang, and I drop the bag and start taking off my shirt. Brothers stares at the opposite platform, eyes moving like searchlights.

"Who's their fighter?" I ask.

He shakes his head. "Don't know him. Not local, out of the Carolinas."

"What's his scorecard?"

He shakes his head again. "Don't know, but he's sort of in your weight class, so he won't turn you into Swiss cheese."

"I'm not worried about it," I say. "I've been fighting out in Montana for years. I think I can take whatever they throw at me."

"Don't get cocky, Jen," he says.

I sink down onto the bench and start wrapping my hands. My muscle memory takes over. That's a confidence boost. I've always been agile and strong. This shouldn't be a big deal. All I need to do is warm up, get out there, and clean house. Then, I'll get the fuck out of dodge so I can get to Byway and pick up Della. I glance around at the crowd. It's thick and restless, but Brothers has enough soldiers to escort us out fast.

I'll have her back by morning.

"Shit," says Brothers.

I look up. He's staring at the opposite platform, stone faced. I rise, trying to see through the flickering light and shadows.

"What?"

He beckons, stepping to the side so I can stand in his place. From this angle, I can see inside the group of men. There's his fighter, a blond man maybe a decade younger but of equitable size. He's shifting back and forth, shaking out his shoulders. Then, my gaze moves to the side, and I see Leland talking to a slender, short figure in red.

Fuck.

"He brought Della," says Brothers.

My stomach goes ice cold. "No... Fuck, this fucks up everything."

He doesn't answer. His eyes dart over the clearing like he's thinking fast.

"Della wouldn't leave Landis behind without a plan," he says finally. "I need to leave, stall this, until I can get to the state route and call Kayleigh."

There's no service in the pit for a reason.

"You can't leave," I say. "We have to get to Della and talk to her before the fight, figure out what's going on. What if you draw Leland aside and give me a chance to talk to her?"

"That's a possibility," he says.

"That's our best bet."

I half expect Brothers to argue, but he goes to the bag and takes out a white handkerchief. He leans off the platform and waves it hard, back and forth, until one of the soldiers on the opposite side points. The crowd shifts, turning to look. Leland pushes through and leans on the railing. There's a second when I think he's going to shake his head. Then, he lifts a hand and beckons.

"You keep the AK," I say.

He jerks his head, leaning over to one of his men, Angie, the younger brother of Angus. He's a tall guy with colorless hair and tattoos up to his jaw. "Angie, you come along with us."

Angie nods, circling behind me as we alight the platform. The crowd murmurs, parting in a slow wave as we work our way through it.

"I don't understand why he'd bring her," says Brothers.

"I've got a couple ideas," I say.

I don't know Leland well, but from what I do know, he's a proud man. The humiliation of having his wife leave him publicly must have stung. Taking her back was likely a bitter pill. For him, this is parading a trophy. For her, it's a walk of shame, a warning.

Do you see what I'm capable of without getting my hands dirty?

It's no wonder she's desperate to be rid of him.

We get close to their platform. Here, the crowd gets sparse and becomes a fortification of soldiers. Brothers slips in front, AK over his arm. He's like a wily cat, head down, eyes up, watching everything as if he's hunting.

I climb the steps to the platform. Leland steps up, and it takes everything I have not to look past him at Della. I know she's there, but I can't meet her eyes. He can't know I know her, much less how intimately. So, I fix my eyes on Leland, squaring him up like he's my opponent.

He's a big, broad man, but it sits on him like he earned it in the gym, bulkier up top, packed on a little too carefully. Tonight, he's dressed casual, work pants and a t-shirt. It's burning hot in the pit with all the barrel fires, and he's already glittering in sweat. I am too. It's dripping into my eyes and making my hair curl.

Leland extends a hand. Brothers shakes it.

"What do you want?" Leland says.

"You got a younger fighter than I do," says Brothers, gesturing. "What's his scorecard?"

"Two losses," Leland says. "Twelve wins."

His gaze swings to me, and I meet it. Deep inside, I want to walk up to him and shake his hand, introduce myself as the man who has fucked Della in about every position known to man. That she comes for me when she never did for him. That I think I still taste his wife's pussy in my mustache. But I don't. I just meet his gaze head on and don't flinch.

"Who's this?" he drawls.

I step forward. "Jensen Childress. I've fought for Brothers before."

His jaw works. "I don't remember you. Where do you hail from?"

"Harlan," I say.

He snorts. "You Harlan fighters are scrappy."

It's pissing me off the way he gets that high and mighty expression at the mention of my county.

"I get the job done," I say shortly.

Watch it. I'll fuck up your fighter then fuck your wife when I'm done.

"Oh yeah?" His jaw goes tight, like he can feel my thoughts rolling off me.

"Yeah."

The tension crackles. Brothers puts a hand on his elbow and murmurs something. Leland nods, backing to the side with Brothers. That clears the path right to Della. There's no way in hell I can conceal what I feel as my eyes fall on her, but I have to. Tonight depends on it.

Warmth blossoms then erupts in my chest, followed by pain.

She's in a cage. Her body is wrapped in a short, tight dress that comes to mid-thigh. It's dark red. I don't know much, but that's not her color. Or maybe she's just washed out from nerves.

Our eyes meet.

My God, she's beautiful.

I'm back in that loft, tangled up in her, lost in my sweet Harlan girl. Everything around us fades. The crowd is a shadow in my periphery. I'm standing in the doorway of Cherry's trailer, bodies all over the floor. Della is there too. She doesn't speak, but I hear what she's saying.

I know what my heart is telling me.

Don't lose her too.

All at once, I know what I said to Brothers in the barn was a lie. I don't have it in me to forgive the Caudills. I don't have it in me to forget either. No, tonight, I'm going to lay it all out. It's time to wrap this up and move on.

I came to stand and deliver, and by God, I will.

For the kid nobody protected.

For Cherry, for Kyle.

But most of all, for Della and Landis, a boy I've never met. An echo of myself years ago.

The crowd on the platform shifts. Brothers glances over his shoulder and blinks slowly, his hand falling on Leland's shoulder. Now's your chance, his eyes say. I shift closer but don't face her. She keeps her back to me, spine stiff.

"Who is with Landis?" I whisper.

She turns briefly, like she's just looking around. "Kayleigh."

"What's her plan?" I say.

"She said she's got this. I think she means to take him to Byway herself."

There's a low whine in the distance of my mind. From the corner of my vision, I see Leland break away from Brothers and go back to Della. I back up, jostled by the soldiers behind me. All I can see is his hand sliding around her waist, the way his mouth almost grazes her temple as he says something in her ear.

She shrinks.

My stomach turns. The Della I know is bright, quick, brave. Standing beside Leland, she's a shadow of herself. Her denial to label what Leland did to her as assault is understandable, but it's clear she metabolized it as such. He might not have done it violently, but what he did was still intimately violent. Her body knows.

I want to kill him.

Brothers appears at my side, eyes wide. "Jen, do you trust me?"

"No," I say.

He takes me by the shoulder, pulling me off the platform and into the crowd. "I need you to trust me just this once. For Della."

Our eyes meet, and I see everything that went down between us. It's sad we're so broken that even with wolves at our heels, I still can't trust him.

"Della thinks Kayleigh is taking Landis out of the house tonight," I say.

"I guessed. That girl is so fucking stubborn." His pupils are blown. Goddamn, he's afraid for her. "If Kayleigh is caught, if he finds out it was her, he'll kill her when he gets back tonight. We can't just fight here tonight, Jen. We have to finish this."

"For her? Or for you?"

He glances sideways at me, eyes sharp. "I've lost a lot of people. I'm not losing her."

He turns on his heel and starts moving back to our platform. I go after him, taking him by the shoulder and pulling him to face me. He's sweating, his shirt drenched, but not from heat. I've never seen him like this before. I didn't know Brothers Boyd knew how to be afraid.

"He might not know it was her who took Landis if we can get her back to the house in time," I say.

"There's no one else it could be. Kayleigh is the only person in that house with Landis tonight," he says.

My stomach sinks. "Kayleigh is... She knows how this is going to end."

"Either we all keep running from the Caudills forever, or we finish this tonight," he says. Sweat etches down his temple. "I was...I was thinking about marrying her, but now...I just want her to live. That's all I'm asking."

I see him, not as the Good God Boyd, but as a man, not unlike myself. It breaks through the bitterness inside.

"You really love her," I say.

His throat bobs, lids flickering. "Fight Leland instead. I can convince him to get in the pit with you. If you get the chance, kill him."

"Fine," I say. "But whatever you do, don't tell him Della and I were together, not while she's still in his hands."

He nods, disappearing back into the crowd. I turn my back. There's a lot of pain in this clearing tonight, on his shoulders, on mine, sitting in Della's fragile heart. Brothers is right. It needs to end. There's a debt that needs to be paid between the Childresses and the Caudills.

Tonight, I'm going to collect on it.

Then, I'll take my family and go home.

CHAPTER THIRTY-SEVEN

DELLA

I'm a perfect statue, standing with Leland's hand on my waist. But my eyes follow the tanned skin of Jensen's shoulders as they move back into the crowd.

They pause on the other side of the pit. He's close to Brothers, talking earnestly. Then, his pale eyes find me. Heat and electricity pour through my veins. Under my constricting dress, my body responds to him. It knows him, deeply, intimately. I want him so goddamn badly. If I can't have him, there will never be another man.

Jensen Childress is it.

Then, he disappears, swallowed by the crowd. Emptiness settles in my chest.

"Della."

I blink, hazy stare adjusting to Leland. He's frowning, mean as a snake.

"What are you doing?" he asks.

I shake my head, confused. "I'm...just standing," I say.

He steps closer, so he's directly over me. "Why are you looking at Brothers? Did he say something to you?"

I turn to face him. "No, sorry. I'm just tired."

The edge of his jaw brushes my temple as he leans in to speak into my ear.

"I don't know if I trust you, Della," he says.

There's a dangerous edge to his voice, soft and deadly. It reminds me of the handful of times I've witnessed him lose his cool and put a bullet in some poor man's head. It also reminds me of the days leading up to the condom incident. A few months into our relationship, he saw I was pulling back from him, trying to shake him off, and he took away my options without saying a word.

I wonder if he knows what he did.

Or if that's just him.

"I'm tired, I swear," I whisper. "I'm uncomfortable being at the fight, but it's fine."

He touches my sternum with his fingertips. "That's alright."

"Are they fighting?" I ask, trying to sound casual.

He turns back to the crowd. To my surprise, Brothers is coming back over, sweat-drenched face hollow. Jensen is gone. He must be lost in the crowd, prepping for the fight. Leland watches him, stare narrowed. Then, he moves down to meet him at the bottom of the steps.

I follow, leaning on the pillar.

"We want to change fighters," Brothers says, taking the cigarette from his lip.

He's nervous. I see it in the flash of the whites of his eyes.

"Why would I do that?" Leland drawls.

Brothers points directly at me with the cherry tip.

"Because my fighter fucked your wife," he says.

My entire body freezes. No, no, what is he doing? There's no way Jensen agreed to revealing that information.

"What?" Leland breathes.

Brothers looks him dead in the eye. "Jensen Childress fucked your wife. If you had any honor at all, you'd take your fighter's place."

I'm sinking. This is the flip side of Brothers Boyd, the one Jensen warned me about. Still, it feels like a punch to the gut. It feels soiled, dirty, laid out in front of Leland like it's no longer this sweet secret between me and Jensen anymore.

My porcelain teacup heart cracks, dozens of fine threads running through it.

Leland turns slowly, and a shudder moves down my spine. "Della," he says. "Care to chime in?"

I can't speak, feet rooted to the spot.

"Come now, Leland," Brothers taunts. "Solve this like a gentleman. She can't help what he did."

I'm so sick, my vision is blurred. Leland walks up the stairs. I see him coming like we're in a tunnel. Then, his iron grip wraps around my throat.

"Did he fuck you?" he says grimly.

A lie feels stupid at this point. Brothers wasn't dressing me for sacrifice the night he sent me back to Leland. No, that was just the appetizer. Tonight, I'm laid out with my throat slit.

I see Brothers in the background through my blurry vision. He mouths something, and I think he's telling me to trust him.

I want to, I do. The comfort of complete trust is a distant concept. I've felt it exactly twice in my life. When my father was alive and that day in the swamp with Jensen's hand on the wheel.

"Della," Leland snarls, dragging me back.

I twist, trying to get my throat free. He holds tight.

"He did," I gasp.

Leland pushes me, hard. I hit the ground and roll to my side. Everything is turned upside down, but I hear Brothers' voice cut through the confusion.

"She didn't want it," he says. "Trust me on that."

Leland is tearing at the seams, trying to keep in control of himself. I'm a puppet on Brothers' strings, my fate changing every time he speaks. Is that what he did to Jensen too? I don't have time to think about it, because Leland takes me by the upper arm and drags me to my feet, pulling me to the far corner of the platform. Behind him, I see Brothers surge forward, like he thinks he can intervene, but Leland's guards cut him off.

"Lelend, please," I beg. His grip is cutting off circulation. "He didn't."

"You just said he did," he spits. "Tell me."

He pushes me against the wooden pillar, hand between my breasts. I'm so fucking scared, I can't stop shaking.

After the way he got me pregnant, Leland scares me more than anyone in this world. If it wasn't an accident, he assaulted me, and then he made me live with him in his perfect house knowing what he did the whole time.

He made me sleep in the same bed with a predator.

That's colder than ice.

"Tell you what?" I breathe.

"What did he do to you?" he snaps.

Under his arm, I see Brothers. He's mouthing those words again. *Trust me, Della.*

My broken heart starts back up.

Thump.

Thump.

I turn back to Leland, tilting my chin up.

"He fucked me," I whisper.

I don't see his hand, but it stings across my face, knocking the breath from my lungs. Anger pours through me. I wrench my head back, shoving my face close to his.

"You can't fight him? You fucking scared, Leland?" I hiss.

He's struggling with his own anger, but I see I hit a sore spot for him. Leland is the same height as Jensen, but he's bulkier, so that puts him in a different weight class. He's not used to doing more than working out though, which gives Jensen an enormous advantage.

He doesn't know that. All he knows is, he shouldn't be scared to fight Jensen and his wife is implying he's a pussy, which I am.

"I fucking hate that I love you," he seethes.

"I know. You've made that clear."

"You had everything given to you, and you throw it away on...what? Who is he?" he roars.

I don't back down. "Jensen Childress, from Harlan County."

He's speechless. I've never spoken to him like this before. If this is my chance, I'm taking it. There's a lot sitting on my chest, and I'm going to unload every damn thing.

"You fucking hate me, Leland," I spit. "You want me, you don't love me. I never wanted to marry you—"

I'm about to launch into a tirade about him using Landis against me, but he cuts me off by raising his hand. I flinch, knowing he can hurt me.

"You stupid bitch," he whispers.

"Fight him, Leland," I hiss. "Maybe you can get an ounce of respect from me for finally getting your hands dirty instead of sending your men to do it for you."

His hand shoots out and grips my throat, pressing me back against the pillar. "I will kill this son of a bitch," he says through gritted teeth. "And you'll pay for what you did."

"Fight him then," I manage.

He twists his arm, and I'm on the ground in a second, gasping. Pain splinters up my thigh, the cloth of my dress tearing as I land at an awkward angle. He's walking away, stopping to talk to one of his bodyguards. Slowly, sick from being manhandled, I push myself to my feet. One of my boots is gone. I kick the other off and pad barefoot to the edge of the platform.

Leland is in the crowd, pulling his shirt off as he walks to the pit. From the corner of my eye, I catch the slender figure of Brothers Boyd. Jensen must still be in the pavilion, because he's nowhere in sight. Brothers turns, looking back at me. My stomach lurches as the firelight glows in a ring around his head. His hooded eyes are soft, sorrowful, paternal.

I hope he knows what he's doing, because this is my last hope.

Father.

Son.

And Holy Ghost.

CHAPTER THIRTY-EIGHT

JENSEN

After Brothers leaves, I go to the back of the pavilion to have a cigarette. Once my nerves are calm, I circle around to find Brothers heading my way. The doors to the cage are being pulled ajar. The pit is deeper than I remembered, the bars overtop thicker, the spikes along the edge sharper. Once they lock that gate, nobody's getting out.

For the first time, I'm afraid of dying.

I can't die. I have something to live for now. I look across the clearing and see her, standing at the top of the steps. She's roughed up, hair falling over her shoulder, skirt torn. My stomach lurches with pure rage, fists clenching at my sides.

Brothers appears at my elbow. "He'll fight you," he breathes.

"What's the price?" I say.

He looks me in the eyes, unflinching. "Fight for her life, Jen."

Right away, I know he told Leland.

We're at the crossroads where I first met the devil, in my front yard, offering to help fix my truck. The Good God Boyd has done it again, pulling at my strings until I have no choices left. I round on him, gripping his arm and pulling him to look at me.

He's so tired, face hollowed, sweat dripping down his forehead.

I'm sick of this, sick of deception, sick of secrets.

"Tell me what you did," I whisper. "The night I can't remember. Tell me now, and I'll fight."

He blinks, slow. "Why does it matter, Jen?" he drawls.

"It matters to me," I grit out.

He looks down, then back up. "I put a gun in your fist and told you to shoot Holly if you wanted to be my right hand. You couldn't do it, we fought, and you left drunk and angry."

One second, I'm in the here and now. The next, everything is flooding back with so much clarity, it could be a movie reel. A dam shatters, and an ocean pulls me under, deep into a part of my past my brain worked hard to keep from me.

BEFORE

"Jen, can you come in here, please?"

I'm moving down the hall, on a high. Everything in my life is going right. Brothers and I are running this operation like Kentucky's criminal dream team. I finally told Holly we're done, and I even sort of meant it. Brothers says he's going to give me another promotion as soon as I can prove myself.

I veer left and step into the dining room, closing the door. My steps falter. The room is empty, save for Brothers sitting at the head of the table and Holly in a chair by the fireplace. Something is off. Why is everyone so serious?

"Everything okay?" I ask.

"Of course," Brothers says, standing. "But it's time we talk about that promotion."

"Okay, but...why is Holly here?"

I glance at her, meeting her eyes. They're huge, brimming with nerves like she wants to say something, but she can't. Brothers walks past her and stands toe to toe with me at my end of the table. He reaches into his jacket and takes out a gun. It's an original Ruger, still in mint condition. He lays it on the table.

"I want you to be my right hand," he says.

That catches me off guard. I thought his brother, Jem, had that spot on lockdown on account of being his blood.

"What?" I breathe.

"I want me and you to do this together, Jen," he says, putting a hand on my shoulder. "Brothers Boyd and Jensen Childress. We can own this city."

"Do you mean that?" I ask.

He nods, lazy smile turning up his mouth. "I mean it."

"Thank you."

"There is a catch," he drawls, turning to face Holly. She swallows, lips parting. "I do need you to prove yourself, prove you can take orders without questioning me."

"Okay," I say slowly. "What do you need me to do?"

Brothers circles until he's standing over my shoulder. "You fell in love with this woman, gave her everything. Now, I'm asking you for something more, and in return, I will give you everything, Jen."

My gut churns. Brothers leaves me, crossing to Holly. She doesn't move, frozen to her chair, and he rests his elbows on the back of it, hands on her shoulders.

"There's one last test of loyalty," he says. "Take that Ruger and put a bullet in her."

The low whine in the back of my mind erupts into an explosion. The world shatters. He puts it in my hand, and the subtle shift in weight tells me there's a single bullet in the chamber. I go from looking at him like the father I never had to recoiling in pure disgust.

"What?" I breathe.

His eyes glint. Holly is frozen, eyes huge. Brothers has her by the shoulders, keeping her pinned to the chair.

"Go on," he says. "I require loyalty, Jen. Undying loyalty. You follow my orders, you trust me, or we can't do this together."

"Fuck no," I snap.

He straightens, fire roaring in his face. "Then walk, Jen. Get out of my house."

No, this isn't right.

He's supposed to be the man who stepped in, who stepped up. He fixed my truck with me. He took me in when I had nothing. He sat in that diner and promised me I could tell him anything. In his place is a man I don't recognize, one who's holding the bond I valued so deeply above my head, telling me to jump for it. A master manipulator.

I'd hoped that love was free. Turns out, it costs my soul.

I'm done, really done this time.

"Fuck you," I whisper, tossing the gun onto the table.

NOW

I snap back to the present. He's standing inches from me, the same man, just a few more lines on his face. The rest is falling into place. We fought, I remember throwing something at him. He told me we'd discuss things in the morning. I said I was going to finish a job and I left, but not before taking the bourbon off the table and walking out.

I can't speak.

He flicks the inside of his cheek with his tongue.

"I take it you remember now," he says finally.

All those years, and the truth is still worse than I imagined. The utter cruelty of it leaves me breathless. He takes a step closer. He's struggling, eyes flickering back and forth, jaw tensing.

"There was no bullet, Jen," he says, barely audible.

"What?"

He shakes his head. "There was no bullet."

"I felt the weight of it."

"Weighted gun," he murmurs, not looking at me. "You had to believe it."

That's less horrifying for Holly, but somehow crueler to past Jensen. A whistle splits through the crowd, and I reel back. The referee from the Caudill side is in the pit. At the edge looms Leland, standing while they tape his hands. The crowd starts chanting, urging me to get in the ring. It's time.

I turn back to Brothers.

When I look at him, I don't want to hurt him.

No hate.

No anger.

Just deep sadness for the man I could have been.

"I'm doing this for Della," I say. "Not for you."

He opens his mouth to say something, but I already have my back to him. Before me is the possibility of Della, of having her become my family. We can go west. I'll be a cowboy, and she'll be my wife. We'll raise her son together, maybe have a few more babies. Behind me is the past, full of death and grief and lost innocence.

I'm ready to leave it all behind in the cage tonight.

I'll fight for that kid from Harlan who never stood a chance. I'll fight for Cherry, for Kyle, who never deserved to be caught between me and the Caudills.

But more than anything, I'll fight for my woman.

CHAPTER THIRTY-NINE

DELLA

He enters the cage like a gladiator walking into an arena, Brothers a step behind. Leland doesn't go in until he's firmly in his corner and they're separated by the entire length of the pit. The referee starts walking to the upper end to check the gate.

I have no faith in his ability to monitor this fight. I'm so scared that once they start, it's not going to end until someone is dead.

I think I might faint.

My nails dig into the post, keeping me upright. The referee comes to the middle of the pit. My breathing shallows. Never did I think this would end with my ex-husband and the man I love fighting in a cage. The world is upside down. Tonight is a blurred, bad dream.

I wonder if Leland has ever fought anyone outside of sparring partners at the gym. If I had to guess, he has, but I know he's never fought anyone like Jensen.

My heart feels distant, a desperate patter, like it's out there with him.

"Move in, move in," the referee calls.

Leland goes, confidently, to the center. Jensen takes two steps to the side, like he's checking his vantage point, and then he starts walking in. He's just like he was that day in the swamp—calm, confident, focused. The firelight catches the tattoo on his side, casting shadows down the ridges and scars of his body.

They stop, face to face, and Leland shakes out his shoulders. Jensen doesn't move, but his eyes track Leland's, his lips parted.

Leland says something.

Jensen laughs once, but he's not amused.

They're not a fair fight to the naked eye. Leland is broader and the audience notices. Money starts changing hands, moving in a wave toward the bucket with Leland's number on it. My stomach roils with unease. They're all here for a show, to win some cash. This is a game to them, but not to me.

My life depends on Jensen winning.

If I go home with Leland tonight, I'm done.

He might kill me, but I don't think so. More likely, he'll keep me alive, keep me sedated beneath his boot, and I'll get to live knowing he got what he wanted. Every day will be hell, my mind wearing thin from the stress of him on my body every night, his eyes following my every move, his relentless need to control everything I say and do.

He's too proud to give me up.

Or too sadistic.

Someone is behind me. I glance over my shoulder, cowed by the two bodyguards standing with their arms crossed, their eyes straight ahead. Neck prickling, I turn to face the pit again.

The referee is speaking to them, gesturing. Leland jerks his head, but Jensen doesn't move, eyes never leaving my ex-husband. Finally, he extends his hand. Leland hesitates before he shakes it, and Jensen leans in, his lips moving.

No, no, please don't.

Lord, I know Jensen just rubbed salt in Leland's wound.

Right on cue, Leland surges at him. I surge too, even though I don't know what I'm doing. The bodyguards take a step to keep me from running. In the pit, the referee steps between them, palms up, and Leland backs off.

Jensen turns, a cocky little smile on his face, and starts walking back to his corner. There's a swagger in his step that wasn't there before.

My God, this man has a death wish.

The referee steps back to the gate, puts two fingers in his mouth, and whistles. The crowd roars, moving in a wave to the edge of the cage. I've never felt anything like this before. My heart is in my mouth, off beat. Everything tastes like metal. I think I'm biting my tongue. The energy is thicker than smoke, and it's making me sick to my stomach.

I can't pass out, not while Jensen is in the pit, fighting for our lives.

I can't go and faint on him.

Desperate, I lean back to the bodyguard. "You got any whiskey on you?"

His jaw twitches, but to my surprise, he pulls a flask out of his pocket and hands it over. Grateful, I drain the little left and pass it back.

Leland starts moving in. Jensen goes sideways, a slow evasion. Why is he doing that? He didn't fight like that back in Montana. Is it because Leland has the advantage? Or is there something I don't see?

Leland comes a few yards in. Jensen starts heading his way, halfway between his corner and the gate. From the corner of my eye, I see Brothers standing by the platform, arms crossed. He looks like he just did a line of coke with his eyes blown out like that, wider than an owl.

Leland puts his fists up. Jensen mirrors him.

They circle for a half a beat. Then, Leland swings, and Jensen side steps. I don't know a lot about fighting, but it seems to me, Leland is leaving too much of his body open. His defense is looser than Jensen's, just from having watched him fight twice before.

Bam.

The crowd roars as Jensen catches Leland in the ribs, darting back before he can retaliate. His strategy is starting to make more sense now. He's got the advantage of being quicker, and he's leaning into it.

Leland surges, and Jensen parries him back using his palms. He's light, swift, but more importantly, he's in control of his emotions, and it's working. He swings, hitting the same spot on Leland's ribs. The rage, the tension, from Leland is palpable, and it scares me.

The referee holds up the chalk scorecard.

Two to zero.

Leland doesn't like that, and he pulls back, circling. His eyes meet mine across the pit, and the look he gives me chills me to my core.

Just brutal rage.

I shrink back until I can't go any further. The bodyguards are an iron wall behind me. There's no way out of this but forward.

Leland circles back, and Jensen mirrors him again. It's impossible to tell if he's playing with Leland or fighting in earnest. This time, they get close, but neither of them give up the defensive position. They just circle, feigning a few times, then back up. Nothing happens for a couple of agonizing minutes. Then, it all happens at once.

Leland comes in with a right hook. Jensen ducks, but not far enough. It catches him in the forehead, sending him stumbling.

No, God, please.

The crowd gasps then roars. They're screaming, beating on the spiked fence. More money pours into Leland's bucket on the betting table.

Jensen recovers fast. He's not bleeding, but there's a mark above his left brow. He shakes his head once, and they circle again until the pressure gets too intense and they have to move in. Every step they take, the crowd screams. It makes me sick, the way they're eating this up, not knowing how much is on the line.

My vision goes hazy. I blink hard, trying to clear the tears.

Jensen moves in to meet Leland, but this time, Jensen swerves to the other side. Leland's right side is open for a fleeting second, and Jensen takes it, swinging and hitting with a crunch that echoes over the clearing. Leland reels, but Jensen keeps going, raining down blows until my husband falls to his back with a thud, throwing up dust.

Jensen turns around, spitting into the dirt.

The crowd goes silent.

The referee starts counting with big, exaggerated gestures. Leland scrambles to a crouch, eyes dark and narrowed. Then, he's up and coming at Jensen fast. Jensen stumbles, backing up, moving to the side to avoid being hit head on. Leland's fist catches him in the same place as before, but this time, the skin splits. He lurches back, jaw rippling as he clenches his teeth.

Crimson trickles down his face and neck.

The crowd goes wild.

Hot tears pour from my eyes, soaking the red of my dress, turning it darker. God, I fucking hate this dress and this color.

But Jensen's back on his feet, unfazed save for the blood. A long, sharp whistle splits over the crowd, and both men relax, backing up to their corners. Thank God, a moment to breathe. Jensen returns to his corner. Brothers is waiting, holding out a crushed water bottle. Jensen takes it, drinking then spattering the rest over his head. He shakes like a dog, eyes squeezed shut.

That had to hurt.

Leland is doing a loop, pacing the side of the cage closest to me. Our eyes meet, and the corner of his mouth turns up.

Got him, he says without speaking.

My hands are cold, and I can't move. Leland turns his back to me, running his hands over his face to clear the sweat. I look past him, watching Jensen talk with Brothers in the far corner. Brothers is touching his temple with a balled up rag, talking earnestly, while Jensen is listening, nodding.

The referee whistles, tapping his wrist. Jensen pulls back from Brothers and starts circling to the center of his side. Leland shakes his shoulders out again. They're both glistening with sweat, but to my untrained eye, it seems like Jensen is less fatigued. Or maybe that's just me hoping too much.

The whistle blows. Round two.

This time, Jensen goes right on defense. Leland, clearly bolstered by the sight of blood, is more aggressive. He's moving in, swinging, darting back out, but Jensen is holding his own, battering him back while barely making contact.

They do this for what feels like forever.

What is Jensen doing?

Back in Montana, I saw him drop both those fighters like it was nothing. If he really wanted to, he could do some damage to Leland, but he's doing everything he can to not take or throw a punch.

The whistle blows. They part, shoulders sagging.

This time, when Leland goes to his corner, he's winded. Our eyes meet, and I still shrink back, but it's a small victory that he's struggling to catch his breath. Jensen has his back to me, tired but more collected than Leland.

The referee whistles. They walk back in.

Jensen cracks his neck. Leland's fists go up fast. In a second, they're back at it, sidestepping and sparring in the center. I lean closer, going as far as the first step. The bodyguards move in, encircling me, but I ignore them.

Leland is wearing down.

The crowd is turning on them. They want blood, not a boxing match. People hang over the edge, arms between the spikes as they beat on the cage in a driving rhythm. I swear, it's matching the swift pump of my blood in my ears.

It hits me all at once. Of course, how did I not see it? I'm so terrified, I can't think straight.

He's buying time for Kayleigh to get Landis out.

My lower lip trembles.

If I get out of this, I'm going to marry this man. I'm going to make sure he wakes up to a fresh cup of coffee and a blowjob every morning for the rest of his life.

He didn't need to help me. His life was fine in Montana. But he hauled himself to the other side of the country, faced down his demons, and now he's cage fighting my piece of shit ex-husband so I have a shot at getting my son back. Flowers and diamonds can go to hell. This is the most romantic thing anybody has ever done in all of history.

Everything goes still.

The crowd is a million miles away.

Jensen Childress loves me.

Maybe he's not good with his words, and he's pretty prickly sometimes, but his actions are loud and clear, and they have been for a while. I think he's been in love with me since the beginning—he's just too damn stubborn to acknowledge it.

Crack.

I blink, the cage coming into focus. Leland stumbles backward, and Jensen sprints to the side. Crimson streams down the side of Leland's neck—Jensen made contact good and hard this time. Hope rises.

Please, finish him off.

Leland shakes his head, seething blood and spit out from between his teeth. He's like a bull going for a red flag, charging at Jensen and reeling as he sidesteps, flipping sides of the pit. Dust rises under their feet. Sweat gleams down their skin, glittering in their soaked hair. Jensen is on defense again, going in, going back, never letting Leland make contact.

The crowd is livid.

They're screaming, rattling the edges of the pit like animals.

There's a brief moment when they both pull back. Then, Leland surges, raining down punches like it's his last stand. Jensen's eyes widen, flashing in the firelight. He sidesteps, catching a hit to the shoulder. It's a graze, barely throwing him off balance.

Bolstered, Leland swings wide.

Jensen ducks and—

Bam.

Jensen goes in so fast, I can barely follow his punches. But I think he hits Leland in the chest, in the throat, in the right side of his ribcage. Leland stumbles, body jerking as he takes the blows. Jensen drives forward without missing a beat. This is the Jensen I saw in the ring in Montana—brutal, relentless, beating his opponent without mercy.

The last hit spins Leland halfway sideways. Lightning fast, Jensen hits him in the back of the head, turning him the rest of the way around, and takes out his left knee with his boot.

Crunch.

Leland's upright for a moment, suspended in time. I see Jensen's eyes flare, and he spits. Then, he swings hard.

Boom.

Leland goes down like a building collapsing. One second, he's upright, and then, he's in the dirt. It happens so fast, and it's so neat, like folding up a lawn chair.

Jensen turns his back on him for a half step. Then, he reels around, drops to his knees straddling Leland, and starts beating the shit out of him. The crowd takes a unanimous breath. The only sound is a meaty crunch over and over. Then, they start screaming and rattling the fence and overhead cage.

They're losing money, but they don't care. This is the blood they were promised.

My stomach roils.

I saw Jensen take out those men with an AK, but I've never seen him like this. One boot braced, one knee cocked. Arm going down like a machine, just pounding. Blood spatters, beading in the dust. He's red from hand to elbow.

My shaking hands are over my mouth.

Oh my God, he's going to kill him.

Everyone seems to realize at the same time I do that Jensen is not letting Leland walk away from the pit tonight. They get quiet and start murmuring. Then, there's a commotion in the crowd. Men in dark shirts with rifles strapped to their backs start pushing through. They kick down the gate, breaking the lock, and stream into the ring before anyone can react.

Brothers runs in from his corner, hands up, shouting, but the Caudill soldiers get there first.

Two of them grip Jensen's upper arms and haul him back. Another pulls Leland to his feet. He's conscious but bleeding badly. Jensen starts fighting as they force him down to his knees.

No, no, please, don't hurt him.

I dash down the steps and enter the crowd. I'm at the edge of the pit when the bodyguards catch me in an iron grip. I'm no match for their brawn. It takes only one of them to pin my arms behind my back.

"Jensen," I scream.

His gaze flickers up, locking with mine.

I've never seen his eyes so dark.

Brothers breaks into the center of the ring, reaching for Jensen, but he's too late. Two more of Leland's soldiers haul him away, pinning his arms behind his back. I've never seen Brothers like this before. He reminds me of the Pentecostal preacher in the church down the road from Mama's. Eyes of fire and brimstone. Righteous anger burning so bright.

Leland wipes the blood from his face and turns to face Brothers.

"Get him out of here," he says. "Get everyone out of the clearing."

They start pulling Brothers back, but he fights hard.

"You have no fucking honor," he spits. "You are no fucking gentleman, you fucking piece of shit."

That means something, coming from him.

"Get him out," Leland shouts, throwing his arm towards the gate.

"I will fucking gut you," Brothers roars, veins standing out in his flushed neck. "And when I send you to the fucking devil, tell him Brothers Boyd sent you to burn, you fucking evil son of a bitch."

Leland turns and strides from the pit. The crowd is in utter confusion, moving this way and that, trying to figure out if they need to clear out or not. The Caudill soldiers hold Jensen and Brothers, but they don't hurt them. Maybe Leland has a trace of honor in him after all.

The bodyguards pull me back, stumbling over my bare feet, to the platform. They force me down, holding me steady. That's when it starts to really sink in that I'm in danger. I was so worried about Jensen, I couldn't think straight. But as I lift my eyes from where I'm on my knees, I see Leland coming up the steps, looking right at me with an expression I know very well.

It's done. It's over.
We won, but it doesn't matter.
I still lost.

CHAPTER FORTY

JENSEN

Leland's men pull back just as Brothers' soldiers start pouring over the edge of the pit. They part, leaving us in the bloodied dust. My vision wavers. My body is exhausted, but in me is a fire I've never felt.

Pushing myself up, I stride to the fence. Brothers is at my heels, shouting to his men. He's far away and right up in my ear all at once, voice blaring in my ears. We're almost to the gate when I look back as the crowd melts away, and I see her for a moment.

She's being dragged. Her dark hair falls around her beautiful face. Her eyes are big, terrified. Her lips move, pleading. I think she might be calling my name as they haul her away into a wave of bodies.

Right then, I think my heart breaks.

She's so fucking brave, and she doesn't even know it. I've seen courage like hers before, a long time ago, in the face of a kid who kept peeling himself off the pavement thinking he was really going someplace.

This time, that look won't go unnoticed.

Tonight, the Caudills are going down. I've got blood on my tongue and nineteen years of anger in my chest. Hellfire is going to sweep through this town, and there won't be a damn thing they can do to save themselves.

Turning on my heel, I head through the clearing and out into the woods where the truck is parked. Brothers is mobilizing his men as he follows me, and it's giving me a head start. I yank open the door, but he appears behind me, grabbing my arm.

I turn on him. "Don't you fucking stop me."

"I'm not," he pants. "I got horses in the woods. We can't make it in time by road. We have to ride."

"And then what?" I spit.

His eyes flash. "Jen," he snaps. "We need to get the women out of that house before Leland hurts them. This isn't the time to argue."

He's right. The fear in his face isn't for Della or me.

"Where are the horses?" I say.

"Get in the truck," Brothers says. "They're about five minutes from here. The men are going to meet us there by road."

Heart pounding, I slide into the passenger side. In the back seat, something glints. He gets in and puts the truck in drive, screeching it back and around like hell is on his heels. I reach back and rip the canvas cover off a stack of AKs halfway up the seat.

"You came prepared." I turn around.

His fingers flex on the wheel. "I'm always prepared," he says.

We're going ninety on the dirt road, truck bouncing so hard, it might pop the hubcaps off. Brothers is tensed up like a bow. I've never seen him afraid before. My cheek stings, and I wipe it, blood and sweat covering my palm.

"Christ," I murmur.

He pulls a handkerchief from his pocket and hands it over. I mop up my face, trying to get a feel for how bad the cut on my cheek is. It's soft, swollen. Maybe that'll keep it from bleeding too bad.

"You all good, Jen?" he says hoarsely.

I nod. "Yeah."

"Took some hard hits out there."

"Nothing much."

He turns the truck at a hairpin bend, veering the opposite direction we came from. "Not the way he took them."

"I had it handled out there," I say.

"You get the women out tonight, I'll be your spotter," he says.

"Sounds like a plan."

My confidence doesn't come from cockiness. No, it's made of all the anger I've carried on my back. I've fought for a break for thirty-nine years. Then, she appeared. Now, I see the light coming through the trees. The opening of the clouds.

I want a family. I want her. I want to feel what it's like to fix a truck with that little boy of hers. Maybe nobody did that for me, but I can sure as hell make sure somebody does it for him.

The trees blur, the headlights a smear across my vision.

I'm so fucking angry.

I think I got real angry down in my marrow the day I came home and saw Cherry, Holly, and Kyle dead on the floor. There was no path to revenge, so I tamped it down, pretended it didn't exist. But I lived with that rage, not realizing it was still growing inside me. Brothers bringing me back here activated it like a sleeper cell. Tonight, it all came spilling out in the pit.

I can't put it back. I've been gutted, and I'm holding everything that used to live inside me in my hands.

Brothers hits the brakes, pulling off the road. He reaches in the back and pulls something out, tossing it in my lap before getting out of the truck. I look down, lifting it—soft felt, a little worn and smells like a barn. It's a cowboy hat, dark brown, the kind I might wear out in wintertime.

There's a tingle of emotion in my chest as I get out of the truck. Just off the road sits a silver horse trailer. Brothers' horse and Godspeed are tied to the side.

"You wanted to be a cowboy, Jen," Brothers says. "Go on, be one."

I put the hat on, and it fits. "So what do we do when we get the women out?"

"Angus is going to have the plane ready at the gravel park at the park-and-ride, off seventy-five," he says, untying his horse. "You get Della and Landis to it, and they'll take you back to Montana."

I stare at him.

"You're just letting me go?" I say. "Just like that?"

His face is shadowed as he checks the cinch of his saddle. "I made a mistake when I took you on for the business. I should've taken one look at you the day we fixed your truck and left you the fuck alone. Hell...life had already kicked you around enough. But I got selfish. We really clicked, and I felt like maybe I could step in and fix some of the shit people did to you."

I don't know what to say.

"I hurt you, Jen, but not on purpose," he says, voice hoarse. "I'm sorry for that."

The people pleasing part of me that used to take precedence back in the day wants me to forgive him the way I did in the diner, but grown Jensen is a different story.

"You got your family with Della and her boy," he says. "Take them and go. I'm sorry I played a part in yours dying."

I clear my throat. "You hauled me all the way back here to say sorry, huh?"

He mounts his horse, turns him, and stacks his hands on the saddle horn.

"No," he says. "I hauled your ass back here to help me take down the Caudills and settle my debt."

"You dying or something?"

"No," he says, frowning. "Tell me we're even and go home, Jen."

My hand finds Godspeed's side. He throws his head, and I take a second to gather myself, untying him and mounting up. I'm on eye level with Brothers now.

"Get me Della and Landis. Get me to that plane," I say. "Then, we're even. But we're also done. You go your own way with Kayleigh, and I'll go mine. Don't contact me again."

His jaw twitches like he's wincing.

"It's a deal," he says.

CHAPTER FORTY-ONE

DELLA

The drive to the Caudill mansion is a nightmare. Leland is in the back seat, being patched up. He's bruised, but he's not gravely injured. I'm huddled against the door, arms wrapped around my cold body.

Leland won't look at me, but I'd rather not look at him either. I press my forehead to the window and pray to anybody or anything who will listen that, at the very least, Kayleigh got Landis out.

This is my final stand.

I'm staring it right in the eyes, and this time, there's no Jensen between me and Leland.

My nails pierce my palms.

He is my own personal hell I have to face tonight.

We pull up to the front doors, and the world goes completely quiet as I see Kayleigh at the end of the hall. Her lashes are wet, her head shaking. Please, no. Hands move me roughly inside, hauling me by the elbow upstairs. To my surprise, they put me in my and Leland's old bedroom instead of the guestroom.

The lock clicks, and I'm alone. Limply, I sink to my knees between the bed and the fireplace. My head is a mess of everything I just witnessed. Blood, rage, revenge. If I die and go to hell, I'll wake up right back by the edge of that pit, just replaying it again and again.

Tears leak down. They fall on the fine hardwood flooring.

I never wanted any of this. Leland forced me open and molded me into the woman he wanted, but that's not what makes me hate him the most. It's the way he looks at our son and doesn't see Landis. He sees himself, just another person he can make in his own image. I lost tonight, and now my sweet little boy will become a man who passes on his violence to the next generation.

My mind goes quiet.

No, I can't give up.

I have a weapon to use against Leland no one else can wield. He might be the most powerful man in this city, but I'm the woman he wants.

It takes me a second to peel myself off the floor. My steps are unsteady as I rip open the closet. All my old clothing still hangs on my side. My beautiful dresses, my shoes, they're all lined up. I push the door open wide and step inside, turning on the light.

There are his weaknesses, all hanging in a row.

Leland is simple. He likes feeling like he won, and he likes submission. Tonight, I'm going to give him his fantasy.

I run my fingertips over the lingerie until I get to the set he likes the best. It's white lace with delicate appliqué. My cut, my colors. Hands steady, I take it down and go into the bathroom. In the cupboard sit all his favorite things. He likes me to smell sweet, to feel soft. I take down the little gold pots and bottles of vanilla scented sugar scrub and lotion.

Working quickly, I shower, wash and dry my hair, and do my makeup. The bra has his initials between the cups, a single diamond in the center. The set was a first anniversary gift from him. I clasp it, slip on the panties, and fasten on the garter belt, drawing the silk tights up to the middle of my thighs.

I lift my head, gazing at my reflection. I've never really looked at myself without picking my face and body apart.

But tonight, I look.

I am beautiful, powerful.

Voices and footsteps sound downstairs. My heart picks up, and I fling open the medicine cupboards. Adderall, painkillers. I frantically sort through the bottles, trying to read through blurred vision. There's a pharmacy in here, but not what I need.

My eyes fall on a little bottle on the counter. Allergy medicine. Leland takes it when he can't sleep sometimes.

Will that work?

I don't think I have a choice. Snatching it up, I shake a handful of pills out and replace the bottle. Then, I leave the bathroom and run in my stockinged feet to the bar on the far end of the table.

This is a wild card, my biggest gamble, somehow bigger than the one I took when I flew out to Montana to find Jensen.

But it's all I have.

The wall behind the bar is covered in bottles from floor to ceiling. Leland loves good alcohol, and like a true Kentucky man, he's got a taste for expensive bourbon. If I pour him a glass, he won't waste it. I scan the shelves, my eyes falling on a bottle on the very top shelf.

It's never been open, not in all the years we were married.

I scramble onto the bar, teetering as I balance on the shelf. My fingertips graze the glass. Fuck, I'm not quite tall enough. Taking a breath, I stretch, bracing my weight between the wall and counter. My fingers close around the glass bottle neck, and I push back, falling sharply on my ass on the counter.

That was so fucking close.

Footsteps sound on the stairs. I slide down and duck behind the bar, grabbing two short glasses. Fuck, my hands are shaking. I take a short breath, open and close my eyes, and dump the pills in my fist in. Pink flood the bottom of the glass. I rip the top of the bourbon off and dump it in. It swirls, and the pills start dissolving.

I need ice.

Leland drinks his bourbon neat, but for tonight, I'm going to plead ignorance. I need to dull the taste of the drugs. So, I take a handful from the mini cooler and dump the cubes into his glass.

Someone is walking down the hall.

Blindly, I pull down the closest bottle of red wine and pour myself some. Then, grabbing both glasses, I sink down on the edge of the bed.

Time to put on the performance of my life.

The knob turns. The room sways. I'm not good in situations like this, but tonight, that can't matter. Tonight, we're going head to head, and then I am running as far and as fast from him as I can. Leland's voice sounds. He's talking to one of the security guards.

The door opens.

I lift my eyes. He steps in and shuts it.

All at once, I'm eighteen years old, back in that dark room with him. My heart pounds in my chest like a hurt animal, but alongside the wound he left in me burns a vengeful anger that wasn't there before this moment.

He hurt me.

And I want him to know how that feels.

He turns to me, his expression unreadable. They patched up his face, put two stitches over his brow. Otherwise, he looks far better than I'd hoped. He must have showered downstairs, because he's in sweats and a t-shirt, and his hair is wet.

"Where's our son?" I whisper.

He clears his throat. "Sleeping. Kayleigh's in the guestroom," he says coldly. "For some reason, she still had him up."

"Maybe he couldn't sleep."

He shrugs, taking a step in. I twitch back but keep myself steady. He comes to stand before the hearth. I keep still as he stares down at the electric fireplace, waiting, wondering what he'll do next. He hits the button and turns the flames on. He keeps looking at it, brow furrowed like he's thinking hard.

What is he doing?

Finally, he sighs then turns around. His eyes are darker than night, brows lowered.

"Leland," I manage.

"Della," he says, voice dropping. "The only thing keeping you alive is the fact that you are the mother of our son. Otherwise, I would break your neck right here on our bed."

My blood goes cold. "I'm sorry. Please let me stay. Please don't take Landis away."

His brows go even lower, shadowing his eyes. "Tell me the truth about what you did with that man," he says.

My lower lip trembles. A tear etches out.

"He fucked me in exchange for getting me back to Kentucky," I say. "I'm sorry about what I said. It wasn't true. I was just angry with you."

His jaw ripples as he clenches it. Then, he comes close and kneels in front of me, looking up into my tearstained face. His mouth is a thin line. His eyes burn into me, trying to dig the truth from my face.

"Is that the truth, Della?" he says softly.

I nod, mouth dry.

"Then tell me what he did to you."

My lips crack open. "What?"

"When he fucked you," he says, cocking his head. "Tell me exactly what he did to you. How did he do it?"

"Oh," I whisper. "Leland, you don't want to hear that."

His brows rise, forehead creasing. "Yes, I do. Whatever he did to you, I want to hear it. Tonight, this waiting bullshit is over. You will sleep in my bed, as my wife, and you will fucking like it."

My jaw is slack.

"Talk to me," he barks.

I jump, the bourbon sloshing. He notices the glass and takes it, rising to his feet so he's towering over me. The waistband of his pants wavers before my eyes.

"I...I ran away, and he offered to help me get back, but he said I had to pay up for it," I say.

"Talk faster, Della, or I might think you're lying," he drawls, composed again. He lifts the glass and has a sip. I tense, but he doesn't make a face.

Maybe this could work.

Bolstered, I clear my throat. "He took me to his house, a ranch out in the country," I burst out, trying my best to make this sound real. "I said he had to get me a plane ticket first, so he did. Then, he took me back to the bedroom and...had sex with me."

His jaw ripples. "How?" he says, tone brittle.

"Leland," I beg.

"How, Della?" he roars.

My hands shake so badly, my wine spatters down my arm. The tear that etches out is very real. Leland's chest rises and falls, like he's trying to get ahold of himself. I've seen him like this many times with other men. He's all calm, collected. Then, he strikes.

"He laid down and had me on top of him," I burst out.

"Jesus," he breathes, turning away.

"It wasn't the same," I gasp. "Not like you and me."

He freezes, staring into the hearth. Then, he turns his head slowly to face me again. "He said you liked it, that you...came from it."

"It's not true."

He drains the glass and throws it into the electric fireplace. It smashes on the ground, spraying glass shards. Panicked, I drop my wine to the floor and pull back, scrambling onto the bed. Leland turns, striding closer like a hunting animal.

"It doesn't matter," he says. "You'll pay for everything with your freedom."

My heart is in a hundred thousand different pieces of fine porcelain. Before he got his hands on it, it was whole. Simple but beautiful, just like the little house I grew up in, the one he tore me from. I never asked for much from him, just that he leave me alone.

That's all I wanted.

To be left in peace. To not be wanted, to not be desired. To not be taken against my will because of it.

"Leland." My voice breaks.

He looks but doesn't respond.

"Why do you want to keep me at all?" I whisper, another tear slipping down my face.

He reaches out and cups my chin. I look up at him, but he's not seeing me, not the way Jensen does. It takes everything I have not to shudder as his hand drags down my neck, down over my collarbones to the satin bra cupping my breasts. His middle finger runs a straight line to the diamond tucked between them. His lids are lowered, eyes focused on my body wrapped in gold and silk.

"Because I like beautiful things," he says finally.

All at once, I'm back in the river by the church. I'm desperate, trying to scrub the blood out, trying to wash Leland from my sheets. He did that like it was nothing. I know that to him, it was truly nothing, a shallow river in the light of the rest of his life.

He is a boy reaching for the best toy, holding it up so everyone can see what he owns. He is a consumer, a destructor, hungry for everything and nothing at all.

He took me. He took this city. God knows what he'll take next.

His ego will burn the world down if nobody stops it.

All these years, I showed him the wounds he put on me. I begged for understanding. I made myself soft and vulnerable, hoping he'd look into my eyes and really see my pain. He never did because he never wanted to understand.

"Leland," I whisper. "The night you got me pregnant...why didn't you wear a condom?"

He's not listening, stroking over my stomach. With slow pressure, he slides his other hand around my body and lays me down against the pillows. The heat of his mouth burns my stomach as he kisses me.

"Leland," I repeat. "Please tell me."

"I don't remember." He lifts his head. "Why does it matter, Della? You'd have gotten pregnant eventually after we married."

Crack.

I was wrong that there's no more heart left in me to break. Right now, he's grinding the final shards of it to dust with his heel. Biblical anger pours through me, mixing with a deep sadness, deeper than the river I tried to wash him away in.

Maybe he's lying. Or maybe that's the God honest truth.

It doesn't matter. His time is up.

"You will behave tonight," he says against my bare skin.

The ceiling swims overhead. My only prayer is that the drug works fast, and that I gave him enough to sedate him.

A hot tear etches into my hair. "I understand," I whisper.

He flips us with effort, like his hands are unsteady. I'm on top of him, straddling his body, and his arousal beneath my bare thigh sends waves of sickness through my stomach. Are his eyes heavy? Or is that just the light?

"Do what you did to him," he says. "Do it to me, but make it better."

He slurs, and I swear I can hear it. Slowly, I bend and touch his forehead with my lips, then his cheekbone where Jensen broke the skin. He makes a noise in his chest, and this time, I know for certain he's fading.

"Fuck," he says, eyelids flickering.

His body slowly weakens beneath mine, like the energy is being drained from him. The hands on my waist loosen but don't let go. I straighten and look down at his face.

He's a handsome man, beautiful like one of the marble busts in his library. A real gentleman on the outside. It's such a pity he's so ugly inside.

"Della," he murmurs.

His eyes roll back, and he's gone but still breathing.

I need to go. It's time to take Landis and run. But something stops me, keeps me sitting on his inert body.

What Leland did to me meant nothing to him. He said he couldn't even remember it. In the confusion of being so young, so vulnerable, I still don't know for certain if he meant to do it, or if Landis was the result of pure negligence. But either way, it doesn't matter. He still did it.

It still hurt me.

And now, I have to carry my broken, porcelain heart everywhere in my hands.

All the nervousness seeps out. In my mind's eye is the sight of Jensen beating Leland with a terrifying anger in the pit. My own rage is so calm now. I'm sinking in a river of it. And I understand what he felt in that moment.

Brothers Boyd told Leland to tell the devil who sent him, but no man will send him to hell. That privilege is only for the most broken, for the woman he loved and destroyed with that love.

And yet, I'm still alive.

My broken heart is still beating.

Tears welling in my eyes, I lift my head. Hanging on the wall is Leland's most prized heirloom, the dagger with the Caudill family crest, handed down from son to son.

Slowly, I reach out, gripping the headboard I've gripped many times before, and pull it from the sheath. The hilt is so cold. A sob works its way up my throat. Maybe anger, maybe sadness. I shake as I draw the knife to the side, but the hand that grips his dark hair and pulls his head back to expose his throat is steady.

Brothers tried to outwit him.

Jensen beat him.

But I will kill him.

I might be a woman who came from nothing, but I know every empire ends.

It's time for his to fall.

Crimson spreads across the white sheets, spilling over the pillows, a bright red flower that keeps blossoming. Burning tears pour down my face, but I don't stop until Leland Caudill is in two pieces.

In the distance, I hear a gunshot. At first, I think it's nothing, a firework maybe. Then, it comes again, loud and clear this time. Someone's shooting in the back field. It snaps me out of my trance, sending me running to the bathroom to wash the blood from my hands. It ripples down the drain, pink, sticky. Stumbling into the bedroom, I snatch one of my dressing gowns out of the closet and pull it on.

I don't look at the body on the bed. There's no desire in me to ever look back again. Stepping into the hall, I pull the door shut, but not before locking it. Another shot rings out. Someone is yelling, rattling the fence.

I run down the hall and push open the nursery. Landis is upright in bed, eyes enormous.

"Mommy, what's happening," he croaks.

I'm at his bedside, gathering him in my arms. He's big for his age, heavy, but right now, he feels like he weighs nothing. Clasping him to my chest, I wrap a throw blanket around his head.

"Keep your eyes down," I order. "Just look at Mommy. Don't look anywhere else."

"Mommy," he cries out, arms wrapping around my neck. "I'm scared."

"You're safe," I breathe. "Just hold me."

I don't have courage, not really. I've let myself be pushed around. I've been a doormat for people all my life. But when it comes to my son, I am the bravest woman who ever lived. I fled to Montana for him. I faced my worst fear and cut its head off for him. There's no world in which I don't get my son out alive.

Holding him tight, I run as fast as I can down the stairs.

God help anyone who gets in my way.

We make it to the front door before Georgie tears down the hall. I whirl to call out to her, and in that second, the glass breaks behind me. She screams, hands clawed and covering her mouth. Frantically, I spin from left to right, desperate for a way out.

If I can get through the kitchen, I can run out the back door.

Surging, I flee down the hall.

Glass splinters again, sounding like something exploded on the porch. The hinges of the front doors blow open. I don't know why, but I stop and look back. My heart stops. He's coming, riding up the drive on horseback. The front gates are burning. A whistle goes off in the distance. He's just a shadow, AK on his back, but I know it's him.

I'd know him anywhere.

Godspeed skids to a halt at the end of the walkway. He swings down, and he's running up the steps, taking them two at a time.

"Jensen," I breathe.

No sound comes out. This is a nightmare, one where my voice doesn't work. The yard is ablaze, Caudill soldiers are shooting in the

Magnolia grove. My son is sobbing in my arms, and my feet won't move.

The firelight flares, catching the side of the house.

It bathes Jensen in a red glow as he bursts through the shattered doorway. I see his face like it's burned into my eyelids—lowered brow, mouth a grim line.

"Jensen," I scream, louder than I've ever screamed in my life.

Our eyes lock through the chaos. He breaks into a run, getting to me in seconds. Overhead, the chandelier sways. Without hesitating, he takes Landis in his arms and grabs my hand.

Right away, Landis stops crying. His tiny arms wrap around Jensen's neck, holding tight like he knows him. My stomach jerks, warmth trickling through the searing fear.

"Kayleigh is upstairs," I pant. "She's in the guestroom."

Another figure skids to a halt on horseback and comes barreling up the stairs. Brothers Boyd, bathed in sweat, eyes wide, blown out.

"Brothers," Jensen roars. "She's upstairs."

The words haven't left his lips before Brothers is running, tripping up the stairs, ripping his AK from his shoulder as he goes. I whirl, heart in my throat. Georgie is gone—I hope to God she gets away safe, but I can't think about that now. We need to get out of here before the fighting gets to the house.

"Back door?" Jensen pants. "Where is it?"

"Both to the left and right. The right exit leads to the kitchen and back door."

"And the left?"

"The dining room and back hallway."

He does a quick circle, pale eyes roaming the room. "No side exits?"

"There's one from the basement," I say. "Left hallway, turn at the end."

He goes ahead, pulling me by the hand. We enter the dining room with the table where I used to sit with Leland while he had meetings. The porcelain set of dishes used to belong to his mother, untouched in their cabinet. A little part of me hopes they burn tonight.

Jensen ushers us down the hallway to the window looking out over the back lawn. My mouth drops, my steps falter. Across the lawn, the fence is burning in tall streaks of orange. Gunshots pop back and forth like fireworks.

This was my life for four years. I thought it would be my life forever, but tonight, I'm watching it go up in flames, burning my past to ashes.

There's no time to understand what I'm feeling. Jensen has my arm, and he's guiding me to the door at the far end to the basement. Landis is quiet for the first time since I pulled him from bed. Maybe he thinks Jensen is his father, but I doubt it. I think it's the strength of his presence. It calmed me the moment he appeared.

"This door," I gasp, pulling it open.

He pushes me through first and shuts it after us. For a second, we're in the dark. Then, the automatic lights flicker on, revealing the enormous cellar that houses all the food, wine, and bourbon for the estate. We make it to the bottom of the stairs before he adjusts Landis to sit in the crook of his arm and ushers us beneath the steps.

"You okay, baby?" His eyes glint, inches from mine.

"Yeah," I whisper.

"Mommy," Landis says, staring up at Jensen. He's just realizing he doesn't know him.

I touch his face. "This is Mommy's friend. He's going to keep us safe, okay?"

He stares at Jensen, hard. Jensen's looking right back at him, but I can't tell what he's feeling at all. His eyes are wide, lips parted. He could be astonished or devastated. It's impossible to know with him.

"Jensen," I whisper.

He swings his eyes to mine. "Where's Leland?"

I open my mouth, but I can't get the words out for a second. All I can do is shake my head.

"Talk to me, baby." His whisper is low and urgent.

"He's dead," I mouth. "Upstairs."

His brows rise. "You kill him?"

I can't speak. I don't want to say the words in front of Landis. Someday, I might tell my son what I did to gain our freedom. Or I might let him live in blissful ignorance. I don't know yet.

"Take Landis," he says hoarsely. "I need to find a way out of here."

"What about Kayleigh and Brothers?"

He eases Landis back into my arms and ducks out. "Brothers knows what he's doing. Stay put, baby."

The way he calls me baby is so soft this time. Heart in my throat, I watch him move among the shelves. There's a flicker of orange as he opens the door to scan the yard. Then, he's back, holding out his hand.

"We have a window of time right now," he says. "Give Landis to me."

I slide from beneath the stairs and put my son in his arms. This time, Landis grips his shirt, holding on. Jensen takes my hand for the second time tonight and pulls us through the back door into the side yard. It's empty, sheltered by the porch. The hydrangea bushes wall off the back area where the commotion still rages.

"Where are we going?" I whisper.

He shifts Landis to his left side and pulls his AK out of the way, reaching to the small of his back to remove his pistol. It glints in the firelight, and Landis makes a muffled sound, like it frightens him. Jensen turns to him, pulling the pistol down and out of sight.

"Hey, it's okay," he says, voice dropping. "I got you, kid."

Landis opens his eyes. "What's your name?" he whispers.

"Jensen," he says, voice cracking.

Landis sniffs. "My name is Landis. It's nice to meet you," he whispers, his words rehearsed the way I taught him. "I'm four years old."

"That's good. That's the best age," Jensen says, eyes glittering.

The fighting fades into nothingness, and I'm back in my bed in Harlan, my daddy sitting on the edge of the mattress. He's using that voice he'd use to calm me down after a bad dream, and it sounds so damn much like the one Jensen is using right now.

Footsteps hammer, snapping me out of it.

“We need to go,” Jensen says. “Stay close, baby.”

CHAPTER FORTY-TWO

JENSEN

We are getting out of this alive.

I don't care what I have to do.

The ground crunches to the right. Two figures careen around the side of the house. I raise my pistol, ready to shoot. Then, the light catches the shadow in front—it's Kayleigh, still in her nightgown. Brothers skids to a halt beside her, AK in hand.

"Is the front—" I start.

"Leland's dead," he pants. "I saw him."

"I know—"

"We need to pull back, Jen," he interjects. "I don't have the guys for this. We need to pull back now. It's over, for now."

"I'll take Kayleigh, Della, and Landis," I say. "You pull your men back and meet us by the north entrance."

"No," Kayleigh says, falling against Brothers' side. Her right knee is bloody, crimson and dirt smeared up her shin. "I'm not leaving you."

He steps into the light, his hand coming up to touch her face. Her lower lip trembles. I see a flash of what I witnessed in the office, a real bond, a depth of feeling.

"Go with them, darling," he begs.

She shakes her head. I know that look—she's not leaving without him.

"We don't have time to stall," Brothers says. "Kayleigh, you go with them. I'm going to pull my men back and make a run through the front to the north."

"Good," I say. "Go."

He bends in, kissing Kayleigh on the forehead. His eyes flutter shut, like he's wondering if this is the last time he'll get to kiss her. Beside me, it looks like Della is about to burst into tears. Then, Brothers turns and disappears into the shadows. There's a half second of silence, then shooting, like a machine gun, rips through the night.

"No, no," Kayleigh whimpers..

I reach for her, but she slips through my fingers like a ghost, disappearing the same way Brothers went. I lurch forward and stop myself. I can't go after her. I have Della and her son to protect. Della gasps, hand going to her mouth. She swings her gaze to me like she's expecting me to do something, but I shake my head.

"Jensen—"

"No, my job is getting you and Landis out," I say. "Take your son, baby. We're running to the side exit. I'm going to spot us."

"Jensen," she whispers, voice breaking.

"You hear me, Della?"

She nods, her face white. I ease Landis back into her arms. Then, we both take a breath and hold. I wait, listening for a lull.

"Go," I order.

We burst into the side yard, running hard for the side exit. The gate is hanging open, but as we get close, a pair of dark figures appear. Caudill soldiers. Reflexively, I lift my pistol and take them both out. Their bodies drop like bricks, but the second they do, footsteps ring out, heading in our direction.

"Right, to the right," I hiss. "Stay in the shadow of the fence."

We move along the fence, making our way into the front of the yard. That's when I see it, and my steps falter. In the yellow light from the burning front door is the shadow of Brothers on his knees, a woman's body in his arms.

His head is bowed. She's not moving.

Fuck.

Della hasn't seen them. I push between her and the horror in the front lawn, keeping my arm around their bodies as I usher them towards the north end. The fence there is open, shattered and half burnt. I put my pistol into my belt and take my AK out. We're getting out this way, and anyone who stops me is dying.

A group of soldiers appears. They're down before they even see us, bodies twisting as they hit the dirt. We burst through the burning gates and into the road. A heavy thud and thundering crash shakes the ground. The house is starting to fall. I can't see anything through the smoke, but it sounds like the bullets have died down. We pause at the bend where the road branches out, and I make the mistake of turning back.

Smoke rises, orange and gray.

In the middle of it, I see the shadow of Brothers laying Kayleigh down and picking up his gun.

Everything is quiet. He turns, lifting a hand.

Waving us on.

"Who is that?" Della gasps.

I take her arm, putting my body between hers and the house. "I don't know," I say. "We need to move and find the horses. We have to go now."

We're less than five steps in when the shooting starts again. This time, it's not the sound of warfare. It sounds like vengeance. This is no place for us tonight. If there is a God, he is long gone by now. All that's left is what I choose to do from here on out, and I choose to protect my family.

I whistle, sharp and loud, into the smoke. The shape of Godspeed appears in the distance. He comes running, hooves sending up sparks as he skids on the pavement. I lift Della up first and hand Landis to her before swinging up behind.

My heels dig in, and Godspeed does what he does best.

He runs.

CHAPTER FORTY-THREE

DELLA

I don't remember much of the ride. All I know is he's holding me, and I'm holding Landis.

And we're safe.

We slow after a good half hour of running. Jensen slides off Godspeed, and someone takes his reins. I see a flash of bright eyes and dark beard—it's Angus. My lips crack, and I try to speak, but Jensen is pushing me across a grassy clearing. Metal glints in the moonlight as a birdlike structure rises into my vision.

"That's a plane?" I ask, stumbling.

"Brothers sent it for us, to get us back to Montana," Jensen says.

"What about Kayleigh?"

He hesitates, dipping his head. "Brothers will keep her safe."

Before I can respond, I see Angus pulling down the airplane steps, Jensen lifting Landis. He doesn't speak as he helps me into the back seat of the tiny plane. It's cramped, the pilot just a few feet from the back row. Jensen slides in, and Angus slams the door, slapping the pilot's side.

The plane rises. Landis whimpers, clinging to me, and I kiss his forehead.

"Is this safe?" I breathe.

"It's all we have, but yes, I think so."

I glance sideways at him. He's wounded from the fight, his face still leaking blood. There's a fine crust of mud scabbed over his bare arms from the ring, but he's never looked so beautiful to me.

He did this. He told me he was going to get my baby back, and he did it. I take my left hand from Landis and reach for Jensen, twining my fingers through his. He's subdued, but his eyes flicker warm in the night, connecting with mine for a breathless second.

The plane curves, and down below, I see fire. Orange, hazy smoke rises from the Caudill estate.

It's gone. It's over.

The hell I went through since the moment I became a woman is finished. It will burn away through the night, but what it leaves behind doesn't matter to me anymore. We're flying toward a new life.

I hold them both close, closing my eyes.

I feel nothing, just numbness. But as the night goes on for hours, there comes a moment when the horizon finally lightens. It goes from mountain blue to the first golden rays of the sun breaking. That's when I finally feel something in the shattered remains of my porcelain heart.

Hope.

I sleep on and off, Landis snoring in my arms, until we touch down at a private airport in Montana. Jensen helps us out and thanks the pilot. He says something to him, but I can't hear it over the engine still running. Then, he strides across the tarmac to us, and the plane rises in the air.

We don't speak. I just touch his chest, and he leans down to kiss my temple.

He takes us from the airport in a rental truck. There's no car seat, so I lay in the back against the door, my arms wrapped around Landis. He sleeps soundly, his head on my chest. Jensen is silent as the grave the entire drive out to his ranch. His thumb moves on the wheel, tapping the entire time until we pull up the driveway.

He cuts the engine.

"You okay?" I ask.

He nods, running a hand over his face. His stubble is growing in, giving him more of a beard than just a mustache. The eyes that meet mine in the rearview mirror are so damn tired.

"Let's get the kid to bed," he says.

He gets out, opening the side door. Gently, reverently, he accepts Landis into his arms. The way he holds my son is the most beautiful thing I've ever seen, like a new morning, a new gasping breath on Earth. It's what I wanted to see the day I gave birth to him.

He carries him inside, locking the door. Landis sleeps hard, his cheek squishing on Jensen's shoulder.

"Where should I put him?" he whispers.

"Do you have a guestroom?" I turn the hall light on.

He nods. "It's next door to mine."

"That's perfect," I say, moving to the stairs. "If he wakes up, we can leave the door open."

He follows me, and all I can think about is how much has changed since I was last in this house. I was desperate and scared. Now, I'm hopeful for the first time since eighteen. My heart flutters as I stand in the doorway and watch Jensen lay Landis down in the big bed against the far wall. He comes back, touching my waist and pulling me near.

"Do you want to sleep here with him?" he asks.

I shake my head. "He's not used to it. I'd like to sleep with you, if that's alright."

"Yeah," he says. "We'll be able to hear him if he calls out."

I nod, stumbling a little as we back into the hall. My legs are so wobbly, it's a wonder I've been upright this entire night. He guides me to his bedroom and closes the door. I turn, and he grips my wrists gently. His face hovers close to mine, eyes heavy lidded.

"What happened?" he rasps.

"What?"

"How did Leland die? Did he touch you?"

Disgust churns in my stomach, and I have to force my mind not to spiral. I shake my head.

"What happened?" he presses.

My tongue flicks out to wet my cracked lips. "He took me back to his bedroom and...I drugged him."

That crease appears between his brows.

"I cut—oh God, I cut his head off with the knife above the bed," I burst out, tears erupting for the first time in hours. "I'm a murderer, I killed him, I killed someone."

His arms are around me, pressing my head to his shoulder. He's shushing me, the sound rumbling in his chest. The sobs rip through me, so violent it's painful. But at the center of it, he's burning as warm as summertime back home on the front steps of my trailer, golden, bright.

If I just close my eyes and sink into him, the world outside seems so much kinder.

I sob until I'm spent.

"Baby, I think he had that coming," he says finally.

"I know," I manage. "It's just a shock."

"I'm sorry you had to be the one to do it. I tried to shield you from it."

"None of this is your fault."

"Nothing is your fault either."

That's the simple truth of it. Nothing that's happened to either of us was our fault, and yet, we still have scars we'll always carry. But that doesn't seem so bad if I just have someone to share that burden with. He lifts his head, turning to kiss my forehead. I turn at the same moment, and by happy accident, our mouths graze.

Heat singes my lips, spreading through my veins.

He kisses me deeply, like he'll never let go. I kiss him back, gripping his shoulder, sliding my other hand around his back. The room is still dark, the sun climbing from behind the mountains. Slowly, he starts to move, rocking me in his arms.

Back and forth, our bodies fall into a soundless rhythm. We stay that way until the world stops spinning and my heart hurts just a little less.

"Tomorrow," he says.

"What happens then?"

"Tomorrow, you and Landis are going downtown to the courthouse," he says firmly. "None of this waiting around bullshit. And tomorrow night, you and I are going to seal the deal."

My heart speeds up. He slows down until he's barely moving.

"You talking about marrying me, cowboy?" I whisper.

"I'm not talking about it," he says. "I'm saying it. Tomorrow morning, I'm taking your ass to the courthouse. I've been through hell and back, baby, just fucking marry me."

My face cracks in a smile. "You're so romantic."

"I can be, but this isn't about romance. This is about locking down what's mine."

"Oh, really?"

"Yeah, I won that fight fair and square."

"Yeah," I say, wrapping my arms around his neck. "You did."

He kisses the top of my head. "Let's clean up and sleep."

I've never felt safer in my life than crawling into bed with him, freshly showered and burrowing into his arms. He opens the adjoining door, and I can make out the shape of Landis fast asleep, never knowing what I had to endure to set him free.

That's how it will stay. He'll grow up with Jensen as his father. If he ever asks, I'll tell him the truth.

But for now, I want us all to heal.

CHAPTER FORTY-FOUR

JENSEN

I'm woken by the sensation of being watched. The hair on the back of my neck prickles. Carefully, I open my eyes and meet a pair of little ones, narrowed. Abruptly, I push myself upright. He's holding the blanket from the guest room tightly in both arms like it's a stuffed animal.

"Hi," he whispers.

"Hey, kid," I say, clearing my throat. I glance over at the inert lump on Della's side of the bed.

"I'm hungry," Landis says. "Can I have pancakes?"

Still confused from sleep, I nod, pushing the covers back. "Yeah, let's go make breakfast."

He waits while I pull on a t-shirt, then he follows me down to the kitchen. My heart is damn near pumping out of my chest. I've never been shy, but suddenly, I'm feeling it, wondering if he's going to take a good look at me and decide I'm not father material.

I pull out the chair. He scrambles into it. He's in his pajamas, which still smell like smoke. Before we go to the courthouse, we're going to have to buy both him and Della a new wardrobe.

"Do you know where my fox is?" he asks.

I freeze. "Your fox?"

"My toy I sleep with. It's a stuffed fox," he explains.

"So, uh, I think it might have gotten lost last night," I say. "But I'll take you and let you pick out whatever you want from the general store. They have toys."

I can tell that only half satisfies him, but he nods. "Okay, that's fine."

Unsure of myself, I take the pan out and start making pancakes from a mix I keep in the freezer. Landis' eyes follow me like tractor beams, soaking in my every move. Finally, I set his plate down in front of him and get to making coffee.

"You're probably wondering where your dad is," I say. "Your mom and you should talk later."

He shakes his head. "My dad is always gone until bedtime."

I falter, burning my hand on the percolator as I set it down. "He was never at home?"

He shakes his head, picking up his fork. "It was just me and Georgie, but she was going to quit and go away. That's what Aunt Kayleigh said. Where's Aunt Kayleigh?"

I clear my throat. "She...she had to leave for a bit."

"Okay," he says, face falling. "Did everyone have to go away?"

I pick up my coffee and sit opposite him. "I'm not going away, and neither is your mom. We're staying."

He starts sawing at the pancakes with the side of his fork. "Okay. That's okay," he says. "Can you cut this for me?"

I lean over, cutting the pancakes for him. It didn't occur to me that kids can't do much for themselves at age four. He watches until it's done, then takes his fork back.

"Thanks," he says. "My house set on fire last night."

I sink down again, feeling like I'm in a game of dodgeball. "Yeah, that's true."

"I like this house," he says.

"Thanks. I made it."

His brows lift, attention piqued. "You made the whole house?"

He's impressed. That's a win for me. "Yeah, I did."

"Can you make me a house?"

"Sure, a treehouse, if that's what you want," I say. "So long as your mom says it's fine."

"She probably will," he says.

He eats some more, cleaning the plate with alarming quickness. I get him some water because the milk is expired, making a mental note to ask Della to come up with a list of food for him later. He accepts the cup, checking it over before taking a careful sip from the open top.

"I like juice," he says.

"Sorry, little guy. We don't have any."

The stairs creak, and it's a relief to see Della appear, in my shirt and shorts. Last night, after we showered, she balled up the lingerie and dressing gown and asked me to throw it into the trash outside. I just never want to see anything from him again, she whispered. I get that.

She goes right to Landis, bending to kiss the top of his head.

"How'd you sleep, sweetie?" she murmurs.

"Good," he says. "Jensen's going to make me a treehouse."

She looks up, brow arching. "Oh, really?"

"Not very high off the ground," I amend.

She circles, her soft hand skimming my shoulders as she leans into me. Landis watches us, not missing a thing. He's a smart kid, I can tell by the way he soaks everything in around him. That means Della is going to have to do a lot of explaining to make sense of what happened and why everything is changing. I wish I could help, but that's not my place. Yet.

"I'm gonna run into town and get you both clothes," I say. "Then, we have a date at the courthouse."

She blushes, kissing my hair. "Thank you for taking care of us."

"Of course, baby," I say.

I squeeze her arm, and she rests her chin on my head. We stay like that for a second before I shift, getting to my feet. Landis puts his cup down and looks up at me.

"Where are you going?" he asks.

"To the store to get you some new clothes," I say, reaching for a piece of scrap paper and a pen. "You want me to see if they have a stuffed fox at the store?"

"Yeah," he says, face lighting up.

Della sinks down in my chair. "Oh no, I didn't get his fox."

"Don't worry," I say. "I'll find something."

I go into town with the list of everything we need in hand. Most of the groceries and clothes are easy to find, but it takes a half hour to find a stuffed fox. I'm about to give up and face a hard conversation with Landis, but just as I'm getting into my truck, I look across the road at a little boutique in South Platte and see one sitting in the window.

I'm across the street in seconds, opening my wallet. The damn thing is thirty dollars, but that's fine. No way in hell I'm leaving without it.

When I get back, they're both showered and ready. Della is quieter than usual, and there's a flush to her face. She gets Landis dressed, not meeting my eyes, and sends him downstairs to get a snack before we leave. I catch her around the waist, her slip silky under my fingers.

"You're feeling some kind of way," I say.

She gives me a look, but she's blushing even harder.

"Is it wrong for me to be excited for my wedding?" she says.

"It's the only way I want you."

She lets me kiss her, nice and deep. Then, she's ducking into the bathroom and locking the door. I'm in my Sunday clothes, pants with suspenders to keep them horizontal and a crisp blue shirt. I don't own a suit, never had a reason to, but this is good enough. I think she'll take me as I am.

Downstairs, Landis stands in the kitchen, eating the sandwich Della left out for him. I pour him a glass of milk. He chugs the entire thing in one go then hands it back to me, nodding his appreciation.

Impressed, I put it in the sink. When he's grown, I have a few bars we can hit up.

"Can we wait on the porch?" he asks.

"Sure thing," I say, leading the way down the hallway.

He scampers after me, perching on the top step. "My mom takes a while to get ready," he says.

"That's alright," I say, sitting beside him. "I got nowhere to be but here."

We sit in silence. Then, he starts going at it with the questions. That's a big field, he points out. How long is it? Can he go into the barn? How many horses do I own? Can he have a horse with a long mane and tail? What are the mountains called, especially the great big one in the distance? That's Sovereign Mountain, I tell him. I'll take you out there real soon. He says that's fine, but why can't we go today? And can he ride in the back of the truck? That one, I go ahead and give him a firm no. He pushes out his lower lip but recovers at light speed.

"I like my room upstairs. Can I keep it?" he asks.

"Yeah, reckon you can," I say.

It's like being in the ring, just one after another. It's a relief when Della steps outside. Then, I forget all about whether I'm doing a good job answering Landis' questions, because the prettiest girl in the world is right here.

She's glowing in her white sundress with little purple flowers. It's like looking right into the sun.

I open my mouth to say something inappropriate, but then I remember Landis is right there, and I need to start watching my words. Instead, I get up and hold out my hand. She gives me a shy smile.

"You ready?" she says.

"More than ready," I say. "Come on. Let's go before you change your mind."

CHAPTER FORTY-FIVE

JENSEN

She doesn't change her mind.

She marries me in the courthouse in South Platte that afternoon. Then, we go down to the diner to get Landis some ice cream. He's chattering a mile a minute about anything and everything he can think of. Della answers him, her arm around his shoulders. Her hand in mine is tight, like she never wants to let go.

I thought today might feel like the aftermath of a disaster, but it doesn't. It feels like waking up after a long nightmare and remembering I'm safe. The relief is overwhelming.

That night, after Landis is fast asleep with his new stuffed fox tucked under his arm, I take her into the bedroom and lock the door. It isn't like in the loft, or even our first time together. It's quiet, no words spoken, no need for them. We undress each other, and I lay her on her back, kissing her mouth until her body blossoms, opening for me.

In the dark, I fuck her as my wife for the first time.

The next morning, I get up and take my truck down to Ryder Ranch. I didn't realize it until late last night, but Chicken has been living out there this entire time. When I pull into the drive, there he is, sitting on the porch like he never moved. I get out and whistle, but he just stares at me, eyes unfocused.

"Goddamn," I say, putting my hands on my hips.

"About time."

I turn to find Deacon striding out of the barn, wiping his hands on a grease rag. "I thought you were never going to pick up your dog."

"Sorry, I was out of town," I say.

He pauses next to me, looking me from head to foot. "What happened to you? You look like somebody hit you in the face with a brick."

"I went back to Kentucky."

"You did? Why?"

Everything comes pouring out, in the simplest of terms. I tell him about meeting Della at the stockyards, that Brothers had sent him, about Leland and Landis. He listens, brow lowered like he's really absorbing it. At the end, he whistles low.

"Damn. So you're married now," he says. "You got a kid."

I nod. "Yeah, that's how it shook out."

He looks like he wants to say something.

"You good?" I ask.

He rubs the back of his neck. "Listen, do you remember a while back when I needed to talk to Brothers Boyd about killing some guy who had fucked my wife years ago?"

"What?"

"He was like an old boyfriend sort of," Deacon explains, like that makes sense. "You gave me Brothers' number on the condition I don't tell him I got it from you."

"Yeah?"

He squints at the sun. "I sort of recall him implying he knew you were out here in Montana. I just had a lot of my own shit going on, with the baby and all, and I forgot to bring it up."

I put my hands on my hips and stare. "Oh yeah? That seems like important information."

"In hindsight, it probably was," he admits.

Out of every wild escapade and harebrained scheme Deacon Ryder and I have shared, this might be the dumbest thing he's ever done. Old Jensen would have punched him in the jaw, but right now, still in the afterglow of marriage, I don't even care anymore.

"Just for that, I'm gonna make you keep Chicken," I say.

He lifts a hand. "Please don't do that."

There's a low whine from the porch, and we both turn. Chicken heaves his haunches off the porch and ambles over, sniffing my pant leg. He does a circle around us, stares at Deacon like he could care less, and heads towards my truck.

"I think he's ready to get out of here," Deacon says.

"I better get back," I say. "Next time you get info like that, at least clue me in."

"Will do," he says, standing back.

On the drive back, it's hard to focus. Chicken is panting like he just ran the derby, but I turn everything over in my head. It doesn't matter that Deacon knew. It's an irrelevant detail at this point. Everything that happened, happened for a reason, and that reason led me straight to my family.

I'm lighter than air.

Back at the house, Della sits in the front yard, watching Landis play in the driveway. I pull up and circle the car, opening the door.

"You want a dog, Landis?" I call.

His eyes light up, and he's up and running, skidding to a halt. Chicken heaves himself to the ground, sniffing and flinging drool everywhere as he licks his lips. The yell of delight from Landis as he drops to a crouch and flings his arms around Chicken brings Della running.

She looks from me to Chicken, her brows knitting.

"You bought him a dog?" she whispers.

"I already owned a dog," I say, wrapping my arm around her waist. "He was staying with some friends, but it was time for him to come home."

Landis starts running, clapping his hands for Chicken to follow. For the first time in his life, Chicken gets some life in him and runs after him. They start circling the yard until Landis throws himself into the grass, and Chicken collapses next to him, panting hard.

"What is he?" Della asks.

"Some kind of hound mix," I say. "Hard to say, I found him a while back, and he just kind of stayed."

She lays her hand on my chest, looking up with a smile. "He's always wanted a dog. You scored some points today."

"With you or him?"

"Both."

I kiss her, and she kisses me back.

The days pass in a golden haze as we slowly adjust to being a family together, but there's always an image in the back of my brain I can't shake. It's Brothers Boyd, holding Kayleigh's body as the fire raged behind him. It's the realization he wasn't lying when he said he was truly sorry for the part he played. And that he'd done his best back then to keep me safe.

It's this nagging feeling there's still one more step in tying up all my loose ends.

A week passes, then another. The fields are growing golden, ready for the haying season. I don't say anything until one Sunday night after Landis has gone to bed. We're on the porch. She's laying in my lap on the steps. That's when it all spills out, and I tell her what I saw.

She sits up, open-mouthed. A tear slips down her cheek. "You have to find out what happened to her," she whispers.

I turn to look up at the dark peak of Sovereign Mountain towering in the distance.

"I need to go back one more time," I say.

It's a relief to hear the words after carrying them inside me for weeks. She leans into me, wrapping her arms around my torso. We both know how hard it will be for me to return after finally getting away, but the need for closure is stronger. Della loved Kayleigh, and we both owe her a debt for the part she played in saving our family. If I don't return and find out what happened, we'll live with that shadow over us forever.

"I just need to know," she says, voice breaking.

"I know, baby, and I'll go," I say. "When the haying season is over in a few weeks. The fall meet starts up then. I know where Brothers will be on the first day of the races."

"Thank you."

I bend to press my lips to her head. We stay like that for a long time as the sun drops below the mountain.

Then, we go upstairs to bed.

CHAPTER FORTY-SIX

JENSEN

ONE MONTH LATER

I don't know if I feel anything at all, standing on the edge of the road. It's the beginning of fall. It smells like it, a little burnt, a little cool. Straight ahead is Brothers' office building. I know I'll find him here on the first day of the fall meet.

I feel older, but I think I'm at peace.

Leaves skitter over my boots. I tap the cowboy hat he gave me against my thigh. A car horn beeps. The streets are more empty than usual today, with everyone at the racetrack.

In the past, I never visited the downtown office. Now, I realize why Brothers never brought me here. There's an aura of sadness around it, like it's a point in time that stood still. The row house walls are gray brick, clean but well worn. The antique windows are shuttered with dark cherry wood that looks like it was placed decades ago.

Over the door hangs a sign.

Brothers Boyd.

I can make out the faint spot where the first word wore out—the origin story of the man who made me, who broke me, and gave me everything back in the end.

A car moves slowly. I wait until it's gone before crossing the street. The short stairs are painted deep green to match the door. There's a brass plaque below the porch light that reads Private Residence, No Solicitors. Ignoring it, I lift the knocker and let it fall with a bang that echoes up and down the road.

A woman opens the door. She's in work clothes, a pencil dress and short heeled shoes.

"Can...I help you?" she says.

I clear my throat. "Jensen Childress to see Brothers Boyd. Is he here?"

She shakes her head. "No, you just missed him."

"Where is he? I flew in. I can't miss him."

"I can't just tell people where he's at. It's not safe."

"He knows me," I say, dipping into my pocket to pull out the picture. She takes it and stares down at it. Then, she glances up at me with narrowed eyes.

"Wait a minute...I know who you are," she whispers. "He said you went home, that you weren't coming back."

"Are you his...woman?"

She shakes her head. "No, I'm his secretary. Brothers doesn't... He doesn't have anyone. I don't know if he ever will again."

Her voice goes soft and sad.

"I promise I'm not here to hurt him," I say. "Just tell me where he is."

She chews her lip. "Alright, he's down at Masterhill Station. Took his dog to shoot some ducks for a dinner he's got going on tonight."

"Thank you," I say, putting my hat back on. "You have a good day, ma'am."

She wraps her arms around herself as a chilly breeze sweeps down the road. "He's not...the same. Not since she's gone."

"I know," I say. "I didn't think he would be."

I cross the street, heading to the rental car. Her eyes follow me beneath knitted brows as I get in and pull out onto the street. Everything feels different, grimmer, like the city is hunkering down for the winter. I wonder what Brothers did when Kayleigh died. I have a pretty good idea he became a darker, more powerful version of himself. That can't be good.

The road takes me out to horse country. It's golden, the trees rustling. The black tar road winds, cutting through the hills. After a while, I come up on the turn off for the hunting area of the Station. Parked in the gravel is a white SUV. It's not the same one he was driving before, but I can tell it's his by the darkened windows.

I park, getting out. The temperature is dropping, so I pull my Carhartt from the car. Then, slowly, because I still don't know what to say when I find him, I climb the ridge and look down the hill. Below stretches a green-brown field with a pond at the center.

There he is, at the edge of the rushes. A lone figure in a plaid suit stands with his hands in his pockets. It's been a month and two weeks since we last spoke, but it feels like years. Decades, even.

I start walking, striding through the grass. He doesn't look up until I'm almost upon him. Then, he turns to glance at me, his face not changing. An open shotgun hangs in the crook of his arm. Pulling up beside him, I look out over the pond, unable to face him head on.

Nobody speaks.

Finally, I clear my throat. "Sorry about Kayleigh."

His jaw flexes. "Which part, Jen?"

"Well, she died," I say.

He smiles, face creasing. "No, she didn't. She took everything in the Caudill accounts—after I slaughtered her whole family—and left. Dumped me harder than I've ever been dumped. Actually, I don't know if I have been dumped before now. I think she was a first."

A wave of relief moves over me. Della is going to be in happy tears when I tell her. She's been so cut up for the last few weeks over Kayleigh. I start to say that, then shut the hell up at the expression on his face. His jaw is set, he's got a beard now, and his eyes are overcast.

"How was she still alive?" I say finally.

"Bullet missed her heart by an inch. I killed every person in that house, brought her to the hospital, and went back to kill the rest. Her family is gone. There was blood in the street. When she woke up, we were done."

"I'm sorry," I say.

He turns. "Don't be. I got everything I wanted."

The edges of his face, the corners of his eyes, are made of stone. He might have gotten everything he wanted, but I think he lost what he needed.

"Why are you here, Jen?" he says.

"Della thought Kayleigh was dead. She asked me to come back."

"Well, she's not."

"And I came to forgive you," I say, the words coming out on accident.

There it is—a hint of softness. He turns, whistling sharply. An Irish Setter jumps from the rushes and comes running. Brothers pats it on the head, giving it a treat from his pocket. Then, he puts his hat on, a plaid newsboy cap I haven't seen him wear in decades, and starts climbing the hill. I go after him, keeping pace at his side.

"You said we were even," he says.

"Even's not the same as forgiven."

"Ain't that the truth."

We pause at the crest of the hill. Down below rolls the bluegrass, and in the distance are the pinnacles, a hazy slate gray. Everything is still clinging to that last bit of green from the summer. His eyes are narrowed as they skim over the horizon, and the lines around them are a little deeper than I remember.

"Thanks for the forgiveness," he says finally.

"Thanks for the family."

He laughs once. "Yeah, how's that going?"

I nod. "Good. We're getting her little boy settled in."

My throat tightens, and I have to clear it before I can tell him something I've never spoken out loud, save for behind the closed doors of my room back home. Nobody knows, not Jack, not Deacon.

"Della's pregnant," I say.

His brows rise. "Really? That was fast."

"I think she got pregnant while we were here," I say. "We just found out a few days ago."

He's smiling, and I see a little bit of the old Brothers come through.

"You know...I got that truck you used to drive in my barn," he says. "I'll ship it out to you. Maybe you can fix it with Landis...and whatever the next one turns out to be."

We look at each other, and everything is behind us, finally laid to rest. It's over this time. Nothing can fix what happened to me. Nobody can make Brothers anything other than the man he is. I've made peace with it, and in my own way, I do forgive him. He hurt me, but I don't think he set out to cause harm. For my own sake, I have to move on. I'm over being angry, and I wish him well from a distance.

"Thanks," I say finally.

He waves a hand. "You go on home, Jen. I might just stay here for a while, see if I can't get one of those ducks after all."

Neither of us speak for a minute or two. Then, I hold out my hand. He shakes it, winking the way he used to. A million times lighter, I walk down the hill and get into my car. He got everything he wanted and lost everything that mattered, but there's nothing I can do now. I tried to tell him. It's time for me to walk away.

The last thing I see in my rearview mirror is Brothers Boyd standing with his head bowed, looking out over the gently shimmering bluegrass.

A lonely figure on a lonely hill.

CHAPTER FORTY-SEVEN

DELLA

A YEAR LATER

The rocking chair creaks gently. Through the window comes a faint breeze that smells like the fields will need to be hayed soon. A little scuffle comes from the windowsill, then through the open window, a wren pokes its head. I stop rocking with my bare foot and watch. Carefully, it looks around. Then, it's gone, darting away in the sunlight.

There's a quiet cry from the bundle in my arms. I shift her with my elbow, tucking the front of my dress closed. My daughter is just a few months old, already the perfect addition to our family. I lift her, supporting her head, and lay her against my shoulder.

"Delia Rose," I whisper. "You are beautiful."

She blinks, looking up at me with her daddy's eyes. We named her after my father's two grandmothers. I looked at those graves so many times, all the names are burned into my brain. Jensen, knowing I never got a hand in naming Landis, told me to pick out what I liked. It's enough she's a Childress, he said.

I love that she looks like him, that she's got his eyes, his surname. They both get the same crease in their forehead when they're angry. It fills me with overwhelming happiness every time I see it.

We rock until she falls asleep, snoring just like her father. Working carefully, I transfer her to the crib. I close the window, tiptoe over to turn on the fan, and slip out of the room to head for the kitchen.

The kitchen is different than it was when we met. Now, it's pale sage green with sanded pine baseboards. When I moved in, Jensen let me do whatever I wanted. We sketched out plans to renovate on the back of junk mail because he didn't have anything else, late one night, spread out on the bedroom floor. I was on my back, feeling the first kicks from Delia, letting him talk about construction late into the night. I felt like the richest woman in the world.

Crash.

I jump, freezing. The side door to the left of the kitchen leads out to the attached garage. It's halfway open, and through it comes a frustrated grunt. I know what that is—that's what my husband sounds like when he's trying not to swear in front of Landis.

Biting back a smile, I make a cup of black coffee and carry it to the door. Through it, I can see into the garage. Chicken is sleeping on his back on the doormat, twitching and snoring. Parked in the middle is an ancient truck that Brothers Boyd sent to Jensen a few months after he visited Kentucky for the last time. It's a rust bucket, more parts broken than fixed. They couldn't work on it during the winter, but now that it's warm out, they've been messing with it a few nights a week. Landis loves it, especially when it means he can stay up late.

"You want some coffee?" I call out.

Jensen rolls out from underneath, on his back on a board on wheels. Right alongside him comes Landis on his child-sized board. He's wearing goggles far too big for him. He tries to take them off, but they get stuck on his nose.

"Come here," Jensen says, pulling him over and working the goggles off. He sets them aside and accepts the coffee.

"Can I have coffee?" Landis says.

"Nope," Jensen says, reaching out to ruffle his hair. "You've got all the energy you need as it is."

All the cracks in my heart mend every time I see them together. It only took a few months for Landis to start following Jensen around like a lost puppy. Leland rarely interacted with him except at dinner, so the prospect of a man spending time with him, especially one who knows as many neat things as Jensen does, was a whole new world.

I kept apologizing to Jensen for how Landis was shadowing him, talking a mile a minute.

"I'm sorry. He's just really taken with you," I said.

He kissed my forehead. "You want me to be his father or not?"

Sniffing, I nodded. "Yeah, I do."

"Then don't apologize."

That healed me. It made me realize having a son from my first marriage isn't a negative to him, it's a bonus. The more I watched them together, the more I realized Landis might be the best thing to ever happen to Jensen after what he went through.

"Can I have some of that cake from the fridge?" Landis says, interrupting me from my thoughts.

"Nope. It's almost dinner," I say.

Jensen stands, coffee in hand. "What's for dinner?"

"Pork belly," I say. "Greens and rice."

He gives me a look that says everything without him having to speak a word. Draining the mug, he hands it back.

"We're just finishing up in here," he says. "I'll get Landis cleaned up when we're done."

"Yeah, Mom, we're fixing the carburetor," says Landis, sitting back down on his board.

I open my mouth, but he snaps his goggles on and lifts a hand.

"Don't worry. It's okay if you don't know what that is," he says.

My jaw drops. Jensen is biting the inside of his cheek so hard, it hallows. The way my son has soaked up every ounce of Jensen's sass is incredible. Landis scoots back under the truck and starts whistling tunelessly. Jensen dips his head, but I see that dimple come out. Lord, do I love seeing it.

"I'm going out to get the greens from the garden," I say. "I'm leaving the door open. Keep an ear on Delia. The monitor is on the counter."

I turn, but he catches me, pulling me close and kissing my mouth. Quick as a flash, he grabs my ass before ducking down and sliding under the truck. My face is flushed when I go back into the kitchen to make more coffee, this time for myself. The coffee maker hums, sputtering. The rich scent fills the room as I carry it through the front hall out to the porch.

There's a truck coming up the drive, hauling a trailer. I squint, shading my eyes. It slides to a halt, and the door busts open, Deacon Ryder stepping out.

I met him a few weeks after Jensen came back. He's the human equivalent of a right hook. Big, bold, tattooed from head to foot, and unashamed of anything. His wife, Freya, is from Eastern Kentucky, the same as me. She's the sweetest thing I've ever met, and we hit it off right away. Together, they own Ryder Ranch, one of the biggest suppliers of top-tier barrel racers in Montana.

Deacon touches the brim of his hat. "Mrs. Childress."

I smile. I never wanted Leland's last name, but when I get called by Jensen's, it makes my toes curl, just thinking about how he's all mine. It helps he's got a good, strong mountain name, the kind that makes me proud to be where I'm from.

Deacon opens the side door and lifts Freya out. She's wearing one of his hats and a sundress, boots on her feet. Usually, she has her baby in her arms, but I don't see him today.

"Where's Slate?" I call.

"He's with Bittern and Janie," she says. "It's date night for us."

That's her brother and his wife, who live out on Ryder Ranch. I climb down the steps, walking up to where Deacon fusses with something in the back of the truck.

"What brings you all up here on date night then?" I ask.

"Deacon's got that filly Jensen wanted," Freya says, jerking her head at the silver trailer.

I put my hands on my hips.

"He didn't tell me about no filly," I say, frowning. "Who's the filly for?"

"Fuck if I know," says Deacon, sauntering around the trailer and unlatching the door. "Don't shoot the messenger, shoot your damn husband."

Freya and I follow him, keeping back so he can swing the door open wide. Inside, there's a chestnut horse with white socks blinking in the sunlight.

"Oh, she's pretty," I say.

"Pretty expensive," says Jensen, appearing out of nowhere with Landis glued to him like usual. My son stares up at the horse but doesn't reach for it. He knows better now that Jensen has taught him the ropes of staying safe on the ranch.

"Hey now, you got a friends and family discount," says Deacon, leading the filly down and out of the trailer. She looks around, ears swiveling.

"What's she for?" I ask.

Jensen's hand rests on my waist. "She's for you, baby."

"For me?"

He nods. "I was up at Ryder Ranch the other week and saw Deacon working with her. Thought she looked like she might be your horse."

My jaw is on the floor. I set my coffee aside and step up to the filly, holding my palm out flat. Of course, I rode a little back home, but not enough to warrant having a horse all to myself. She dips her head and sniffs my hand, nuzzling it with her prickly nose. The late afternoon sun hits her just right, making her hair glow red.

"She's beautiful," I whisper.

"Yeah, she's one of my best this year," says Deacon.

Jensen puts his hand on my elbow. My heart melts in my chest, but I don't want to embarrass myself in front of Deacon and Freya by crying.

"Y'all want to stay for dinner?" I ask, clearing my throat.

"Nah, there's a new place in town Freya wanted to check out," says Deacon. "But we'll be by Sunday night to check on the filly. We can stay then."

"Deacon, don't invite yourself," Freya chides.

Jensen laughs. "You know you can come by anytime."

I'm distracted by the filly, a little relieved they aren't staying tonight. Inside, I'm overwhelmed. Of course, Jensen has gotten me plenty of things over the last year, the rock glittering on my finger chief among them, but there's something so sweet about this filly. Knowing he saw her and thought of me has me choked up.

"We better go, speaking of," says Freya.

They pile into the truck, leaving us with the filly. On the way out, Deacon hits the gatepost with the edge of the trailer tire, and Jensen has to go over to inspect it. Landis follows, imitating the way they're both standing with their hands on their hips. They talk for another twenty minutes. I run my hand down the filly's neck. She's blinking, looking around the ranch.

Bored with waiting, I take her into the barn. There are a few open stalls at the back, one with pasture access. I clip her to the mounting station and fix up one of the stalls so she can be comfortable until we decide where we want her to stay for good. Then, carefully because she's young, I lead her into the stall and slip her halter off, standing back to give her space.

She snorts, dipping her head. Sunlight filters in through the window, catching her brilliant coat.

"You like her, baby?"

I look up to find Jensen leaning on the door, hat pulled low. Lord, him doing sweet things for me gets me more fired up than when he talks dirty, trying to get me upstairs. I go to him, tilting my head back so he can kiss me. He tastes a little bit like the gum between his back teeth.

His mustache tickles. I pull back, tapping the brim of his hat.

"I love her," I say. "I better go check on Delia though."

"I've got the monitor in my pocket," he says. "She's been rustling, but she's not up yet."

"Where's Landis?"

"Back in the garage. I told him to check on Chicken and get him dinner," he says, opening the stall door to let me out. I start to walk past him, but his arm shoots out and wraps around my waist, pulling me against his body.

"I've been thinking," he says.

"Uh oh."

"It's nothing bad. I just wanted to get a timeline on your plans for the next few years."

I stare, trying to figure out what he's getting at. "Why? You planning on doing some complicated project?"

"Yeah," he says. "Planning on doing this pussy."

"It ain't that complicated, but you're welcome to it."

"Not for me, anyway," he drawls.

I roll my eyes, hands on his chest. "So what are you wanting to get into?"

"I'm just trying to figure out what you want your family to look like," he says. "When we might want to have another baby."

"Oh? What's got you thinking about that?"

"Deacon's already talking about it."

"He's talking about us having another baby?"

"No, he's talking about knocking Freya up again. And he's got some pretty valid points."

I pull back, hands on my hips. "Oh, really? What points?"

He shrugs. "About staggering out ages and taking into account I'm a fair bit older than you."

"Well, I'm not ready to get knocked up again," I say. "But I'm open to it. So come and ask me in about six months, and then we can negotiate. Deal?"

I hold out my hand. His face breaks into that smile I love more than anything, and he shakes my hand. Before I can pull back, he tugs me close, picks me up, and slings me over his shoulder. The world spins as I hang upside down, and I'm blushing like crazy.

He carries me up the front walkway and deposits me in the kitchen. I'm flustered, my hair all messed up. He steps back to peer at Landis through the garage door before pushing me against the fridge to go in for another kiss.

I'm falling hard every day, again and again.

A rustle comes from his pocket, and we break apart, knowing naptime is over. "Go on upstairs and get Delia," I whisper. "I'll start dinner."

He kisses me one more time before heading to the nursery. I lay out my pork belly and start cutting it in chunks, the oil heating up in my big pan. He's back in a few minutes with Delia in his arms, walking carefully, trying not to jostle his girl.

"I think she's hungry," he says.

I wipe my fingers on a rag. "You want to get her a bottle? I pumped earlier."

He's already opening the fridge to retrieve it. While it warms, he sinks down at the kitchen table and shifts Delia to his hands. She fits perfectly in them, looking up at him with sleepy eyes.

"I don't know, but I think we got the cutest baby ever made," he says.

"I reckon so," I say.

"Reckon that comes from you," he says, taking the bottle out of hot water and wiping it on his shirt.

"I think you did some contributing."

"A few minutes of it, yeah."

I laugh and shake my head. Landis walks in, talking to Jensen. He wants to hold Delia and help feed her. Jensen says that's alright, but he's got to wash all the grease off his hands first. Their conversation dulls to a comforting background sound as I make dinner.

Sometimes, I have moments like this, when I'm fully aware, out of nowhere, that I got everything I want. I don't have words to describe it, so I just smile and try to soak it all in.

After dinner, I nurse Delia to sleep. Then, I slip downstairs to find Jensen on the porch again, watching the sun make its way down behind the great shadow of Sovereign Mountain.

He holds out his arm, and I sit, leaning into his side. His fingers stroke through my hair, playing absently with it. We don't speak.

Jensen and I can go at it like cats and dogs, bantering until the cows come home, but at the end of the day, when my heart is full, we don't have to say anything at all to be understood. We've always been two halves of each other.

That was all I really wanted in the end.

To be loved, to be known.

CHAPTER FORTY-EIGHT

JENSEN

It's evening. The kids are asleep. All the doors are locked, including our bedroom. I'm in the chair by the window. She's on her knees on the bare floorboards. Her beautiful hair is pulled high, tumbling down to her waist. Her eyes are wrapped in white cloth and her arms are bound behind her back.

Her nipples are hard, pinched red beneath silver clamps. A thin silver strand connects them to the clip on her clit.

She hurts, but she's such a good girl. Despite the unforgiving grains of rice pressing into her knees and shins, she hasn't moved.

I glance up at the clock hanging over the bed. The face of it is plain white. It's been ten minutes—that's long enough. I don't want her getting fatigued.

Slowly, I move to crouch before her. Her lip quivers. She senses my closeness, but she keeps still. I'm so hard from denial, from looking at her naked and tortured.

I dip my fingers between her legs, playing with the clip before sliding them to her cunt.

Soaked.

Her gasp sends a shiver down my spine as I trace her sex. That turns into a whimper when I slip two fingers inside and find the soft ridge of the spot that drives her wild. Starting slow, I tap and rub with growing intensity. Her teeth dig at her lower lip. Gently, I stroke, easing down. Her thighs are tight, forcing her shins harder into the rice, getting her so wet, it drips down my knuckles.

"You want to come for me, baby?" I murmur.

"Yes," she gasps. "Please."

"Don't move."

She nods, sinking back onto her heels as I pull my fingers out and stand. From the end of the bed, I grab a cloth acupressure mat about the size of my upper back. It's perfect for when I want to lay it out and have her kneel on the little spikes all over the inside, but it also fits between her legs for when I want to use it.

I unfurl it, sliding it between her knees. Then, I pull her blindfold off. Big, dark eyes flutter open and fix on me, hazy with desire. I start unbuttoning my shirt.

"God," she moans.

I let it drop on the chair behind me. "What?"

She shakes her head. I turn and lay myself down on my back, spikes digging into the skin over my shoulders. Pain sets everything on edge and lights up all my nerve endings. My cock throbs, tight behind my zipper. Delirious for her, I press my head between her thighs, forcing her to back to kneel over my face.

"You just...you're so pretty," she breathes.

When she says that, I know what she means now.

"I'll be prettier with you squirting on my face, baby," I say.

She moans, head falling to the side. Her thighs lower until she's an inch over my mouth. We've done this before, and we both know what I want. I kiss her thigh then bare my teeth and sink them into the soft skin. She writhes, spine twisting, body shaking with effort to hold steady.

"You are a needy little bitch," I tell her, sliding my hand around her thigh to her ass.

"Oh God," she bursts out. "I need to come."

Pain is a hot throb down my spine. The heels of my boots grit in dry rice. Her cunt is so close, I can almost taste it, hovering an inch from my lips. I wet my fingers and slide them in, parting her pussy, dipping into her tight, hot wetness. Her hips pulse, pulling me deep.

"I'm going to fingerfuck you," I say. "And you're going to come on my face. Understood?"

"Yes," she gasps, shivering.

I go hard on that spot inside her cunt, and she shakes so hard, it takes only a few seconds before I have to hold her up with one hand. Little whines slip out from between her teeth.

Give it to me.

Her spine curls. She's so goddamn tight around my fingers. I'm stroking, coaxing hard. I see it, even in the dim light, the way her cunt tightens.

Take me. Wash me away.

Her spine locks. My eyes close, and I feel it flood over me, hot and tasting of my wife on my tongue. It hits my face, my mustache, spattering over my face and neck, soaking the rice around my head.

She sinks down onto my face, pushing me hard into the rice and spikes beneath my back. Pain grounds me, keeping me from going over the edge most of the time, but tonight, it's too much.

Pleasure runs in a wave through my body, and there's a harsh accumulation of it behind my zipper. A flood, a dam breaking.

"Oh God," she whimpers. "Untie me."

Face still in her cunt, I undo her binds. Her nails scrabble at my belt, tearing my pants open. Her hot tongue runs over me, cleaning my cum from my cock. She's the most beautiful woman in the world, and sometimes, I can't hold back, but that's never mattered to her. She takes all of me, fuck-ups and everything.

Her pussy pulses on my lips as she pushes my cock to the back of her throat, loving me the way I need.

There was never anything sick, nothing twisted, in me to begin with. Della made me understand that. Here in our bedroom, she indulges my fantasies, and I hold the space for hers, every single one. Even the ones she's embarrassed to say aloud.

In this place, we've both finally let go of the past.

It will always exist, but it doesn't control us anymore.

I pull myself from between her thighs with difficulty. My skin burns as I peel it off the mat. Despite having just come, I need to be inside her, to look in her eyes, to feel her in my arms. I lift her, carrying her to the bed. We tumble back against the headboard, both shoving off the last bits of clothing as we go.

I push her thighs open with my knee and sink into her pussy.

"Yes," she breathes, lids flickering.

My hand grips the nape of her neck, steadying her body so I can fuck her. Her nipples are twisted, hot and red. I know her clit aches—I feel how she's gripping me against the pain.

"Come for me, baby," I urge. "Come on my cock."

I unclip her clit, and she cries out at the release. My fingers stroke over it, slick and swollen, teasing it the way she likes. She's so wet, and the sound has me rock hard.

"Hit me, baby," I pant.

She hesitates. She always does. I grip her throat, rutting my hips. The look in my eyes cows her, forcing her to obey. From the corner of my eye, her hand blurs. The pain explodes, and I'm rock hard, right on the edge.

Our mouths are so close.

"Blood, baby," I breathe out. "I want to taste blood."

This time, the pain is white hot, the aftermath bloody metal on my tongue as my lip splits just enough to give me what I need. Fuck, that's better than good.

My cock pushes so deep in her, I feel resistance. Her throat bobs beneath my grip. Our gazes lock, and she looks me deep in the eyes as I come inside her.

"That's right, baby," I grit out. "Take it all. Take all of me."

She kisses me, mouth open, her hips riding up, legs locked around me until I'm done. When I pull back and out of her, I notice a smear of crimson on her chin. Cradling her face, I wipe it away with my thumb.

"Fuck," she says, shivering as she stretches and flexes her legs.

"Hey, lay on my chest," I say.

She crawls into my arms. Her comedown is rough sometimes, but she enjoys it so long as I'm there to help her through. She lays her head on my shoulder, her face against my neck.

"I love you," I murmur, stroking her hair.

"God, I fucking love you," she whispers back.

We don't move for a while. Then, I put her in the shower and get the room back in order. When everything is clean, I join her, and she washes me, paying careful attention to my split lip. She's always worrying about me when there's blood, but it never bothers me much.

We fall asleep not long after our bodies touch the bed.

Both exhausted, both safe.

The morning comes too fast, as it always does on the ranch. I extract myself from my wife's embrace and get up. In the nursery, Delia is already chattering. I get dressed in my work clothes—I've got a long list of chores this morning. Then, I move noiselessly down the hall into the nursery.

My daughter is in her crib, waving her arms and legs. She swivels, looking at me through the bars.

"Morning," I say.

She gurgles, smiling as I lift her, easing her onto my shoulder. For a moment, I close my eyes and just hold her close, breathing in her baby shampoo scent. Time already feels like it's slipping through my fingers. Someday, she'll be grown, along with her brother, and I'll be watching them from afar. But for now, she's so small, she fits in my hands, and I soak in the time when I can keep her safe.

Della rolls over, blinking sleepily as I bring Delia to nurse. She pushes the blankets aside, making room. I lay our daughter down and press a kiss to my wife's temple.

"I'm going to do the chores," I say. "I'll be right back."

"No hurry," she says. "I'll start breakfast when she's done."

There's never been a time when I have the right words to tell her what the family she gave me means. So, I just brush my fingertips through hers, and she understands.

Out on the porch, I'm surprised to find Landis already awake. He's crouched on the stoop, my hat on his lap.

"You're up early," I say.

He looks up, squinting. "I wanted to feed the horses."

"Let's go then."

He smiles, handing me my hat. We cross the yard where I once laid with Della, long before I knew what the future held. The barn is still cool. The horses line the stalls, throwing their heads, waiting for breakfast. I gather the buckets and help Landis measure the right amount of feed.

"Can I ask you a question?" He stops after the last bucket and puts his hands on his hips.

"Sure," I say, hoping this isn't one of those awkward parenting moments.

He hesitates, face screwed up in concentration.

"Penny for your thoughts?" I say lightly.

"Can I call you my dad?" he asks, not looking at me.

Well, damn, that one hurts. I knew it was coming eventually, but it's like getting kicked in the chest, like tripping and falling all the way down to a place I don't want to leave. I clear my throat and try to answer, but nothing comes out. He's staring up at me, nervous. Finally, I take my hat off and put it on his head.

"Yeah," I say. "Reckon you can."

He smiles. "Really?"

"Yep. You can keep the hat. It'll fit you someday."

He's smiling as he reaches for a bucket. We don't talk while we fill up the feed bins. That's how I know he's serious, when he's used up all his words. Pretty soon, the barn is filled with the sounds of horses chewing. I pile up the buckets for tomorrow as he stands in the far end of the barn, staring up at the mountains in the distance.

"What're you thinking?" I ask, coming up beside him.

"I was thinking about the truck," he says.

"Yeah? What about it?"

He squints up at me. "How long will it take to fix?"

Truthfully, I could get it done in a few weeks on my own, but I think I'll take my time with it.

"Maybe a few years," I say.

"Years?" His jaw drops.

"Well, you can't drive until you're older anyway. What's it matter?"

He thinks that through and nods slowly. "I guess that's okay."

"It's a real old truck. It was mine when I was a teenager," I say. "It needs a lot of work."

He nods. From the front porch, we both catch the faint sound of Della calling for us. Without speaking, we head back through the barn and up the driveway to the porch. She's standing on the top step, Delia in her arms.

"Y'all coming?" she calls. "Breakfast is gonna be ice cold."

Landis scrambles up the stairs. She tilts his chin up, checking if his face is dirty.

"You wash your hands," she says. "Where'd you get that hat?"

"It's Dad's hat," he says, ducking around her and disappearing inside.

Della freezes. "What did he say?"

I shrug, but really, I'm taking that extra second to compose myself. "He asked if he could call me his dad this morning, and I said yes. That alright by you, baby?"

She swallows, eyes wide. I touch her cheek. "You okay?" I press.

She nods, sniffing. "Yeah, I just...I hoped he'd ask you that."

I bend to kiss her forehead. When I pull back, Delia makes a vicious grab for my mustache. I catch her tiny hand, letting her grip the tip of my finger instead. Della is smiling like she'll never stop, her lashes wet.

"Things change for the better," she says. "I guess we just had to wait."

"We worked for it too," I say.

She nods, her face sobering. There's a breath on the wind that smells like summer flowers and field grass. For a second, it feels like being back where I grew up, but without all the hurt. She notices it too. I see the distance in her eyes as she looks out towards the mountains.

"Do you think about them sometimes?" she whispers.

"Who?"

"Kayleigh and Brothers."

"Kayleigh is living high, probably somewhere glamorous," I say. "I don't think about it because I know she's doing just fine."

"And Brothers?"

"Brothers Boyd is like a cat," I say. "He'll always land on his feet."

She nods, like she's ready to move on. I hold the door for her, guiding her into the hallway with our daughter in her arms. Before I step inside, I pause in the doorway and look out over my ranch.

I got everything I wanted in the end. Now, when I think of home, it's just bittersweetness on my tongue. For the hills, for the people who made me, for better and for worse.

Those feelings of bittersweetness come, but they go, and I'm left knowing only one thing for certain.

I am home.

THE END

OTHER BOOKS BY RAYA MORRIS EDWARDS

The Sovereign Mountain Series

Sovereign

Westin

Deacon

Jensen

Jack - Coming 2026

Sovereign Mountain Bonus Content Series

Redbird

Darling Bride

Sweet Beloved

Into the Sun

The Welsh Kings Trilogy

Paradise Descent

Prince of Ink & Scars

Acknowledgments

Thank you to my husband, who reminds me to eat and breathe when I'm on a deadline. There would be no Sovereign Mountain Series without you.

Thank you to Corinne, who spent hours reading and discussing this book with me. I couldn't have written this series without your insight and advice.

Thank you to Emilie who hyped me up so much about this book. I'm so glad you loved Jensen! Thank you to Sarah, who was able to step in and help at the last minute. And thank you to all my beta readers, early readers, and ARC readers for this book.

A special thank you to Lex who made me give Jensen a mustache. That was the right choice.

Thank you to my editors. To Lexie, for loving this story and hyping me up with your dev edits. And thank you to Alexa, not only for the proof and copy edits, but for navigating me through rough waters.

Thank you to Michelle for your endless patience in my search to find the perfect shot for this cover. Your work, as always, is exemplary. And thank you to Sandra for your wonderful work designing both the model and discreet covers. This is one of my favorites yet!

Made in the USA
Las Vegas, NV
10 December 2025

35759897R00236